AF172600

The "Genius"
Book II The Struggle

by

Theodore Dreiser

Double9
BOOKS

The "Genius"
Book II The Struggle
by Theodore Dreiser

Copyright © 2024

All Rights reserved.

ISBN: 978-93-68091-32-5

Published by

DOUBLE 9 BOOKS

2/13-B, Ansari Road
Daryaganj, New Delhi – 110002
info@double9books.com
www.double9books.com
Tel. 011-40042856

This book is under public domain

ABOUT THE AUTHOR

Theodore Dreiser (1871–1945) was a prominent American journalist and novelist who made important contributions to the literary naturalism movement. Dreiser was born in Terre Haute, Indiana, on August 27, 1871, and was raised in a working-class household. His early life and difficulties with poverty had a big impact on the writing he produced later. Because of his novels' candid depictions of sexuality and social issues, Dreiser faced criticism and restriction, but his writings were vital in forming American literature. His naturalistic approach deviated from popular literary traditions by highlighting the impact of environment and genetics on human behavior. In addition, Dreiser was a journalist who wrote for magazines including Harper's Magazine and The New York Times. Throughout his career, he participated in literary and political circles and was an advocate for social justice. On December 28, 1945, Theodore Dreiser passed away. He is remembered for being a significant figure in American literature and a forerunner of literary naturalism.

CONTENTS

CHAPTER I

The marriage ceremony between Eugene and Angela was solemnized at Buffalo on November second. As planned, Marietta was with them. They would go, the three of them, to the Falls, and to West Point, where the girls would see their brother David, and then Marietta would return to tell the family about it. Naturally, under the circumstances, it was a very simple affair, for there were no congratulations to go through with and no gifts—at least immediately—to consider and acknowledge. Angela had explained to her parents and friends that it was quite impossible for Eugene to come West at this time. She knew that he objected to a public ceremony where he would have to run the gauntlet of all her relatives, and so she was quite willing to meet him in the East and be married there. Eugene had not troubled to take his family into his confidence as yet. He had indicated on his last visit home that he might get married, and that Angela was the girl in question, but since Myrtle was the only one of his family who had seen her and she was now in Ottumwa, Iowa, they could not recall anything about her. Eugene's father was a little disappointed, for he expected to hear some day that Eugene had made a brilliant match. His boy, whose pictures were in the magazines so frequently and whose appearance was so generally distinguished, ought in New York, where opportunities abounded, to marry an heiress at least. It was all right of course if Eugene wanted to marry a girl from the country, but it robbed the family of a possible glory.

The spirit of this marriage celebration, so far as Eugene was concerned, was hardly right. There was the consciousness, always with him, of his possibly making a mistake; the feeling that he was being compelled by circumstances and his own weakness to fulfil an agreement which might better remain unfulfilled. His only urge was his desire, in the gratification of which he might find compensation, for saving Angela from an unhappy spinsterhood. It was a thin reed to lean on; there could be no honest satisfaction in it. Angela was sweet, devoted, painstaking in her attitude toward life, toward him, toward everything with which she came in contact, but she was not what he had always fancied his true mate would be—the be all and the end all of his existence. Where was the divine fire which on this occasion should have animated him; the lofty thoughts of future companionship; that intense feeling he had first felt about her when he had called on her at her aunt's house in Chicago? Something had happened. Was it that he had cheapened his ideal by too close contact with it? Had he taken a beautiful flower and trailed it in the dust? Was passion all there was to marriage? Or was it that true marriage was something higher—a union of fine thoughts and feelings? Did Angela share his with him? Angela did have exalted feelings and moods at times. They were not sensibly intellectual—but she seemed to respond to the better things in music and to some extent in literature. She knew nothing about art, but she was emotionally responsive to many fine things. Why was not this enough to make life durable and comfortable between them? Was it not really enough? After he had gone over all these points, there was still the thought that there was something wrong in this union. Despite his supposedly laudable conduct in fulfilling an obligation which, in a way, he had helped create or created, he was not happy. He went to his marriage as a man goes to fulfil an uncomfortable social obligation. It might turn out that he would have an enjoyable and happy life and it might turn out very much otherwise. He could not face the weight and significance of the social theory that this was for life—that if he married her today he would have to live with her all the rest of his days. He knew that was the generally accepted interpretation of marriage, but it did not appeal to him. Union ought in his estimation to be based on a keen desire to live together and on nothing else. He did not feel the obligation which attaches to children, for he had never had any and did not feel the desire for any. A child was a kind of a nuisance. Marriage was a trick of Nature's by which you were compelled to carry out her scheme of race continuance. Love was a lure; desire a scheme of propagation devised by the way. Nature, the race spirit, used you as you would use a work-horse to pull a load. The load in this case was race progress and man was the victim. He did not think he owed anything to nature, or to this race spirit. He had not asked to come here. He had not been treated as generously as he might have been since he arrived. Why should he do what nature bid?

When he met Angela he kissed her fondly, for of course the sight of her aroused the feeling of desire which had been running in his mind so keenly for some time. Since last seeing Angela he had touched no woman, principally because the right one had not presented herself and because the memories and the anticipations in connection with Angela were so close. Now that he was with her again the old fire came over him and he was eager for the completion of the ceremony. He had seen to the marriage license in the morning,—and from the train on which Angela and Marietta arrived they proceeded in a carriage direct to the Methodist preacher. The ceremony which meant so much to Angela meant practically nothing to him. It seemed a silly formula—this piece of paper from the marriage clerk's office and this instructed phraseology concerning "love, honor and cherish." Certainly he would love, honor and cherish if it were possible—if not, then not. Angela, with the marriage ring on her finger and the words "with this ring I thee wed" echoing in her ears, felt that all her dreams had come true. Now she was, really, truly, Mrs. Eugene Witla. She did not need to worry about drowning herself, or being disgraced, or enduring a lonely, commiserated old age. She was the wife of an artist—a rising one, and she was going to live in New York. What a future stretched before her! Eugene loved her after all. She imagined she could see that. His slowness in marrying her was due to the difficulty of establishing himself properly. Otherwise he would have done it before. They drove to the Iroquois hotel and registered as man and wife, securing a separate room for Marietta. The latter pretending an urgent desire to bathe after her railroad journey, left them, promising to be ready in time for dinner. Eugene and Angela were finally alone.

He now saw how, in spite of his fine theories, his previous experiences with Angela had deadened to an extent his joy in this occasion. He had her again it was true. His desire that he had thought of so keenly was to be gratified, but there was no mystery connected with it. His real nuptials had been celebrated at Blackwood months before. This was the commonplace of any marriage relation. It was intense and gratifying, but the original, wonderful mystery of unexplored character was absent. He eagerly took her in his arms, but there was more of crude desire than of awed delight in the whole proceeding.

Nevertheless Angela was sweet to him. Hers was a loving disposition and Eugene was the be all and end all of her love. His figure was of heroic proportions to her. His talent was divine fire. No one could know as much as Eugene, of course! No one could be as artistic. True, he was not as practical as some men—her brothers and brothers-in-law, for instance—but he was a man of genius. Why should he be practical? She was beginning to think already of how thoroughly she would help him shape his life toward success—what a good wife she would be to him. Her training as a teacher, her experience as a buyer, her practical judgment, would help him so much. They spent the two hours before dinner in renewed transports and then dressed and made their public appearance. Angela had had designed a number of dresses for this occasion, representing the saving of years, and tonight at dinner she looked exceptionally pretty in a dress of black silk with neck piece and half sleeves of mother-of-pearl silk, set off with a decoration of seed pearls and black beads in set designs. Marietta, in a pale pink silk of peachblow softness of hue with short sleeves and a low cut bodice was, with all her youth and natural plumpness and gaiety of soul, ravishing. Now that she had Angela safely married, she was under no obligations to keep out of Eugene's way nor to modify her charms in order that her sister's might shine. She was particularly ebullient in her mood and Eugene could not help contrasting, even in this hour, the qualities of the two sisters. Marietta's smile, her humor, her unconscious courage, contrasted so markedly with Angela's quietness.

The luxuries of the modern hotel have become the commonplaces of ordinary existence, but to the girls they were still strange enough to be impressive. To Angela they were a foretaste of what was to be an enduring higher life. These carpets, hangings, elevators, waiters, seemed in their shabby materialism to speak of superior things.

One day in Buffalo, with a view of the magnificent falls at Niagara, and then came West Point with a dress parade accidentally provided for a visiting general and a ball for the cadets. Marietta, because of her charm and her brother's popularity, found herself so much in demand at West Point that she extended her stay to a week, leaving Eugene and Angela free to come to New York together and have a little time to themselves. They only stayed long enough to see Marietta safely housed and then came to the city and the apartment in Washington Square.

It was dark when they arrived and Angela was impressed with the glittering galaxy of lights the city presented across the North River from Forty-second Street. She had no idea of the nature of the city, but as the cab at Eugene's request turned into Broadway at Forty-second Street and clattered with interrupted progress south to Fifth Avenue she had her first glimpse of that tawdry world which subsequently became known as the "Great White Way." Already its make-believe and inherent cheapness had come to seem to Eugene largely characteristic of the city and of life, but it still retained enough of the lure of the flesh and of clothes and of rush-light reputations to hold his attention. Here were dramatic critics and noted actors and actresses and chorus girls, the gods and toys of avid, inexperienced, unsatisfied wealth. He showed Angela the different theatres, called her attention to distinguished names; made much of restaurants and hotels and shops and stores that sell trifles and trash, and finally turned into lower Fifth Avenue, where the dignity of great houses and great conservative wealth still lingered. At Fourteenth Street Angela could already see Washington Arch glowing cream white in the glare of electric lights.

"What is that?" she asked interestedly.

"It's Washington Arch," he replied. "We live in sight of that on the south side of the Square."

"Oh! but it is beautiful!" she exclaimed.

It seemed very wonderful to her, and as they passed under it, and the whole Square spread out before her, it seemed a perfect world in which to live.

"Is this where it is?" she asked, as they stopped in front of the studio building.

"Yes, this is it. How do you like it?"

"I think it's beautiful," she said.

They went up the white stone steps of the old Bride house in which was Eugene's leased studio, up two flights of red-carpeted stairs and finally into the dark studio where he struck a match and lit, for the art of it, candles. A soft waxen glow irradiated the place as he proceeded and then Angela saw old Chippendale chairs, a Heppelwhite writing-table, a Flemish strong box containing used and unused drawings, the green stained fish-net studded with bits of looking glass in imitation of scales, a square, gold-framed mirror over the mantel, and one of Eugene's drawings—the three engines in the gray, lowering weather, standing large and impressive upon an easel. It seemed to Angela the perfection of beauty. She saw the difference now between the tawdry gorgeousness of a commonplace hotel and this selection and arrangement of individual taste. The glowing candelabrum of seven candles on either side of the square mirror surprised her deeply. The black walnut piano in the alcove behind the half draped net drew forth an exclamation of delight. "Oh, how lovely it all is!" she exclaimed and ran to Eugene to be kissed. He fondled her for a few minutes and then she left again to examine in detail pictures, pieces of furniture, ornaments of brass and copper.

"When did you get all this?" she asked, for Eugene had not told her of his luck in finding the departing Dexter and leasing it for the rent of the studio and its care. He was lighting the fire in the grate which had been prepared by the house attendant.

"Oh, it isn't mine," he replied easily. "I leased this from Russell Dexter. He's going to be in Europe until next winter. I thought that would be easier than waiting around to fix up a place after you came. We can get our things together next fall."

He was thinking he would be able to have his exhibition in the spring, and perhaps that would bring some notable sales. Anyhow it might bring a few, increase his repute and give him a greater earning power.

Angela's heart sank just a little but she recovered in a moment, for after all it was very exceptional even to be able to lease a place of this character. She went to the window and looked out. There was the great square with its four walls of houses, the spread of trees, still decorated with a few dusty leaves, and the dozens of arc lights sputtering their white radiance in between, the graceful arch, cream white over at the entrance of Fifth Avenue.

"It's so beautiful," she exclaimed again, coming back to Eugene and putting her arms about him. "I didn't think it would be anything as fine as this. You're so good to me." She put up her lips and he kissed her, pinching her cheeks. Together they walked to the kitchen, the bedroom, the bathroom. Then after a time they blew out the candles and retired for the night.

CHAPTER II

After the quiet of a small town, the monotony and simplicity of country life, the dreary, reiterated weariness of teaching a country school, this new world into which Angela was plunged seemed to her astonished eyes to be compounded of little save beauties, curiosities and delights. The human senses, which weary so quickly of reiterated sensory impressions, exaggerate with equal readiness the beauty and charm of the unaccustomed. If it is new, therefore it must be better than that which we have had of old. The material details with which we are able to surround ourselves seem at times to remake our point of view. If we have been poor, wealth will seem temporarily to make us happy; when we have been amid elements and personages discordant to our thoughts, to be put among harmonious conditions seems, for the time being, to solve all our woes. So little do we have that interior peace which no material conditions can truly affect or disturb.

When Angela awoke the next morning, this studio in which she was now to live seemed the most perfect habitation which could be devised by man. The artistry of the arrangement of the rooms, the charm of the conveniences—a bathroom with hot and cold water next to the bedroom; a kitchen with an array of necessary utensils. In the rear portion of the studio used as a dining-room a glimpse of the main studio gave her the sense of art which dealt with nature, the beauty of the human form, colors, tones—how different from teaching school. To her the difference between the long, low rambling house at Blackwood with its vine ornamented windows, its somewhat haphazard arrangement of flowers and its great lawn, and this peculiarly compact and ornate studio apartment looking out upon Washington Square, was all in favor of the latter. In Angela's judgment there was no comparison. She could not have understood if she could have seen into Eugene's mind at this time how her home town, her father's single farm, the blue waters of the little lake near her door, the shadows of the tall trees on her lawn were somehow, compounded for him not only with classic beauty itself, but with her own charm. When she was among these things she partook of their beauty and was made more beautiful thereby. She did not know how much she had lost in leaving them behind. To her all these older elements of her life were shabby and unimportant, pointless and to be neglected.

This new world was in its way for her an Aladdin's cave of delight. When she looked out on the great square for the first time the next morning, seeing it bathed in sunlight, a dignified line of red brick dwellings to the north, a towering office building to the east, trucks, carts, cars and vehicles clattering over the pavement below, it all seemed gay with youth and energy.

"We'll have to dress and go out to breakfast," said Eugene. "I didn't think to lay anything in. As a matter of fact I wouldn't have known what to buy if I had wanted to. I never tried housekeeping for myself."

"Oh, that's all right," said Angela, fondling his hands, "only let's not go out to breakfast unless we have to. Let's see what's here," and she went back to the very small room devoted to cooking purposes to see what cooking utensils had been provided. She had been dreaming of housekeeping and cooking for Eugene, of petting and spoiling him, and now the opportunity had arrived. She found that Mr. Dexter, their generous lessor, had provided himself with many conveniences—breakfast and dinner sets of brown and blue porcelain, a coffee percolator, a charming dull blue teapot with cups to match, a chafing dish, a set of waffle irons, griddles, spiders, skillets, stew and roasting pans and knives and forks of steel and silver in abundance. Obviously he had entertained from time to time, for there were bread, cake, sugar, flour and salt boxes and a little chest containing, in small drawers, various spices.

"Oh, it will be easy to get something here," said Angela, lighting the burners of the gas stove to see whether it was in good working order. "We can just go out to market if you'll come and show me once and get what we want. It won't take a minute. I'll know after that." Eugene consented gladly.

She had always fancied she would be an ideal housekeeper and now that she had her Eugene she was anxious to begin. It would be such a pleasure to show him what a manager she was, how everything would go smoothly in her hands, how careful she would be of his earnings—their joint possessions.

She was sorry, now that she saw that art was no great producer of wealth, that she had no money to bring him, but she knew that Eugene in the depth of his heart thought nothing of that. He was too impractical. He was a great artist, but when it came to practical affairs she felt instinctively that she was much the wiser. She had bought so long, calculated so well for her sisters and brothers.

Out of her bag (for her trunks had not yet arrived) she extracted a neat house dress of pale green linen which she put on after she had done up her hair in a cosy coil, and together with Eugene for a temporary guide, they set forth to find the stores. He had told her, looking out the windows, that there were lines of Italian grocers, butchers and vegetable men in the side streets, leading south from the square, and into one of these they now ventured. The swarming, impressive life of the street almost took her breath away, it was so crowded. Potatoes, tomatoes, eggs, flour, butter, lamb chops, salt—a dozen little accessories were all purchased in small quantities, and then they eagerly returned to the studio. Angela was a little disgusted with the appearance of some of the stores, but some of them were clean enough. It seemed so strange to her to be buying in an Italian street, with Italian women and children about, their swarthy leathern faces set with bright, almost feverish eyes. Eugene in his brown corduroy suit and soft green hat, watching and commenting at her side, presented such a contrast. He was so tall, so exceptional, so laconic.

"I like them when they wear rings in their ears," he said at one time.

"Get the coal man who looks like a bandit," he observed at another.

"This old woman here might do for the witch of Endor."

Angela attended strictly to her marketing. She was gay and smiling, but practical. She was busy wondering in what quantities she should buy things, how she would keep fresh vegetables, whether the ice box was really clean; how much delicate dusting the various objects in the studio would require. The raw brick walls of the street, the dirt and slops in the gutter, the stray cats and dogs hungry and lean, the swarming stream of people, did not appeal to her as picturesque at all. Only when she heard Eugene expatiating gravely did she begin to realize that all this must have artistic significance. If Eugene said so it did. But it was a fascinating world whatever it was, and it was obvious that she was going to be very, very happy.

There was a breakfast in the studio then of hot biscuit with fresh butter, an omelette with tomatoes, potatoes stewed in cream, and coffee. After the long period of commonplace restaurant dining which Eugene had endured, this seemed ideal. To sit in your own private apartment with a charming wife opposite you ready to render you any service, and with an array of food before you which revived the finest memories in your gustatory experience, seemed perfect. Nothing could be better. He saw visions of a happy future if he could finance this sort of thing. It would require a lot of money, more than he had been making, but he thought he could make out. After breakfast Angela played on the piano, and then, Eugene wanting to work, she started housekeeping in earnest. The trunks arriving gave her the task of unpacking and with that and lunch and dinner to say nothing of love she had sufficient to do.

It was a charming existence for a little while. Eugene suggested that they should have Smite and MacHugh to dinner first of all, these being his closest friends. Angela agreed heartily for she was only too anxious to meet the people he knew. She wanted to show him she knew how to receive and entertain as well as anyone. She made great preparations for the Wednesday evening following—the night fixed for the dinner—and when it came was on the qui vive to see what his friends were like and what they would think of her.

The occasion passed off smoothly enough and was the occasion of considerable jollity. These two cheerful worthies were greatly impressed with the studio. They were quick to praise it before Angela, and to congratulate him on his good fortune in having married her. Angela, in the same dress in which she had appeared at dinner in Buffalo, was impressive. Her mass of yellow hair fascinated the gaze of both Smite and MacHugh.

"Gee, what hair!" Smite observed secretly to MacHugh when neither Angela nor Eugene were within hearing distance.

"You're right," returned MacHugh. "She's not at all bad looking, is she?"

"I should say not," returned Smite who admired Angela's simple, good-natured western manners. A little later, more subtly, they expressed their admiration to her, and she was greatly pleased.

Marietta, who had arrived late that afternoon, had not made her appearance yet. She was in the one available studio bedroom making her toilet. Angela, in spite of her fine raiment, was busy superintending the cooking, for although through the janitor she had managed to negotiate the loan of a girl to serve, she could not get anyone to cook. A soup, a fish, a chicken and a salad, were the order of procedure. Marietta finally appeared, ravishing in pink silk. Both Smite and MacHugh sat up and Marietta proceeded to bewitch them. Marietta knew no order or distinctions in men. They were all slaves to her—victims to be stuck on the spit of her beauty and broiled in their amorous uncertainties at her leisure. In after years Eugene learned to speak of Marietta's smile as "the dagger." The moment she appeared smiling he would say, "Ah, we have it out again, have we? Who gets the blade this evening? Poor victim!"

Being her brother-in-law now, he was free to slip his arm about her waist and she took this family connection as license to kiss him. There was something about Eugene which held her always. During these very first days she gratified her desire to be in his arms, but always with a sense of reserve which kept him in check. She wondered secretly how much he liked her.

Smite and MacHugh, when she appeared, both rose to do her service. MacHugh offered her his chair by the fire. Smite bestirred himself in an aimless fashion.

"I've just had such a dandy week up at West Point," began Marietta cheerfully, "dancing, seeing dress parades, walking with the soldier boys."

"I warn you two, here and now," began Eugene, who had already learned to tease Marietta, "that you're not safe. This woman here is dangerous. As artists in good standing you had better look out for yourselves."

"Oh, Eugene, how you talk," laughed Marietta, her teeth showing effectively. "Mr. Smite, I leave it to you. Isn't that a mean way to introduce a sister-in-law? I'm here for just a few days too, and have so little time. I think it cruel!"

"It's a shame!" said Smite, who was plainly a willing victim. "You ought to have another kind of brother-in-law. If you had some people I know now—"

"It's an outrage," commented MacHugh. "There's one thing though. You may not require so very much time."

"Now I think that's ungallant," Marietta laughed. "I see I'm all alone here except for Mr. Smite. Never mind. You all will be sorry when I'm gone."

"I believe that," replied MacHugh, feelingly.

Smite simply stared. He was lost in admiration of her cream and peach complexion, her fluffy, silky brown hair, her bright blue eyes and plump rounded arms. Such radiant good nature would be heavenly to live with. He wondered what sort of a family this was that Eugene had become connected with. Angela, Marietta, a brother at West Point. They must be nice, conservative, well-to-do western people. Marietta went to help her sister, and Smite, in the absence of Eugene, said: "Say, he's in right, isn't he? She's a peach. She's got it a little on her sister."

MacHugh merely stared at the room. He was taken with the complexion and arrangement of things generally. The old furniture, the rugs, the hangings, the pictures, Eugene's borrowed maid servant in a white apron and cap, Angela, Marietta, the bright table set with colored china and an arrangement of silver candlesticks—Eugene had certainly changed the tenor of his life radically within the last ten days. Why he was marvellously fortunate. This studio was a wonderful piece of luck. Some people—and he shook his head meditatively.

"Well," said Eugene, coming back after some final touches to his appearance, "what do you think of it, Peter?"

"You're certainly moving along, Eugene. I never expected to see it. You ought to praise God. You're plain lucky."

Eugene smiled enigmatically. He was wondering whether he was. Neither Smite nor MacHugh nor anyone could dream of the conditions under which this came about. What a sham the world was anyhow. It's surface appearances so ridiculously deceptive! If anyone had known of the apparent necessity when he first started to look for an apartment, of his own mood toward it!

Marietta came back, and Angela. The latter had taken kindly to both these men, or boys as she already considered them. Eugene had a talent for reducing everybody to "simply folks," as he called them. So these two capable and talented men were mere country boys like himself—and Angela caught his attitude.

"I'd like to have you let me make a sketch of you some day, Mrs. Witla," MacHugh said to Angela when she came back to the fire. He was essaying portraiture as a side line and he was anxious for good opportunities to practice.

Angela thrilled at the invitation, and the use of her new name, Mrs. Witla, by Eugene's old friends.

"I'd be delighted," she replied, flushing.

"My word, you look nice, Angel-Face," exclaimed Marietta, catching her about the waist. "You paint her with her hair down in braids, Mr. MacHugh. She makes a stunning Gretchen."

Angela flushed anew.

"I've been reserving that for myself, Peter," said Eugene, "but you try your hand at it. I'm not much in portraiture anyhow."

Smite smiled at Marietta. He wished he could paint her, but he was poor at figure work except as incidental characters in sea scenes. He could do men better than he could women.

"If you were an old sea captain now, Miss Blue," he said to Marietta gallantly, "I could make a striking thing out of you."

"I'll try to be, if you want to paint me," she replied gaily. "I'd look fine in a big pair of boots and a raincoat, wouldn't I, Eugene?"

"You certainly would, if I'm any judge," replied Smite. "Come over to the studio and I'll rig you out. I have all those things on hand."

"I will," she replied, laughing. "You just say the word."

MacHugh felt as if Smite were stealing a march on him. He wanted to be nice to Marietta, to have her take an interest in him.

"Now, looky, Joseph," he protested. "I was going to suggest making a study of Miss Blue myself."

"Well, you're too late," replied Smite. "You didn't speak quick enough."

Marietta was greatly impressed with this atmosphere in which Angela and Eugene were living. She expected to see something artistic, but nothing so nice as this particular studio. Angela explained to her that Eugene did not own it, but that made small difference in Marietta's estimate of its significance. Eugene had it. His art and social connections brought it about. They were beginning excellently well. If she could have as nice a home when she started on her married career she would be satisfied.

They sat down about the round teak table which was one of Dexter's prized possessions, and were served by Angela's borrowed maid. The conversation was light and for the most part pointless, serving only to familiarize these people with each other. Both Angela and Marietta were taken with the two artists because they felt in them a note of homely conservatism. These men spoke easily and naturally of the trials and triumphs of art life, and the difficulty of making a good living, and seemed to be at home with personages of repute in one world and another, its greatest reward.

During the dinner Smite narrated experiences in his sea-faring life, and MacHugh of his mountain camping experiences in the West. Marietta described experiences with her beaux in Wisconsin and characteristics of her yokel neighbors at Blackwood, Angela joining in. Finally MacHugh drew a pencil sketch of Marietta followed by a long train of admiring yokels, her eyes turned up in a very shy, deceptive manner.

"Now I think that's cruel," she declared, when Eugene laughed heartily. "I never look like that."

"That's just the way you look and do," he declared. "You're the broad and flowery path that leadeth to destruction."

"Never mind, Babyette," put in Angela, "I'll take your part if no one else will. You're a nice, demure, shrinking girl and you wouldn't look at anyone, would you?"

Angela got up and was holding Marietta's head mock sympathetically in her arms.

"Say, that's a dandy pet name," called Smite, moved by Marietta's beauty.

"Poor Marietta," observed Eugene. "Come over here to me and I'll sympathize with you."

"You don't take my drawing in the right spirit, Miss Blue," put in MacHugh cheerfully. "It's simply to show how popular you are."

Angela stood beside Eugene as her guests departed, her slender arm about his waist. Marietta was coquetting finally with MacHugh. These two friends of his, thought Eugene, had the privilege of singleness to be gay and alluring to her. With him that was over now. He could not be that way to any girl any more. He had to behave—be calm and circumspect. It cut him, this thought. He saw at once it was not in accord with his nature. He wanted to do just as he had always done—make love to Marietta if she would let him, but he could not. He walked to the fire when the studio door was closed.

"They're such nice boys," exclaimed Marietta. "I think Mr. MacHugh is as funny as he can be. He has such droll wit."

"Smite is nice too," replied Eugene defensively.

"They're both lovely—just lovely," returned Marietta.

"I like Mr. MacHugh a little the best—he's quainter," said Angela, "but I think Mr. Smite is just as nice as he can be. He's so old fashioned. There's not anyone as nice as my Eugene, though," she said affectionately, putting her arm about him.

"Oh, dear, you two!" exclaimed Marietta. "Well, I'm going to bed."

Eugene sighed.

They had arranged a couch for her which could be put behind the silver-spangled fish net in the alcove when company was gone.

Eugene thought what a pity that already this affection of Angela's was old to him. It was not as it would be if he had taken Marietta or Christina. They went to their bed room to retire and then he saw that all he had was passion. Must he be satisfied with that? Could he be? It started a chain of thought which, while persistently interrupted or befogged, was really never broken. Momentary sympathy, desire, admiration, might obscure it, but always fundamentally it was there. He had made a mistake. He had put his head in a noose. He had subjected himself to conditions which he did not sincerely approve of. How was he going to remedy this—or could it ever be remedied?

CHAPTER III

Whatever were Eugene's secret thoughts, he began his married life with the outward air of one who takes it seriously enough. Now that he was married, was actually bound by legal ties, he felt that he might as well make the best of it. He had once had the notion that it might be possible to say nothing of his marriage, and keep Angela in the background, but this notion had been dispelled by the attitude of MacHugh and Smite, to say nothing of Angela. So he began to consider the necessity of notifying his friends—Miriam Finch and Norma Whitmore and possibly Christina Channing, when she should return. These three women offered the largest difficulty to his mind. He felt the commentary which their personalities represented. What would they think of him? What of Angela? Now that she was right here in the city he could see that she represented a different order of thought. He had opened the campaign by suggesting that they invite Smite and MacHugh. The thing to do now was to go further in this matter.

The one thing that troubled him was the thought of breaking the news to Miriam Finch, for Christina Channing was away, and Norma Whitmore was not of sufficient importance. He argued now that he should have done this beforehand, but having neglected that it behoved him to act at once. He did so, finally, writing to Norma Whitmore and saying, for he had no long explanation to make—"Yours truly is married. May I bring my wife up to see you?" Miss Whitmore was truly taken by surprise. She was sorry at first—very—because Eugene interested her greatly and she was afraid he would make a mistake in his marriage; but she hastened to make the best of a bad turn on the part of fate and wrote a note which ran as follows:

"Dear Eugene and Eugene's Wife:

"This is news as is news. Congratulations. And I am
coming right down as soon as I get my breath. And then
you two must come to see me.
"Norma Whitmore."

Eugene was pleased and grateful that she took it so nicely, but Angela was the least big chagrined secretly that he had not told her before. Why hadn't he? Was this someone that he was interested in? Those three years in which she had doubtingly waited for Eugene had whetted her suspicions and nurtured her fears. Still she tried to make little of it and to put on an air of joyousness. She would be so glad to meet Miss Whitmore. Eugene told her how kind she had been to him, how much she admired his art, how helpful she was in bringing together young literary and artistic people and how influential with those who counted. She could do him many a good turn. Angela listened patiently, but she was just the least bit resentful that he should think so much of any one woman outside of herself. Why should he, Eugene Witla, be dependent on the favor of any woman? Of course she must be very nice and they would be good friends, but—

Norma came one afternoon two days later with the atmosphere of enthusiasm trailing, as it seemed to Eugene, like a cloud of glory about her. She was both fire and strength to him in her regard and sympathy, even though she resented, ever so slightly, his affectional desertion.

"You piggy-wiggy Eugene Witla," she exclaimed. "What do you mean by running off and getting married and never saying a word. I never even had a chance to get you a present and now I have to bring it. Isn't this a charming place—why it's perfectly delightful," and as she laid her present down unopened she looked about to see where Mrs. Eugene Witla might be.

Angela was in the bedroom finishing her toilet. She was expecting this descent and so was prepared, being suitably dressed in the light green house gown. When she heard Miss Whitmore's familiar mode of address she winced, for this spoke volumes for a boon companionship of long endurance. Eugene hadn't said so much of Miss Whitmore in the past as he had recently, but she could see that they were very intimate. She looked out and saw her—this tall, not very shapely, but graceful woman, whose whole being represented dynamic energy, awareness, subtlety of perception. Eugene was shaking her hand and looking genially into her face.

"Why should Eugene like her so much?" she asked herself instantly. "Why did his face shine with that light of intense enthusiasm?" The "piggy-wiggy Eugene Witla" expression irritated her. It sounded as though she might be in love with him. She came out after a moment with a glad smile on her face and approached with every show of good feeling, but Miss Whitmore could sense opposition.

"So this is Mrs. Witla," she exclaimed, kissing her. "I'm delighted to know you. I have always wondered what sort of a girl Mr. Witla would marry. You'll just have to pardon my calling him Eugene. I'll get over it after a bit, I suppose, now that he's married. But we've been such good friends and I admire his work so much. How do you like studio life—or are you used to it?"

Angela, who was taking in every detail of Eugene's old friend, replied in what seemed an affected tone that no, she wasn't used to studio life: she was just from the country, you know—a regular farmer girl—Blackwood, Wisconsin, no less! She stopped to let Norma express friendly surprise, and then went on to say that she supposed Eugene had not said very much about her, but he wrote her often enough. She was rejoicing in the fact that whatever slight Eugene's previous silence seemed to put upon her, she had the satisfaction that she had won him after all and Miss Whitmore had not. She fancied from Miss Whitmore's enthusiastic attitude that she must like Eugene very much, and she could see now what sort of women might have made him wish to delay. Who were the others, she wondered?

They talked of metropolitan experiences generally. Marietta came in from a shopping expedition with a Mrs. Link, wife of an army captain acting as an instructor at West Point, and tea was served immediately afterward. Miss Whitmore was insistent that they should come and take dinner with her some evening. Eugene confided that he was sending a painting to the Academy.

"They'll hang it, of course," assured Norma, "but you ought to have an exhibition of your own."

Marietta gushed about the wonder of the big stores and so it finally came time for Miss Whitmore to go.

"Now you will come up, won't you?" she said to Angela, for in spite of a certain feeling of incompatibility and difference she was determined to like her. She thought Angela a little inexperienced and presumptuous in marrying Eugene. She was afraid she was not up to his standard. Still she was quaint, piquant. Perhaps she would do very well. Angela was thinking all the while that Miss Whitmore was presuming on her old acquaintance with Eugene—that she was too affected and enthusiastic.

There was another day on which Miriam Finch called. Richard Wheeler, having learned at Smite's and MacHugh's studio of Eugene's marriage and present whereabouts, had hurried over, and then immediately afterwards off to Miriam Finch's studio. Surprised himself, he knew that she would be more so.

"Witla's married!" he exclaimed, bursting into her room, and for the moment Miriam lost her self-possession sufficiently to reply almost dramatically: "Richard Wheeler, what are you talking about! You don't mean that, do you?"

"He's married," insisted Wheeler, "and he's living down in Washington Square, 61 is the number. He has the cutest yellow-haired wife you ever saw."

Angela had been nice to Wheeler and he liked her. He liked the air of this domicile and thought it was going to be a good thing for Eugene. He needed to settle down and work hard.

Miriam winced mentally at the picture. She was hurt by this deception of Eugene's, chagrined because he had not thought enough of her even to indicate that he was going to get married.

"He's been married ten days," communicated Wheeler, and this added force to her temporary chagrin. The fact that Angela was yellow-haired and cute was also disturbing.

"Well," she finally exclaimed cheerfully, "he might have said something to us, mightn't he?" and she covered her own original confusion by a gay nonchalance which showed nothing of what she was really thinking. This was certainly indifference on Eugene's part, and yet, why shouldn't he? He had never proposed to her. Still they had been so intimate mentally.

She was interested to see Angela. She wondered what sort of a woman she really was. "Yellow-haired! Cute!" Of course, like all men, Eugene had sacrificed intellect and mental charm for a dainty form and a pretty face. It seemed queer, but she had fancied that he would not do that—that his wife, if he ever took one, would be tall perhaps, and gracious, and of a beautiful mind—someone distinguished. Why would men, intellectual men, artistic men, any kind of men, invariably make fools of themselves! Well, she would go and see her.

Because Wheeler informed him that he had told Miriam, Eugene wrote, saying as briefly as possible that he was married and that he wanted to bring Angela to her studio. For reply she came herself, gay, smiling, immaculately dressed, anxious to hurt Angela because she had proved the victor. She also wanted to show Eugene how little difference it all made to her.

"You certainly are a secretive young man, Mr. Eugene Witla," she exclaimed, when she saw him. "Why didn't you make him tell us, Mrs. Witla?" she demanded archly of Angela, but with a secret dagger thrust in her eyes. "You'd think he didn't want us to know."

Angela cowered beneath the sting of this whip cord. Miriam made her feel as though Eugene had attempted to conceal his relationship to her—as though he was ashamed of her. How many more women were there like Miriam and Norma Whitmore?

Eugene was gaily unconscious of the real animus in Miriam's conversation, and now that the first cruel moment was over, was talking glibly of things in general, anxious to make everything seem as simple and natural as possible. He was working at one of his pictures when Miriam came in and was eager to obtain her critical opinion, since it was nearly done. She squinted at it narrowly but said nothing when he asked. Ordinarily she would have applauded it vigorously. She did think it exceptional, but was determined to say nothing. She walked indifferently about, examining this and that object in a superior way, asking how he came to obtain the studio, congratulating him upon his good luck. Angela, she decided, was interesting, but not in Eugene's class mentally, and should be ignored. He had made a mistake, that was plain.

"Now you must bring Mrs. Witla up to see me," she said on leaving. "I'll play and sing all my latest songs for you. I have made some of the daintest discoveries in old Italian and Spanish pieces."

Angela, who had posed to Eugene as knowing something about music, resented this superior invitation, without inquiry as to her own possible ability or taste, as she did Miriam's entire attitude. Why was she so haughty—so superior? What was it to her whether Eugene had said anything about her or not?

She said nothing to show that she herself played, but she wondered that Eugene said nothing. It seemed neglectful and inconsiderate of him. He was busy wondering what Miriam thought of his picture. Miriam took his hand warmly at parting, looked cheerfully into his eyes, and said, "I know you two are going to be irrationally happy," and went out.

Eugene felt the irritation at last. He knew Angela felt something. Miriam was resentful, that was it. She was angry at him for his seeming indifference. She had commented to herself on Angela's appearance and to her disadvantage. In her manner had been the statement that his wife was not very important after all, not of the artistic and superior world to which she and he belonged.

"How do you like her?" he asked tentatively after she had gone, feeling a strong current of opposition, but not knowing on what it might be based exactly.

"I don't like her," returned Angela petulantly. "She thinks she's sweet. She treats you as though she thought you were her personal property. She openly insulted me about your not telling her. Miss Whitmore did the same thing—they all do! They all will! Oh!!"

She suddenly burst into tears and ran crying toward their bedroom.

Eugene followed, astonished, ashamed, rebuked, guilty minded, almost terror-stricken—he hardly knew what.

"Why, Angela," he urged pleadingly, leaning over her and attempting to raise her. "You know that isn't true."

"It is! It is!!" she insisted. "Don't touch me! Don't come near me! You know it is true! You don't love me. You haven't treated me right at all since I've been here. You haven't done anything that you should have done. She insulted me openly to my face."

She was speaking with sobs, and Eugene was at once pained and terrorized by the persistent and unexpected display of emotion. He had never seen Angela like this before. He had never seen any woman so.

"Why, Angelface," he urged, "how can you go on like this? You know what you say isn't true. What have I done?"

"You haven't told your friends—that's what you haven't done," she exclaimed between gasps. "They still think you're single. You keep me here hidden in the background as though I were a—were a—I don't know what! Your friends come and insult me openly to my face. They do! They do! Oh!" and she sobbed anew.

She knew very well what she was doing in her anger and rage. She felt that she was acting in the right way. Eugene needed a severe reproof; he had acted very badly, and this was the way to administer it to him now in the beginning. His conduct was indefensible, and only the fact that he was an artist, immersed in cloudy artistic thoughts and not really subject to the ordinary conventions of life, saved him in her estimation. It didn't matter that she had urged him to marry her. It didn't absolve him that he had done so. She thought he owed her that. Anyhow they were married now, and he should do the proper thing.

Eugene stood there cut as with a knife by this terrific charge. He had not meant anything by concealing her presence, he thought. He had only endeavored to protect himself very slightly, temporarily.

"You oughtn't to say that, Angela," he pleaded. "There aren't any more that don't know—at least any more that I care anything about. I didn't think. I didn't mean to conceal anything. I'll write to everybody that might be interested."

He still felt hurt that she should brutally attack him this way even in her sorrow. He was wrong, no doubt, but she? Was this a way to act, this the nature of true love? He mentally writhed and twisted.

Taking her up in his arms, smoothing her hair, he asked her to forgive him. Finally, when she thought she had punished him enough, and that he was truly sorry and would make amends in the future, she pretended to listen and then of a sudden threw her arms about his neck and began to hug and kiss him. Passion, of course, was the end of this, but the whole thing left a disagreeable taste in Eugene's mouth. He did not like scenes. He preferred the lofty indifference of Miriam, the gay subterfuge of Norma, the supreme stoicism of Christina Channing. This noisy, tempestuous, angry emotion was not quite the thing to have introduced into his life. He did not see how that would make for love between them.

Still Angela was sweet, he thought. She was a little girl—not as wise as Norma Whitmore, not as self-protective as Miriam Finch or Christina Channing. Perhaps after all she needed his care and affection. Maybe it was best for her and for him that he had married her.

So thinking he rocked her in his arms, and Angela, lying there, was satisfied. She had won a most important victory. She was starting right. She was starting Eugene right. She would get the moral, mental and emotional upper hand of him and keep it. Then these women, who thought themselves so superior, could go their way. She would have Eugene and he would be a great man and she would be his wife. That was all she wanted.

CHAPTER IV

The result of Angela's outburst was that Eugene hastened to notify those whom he had not already informed—Shotmeyer, his father and mother, Sylvia, Myrtle, Hudson Dula—and received in return cards and letters of congratulation expressing surprise and interest, which he presented to Angela in a conciliatory spirit. She realized, after it was all over, that she had given him an unpleasant shock, and was anxious to make up to him in personal affection what she had apparently compelled him to suffer for policy's sake. Eugene did not know that in Angela, despite her smallness of body and what seemed to him her babyishness of spirit, he had to deal with a thinking woman who was quite wise as to ways and means of handling her personal affairs. She was, of course, whirled in the maelstrom of her affection for Eugene and this was confusing, and she did not understand the emotional and philosophic reaches of his mind; but she did understand instinctively what made for a stable relationship between husband and wife and between any married couple and the world. To her the utterance of the marriage vow meant just what it said, that they would cleave each to the other; there should be henceforth no thoughts, feelings, or emotions, and decidedly no actions which would not conform with the letter and the spirit of the marriage vow.

Eugene had sensed something of this, but not accurately or completely. He did not correctly estimate either the courage or the rigidity of her beliefs and convictions. He thought that her character might possibly partake of some of his own easy tolerance and good nature. She must know that people—men particularly—were more or less unstable in their make-up. Life could not be governed by hard and fast rules. Why, everybody knew that. You might try, and should hold yourself in check as much as possible for the sake of self-preservation and social appearances, but if you erred— and you might easily—it was no crime. Certainly it was no crime to look at another woman longingly. If you went astray, overbalanced by your desires, wasn't it after all in the scheme of things? Did we make our desires?

Certainly we did not, and if we did not succeed completely in controlling them—well—

The drift of life into which they now settled was interesting enough, though for Eugene it was complicated with the thought of possible failure, for he was, as might well be expected of such a temperament, of a worrying nature, and inclined, in his hours of ordinary effort, to look on the dark side of things. The fact that he had married Angela against his will, the fact that he had no definite art connections which produced him as yet anything more than two thousand dollars a year, the fact that he had assumed financial obligations which doubled the cost of food, clothing, entertainment, and rent—for their studio was costing him thirty dollars more than had his share of the Smite-MacHugh chambers—weighed on him. The dinner which he had given to Smite and MacHugh had cost about eight dollars over and above the ordinary expenses of the week. Others of a similar character would cost as much and more. He would have to take Angela to the theatre occasionally. There would be the need of furnishing a new studio the following fall, unless another such windfall as this manifested itself. Although Angela had equipped herself with a varied and serviceable trousseau, her clothes would not last forever. Odd necessities began to crop up not long after they were married, and he began to see that if they lived with anything like the freedom and care with which he had before he was married, his income would have to be larger and surer.

The energy which these thoughts provoked was not without result. For one thing he sent the original of the East Side picture, "Six O'clock" to the American Academy of Design exhibition—a thing which he might have done long before but failed to do.

Angela had heard from Eugene that the National Academy of Design was a forum for the display of art to which the public was invited or admitted for a charge. To have a picture accepted by this society and hung on the line was in its way a mark of merit and approval, though Eugene did not think very highly of it. All the pictures were judged by a jury of artists which decided whether they should be admitted or rejected, and if admitted whether they should be given a place of honor or hung in some inconspicuous position. To be hung "on the line" was to have your picture placed in the lower tier where the light was excellent and the public could get a good view of it. Eugene had thought the first two years he was in New York that he was really not sufficiently experienced or meritorious, and the previous year he had thought that he would hoard all that he was doing for his first appearance in some exhibition of his own, thinking the National Academy commonplace and retrogressive. The exhibitions he had seen thus far had been full of commonplace, dead-and-alive stuff, he thought. It was no great honor to be admitted to such a collection. Now, because MacHugh was trying, and because he had accumulated nearly enough pictures for exhibition at a private gallery which he hoped to interest, he was anxious to see what the standard body of American artists thought of his work. They might reject him. If so that would merely prove that they did not recognize a radical departure from accepted methods and subject matter as art. The impressionists, he understood, were being so ignored. Later they would accept him. If he were admitted it would simply mean that they knew better than he believed they did.

"I believe I will do it," he said; "I'd like to know what they think of my stuff anyhow."

The picture was sent as he had planned, and to his immense satisfaction it was accepted and hung. It did not, for some reason, attract as much attention as it might, but it was not without its modicum of praise. Owen Overman, the poet, met him in the general reception entrance of the Academy on the opening night, and congratulated him sincerely. "I remember seeing that in *Truth*," he said, "but it's much better in the original. It's fine. You ought to do a lot of those things."

"I am," replied Eugene. "I expect to have a show of my own one of these days."

He called Angela, who had wandered away to look at a piece of statuary, and introduced her.

"I was just telling your husband how much I like his picture," Overman informed her.

Angela was flattered that her husband was so much of a personage that he could have his picture hung in a great exhibition such as this, with its walls crowded with what seemed to her magnificent canvases, and its rooms filled with important and distinguished people. As they strolled about Eugene pointed out to her this well known artist and that writer, saying almost always that they were very able. He knew three or four of the celebrated collectors, prize givers, and art patrons by sight, and told Angela who they were. There were a number of striking looking models present whom Eugene knew either by reputation, whispered comment of friends, or personally—Zelma Desmond, who had posed for Eugene,

Hedda Anderson, Anna Magruder and Laura Matthewson among others. Angela was struck and in a way taken by the dash and beauty of these girls. They carried themselves with an air of personal freedom and courage which surprised her. Hedda Anderson was bold in her appearance but immensely smart. Her manner seemed to comment on the ordinary woman as being indifferent and not worth while. She looked at Angela walking with Eugene and wondered who she was.

"Isn't she striking," observed Angela, not knowing she was anyone whom Eugene knew.

"I know her well," he replied; "she's a model."

Just then Miss Anderson in return for his nod gave him a fetching smile. Angela chilled.

Elizabeth Stein passed by and he nodded to her.

"Who is she?" asked Angela.

"She's a socialist agitator and radical. She sometimes speaks from a soap-box on the East Side."

Angela studied her carefully. Her waxen complexion, smooth black hair laid in even plaits over her forehead, her straight, thin, chiseled nose, even red lips and low forehead indicated a daring and subtle soul. Angela did not understand her. She could not understand a girl as good looking as that doing any such thing as Eugene said, and yet she had a bold, rather free and easy air. She thought Eugene certainly knew strange people. He introduced to her William McConnell, Hudson Dula, who had not yet been to see them, Jan Jansen, Louis Deesa, Leonard Baker and Paynter Stone.

In regard to Eugene's picture the papers, with one exception, had nothing to say, but this one in both Eugene's and Angela's minds made up for all the others. It was the *Evening Sun*, a most excellent medium for art opinion, and it was very definite in its conclusions in regard to this particular work. The statement was:

"A new painter, Eugene Witla, has an oil entitled 'Six O'clock' which for directness, virility, sympathy, faithfulness to detail and what for want of a better term we may call totality of spirit, is quite the best thing in the exhibition. It looks rather out of place surrounded by the weak and spindling interpretations of scenery and water which so readily find a place in the exhibition of the Academy, but it is none the weaker for that. The artist has a new, crude, raw and almost rough method, but his picture seems to say quite clearly what he sees and feels. He may have to wait—if this is not a single burst of ability—but he will have a hearing. There is no question of that. Eugene Witla is an artist."

Eugene thrilled when he read this commentary. It was quite what he would have said himself if he had dared. Angela was beside herself with joy. Who was the critic who had said this, they wondered? What was he like? He must be truly an intellectual personage. Eugene wanted to go and look him up. If one saw his talent now, others would see it later. It was for this reason—though the picture subsequently came back to him unsold, and unmentioned so far as merit or prizes were concerned—that he decided to try for an exhibition of his own.

CHAPTER V

The hope of fame—what hours of speculation, what pulses of enthusiasm, what fevers of effort, are based on that peculiarly subtle illusion! It is yet the lure, the ignis fatuus of almost every breathing heart. In the young particularly it burns with the sweetness and perfume of spring fires. Then most of all does there seem substantial reality in the shadow of fame—those deep, beautiful illusions which tremendous figures throw over the world. Attainable, it seems, must be the peace and plenty and sweet content of fame—that glamour of achievement that never was on sea or land. Fame partakes of the beauty and freshness of the morning. It has in it the odour of the rose, the feel of rich satin, the color of the cheeks of youth. If we could but be famous when we dream of fame, and not when locks are tinged with grey, faces seamed with the lines that speak of past struggles, and eyes wearied with the tensity, the longings and the despairs of years! To bestride the world in the morning of life, to walk amid the plaudits and the huzzahs when love and faith are young; to feel youth and the world's affection when youth and health are sweet—what dream is that, of pure sunlight and moonlight compounded. A sun-kissed breath of mist in the sky; the reflection of moonlight upon water; the remembrance of dreams to the waking mind—of such is fame in our youth, and never afterward.

By such an illusion was Eugene's mind possessed. He had no conception of what life would bring him for his efforts. He thought if he could have his pictures hung in a Fifth Avenue gallery much as he had seen Bouguereau's "Venus" in Chicago, with people coming as he had come on that occasion—it would be of great comfort and satisfaction to him. If he could paint something which would be purchased by the Metropolitan Museum in New York he would then be somewhat of a classic figure, ranking with Corot and Daubigny and Rousseau of the French or with Turner and Watts and Millais of the English, the leading artistic figures of his pantheon. These men seemed to have something which he did not have, he thought, a greater breadth of technique, a finer comprehension of color and character, a feeling for the subtleties at the back of life which somehow showed through what they did. Larger experience, larger vision, larger feeling—these things seemed to be imminent in the great pictures exhibited here, and it made him a little uncertain of himself. Only the criticism in the *Evening Sun* fortified him against all thought of failure. *He was an artist.*

He gathered up the various oils he had done—there were some twenty-six all told now, scenes of the rivers, the streets, the night life, and so forth—and went over them carefully, touching up details which in the beginning he had merely sketched or indicated, adding to the force of a spot of color here, modifying a tone or shade there, and finally, after much brooding over the possible result, set forth to find a gallery which would give them place and commercial approval.

Eugene's feeling was that they were a little raw and sketchy—that they might not have sufficient human appeal, seeing that they dealt with factory architecture at times, scows, tugs, engines, the elevated roads in raw reds, yellows and blacks; but MacHugh, Dula, Smite, Miss Finch, Christina, the *Evening Sun*, Norma Whitmore, all had praised them, or some of them. Was not the world much more interested in the form and spirit of classic beauty such as that represented by Sir John Millais? Would it not prefer Rossetti's "Blessed Damozel" to any street scene ever painted? He could never be sure. In the very hour of his triumph when the *Sun* had just praised his picture, there lurked the spectre of possible intrinsic weakness. Did the world wish this sort of thing? Would it ever buy of him? Was he of any real value?

"No, artist heart!" one might have answered, "of no more value than any other worker of existence and no less. The sunlight on the corn, the color of dawn in the maid's cheek, the moonlight on the water—these are of value and of no value according to the soul to whom is the appeal. Fear not. Of dreams and the beauty of dreams is the world compounded."

Kellner and Son, purveyors of artistic treasures by both past and present masters, with offices in Fifth Avenue near Twenty-eighth Street, was the one truly significant firm of art-dealers in the city. The pictures in the windows of Kellner and Son, the exhibitions in their very exclusive show rooms, the general approval which their discriminating taste evoked, had attracted the attention of artists and the lay public for fully thirty years. Eugene had followed their shows with interest ever since he had been in New York. He had seen, every now and then, a most astonishing picture of one school or another displayed in their imposing shop window, and had heard artists comment from time to time on other things there with considerable enthusiasm. The first important picture of the impressionistic school—a heavy spring rain in a grove of silver poplars by Winthrop—had been shown in the window of this firm, fascinating Eugene with its technique. He had encountered here collections of Aubrey Beardsley's decadent drawings, of Helleu's silverpoints, of Rodin's astonishing sculptures and Thaulow's solid Scandinavian eclecticism. This house appeared to have capable artistic connections all over the world, for the latest art force in Italy, Spain, Switzerland, or Sweden, was quite as likely to find its timely expression here as the more accredited work of England, Germany or France. Kellner and Son were art connoisseurs in the best sense of the word, and although the German founder of the house had died many years before, its management and taste had never deteriorated.

Eugene did not know at this time how very difficult it was to obtain an exhibition under Kellner's auspices, they being over-crowded with offers of art material and appeals for display from celebrated artists who were quite willing and able to pay for the space and time they occupied. A fixed charge was made, never deviated from except in rare instances where the talent of the artist, his poverty, and the advisability of the exhibition were extreme. Two hundred dollars was considered little enough for the use of one of their show rooms for ten days.

Eugene had no such sum to spare, but one day in January, without any real knowledge as to what the conditions were, he carried four of the reproductions which had been made from time to time in *Truth* to the office of Mr. Kellner, certain that he had something to show. Miss Whitmore had indicated to him that Eberhard Zang wanted him to come and see him, but he thought if he was going anywhere he would prefer to go to Kellner and Son. He wanted to explain to Mr. Kellner, if there were such a person, that he had many more paintings which he considered even better—more expressive of his growing understanding of American life and of himself and his technique. He went in timidly, albeit with quite an air, for this adventure disturbed him much.

The American manager of Kellner and Son, M. Anatole Charles, was a Frenchman by birth and training, familiar with the spirit and history of French art, and with the drift and tendency of art in various other sections of the world. He had been sent here by the home office in Berlin not only because of his very thorough training in English art ways, and because of his ability to select that type of picture which would attract attention and bring credit and prosperity to the house here and abroad; but also because of his ability to make friends among the rich and powerful wherever he was, and to sell one type of important picture after another—having some knack or magnetic capacity for attracting to him those who cared for good art and were willing to pay for it. His specialties, of course, were the canvases of the eminently successful artists in various parts of the world—the living successful. He knew by experience what sold—here, in France, in England, in Germany. He was convinced that there was practically nothing of value in American art as yet—certainly not from the commercial point of view, and very little from the artistic. Beyond a few canvases by Inness, Homer, Sargent, Abbey, Whistler, men who were more foreign, or rather universal, than American in their attitude, he considered that the American art spirit was as yet young and raw and crude. "They do not seem to be grown up as yet over here," he said to his intimate friends. "They paint little things in a forceful way, but they do not seem as yet to see things as a whole. I miss that sense of the universe in miniature which we find in the canvases of so many of the great Europeans. They are better illustrators than artists over here—why I don't know."

M. Anatole Charles spoke English almost more than perfectly. He was an example of your true man of the world—polished, dignified, immaculately dressed, conservative in thought and of few words in expression. Critics and art enthusiasts were constantly running to him with this and that suggestion in regard to this and that artist, but he only lifted his sophisticated eyebrows, curled his superior mustachios, pulled at his highly artistic goatee, and exclaimed: "Ah!" or "So?" He asserted always that he was most anxious to find talent—profitable talent—though on occasion (and he would demonstrate that by an outward wave of his hands and a shrug of his shoulders), the house of Kellner and Son was not averse to doing what it could for art—and that for art's sake without any thought of profit whatsoever. "Where are your artists?" he would ask. "I look and look. Whistler, Abbey, Inness, Sargent—ah—they are old, where are the new ones?"

"Well, this one"—the critic would probably persist.

"Well, well, I go. I shall look. But I have little hope—very, very little hope."

He was constantly appearing under such pressure, at this studio and that—examining, criticising. Alas, he selected the work of but few artists for purposes of public exhibition and usually charged them well for it.

It was this man, polished, artistically superb in his way, whom Eugene was destined to meet this morning. When he entered the sumptuously furnished office of M. Charles the latter arose. He was seated at a little rosewood desk lighted by a lamp with green silk shade. One glance told him that Eugene was an artist—very likely of ability, more than likely of a sensitive, high-strung nature. He had long since learned that politeness and savoir faire cost nothing. It was the first essential so far as the good will of an artist was concerned. Eugene's card and message brought by a uniformed attendant had indicated the nature of his business. As he approached, M.

Charles' raised eyebrows indicated that he would be very pleased to know what he could do for Mr. Witla.

"I should like to show you several reproductions of pictures of mine," began Eugene in his most courageous manner. "I have been working on a number with a view to making a show and I thought that possibly you might be interested in looking at them with a view to displaying them for me. I have twenty-six all told and—"

"Ah! that is a difficult thing to suggest," replied M. Charles cautiously. "We have a great many exhibitions scheduled now—enough to carry us through two years if we considered nothing more. Obligations to artists with whom we have dealt in the past take up a great deal of our time. Contracts, which our Berlin and Paris branches enter into, sometimes crowd out our local shows entirely. Of course, we are always anxious to make interesting exhibitions if opportunity should permit. You know our charges?"

"No," said Eugene, surprised that there should be any.

"Two hundred dollars for two weeks. We do not take exhibitions for less than that time."

Eugene's countenance fell. He had expected quite a different reception. Nevertheless, since he had brought them, he untied the tape of the portfolio in which the prints were laid.

M. Charles looked at them curiously. He was much impressed with the picture of the East Side Crowd at first, but looking at one of Fifth Avenue in a snow storm, the battered, shabby bus pulled by a team of lean, unkempt, bony horses, he paused, struck by its force. He liked the delineation of swirling, wind-driven snow. The emptiness of this thoroughfare, usually so crowded, the buttoned, huddled, hunched, withdrawn look of those who traveled it, the exceptional details of piles of snow sifted on to window sills and ledges and into doorways and on to the windows of the bus itself, attracted his attention.

"An effective detail," he said to Eugene, as one critic might say to another, pointing to a line of white snow on the window of one side of the bus. Another dash of snow on a man's hat rim took his eye also. "I can feel the wind," he added.

Eugene smiled.

M. Charles passed on in silence to the steaming tug coming up the East River in the dark hauling two great freight barges. He was saying to himself that after all Eugene's art was that of merely seizing upon the obviously dramatic. It wasn't so much the art of color composition and life analysis as it was stage craft. The man before him had the ability to see the dramatic side of life. Still—

He turned to the last reproduction which was that of Greeley Square in a drizzling rain. Eugene by some mystery of his art had caught the exact texture of seeping water on gray stones in the glare of various electric lights. He had caught the values of various kinds of lights, those in cabs, those in cable cars, those in shop windows, those in the street lamp—relieving by them the black shadows of the crowds and of the sky. The color work here was unmistakably good.

"How large are the originals of these?" he asked thoughtfully.

"Nearly all of them thirty by forty."

Eugene could not tell by his manner whether he were merely curious or interested.

"All of them done in oil, I fancy."

"Yes, all."

"They are not bad, I must say," he observed cautiously. "A little persistently dramatic but—"

"These reproductions—" began Eugene, hoping by criticising the press work to interest him in the superior quality of the originals.

"Yes, I see," M. Charles interrupted, knowing full well what was coming. "They are very bad. Still they show well enough what the originals are like. Where is your studio?"

"61 Washington Square."

"As I say," went on M. Charles, noting the address on Eugene's card, "the opportunity for exhibition purposes is very limited and our charge is rather high. We have so many things we would like to exhibit—so many things we must exhibit. It is hard to say when the situation would permit— If you are interested I might come and see them sometime."

Eugene looked perturbed. Two hundred dollars! Two hundred dollars! Could he afford it? It would mean so much to him. And yet the man was not at all anxious to rent him the show room even at this price.

"I will come," said M. Charles, seeing his mood, "if you wish. That is what you want me to do. We have to be careful of what we exhibit here. It isn't as if it were an ordinary show room. I will drop you a card some day when occasion offers, if you wish, and you can let me know whether the time I suggest is all right. I am rather anxious to see these scenes of yours. They are very good of their kind. It may be—one never can tell—an opportunity might offer—a week or ten days, somewhere in between other things."

Eugene sighed inwardly. So this was how these things were done. It wasn't very flattering. Still, he must have an exhibition. He could afford two hundred if he had to. An exhibition elsewhere would not be so valuable. He had expected to make a better impression than this.

"I wish you would come," he said at last meditatively. "I think I should like the space if I can get it. I would like to know what you think."

M. Charles raised his eyebrows.

"Very well," he said, "I will communicate with you."

Eugene went out.

What a poor thing this exhibiting business was, he thought. Here he had been dreaming of an exhibition at Kellners which should be brought about without charge to him because they were tremendously impressed with his work. Now they did not even want his pictures—would charge him two hundred dollars to show them. It was a great come down—very discouraging.

Still he went home thinking it would do him some good. The critics would discuss his work just as they did that of other artists. They would have to see what he could do should it be that at last this thing which he had dreamed of and so deliberately planned had come true. He had thought of an exhibition at Kellner's as the last joyous thing to be attained in the world of rising art and now it looked as though he was near it. It might actually be coming to pass. This man wanted to see the rest of his work. He was not opposed to looking at them. What a triumph even that was!

CHAPTER VI

It was some little time before M. Charles condescended to write saying that if it was agreeable he would call Wednesday morning, January 16th, at 10 A. M., but the letter finally did come and this dispelled all his intermediary doubts and fears. At last he was to have a hearing! This man might see something in his work, possibly take a fancy to it. Who could tell? He showed the letter to Angela with an easy air as though it were quite a matter of course, but he felt intensely hopeful.

Angela put the studio in perfect order for she knew what this visit meant to Eugene, and in her eager, faithful way was anxious to help him as much as possible. She bought flowers from the Italian florist at the corner and put them in vases here and there. She swept and dusted, dressed herself immaculately in her most becoming house dress and waited with nerves at high tension for the fateful ring of the door bell. Eugene pretended to work at one of his pictures which he had done long before—the raw jangling wall of an East Side street with its swarms of children, its shabby push-carts, its mass of eager, shuffling, pushing mortals, the sense of rugged ground life running all through it, but he had no heart for the work. He was asking himself over and over what M. Charles would think. Thank heaven this studio looked so charming! Thank heaven Angela was so dainty in her pale green gown with a single red coral pin at her throat. He walked to the window and stared out at Washington Square, with its bare, wind-shaken branches of trees, its snow, its ant-like pedestrians hurrying here and there. If he were only rich—how peacefully he would paint! M. Charles could go to the devil.

The door bell rang.

Angela clicked a button and up came M. Charles quietly. They could hear his steps in the hall. He knocked and Eugene answered, decidedly nervous in his mind, but outwardly calm and dignified. M. Charles entered, clad in a fur-lined overcoat, fur cap and yellow chamois gloves.

"Ah, good morning!" said M. Charles in greeting. "A fine bracing day, isn't it? What a charming view you have here. Mrs. Witla! I'm delighted to meet you. I am a little late but I was unavoidably detained. One of our German associates is in the city."

He divested himself of his great coat and rubbed his hands before the fire. He tried, now that he had unbent so far, to be genial and considerate. If he and Eugene were to do any business in the future it must be so. Besides the picture on the easel before him, near the window, which for the time being he pretended not to see, was an astonishingly virile thing. Of whose work did it remind him—anybody's? He confessed to himself as he stirred around among his numerous art memories that he recalled nothing exactly like it. Raw reds, raw greens, dirty grey paving stones—such faces! Why this thing fairly shouted its facts. It seemed to say: "I'm dirty, I am commonplace, I am grim, I am shabby, but I am life." And there was no apologizing for anything in it, no glossing anything over. Bang! Smash! Crack! came the facts one after another, with a bitter, brutal insistence on their so-ness. Why, on moody days when he had felt sour and depressed he had seen somewhere a street that looked like this, and there it was—dirty, sad, slovenly, immoral, drunken—anything, everything, but here it was. "Thank God for a realist," he said to himself as he looked, for he knew life, this cold connoisseur; but he made no sign. He looked at the tall, slim frame of Eugene, his cheeks slightly sunken, his eyes bright—an artist every inch of him, and then at Angela, small, eager, a sweet, loving, little woman, and he was glad that he was going to be able to say that he would exhibit these things.

"Well," he said, pretending to look at the picture on the easel for the first time, "we might as well begin to look at these things. I see you have one here. Very good, I think, quite forceful. What others have you?"

Eugene was afraid this one hadn't appealed to him as much as he hoped it would, and set it aside quickly, picking up the second in the stock which stood against the wall, covered by a green curtain. It was the three engines entering the great freight yard abreast, the smoke of the engines towering straight up like tall whitish-grey plumes, in the damp, cold air, the sky lowering with blackish-grey clouds, the red and yellow and blue cars standing out in the sodden darkness because of the water. You could feel the cold, wet drizzle, the soppy tracks, the weariness of "throwing switches." There was a lone brakeman in the foreground, "throwing" a red brake signal. He was quite black and evidently wet.

"A symphony in grey," said M. Charles succinctly.

They came swiftly after this, without much comment from either, Eugene putting one canvas after another before him, leaving it for a few moments and replacing it with another. His estimate of his own work did not rise very rapidly, for M. Charles was persistently distant, but the latter could not help voicing approval of "After The Theatre," a painting full of the wonder and bustle of a night crowd under sputtering electric lamps. He saw that Eugene had covered almost every phase of what might be called the dramatic spectacle in the public life of the city and much that did not appear dramatic until he touched it—the empty canyon of Broadway at three o'clock in the morning; a long line of giant milk wagons, swinging curious lanterns, coming up from the docks at four o'clock in the morning; a plunging parade of fire vehicles, the engines steaming smoke, the people running or staring open-mouthed; a crowd of polite society figures emerging from the opera; the bread line; an Italian boy throwing pigeons in the air from a basket on his arm in a crowded lower West-side street. Everything he touched seemed to have romance and beauty, and yet it was real and mostly grim and shabby.

"I congratulate you, Mr. Witla," finally exclaimed M. Charles, moved by the ability of the man and feeling that caution was no longer necessary. "To me this is wonderful material, much more effective than the reproductions show, dramatic and true. I question whether you will make any money out of it. There is very little sale for American art in this country. It might almost do better in Europe. It *ought* to sell, but that is another matter. The best things do not always sell readily. It takes time. Still I will do what I can. I will give these pictures a two weeks' display early in April without any charge to you whatever." (Eugene started.) "I will call them to the attention of those who know. I will speak to those who buy. It is an honor, I assure you, to do this. I consider you an artist in every sense of the word—I might say a great artist. You ought, if you preserve yourself sanely and with caution, to go far, very far. I shall be glad to send for these when the time comes."

Eugene did not know how to reply to this. He did not quite understand the European seriousness of method, its appreciation of genius, which was thus so easily and sincerely expressed in a formal way. M. Charles meant every word he said. This was one of those rare and gratifying moments of his life when he was permitted to extend to waiting and unrecognized genius the assurance of the consideration and approval of the world. He stood there waiting to hear what Eugene would say, but the latter only flushed under his pale skin.

"I'm very glad," he said at last, in his rather commonplace, off-hand, American way. "I thought they were pretty good but I wasn't sure. I'm very grateful to you."

"You need not feel gratitude toward me," returned M. Charles, now modifying his formal manner. "You can congratulate yourself—your art. I am honored, as I tell you. We will make a fine display of them. You have no frames for these? Well, never mind, I will lend you frames."

He smiled and shook Eugene's hand and congratulated Angela. She had listened to this address with astonishment and swelling pride. She had perceived, despite Eugene's manner, the anxiety he was feeling, the intense hopes he was building on the outcome of this meeting. M. Charles' opening manner had deceived her. She had felt that he did not care so much after all, and that Eugene was going to be disappointed. Now, when this burst of approval came, she hardly knew what to make of it. She looked at Eugene and saw that he was intensely moved by not only a sense of relief, but pride and joy. His pale, dark face showed it. To see this load of care taken off him whom she loved so deeply was enough to unsettle Angela. She found herself stirred in a pathetic way and now, when M. Charles turned to her, tears welled to her eyes.

"Don't cry, Mrs. Witla," he said grandly on seeing this. "You have a right to be proud of your husband. He is a great artist. You should take care of him."

"Oh, I'm so happy," half-laughed and half-sobbed Angela, "I can't help it."

She went over to where Eugene was and put her face against his coat. Eugene slipped his arm about her and smiled sympathetically. M. Charles smiled also, proud of the effect of his words. "You both have a right to feel very happy," he said.

"Little Angela!" thought Eugene. This was your true wife for you, your good woman. Her husband's success meant all to her. She had no life of her own—nothing outside of him and his good fortune.

M. Charles smiled. "Well, I will be going now," he said finally. "I will send for the pictures when the time comes. And meanwhile you two must come with me to dinner. I will let you know."

He bowed himself out with many assurances of good will, and then Angela and Eugene looked at each other.

"Oh, isn't it lovely, Honeybun," she cried, half giggling, half crying. (She had begun to call him Honeybun the first day they were married.) "My Eugene a great artist. He said it was a great honor! Isn't that lovely? And all the world is going to know it soon, now. Isn't that fine! Oh dear, I'm so proud." And she threw her arms ecstatically about his neck.

Eugene kissed her affectionately. He was not thinking so much of her though as he was of Kellner and Son—their great exhibit room, the appearance of these twenty-seven or thirty great pictures in gold frames; the spectators who might come to see; the newspaper criticisms; the voices of approval. Now all his artist friends would know that he was considered a great artist; he was to have a chance to associate on equal terms with men like Sargent and Whistler if he ever met them. The world would hear of him widely. His fame might go to the uttermost parts of the earth.

He went to the window after a time and looked out. There came back to his mind Alexandria, the printing shop, the Peoples' Furniture Company in Chicago, the Art Students League, the *Daily Globe*. Surely he had come by devious paths.

"Gee!" he exclaimed at last simply. "Smite and MacHugh'll be glad to hear this. I'll have to go over and tell them."

CHAPTER VII

The exhibition which followed in April was one of those things which happen to fortunate souls—a complete flowering out before the eyes of the world of its feelings, emotions, perceptions, and understanding. We all have our feelings and emotions, but lack the power of self-expression. It is true, the work and actions of any man are to some degree expressions of character, but this is a different thing. The details of most lives are not held up for public examination at any given time. We do not see succinctly in any given place just what an individual thinks and feels. Even the artist is not always or often given the opportunity of collected public expression under conspicuous artistic auspices. Some are so fortunate—many are not. Eugene realized that fortune was showering its favors upon him.

When the time came, M. Charles was so kind as to send for the pictures and to arrange all the details. He had decided with Eugene that because of the vigor of treatment and the prevailing color scheme black frames would be the best. The principal exhibition room on the ground floor in which these paintings were to be hung was heavily draped in red velvet and against this background the different pictures stood out effectively. Eugene visited the show room at the time the pictures were being hung, with Angela, with Smite and MacHugh, Shotmeyer and others. He had long since notified Norma Whitmore and Miriam Finch, but not the latter until after Wheeler had had time to tell her. This also chagrined her, for she felt in this as she had about his marriage, that he was purposely neglecting her.

The dream finally materialized—a room eighteen by forty, hung with dark red velvet, irradiated with a soft, illuminating glow from hidden lamps in which Eugene's pictures stood forth in all their rawness and reality—almost as vigorous as life itself. To some people, those who do not see life clearly and directly, but only through other people's eyes, they seemed more so.

For this reason Eugene's exhibition of pictures was an astonishing thing to most of those who saw it. It concerned phases of life which in the main they had but casually glanced at, things which because they were commonplace and customary were supposedly beyond the pale of artistic significance. One picture in particular, a great hulking, ungainly negro, a positively animal man, his ears thick and projecting, his lips fat, his nose flat, his cheek bones prominent, his whole body expressing brute strength and animal indifference to dirt and cold, illustrated this point particularly. He was standing in a cheap, commonplace East Side street. The time evidently was a January or February morning. His business was driving an ash cart, and his occupation at the moment illustrated by the picture was that of lifting a great can of mixed ashes, paper and garbage to the edge of the ungainly iron wagon. His hands were immense and were covered with great red patched woolen and leather gloves—dirty, bulbous, inconvenient, one would have said. His head and ears were swaddled about by a red flannel shawl or strip of cloth which was knotted under his pugnacious chin, and his forehead, shawl and all, surmounted by a brown canvas cap with his badge and number as a garbage driver on it. About his waist was tied a great piece of rough coffee sacking and his arms and legs looked as though he might have on two or three pairs of trousers and as many vests. He was looking purblindly down the shabby street, its hard crisp snow littered with tin cans, paper, bits of slop and offal. Dust—gray ash dust, was flying from his upturned can. In the distance behind him was a milk wagon, a few pedestrians, a little thinly clad girl coming out of a delicatessen store. Over head were dull small-paned windows, some shutters with a few of their slats broken out, a frowsy headed man looking out evidently to see whether the day was cold.

Eugene was so cruel in his indictment of life. He seemed to lay on his details with bitter lack of consideration. Like a slavedriver lashing a slave he spared no least shade of his cutting brush. "Thus, and thus and thus" (he seemed to say) "is it." "What do you think of this? and this? and this?"

People came and stared. Young society matrons, art dealers, art critics, the literary element who were interested in art, some musicians, and, because the newspapers made especial mention of it, quite a number of those who run wherever they imagine there is something interesting to see. It was quite a notable two weeks' display. Miriam Finch (though she never admitted to Eugene that she had seen it—she would not give him that satisfaction) Norma Whitmore, William McConnell, Louis Deesa, Owen Overman, Paynter Stone, the whole ruck and rabble of literary and artistic life, came. There were artists of great ability there whom Eugene had never seen before. It would have pleased him immensely if he had chanced to see several of the city's most distinguished social leaders looking, at one time and another, at his pictures. All his observers were astonished at his virility, curious as to his personality, curious as to what motive, or significance, or point of view it might have. The more eclectically cultured turned to the newspapers to see what the art critics would say of this—how they would label it. Because of the force of the work, the dignity and critical judgment of Kellner and Son, the fact that the public of its own instinct and volition was interested, most of the criticisms were favorable. One art publication, connected with and representative of the conservative tendencies of a great publishing house, denied the merit of the collection as a whole, ridiculed the artist's insistence on shabby details as having artistic merit, denied that he could draw accurately, denied that he was a lover of pure beauty, and accused him of having no higher ideal than that of desire to shock the current mass by painting brutal things brutally.

"Mr. Witla," wrote this critic, "would no doubt be flattered if he were referred to as an American Millet. The brutal exaggeration of that painter's art would probably testify to him of his own merit. He is mistaken. The great Frenchman was a lover of humanity, a reformer in spirit, a master of drawing and composition. There was nothing of this cheap desire to startle and offend by what he did. If we are to have ash cans and engines and broken-down bus-horses thrust down our throats as art, Heaven preserve us. We had better turn to commonplace photography at once and be done with it. Broken window shutters, dirty pavements, half frozen ash cart drivers, overdrawn, heavily exaggerated figures of policemen, tenement harridans, beggars, panhandlers, sandwich men—of such is *Art* according to Eugene Witla."

Eugene winced when he read this. For the time being it seemed true enough. His art was shabby. Yet there were others like Luke Severas who went to the other extreme.

"A true sense of the pathetic, a true sense of the dramatic, the ability to endow color—not with its photographic value, though to the current thought it may seem so—but with its higher spiritual significance; the ability to indict life with its own grossness, to charge it prophetically with its own meanness and cruelty in order that mayhap it may heal itself; the ability to see wherein is beauty—even in shame and pathos and degradation; of such is this man's work. He comes from the soil apparently, fresh to a great task. There is no fear here, no bowing to traditions, no recognition of any of the accepted methods. It is probable that he may not know what the accepted methods are. So much the better. We have a new method. The world is the richer for that. As we have said before, Mr. Witla may have to wait for his recognition. It is certain that these pictures will not be quickly purchased and hung in parlors. The average art lover does not take to a new thing so readily. But if he persevere, if his art does not fail him, his turn will come. It cannot fail. He is a great artist. May he live to realize it consciously and in his own soul."

Tears leaped to Eugene's eyes when he read this. The thought that he was a medium for some noble and super-human purpose thickened the cords in his throat until they felt like a lump. He wanted to be a great artist, he wanted to be worthy of the appreciation that was thus extended to him. He thought of all the writers and artists and musicians and connoisseurs of pictures who would read this and remember him. It was just possible that from now onwards some of his pictures would sell. He would be so glad to devote himself to this sort of thing—to quit magazine illustration entirely. How ridiculous the latter was, how confined and unimportant. Henceforth, unless driven by sheer necessity, he would do it no more. They should beg in vain. He was an artist in the true sense of the word—a great painter, ranking with Whistler, Sargent, Velasquez and Turner. Let the magazines with their little ephemeral circulation go their way. He was for the whole world.

He stood at the window of his studio one day while the exhibition was still in progress, Angela by his side, thinking of all the fine things that had been said. No picture had been sold, but M. Charles had told him that some might be taken before it was all over.

"I think if I make any money out of this," he said to Angela, "we will go to Paris this summer. I have always wanted to see Paris. In the fall we'll come back and take a studio up town. They are building some dandy ones up in Sixty-fifth Street." He was thinking of the artists who could pay three and four thousand dollars a year for a studio. He was thinking of men who made four, five, six and even eight hundred dollars out of every picture they painted. If he could do that! Or if he could get a contract for a mural decoration for next winter. He had very little money laid by. He had spent most of his time this winter working with these pictures.

"Oh, Eugene," exclaimed Angela, "it seems so wonderful. I can hardly believe it. You a really, truly, great artist! And us going to Paris! Oh, isn't that beautiful. It seems like a dream. I think and think, but it's hard to believe that I am here sometimes, and that your pictures are up at Kellner's and oh!—" she clung to him in an ecstasy of delight.

Out in the park the leaves were just budding. It looked as though the whole square were hung with a transparent green net, spangled, as was the net in his room, with tiny green leaves. Songsters were idling in the sun. Sparrows were flying noisily about in small clouds. Pigeons were picking lazily between the car tracks of the street below.

"I might get a group of pictures illustrative of Paris. You can't tell what we'll find. Charles says he will have another exhibition for me next spring, if

I'll get the material ready." He pushed his arms above his head and yawned deliciously.

He wondered what Miss Finch thought now. He wondered where Christina Channing was. There was never a word in the papers yet as to what had become of her. He knew what Norma Whitmore thought. She was apparently as happy as though the exhibition had been her own.

"Well, I must go and get your lunch, Honeybun!" exclaimed Angela. "I have to go to Mr. Gioletti, the grocer, and to Mr. Ruggiere, the vegetable man." She laughed, for the Italian names amused her.

Eugene went back to his easel. He was thinking of Christina—where was she? At that moment, if he had known, she was looking at his pictures, only newly returned from Europe. She had seen a notice in the *Evening Post*.

"Such work!" Christina thought, "such force! Oh, what a delightful artist. And he was with me."

Her mind went back to Florizel and the amphitheatre among the trees. "He called me 'Diana of the Mountains,'" she thought, "his 'hamadryad,' his 'huntress of the morn.'" She knew he was married. An acquaintance of hers had written in December. The past was past with her—she wanted no more of it. But it was beautiful to think upon—a delicious memory.

"What a queer girl I am," she thought.

Still she wished she could see him again—not face to face, but somewhere where he could not see her. She wondered if he was changing—if he would ever change. He was so beautiful then—to her.

CHAPTER VIII

Paris now loomed bright in Eugene's imagination, the prospect mingling with a thousand other delightful thoughts. Now that he had attained to the dignity of a public exhibition, which had been notably commented upon by the newspapers and art journals and had been so generally attended by the elect, artists, critics, writers generally, seemed to know of him. There were many who were anxious to meet and greet him, to speak approvingly of his work. It was generally understood, apparently, that he was a great artist, not exactly arrived to the fullness of his stature as yet, being so new, but on his way. Among those who knew him he was, by this one exhibition, lifted almost in a day to a lonely height, far above the puny efforts of such men as Smite and MacHugh, McConnell and Deesa, the whole world of small artists whose canvases packed the semi-annual exhibition of the National Academy of Design and the Water color society, and with whom in a way, he had been associated. He was a great artist now—recognized as such by the eminent critics who knew; and as such, from now on, would be expected to do the work of a great artist. One phrase in the criticisms of Luke Severas in the *Evening Sun* as it appeared during the run of his exhibition remained in his memory clearly—"If he perseveres, if his art does not fail him." Why should his art fail him?—he asked himself. He was immensely pleased to hear from M. Charles at the close of the exhibition that three of his pictures had been sold—one for three hundred dollars to Henry McKenna, a banker; another, the East Side street scene which M. Charles so greatly admired, to Isaac Wertheim, for five hundred dollars; a third, the one of the three engines and the railroad yard, to Robert C. Winchon, a railroad man, first vice-president of one of the great railroads entering New York, also for five hundred dollars. Eugene had never heard of either Mr. McKenna or Mr. Winchon, but he was assured that they were men of wealth and refinement. At Angela's suggestion he asked M. Charles if he would not accept one of his pictures as a slight testimony of his appreciation for all he had done for him. Eugene would not have thought to do this, he was so careless and unpractical. But Angela thought of it, and saw that he did it. M. Charles was greatly pleased, and took the picture of Greeley Square, which he considered a masterpiece of color interpretation. This somehow sealed the friendship between these two, and M. Charles was anxious to see Eugene's interests properly forwarded. He asked him to leave three of his scenes on sale for a time and he would see what he could do. Meanwhile, Eugene, with thirteen hundred added to the thousand and some odd dollars he had left in his bank from previous earnings, was convinced that his career was made, and decided, as he had planned to go to Paris, for the summer at least.

This trip, so exceptional to him, so epoch-making, was easily arranged. All the time he had been in New York he had heard more in his circle of Paris than of any other city. Its streets, its quarters, its museums, its theatres and opera were already almost a commonplace to him. The cost of living, the ideal methods of living, the way to travel, what to see—how often he had sat and listened to descriptions of these things. Now he was going. Angela took the initiative in arranging all the practical details—such as looking up the steamship routes, deciding on the size of trunks required, what to take, buying the tickets, looking up the rates of the different hotels and pensions at which they might possibly stay. She was so dazed by the glory that had burst upon her husband's life that she scarcely knew what to do or what to make of it.

"That Mr. Bierdat," she said to Eugene, referring to one of the assistant steam-ship agents with whom she had taken counsel, "tells me that if we are just going for the summer it's foolish to take anything but absolute necessaries. He says we can buy so many nice little things to wear over there if we need them, and then I can bring them back duty free in the fall."

Eugene approved of this. He thought Angela would like to see the shops. They finally decided to go via London, returning direct from Havre, and on the tenth of May they departed, arriving in London a week later and in Paris on the first of June. Eugene was greatly impressed with London. He had arrived in time to miss the British damp and cold and to see London through a golden haze which was entrancing. Angela objected to the shops, which she described as "punk," and to the condition of the lower classes, who were so poor and wretchedly dressed. She and Eugene discussed the interesting fact that all Englishmen looked exactly alike, dressed, walked, and wore their hats and carried their canes exactly alike. Eugene was impressed with the apparent "go" of the men—their smartness and dapperness. The women he objected to in the main as being dowdy and homely and awkward.

But when he reached Paris, what a difference! In London, because of the lack of sufficient means (he did not feel that as yet he had sufficient to permit him to indulge in the more expensive comforts and pleasures of the city) and for the want of someone to provide him with proper social introductions, he was compelled to content himself with that superficial, exterior aspect of things which only the casual traveler sees—the winding streets, the crush of traffic, London Tower, Windsor Castle, the Inns of court, the Strand, Piccadilly, St. Paul's and, of course, the National Gallery and the British Museum. South Kensington and all those various endowed palaces where objects of art are displayed pleased him greatly. In the main he was struck with the conservatism of London, its atmosphere of Empire, its soldiery and the like, though he considered it drab, dull, less strident than New York, and really less picturesque. When he came to Paris, however, all this was changed. Paris is of itself a holiday city—one whose dress is always gay, inviting, fresh, like one who sets forth to spend a day in the country. As Eugene stepped onto the dock at Calais and later as he journeyed across and into the city, he could feel the vast difference between France and England. The one country seemed young, hopeful, American, even foolishly gay, the other serious, speculative, dour.

Eugene had taken a number of letters from M. Charles, Hudson Dula, Louis Deesa, Leonard Baker and others, who, on hearing that he was going, had volunteered to send him to friends in Paris who might help him. The principal thing, if he did not wish to maintain a studio of his own, and did wish to learn, was to live with some pleasant French family where he could hear French and pick it up quickly. If he did not wish to do this, the next best thing was to settle in the Montmartre district in some section or court where he could obtain a nice studio, and where there were a number of American or English students. Some of the Americans to whom he had letters were already domiciled here. With a small calling list of friends who spoke English he would do very well.

"You will be surprised, Witla," said Deesa to him one day, "how much English you can get understood by making intelligent signs."

Eugene had laughed at Deesa's descriptions of his own difficulties and successes, but he found that Deesa was right. Signs went very far and they were, as a rule, thoroughly intelligible.

The studio which he and Angela eventually took after a few days spent at an hotel, was a comfortable one on the third floor of a house which Eugene found ready to his hand, recommended by M. Arkquin, of the Paris branch of Kellner and Son. Another artist, Finley Wood, whom afterwards Eugene recalled as having been mentioned to him by Ruby Kenny, in Chicago, was leaving Paris for the summer. Because of M. Charles' impressive letter, M. Arkquin was most anxious that Eugene should be comfortably installed and suggested that he take this, the charge being anything he cared to pay—forty francs the month. Eugene looked at it and was delighted. It was in the back of the house, looking out on a little garden, and because of a westward slope of the ground from this direction and an accidental breach in the building line, commanded a wide sweep of the city of Paris, the twin towers of Notre Dame, the sheer rise of the Eiffel tower. It was fascinating to see the lights of the city blinking of an evening. Eugene would invariably draw his chair close to his favorite window when he came in, while Angela made lemonade or iced tea or practised her culinary art on a chafing dish. In presenting to him an almost standard American menu she exhibited the executive ability and natural industry which was her chief characteristic. She would go to the neighboring groceries, rotisseries, patisseries, green vegetable stands, and get the few things she needed in the smallest quantities, always selecting the best and preparing them with the greatest care. She was an excellent cook and loved to set a dainty and shining table. She saw no need of company, for she was perfectly happy alone with Eugene and felt that he must be with her. She had no desire to go anywhere by herself—only with him; and she would hang on every thought and motion waiting for him to say what his pleasure would be.

The wonder of Paris to Eugene was its freshness and the richness of its art spirit as expressed on every hand. He was never weary of looking at the undersized French soldiery with their wide red trousers, blue coats and red caps, or the police with their capes and swords and the cab drivers with their air of leisurely superiority. The Seine, brisk with boats at this season of the year, the garden of the Tuileries, with its white marble nudes and formal paths and stone benches, the Bois, the Champ de Mars, the Trocadero Museum, the Louvre—all the wonder streets and museums held him as in a dream.

"Gee," he exclaimed to Angela one afternoon as he followed the banks of the Seine toward Issy, "this is certainly the home of the blessed for all good artists. Smell that perfume. (It was from a perfume factory in the distance.) See that barge!" He leaned on the river wall. "Ah," he sighed, "this is perfect."

They went back in the dusk on the roof of an open car. "When I die," he sighed, "I hope I come to Paris. It is all the heaven I want."

Yet like all perfect delights, it lost some of its savour after a time, though not much. Eugene felt that he could live in Paris if his art would permit him—though he must go back, he knew, for the present anyhow.

Angela, he noticed after a time, was growing in confidence, if not in mentality. From a certain dazed uncertainty which had characterized her the preceding fall when she had first come to New York, heightened and increased for the time being by the rush of art life and strange personalities she had encountered there and here she was blossoming into a kind of assurance born of experience. Finding that Eugene's ideas, feelings and interests were of the upper world of thought entirely—concerned with types, crowds, the aspect of buildings, streets, skylines, the humors and pathetic aspects of living, she concerned herself solely with the managerial details. It did not take her long to discover that if anyone would relieve Eugene of all care for himself he would let him do it. It was no satisfaction to him to buy himself anything. He objected to executive and commercial details. If tickets had to be bought, time tables consulted, inquiries made, any labor of argument or dispute engaged in, he was loath to enter on it. "You get these, will you, Angela?" he would plead, or "you see him about that. I can't now. Will you?"

Angela would hurry to the task, whatever it was, anxious to show that she was of real use and necessity. On the busses of London or Paris, as in New York, he was sketching, sketching, sketching—cabs, little passenger boats of the Seine, characters in the cafes, parks, gardens, music halls, anywhere, anything, for he was practically tireless. All that he wanted was not to be bothered very much, to be left to his own devices. Sometimes Angela would pay all the bills for him for a day. She carried his purse, took charge of all the express orders into which their cash had been transferred, kept a list of all their expenditures, did the shopping, buying, paying. Eugene was left to see the thing that he wanted to see, to think the things that he wanted to think. During all those early days Angela made a god of him and he was very willing to cross his legs, Buddha fashion, and act as one.

Only at night when there were no alien sights or sounds to engage his attention, when not even his art could come between them, and she could draw him into her arms and submerge his restless spirit in the tides of her love did she feel his equal—really worthy of him. These transports which came with the darkness, or with the mellow light of the little oil lamp that hung in chains from the ceiling near their wide bed, or in the faint freshness of dawn with the birds cheeping in the one tree of the little garden below— were to her at once utterly generous and profoundly selfish. She had eagerly absorbed Eugene's philosophy of self-indulgent joy where it concerned themselves—all the more readily as it coincided with her own vague ideas and her own hot impulses.

Angela had come to marriage through years of self-denial, years of bitter longing for the marriage that perhaps would never be, and out of those years she had come to the marriage bed with a cumulative and intense passion. Without any knowledge either of the ethics or physiology of sex, except as pertained to her state as a virgin, she was vastly ignorant of marriage itself; the hearsay of girls, the equivocal confessions of newly married women, and the advice of her elder sister (conveyed by Heaven only knows what process of conversation) had left her almost as ignorant as before, and now she explored its mysteries with abandon, convinced that the unrestrained gratification of passion was normal and excellent—in addition to being, as she came to find, a universal solvent for all differences of opinion or temperament that threatened their peace of mind. Beginning with their life in the studio on Washington Square, and continuing with even greater fervor now in Paris, there was what might be described as a prolonged riot of indulgence between them, bearing no relation to any necessity in their natures, and certainly none to the demands which Eugene's intellectual and artistic tasks laid upon him. She was to Eugene astonishing and delightful; and yet perhaps not so much delightful as astonishing. Angela was in a sense elemental, but Eugene was not: he was the artist, in this as in other things, rousing himself to a pitch of appreciation which no strength so undermined by intellectual subtleties could continuously sustain. The excitement of adventure, of intrigue in a sense, of discovering the secrets of feminine personality—these were really what had constituted the charm, if not the compelling urge, of his romances. To conquer was beautiful: but it was in essence an intellectual enterprise. To see his rash dreams come true in the yielding of the last sweetness possessed by the desired woman, had been to him imaginatively as well as physically an irresistible thing. But these enterprises were like thin silver strands spun out across an abyss, whose beauty but not whose dangers were known to him. Still, he rejoiced in this magnificent creature-joy which Angela supplied; it was, so far as it was concerned, what he thought he wanted. And Angela interpreted her power to respond to what seemed his inexhaustible desire as not only a kindness but a duty.

Eugene set up his easel here, painted from nine to noon some days, and on others from two to five in the afternoon. If it were dark, he would walk or ride with Angela or visit the museums, the galleries and the public buildings or stroll in the factory or railroad quarters of the city. Eugene sympathized most with sombre types and was constantly drawing something which represented grim care. Aside from the dancers in the music halls, the toughs, in what later became known as the Apache district, the summer picnicking parties at Versailles and St. Cloud, the boat crowds on the Seine, he drew factory throngs, watchmen and railroad crossings, market people, market in the dark, street sweepers, newspaper vendors, flower merchants, always with a memorable street scene in the background. Some of the most interesting bits of Paris, its towers, bridges, river views, façades, appeared in backgrounds to the grim or picturesque or pathetic character studies. It was his hope that he could interest America in these things—that his next exhibition would not only illustrate his versatility and persistence of talent, but show an improvement in his art, a surer sense of color values, a greater analytical power in the matter of character, a surer selective taste in the matter of composition and arrangement. He did not realize that all this might be useless—that he was, aside from his art, living a life which might rob talent of its finest flavor, discolor the aspect of the world for himself, take scope from imagination and hamper effort with nervous irritation, and make accomplishment impossible. He had no knowledge of the effect of one's sexual life upon one's work, nor what such a life when badly arranged can do to a perfect art—how it can distort the sense of color, weaken that balanced judgment of character which is so essential to a normal interpretation of life, make all striving hopeless, take from art its most joyous conception, make life itself seem unimportant and death a relief.

CHAPTER IX

The summer passed, and with it the freshness and novelty of Paris, though Eugene never really wearied of it. The peculiarities of a different national life, the variations between this and his own country in national ideals, an obviously much more complaisant and human attitude toward morals, a matter-of-fact acceptance of the ills, weaknesses and class differences, to say nothing of the general physical appearance, the dress, habitations and amusements of the people, astonished as much as they entertained him. He was never weary of studying the differences between American and European architecture, noting the pacific manner in which the Frenchman appeared to take life, listening to Angela's unwearied comments on the cleanliness, economy, thoroughness with which the French women kept house, rejoicing in the absence of the American leaning to incessant activity. Angela was struck by the very moderate prices for laundry, the skill with which their concierge—who governed this quarter and who knew sufficient English to talk to her—did her marketing, cooking, sewing and entertaining. The richness of supply and aimless waste of Americans was alike unknown. Because she was naturally of a domestic turn Angela became very intimate with Madame Bourgoche and learned of her a hundred and one little tricks of domestic economy and arrangement.

"You're a peculiar girl, Angela," Eugene once said to her. "I believe you would rather sit down stairs and talk to that French-woman than meet the most interesting literary or artistic personage that ever was. What do you find that's so interesting to talk about?"

"Oh, nothing much," replied Angela, who was not unconscious of the implied hint of her artistic deficiencies. "She's such a smart woman. She's so practical. She knows more in a minute about saving and buying and making a little go a long way than any American woman I ever saw. I'm not interested in her any more than I am in anyone else. All the artistic people do, that I can see, is to run around and pretend that they're a whole lot when they're not."

Eugene saw that he had made an irritating reference, not wholly intended in the way it was being taken.

"I'm not saying she isn't able," he went on. "One talent is as good as another, I suppose. She certainly looks clever enough to me. Where is her husband?"

"He was killed in the army," returned Angela dolefully.

"Well I suppose you'll learn enough from her to run a hotel when you get back to New York. You don't know enough about housekeeping now, do you?"

Eugene smiled with his implied compliment. He was anxious to get Angela's mind off the art question. He hoped she would feel or see that he meant nothing, but she was not so easily pacified.

"You don't think I'm so bad, Eugene, do you?" she asked after a moment. "You don't think it makes so much difference whether I talk to Madame Bourgoche? She isn't so dull. She's awfully smart. You just haven't talked to her. She says she can tell by looking at you that you're a great artist. You're different. You remind her of a Mr. Degas that once lived here. Was he a great artist?"

"Was he!" said Eugene. "Well I guess yes. Did he have this studio?"

"Oh, a long time ago—fifteen years ago."

Eugene smiled beatifically. This was a great compliment. He could not help liking Madame Bourgoche for it. She was bright, no doubt of that, or she would not be able to make such a comparison. Angela drew from him, as before, that her domesticity and housekeeping skill was as important as anything else in the world, and having done this was satisfied and cheerful once more. Eugene thought how little art or conditions or climate or country altered the fundamental characteristics of human nature. Here he was in Paris, comparatively well supplied with money, famous, or in process of becoming so, and quarreling with Angela over little domestic idiosyncrasies, just as in Washington Square.

By late September Eugene had most of his Paris sketches so well laid in that he could finish them anywhere. Some fifteen were as complete as they could be made. A number of others were nearly so. He decided that he had had a profitable summer. He had worked hard and here was the work to show for it—twenty-six canvases which were as good, in his judgment, as those he had painted in New York. They had not taken so long, but he was surer of himself—surer of his method. He parted reluctantly with all the lovely things he had seen, believing that this collection of Parisian views would be as impressive to Americans as had been his New York views. M. Arkquin for one, and many others, including the friends of Deesa and Dula were delighted with them. The former expressed the belief that some of them might be sold in France.

Eugene returned to America with Angela, and learning that he might stay in the old studio until December first, settled down to finish the work for his exhibition there.

The first suggestion that Eugene had that anything was wrong with him, aside from a growing apprehensiveness as to what the American people would think of his French work, was in the fall, when he began to imagine—or perhaps it was really true—that coffee did not agree with him. He had for several years now been free of his old-time complaint,—stomach trouble; but gradually it was beginning to reappear and he began to complain to Angela that he was feeling an irritation after his meals, that coffee came up in his throat. "I think I'll have to try tea or something else if this doesn't stop," he observed. She suggested chocolate and he changed to that, but this merely resulted in shifting the ill to another quarter. He now began to quarrel with his work—not being able to get a certain effect, and having sometimes altered and re-altered and re-re-altered a canvas until it bore little resemblance to the original arrangement, he would grow terribly discouraged; or believe that he had attained perfection at last, only to change his mind the following morning.

"Now," he would say, "I think I have that thing right at last, thank heaven!"

Angela would heave a sigh of relief, for she could feel instantly any distress or inability that he felt, but her joy was of short duration. In a few hours she would find him working at the same canvas changing something. He grew thinner and paler at this time and his apprehensions as to his future rapidly became morbid.

"By George! Angela," he said to her one day, "it would be a bad thing for me if I were to become sick now. It's just the time that I don't want to. I want to finish this exhibition up right and then go to London. If I could do London and Chicago as I did New York I would be just about made, but if I'm going to get sick—"

"Oh, you're not going to get sick, Eugene," replied Angela, "you just think you are. You want to remember that you've worked very hard this summer. And think how hard you worked last winter! You need a good rest, that's what you need. Why don't you stop after you get this exhibition ready and rest awhile? You have enough to live on for a little bit. M. Charles will probably sell a few more of those pictures, or some of those will sell and then you can wait. Don't try to go to London in the spring. Go on a walking tour or go down South or just rest awhile, anywhere,—that's what you need."

Eugene realized vaguely that it wasn't rest that he needed so much as peace of mind. He was not tired. He was merely nervously excited and apprehensive. He began to sleep badly, to have terrifying dreams, to feel that his heart was failing him. At two o'clock in the morning, the hour when for some reason human vitality appears to undergo a peculiar disturbance, he would wake with a sense of sinking physically. His pulse would appear to be very low, and he would feel his wrists nervously. Not infrequently he would break out in a cold perspiration and would get up and walk about to restore himself. Angela would rise and walk with him. One day at his easel he was seized with a peculiar nervous disturbance—a sudden glittering light before his eyes, a rumbling in his ears, and a sensation which was as if his body were being pricked with ten million needles. It was as though his whole nervous system had given way at every minute point and division. For the time being he was intensely frightened, believing that he was going crazy, but he said nothing. It came to him as a staggering truth that the trouble with him was over-indulgence physically; that the remedy was abstinence, complete or at least partial; that he was probably so far weakened mentally and physically that it would be very difficult for him to recover; that his ability to paint might be seriously affected—his life blighted.

He stood before his canvas holding his brush, wondering. When the shock had completely gone he laid the brush down with a trembling hand. He walked to the window, wiped his cold, damp forehead with his hand and then turned to get his coat from the closet.

"Where are you going?" asked Angela.

"For a little walk. I'll be back soon. I don't feel just as fresh as I might."

She kissed him good-bye at the door and let him go, but her heart troubled her.

"I'm afraid Eugene is going to get sick," she thought. "He ought to stop work."

CHAPTER X

It was the beginning of a period destined to last five or six years, in which, to say the least, Eugene was not himself. He was not in any sense out of his mind, if power to reason clearly, jest sagely, argue and read intelligently are any evidences of sanity; but privately his mind was a maelstrom of contradictory doubts, feelings and emotions. Always of a philosophic and introspective turn, this peculiar faculty of reasoning deeply and feeling emotionally were now turned upon himself and his own condition and, as in all such cases where we peer too closely into the subtleties of creation, confusion was the result. Previously he had been well satisfied that the world knew nothing. Neither in religion, philosophy nor science was there any answer to the riddle of existence. Above and below the little scintillating plane of man's thought was—what? Beyond the optic strength of the greatest telescope,—far out upon the dim horizon of space—were clouds of stars. What were they doing out there? Who governed them? When were their sidereal motions calculated? He figured life as a grim dark mystery, a sad semiconscious activity turning aimlessly in the dark. No one knew anything. God knew nothing—himself least of all. Malevolence, life living on death, plain violence—these were the chief characteristics of existence. If one failed of strength in any way, if life were not kind in its bestowal of gifts, if one were not born to fortune's pampering care—the rest was misery. In the days of his strength and prosperity the spectacle of existence had been sad enough: in the hours of threatened delay and defeat it seemed terrible. Why, if his art failed him now, what had he? Nothing. A little puny reputation which he could not sustain, no money, a wife to take care of, years of possible suffering and death. The abyss of death! When he looked into that after all of life and hope, how it shocked him, how it hurt! Here was life and happiness and love in health—there was death and nothingness—æons and æons of nothingness.

He did not immediately give up hope—immediately succumb to the evidences of a crumbling reality. For months and months he fancied each day that this was a temporary condition; that drugs and doctors could heal him. There were various remedies that were advertised in the papers, blood purifiers, nerve restorers, brain foods, which were announced at once as specifics and cures, and while he did not think that the ordinary patent medicine had anything of value in it, he did imagine that some good could be had from tonics, or *the* tonic. A physician whom he consulted recommended rest and an excellent tonic which he knew of. He asked whether he was subject to any wasting disease. Eugene told him no. He confessed to an over-indulgence in the sex-relationship, but the doctor did not believe that ordinarily this should bring about a nervous decline. Hard work must have something to do with it, over-anxiety. Some temperaments such as his were predisposed at birth to nervous breakdowns; they had to guard themselves. Eugene would have to be very careful. He should eat regularly, sleep as long as possible, observe regular hours. A system of exercise might not be a bad thing for him. He could get him a pair of Indian clubs or dumb-bells or an exerciser and bring himself back to health that way.

Eugene told Angela that he believed he would try exercising and joined a gymnasium. He took a tonic, walked with her a great deal, sought to ignore the fact that he was nervously depressed. These things were of practically no value, for the body had apparently been drawn a great distance below normal and all the hell of a subnormal state had to be endured before it could gradually come into its own again.

In the meantime he was continuing his passional relations with Angela, in spite of a growing judgment that they were in some way harmful to him. But it was not easy to refrain, and each failure to do so made it harder. It was a customary remark of his that "he must quit this," but it was like the self-apologetic assurance of the drunkard that he must reform.

Now that he had stepped out into the limelight of public observation — now that artists and critics and writers somewhat knew of him, and in their occasional way were wondering what he was doing, it was necessary that he should bestir himself to especial effort in order to satisfy the public as to the enduring quality of his art. He was glad, once he realized that he was in for a siege of bad weather, that his Paris drawings had been so nearly completed before the break came. By the day he suffered the peculiar nervousness which seemed to mark the opening of his real decline, he had completed twenty-two paintings, which Angela begged him not to touch; and by sheer strength of will, though he misdoubted gravely, he managed to complete five more. All of these M. Charles came to see on occasion, and he approved of them highly. He was not so sure that they would have the appeal of the American pictures, for after all the city of Paris had been pretty well done over and over in illustration and genré work. It was not so new as New York; the things Eugene chose were not as unconventional. Still, he could say truly they were exceptional. They might try an exhibition of them later in Paris if they did not take here. He was very sorry to see that Eugene was in poor health and urged him to take care of himself.

It seemed as if some malign planetary influence were affecting him. Eugene knew of astrology and palmistry and one day, in a spirit of curiosity and vague apprehensiveness, consulted a practitioner of the former, receiving for his dollar the statement that he was destined to great fame in either art or literature but that he was entering a period of stress which would endure for a number of years. Eugene's spirits sank perceptibly. The musty old gentleman who essayed his books of astrological lore shook his head. He had a rather noble growth of white hair and a white beard, but his coffee-stained vest was covered with tobacco ash and his collar and cuffs were dirty.

"It looks pretty bad between your twenty-eighth and your thirty-second years, but after that there is a notable period of prosperity. Somewhere around your thirty-eighth or thirty-ninth year there is some more trouble—a little—but you will come out of that—that is, it looks as though you would. Your stars show you to be of a nervous, imaginative character, inclined to worry; and I see that your kidneys are weak. You ought never to take much medicine. Your sign is inclined to that but it is without benefit to you. You will be married twice, but I don't see any children."

He rambled on dolefully and Eugene left in great gloom. So it was written in the stars that he was to suffer a period of decline and there was to be more trouble for him in the future. But he did see a period of great success for him between his thirty-second and his thirty-eighth years. That was some comfort. Who was the second woman he was to marry? Was Angela going to die? He walked the streets this early December afternoon, thinking, thinking.

The Blue family had heard a great deal of Eugene's success since Angela had come to New York. There had never been a week but at least one letter, and sometimes two, had gone the rounds of the various members of the family. It was written to Marietta primarily, but Mrs. Blue, Jotham, the boys and the several sisters all received it by turns. Thus the whole regiment of Blue connections knew exactly how it was with Angela and even better than it was; for although things had looked prosperous enough, Angela had not stayed within the limits of bare fact in describing her husband's success. She added atmosphere, not fictitious, but the seeming glory which dwelt in her mind, until the various connections of the Blue family, Marietta in particular, were convinced that there was nothing but dignity and bliss in store for the wife of so talented a man. The studio life which Angela had seen, here and in Paris, the picturesque descriptions which came home from London and Paris, the personalities of M. Charles, M. Arkquin, Isaac Wertheim, Henry L. Tomlins, Luke Severas—all the celebrities whom they met, both in New York and abroad, had been described at length. There was not a dinner, a luncheon, a reception, a tea party, which was not pictured in all its native colors and more. Eugene had become somewhat of a demi-god to his Western connections. The quality of his art was never questioned. It was only a little time now before he would be rich or at least well-to-do.

All the relatives hoped that he would bring Angela home some day on a visit. To think that she should have married such a distinguished man!

In the Witla family it was quite the same. Eugene had not been home to see his parents since his last visit to Blackwood, but they had not been without news. For one thing, Eugene had been neglectful, and somewhat because of this Angela had taken it upon herself to open up a correspondence with his mother. She wrote that of course she didn't know her but that she was terribly fond of Eugene, that she hoped to make him a good wife and that she hoped to make her a satisfactory daughter-in-law. Eugene was so dilatory about writing. She would write for him now and his mother should hear every week. She asked if she and her husband couldn't manage to come and see them sometime. She would be so glad and it would do Eugene so much good. She asked if she couldn't have Myrtle's address — they had moved from Ottumwa — and if Sylvia wouldn't write occasionally. She sent a picture of herself and Eugene, a sketch of the studio which Eugene had made one day, a sketch of herself looking pensively out of the window into Washington Square. Pictures from his first show published in the newspapers, accounts of his work, criticisms, — all reached the members of both families impartially and they were kept well aware of how things were going.

During the time that Eugene was feeling so badly and because, if he were going to lose his health, it might be necessary to economize greatly, it occurred to Angela that it might be advisable for them to go home for a visit. While her family were not rich, they had sufficient means to live on. Eugene's mother also was constantly writing, wanting to know why they didn't come out there for a while. She could not see why Eugene could not paint his pictures as well in Alexandria as in New York or Paris. Eugene listened to this willingly, for it occurred to him that instead of going to London he might do Chicago next, and he and Angela could stay awhile at Blackwood and another while at his own home. They would be welcome guests.

The condition of his finances at this time was not exactly bad, but it was not very good. Of the thirteen hundred dollars he had received for the first three pictures sold, eleven hundred had been used on the foreign trip. He had since used three hundred dollars of his remaining capital of twelve hundred, but M. Charles' sale of two pictures at four hundred each had swelled his bank balance to seventeen hundred dollars; however, on this he had to live now until additional pictures were disposed of. He daily hoped to hear of additional sales, but none occurred.

Moreover, his exhibition in January did not produce quite the impression he thought it would. It was fascinating to look at; the critics and the public imagined that by now he must have created a following for himself, else why should M. Charles make a feature of his work. But Charles pointed out that these foreign studies could not hope to appeal to Americans as did the American things. He indicated that they might take better in France. Eugene was depressed by the general tone of the opinions, but this was due more to his unhealthy state of mind than to any inherent reason for feeling so. There was still Paris to try and there might be some sales of his work here. The latter were slow in materializing, however, and because by February he had not been able to work and because it was necessary that he should husband his resources as carefully as possible, he decided to accept Angela's family's invitation as well as that of his own parents and spend some time in Illinois and Wisconsin. Perhaps his health would become better. He decided also that, if his health permitted, he would work in Chicago.

CHAPTER XI

It was in packing the trunks and leaving the studio in Washington Square (owing to the continued absence of Mr. Dexter they had never been compelled to vacate it) that Angela came across the first evidence of Eugene's duplicity. Because of his peculiar indifference to everything except matters which related to his art, he had put the letters which he had received in times past from Christina Channing, as well as the one and only one from Ruby Kenny, in a box which had formerly contained writing paper and which he threw carelessly in a corner of his trunk. He had by this time forgotten all about them, though his impression was that he had placed them somewhere where they would not be found. When Angela started to lay out the various things which occupied it she came across this box and opening it took out the letters.

Curiosity as to things relative to Eugene was at this time the dominant characteristic of her life. She could neither think nor reason outside of this relationship which bound her to him. He and his affairs were truly the sum and substance of her existence. She looked at the letters oddly and then opened one—the first from Christina. It was dated Florizel, the summer of three years before when she was waiting so patiently for him at Blackwood. It began conservatively enough—"Dear E—," but it concerned itself immediately with references to an apparently affectionate relationship. "I went this morning to see if by chance there were any tell-tale evidences of either Diana or Adonis in Arcady. There were none of importance. A hairpin or two, a broken mother-of-pearl button from a summer waist, the stub of a lead-pencil wherewith a certain genius sketched. The trees seemed just as unconscious of any nymphs or hamadryads as they could be. The smooth grass was quite unruffled of any feet. It is strange how much the trees and forest know and keep their counsel.

"And how is the hot city by now? Do you miss a certain evenly-swung hammock? Oh, the odor of leaves and the dew! Don't work too hard. You have an easy future and almost too much vitality. More repose for you, sir, and considerably more optimism of thought. I send you good wishes.— Diana."

Angela wondered at once who Diana was, for before she had begun the letter she had looked for the signature on the succeeding page. Then after reading this she hurried feverishly from letter to letter, seeking a name. There was none. "Diana of the Mountains," "The Hamadryad," "The Wood-Nymph," "C," "C C"—so they ran, confusing, badgering, enraging her until all at once it came to light—her first name at least. It was on the letter from Baltimore suggesting that he come to Florizel—"Christina."

"Ah," she thought, "Christina! That is her name." Then she hurried back to read the remaining epistles, hoping to find some clue to her surname. They were all of the same character, in the manner of writing she despised,—top-lofty, make-believe, the nasty, hypocritical, cant and make-believe superiority of the studios. How Angela hated her from that moment. How she could have taken her by the throat and beaten her head against the trees she described. Oh, the horrid creature! How dare she! And Eugene—how could he! What a way to reward her love! What an answer to make to all her devotion! At the very time when she was waiting so patiently, he was in the mountains with this Diana. And here she was packing his trunk for him like the little slave that she was when he cared so little, had apparently cared so little all this time. How could he ever have cared for her and done anything like this! He didn't! He never had! Dear Heaven!

She began clenching and unclenching her hands dramatically, working herself into that frenzy of emotion and regret which was her most notable characteristic. All at once she stopped. There was another letter in another handwriting on cheaper paper. "Ruby" was the signature.

"Dear Eugene:"—she read—"I got your note several weeks ago, but I couldn't bring myself to answer it before this. I know everything is over between us and that is all right I suppose. It has to be. You couldn't love any woman long, I think. I know what you say about having to go to New York to broaden your field is true. You ought to, but I'm sorry you didn't come out. You might have. Still I don't blame you, Eugene. It isn't much different from what has been going on for some time. I have cared, but I'll get over that, I know, and I won't ever think hard of you. Won't you return me the notes I have sent you from time to time, and my picture? You won't want them now.—Ruby."

"I stood by the window last night and looked out on the street. The moon was shining and those dead trees were waving in the wind. I saw the moon on that pool of water over in the field. It looked like silver. Oh, Eugene, I wish that I were dead."

Angela got up (as Eugene had) when she read this. The pathos struck home, for somehow it matched her own. Ruby! Who was she? Where had she been concealed while she, Angela, was coming to Chicago? Was this the fall and winter of their engagement? It certainly was. Look at the date. He had given her the diamond ring on her finger that fall! He had sworn eternal affection! He had sworn there was never another girl like her in all the world and yet, at that very time, he was apparently paying *court* to this woman if nothing worse. Heaven! Could anything like this really be? He was telling her that he loved her and making love to this Ruby at the same time. He was kissing and fondling her and Ruby too!! Was there ever such a situation? He, Eugene Witla, to deceive her this way. No wonder he wanted to get rid of her when he came to New York. He would have treated her as he had this Ruby. And Christina! This Christina!! Where was she? Who was she? What was she doing now? She jumped up prepared to go to Eugene and charge him with his iniquities, but remembered that he was out of the studio—that he had gone for a walk. He was sick now, very sick. Would she dare to reproach him with these reprehensible episodes?

She came back to the trunk where she was working and sat down. Her eyes were hard and cold for the time, but at the same time there was a touch of terror and of agonized affection. A face that, in the ordinary lines of its repose, was very much like that of a madonna, was now drawn and peaked and gray. Apparently Christina had forsaken him, or it might be that they still corresponded secretly. She got up again at that thought. Still the letters were old. It looked as though all communication had ceased two years ago. What had he written to her?—love notes. Letters full of wooing phrases such as he had written to her. Oh, the instability of men, the insincerity, the lack of responsibility and sense of duty. Her father,—what a different man he was; her brothers,—their word was their bond. And here was she married to a man who, even in the days of his most ardent wooing, had been deceiving her. She had let him lead her astray, too,—disgrace her own home. Tears came after a while, hot, scalding tears that seared her cheeks. And now she was married to him and he was sick and she would have to make the best of it. She wanted to make the best of it, for after all she loved him.

But oh, the cruelty, the insincerity, the unkindness, the brutality of it all.

The fact that Eugene was out for several hours following her discovery gave her ample time to reflect as to a suitable course of action. Being so impressed by the genius of the man, as imposed upon her by the opinion of others and her own affection, she could not readily think of anything save some method of ridding her soul of this misery and him of his evil tendencies, of making him ashamed of his wretched career, of making him see how badly he had treated her and how sorry he ought to be. She wanted him to feel sorry, very sorry, so that he would be a long time repenting in suffering, but she feared at the same time that she could not make him do that. He was so ethereal, so indifferent, so lost in the contemplation of life that he could not be made to think of her. That was her one complaint. He had other gods before her—the god of his art, the god of nature, the god of people as a spectacle. Frequently she had complained to him in this last year—"you don't love me! you don't love me!" but he would answer, "oh, yes I do. I can't be talking to you all the time, Angel-face. I have work to do. My art has to be cultivated. I can't be making love all the time."

"Oh, it isn't that, it isn't that!" she would exclaim passionately. "You just don't love me, like you ought to. You just don't care. If you did I'd feel it."

"Oh, Angela," he answered, "why do you talk so? Why do you carry on so? You're the funniest girl I ever knew. Now be reasonable. Why don't you bring a little philosophy to bear? We can't be billing and cooing all the time!"

"Billing and cooing! That's the way you think of it! That's the way you talk of it! As though it were something you had to do. Oh, I hate love! I hate life! I hate philosophy! I wish I could die."

"Now, Angela, for Heaven's sake, why will you take on so? I can't stand this. I can't stand these tantrums of yours. They're not reasonable. You know I love you. Why, haven't I shown it? Why should I have married you if I didn't? I wasn't obliged to marry you!"

"Oh, dear! oh, dear!" Angela would sob on, wringing her hands. "Oh, you really don't love me! You don't care! And it will go on this way, getting worse and worse, with less and less of love and feeling until after awhile you won't even want to see me any more—you'll hate me! Oh, dear! oh, dear!"

Eugene felt keenly the pathos involved in this picture of decaying love. In fact, her fear of the disaster which might overtake her little bark of happiness was sufficiently well founded. It might be that his affection would cease—it wasn't even affection now in the true sense of the word,—a passionate intellectual desire for her companionship. He never had really loved her for her mind, the beauty of her thoughts. As he meditated he realized that he had never reached an understanding with her by an intellectual process at all. It was emotional, subconscious, a natural drawing together which was not based on reason and spirituality of contemplation apparently, but on grosser emotions and desires. Physical desire had been involved—strong, raging, uncontrollable. And for some reason he had always felt sorry for her—he always had. She was so little, so conscious of disaster, so afraid of life and what it might do to her. It was a shame to wreck her hopes and desires. At the same time he was sorry now for this bondage he had let himself into—this yoke which he had put about his neck. He could have done so much better. He might have married a woman of wealth or a woman with artistic perceptions and philosophic insight like Christina Channing, who would be peaceful and happy with him. Angela couldn't be. He really didn't admire her enough, couldn't fuss over her enough. Even while he was soothing her in these moments, trying to make her believe that there was no basis for her fears, sympathizing with her subconscious intuitions that all was not well, he was thinking of how different his life might have been.

"It won't end that way," he would soothe. "Don't cry. Come now, don't cry. We're going to be very happy. I'm going to love you always, just as I'm loving you now, and you're going to love me. Won't that be all right? Come on, now. Cheer up. Don't be so pessimistic. Come on, Angela. Please do. Please!"

Angela would brighten after a time, but there were spells of apprehension and gloom; they were common, apt to burst forth like a summer storm when neither of them was really expecting it.

The discovery of these letters now checked the feeling, with which she tried to delude herself at times, that there might be anything more than kindness here. They confirmed her suspicions that there was not and brought on that sense of defeat and despair which so often and so tragically overcame her. It did it at a time, too, when Eugene needed her undivided consideration and feeling, for he was in a wretched state of mind. To have her quarrel with him now, lose her temper, fly into rages and compel him to console her, was very trying. He was in no mood for it; could not very well endure it without injury to himself. He was seeking for an atmosphere of joyousness, wishing to find a cheerful optimism somewhere which would pull him out of himself and make him whole. Not infrequently he dropped in to see Norma Whitmore, Isadora Crane, who was getting along very well on the stage, Hedda Andersen, who had a natural charm of intellect with much vivacity, even though she was a model, and now and then Miriam Finch. The latter was glad to see him alone, almost as a testimony against Angela, though she would not go out of her way to conceal from Angela the fact that he had been there. The others, though he said nothing, assumed that since Angela did not come with him he wanted nothing said and observed his wish. They were inclined to think that he had made a matrimonial mistake and was possibly artistically or intellectually lonely. All of them noted his decline in health with considerate apprehension and sorrow. It was too bad, they thought, if his health was going to fail him just at this time. Eugene lived in fear lest Angela should become aware of any of these visits. He thought he could not tell her because in the first place she would resent his not having taken her with him; and in the next, if he had proposed it first, she would have objected, or set another date, or asked pointless questions. He liked the liberty of going where he pleased, saying nothing, not feeling it necessary to say anything. He longed for the freedom of his old pre-matrimonial days. Just at this time, because he could not work artistically and because he was in need of diversion and of joyous artistic palaver, he was especially miserable. Life seemed very dark and ugly.

Eugene, returning and feeling, as usual, depressed about his state, sought to find consolation in her company. He came in at one o'clock, their usual lunch hour, and finding Angela still working, said, "George! but you like to keep at things when you get started, don't you? You're a regular little work-horse. Having much trouble?"

"No-o," replied Angela, dubiously.

Eugene noted the tone of her voice. He thought she was not very strong and this packing was getting on her nerves. Fortunately there were only some trunks to look after, for the vast mass of their housekeeping materials belonged to the studio. Still no doubt she was weary.

"Are you very tired?" he asked.

"No-o," she replied.

"You look it," he said, slipping his arm about her. Her face, which he turned up with his hand, was pale and drawn.

"It isn't anything physical," she replied, looking away from him in a tragic way. "It's just my heart. It's here!" and she laid her hand over her heart.

"What's the matter now?" he asked, suspecting something emotional, though for the life of him he could not imagine what. "Does your heart hurt you?"

"It isn't my real heart," she returned, "it's just my mind, my feelings; though I don't suppose they ought to matter."

"What's the matter now, Angel-face," he persisted, for he was sorry for her. This emotional ability of hers had the power to move him. It might have been acting, or it might not have been. It might be either a real or a fancied woe;—in either case it was real to her. "What's come up?" he continued. "Aren't you just tired? Suppose we quit this and go out somewhere and get something to eat. You'll feel better."

"No, I couldn't eat," she replied. "I'll stop now and get your lunch, but I don't want anything."

"Oh, what's the matter, Angela?" he begged. "I know there's something. Now what is it? You're tired, or you're sick, or something has happened. Is it anything that I have done? Look at me! Is it?"

Angela held away from him, looking down. She did not know how to begin this but she wanted to make him terribly sorry if she could, as sorry as she was for herself. She thought he ought to be; that if he had any true feeling of shame and sympathy in him he would be. Her own condition in the face of his shameless past was terrible. She had no one to love her. She had no one to turn to. Her own family did not understand her life any more—it had changed so. She was a different woman now, greater, more important, more distinguished. Her experiences with Eugene here in New York, in Paris, in London and even before her marriage, in Chicago and Blackwood, had changed her point of view. She was no longer the same in her ideas, she thought, and to find herself deserted in this way emotionally—not really loved, not ever having been really loved but just toyed with, made a doll and a plaything, was terrible.

"Oh, dear!" she exclaimed in a shrill staccato, "I don't know what to do! I don't know what to say! I don't know what to think! If I only knew how to think or what to do!"

"What's the matter?" begged Eugene, releasing his hold and turning his thoughts partially to himself and his own condition as well as to hers. His nerves were put on edge by these emotional tantrums—his brain fairly ached. It made his hands tremble. In his days of physical and nervous soundness it did not matter, but now, when he was sick, when his own heart was weak, as he fancied, and his nerves set to jangling by the least discord, it was almost more than he could bear. "Why don't you speak?" he insisted. "You know I can't stand this. I'm in no condition. What's the trouble? What's the use of carrying on this way? Are you going to tell me?"

"There!" Angela said, pointing her finger at the box of letters she had laid aside on the window-sill. She knew he would see them, would remember instantly what they were about.

Eugene looked. The box came to his memory instantly. He picked it up nervously, sheepishly, for this was like a blow in the face which he had no power to resist. The whole peculiar nature of his transactions with Ruby and with Christina came back to him, not as they had looked to him at the time, but as they were appearing to Angela now. What must she think of him? Here he was protesting right along that he loved her, that he was happy and satisfied to live with her, that he was not interested in any of these other women whom she knew to be interested in him and of whom she was inordinately jealous, that he had always loved her and her only, and yet here were these letters suddenly come to light, giving the lie to all these protestations and asseverations—making him look like the coward, the blackguard, the moral thief that he knew himself to be. To be dragged out of the friendly darkness of lack of knowledge and understanding on her part and set forth under the clear white light of positive proof—he stared helplessly, his nerves trembling, his brain aching, for truly he was in no condition for an emotional argument.

And yet Angela was crying now. She had walked away from him and was leaning against the mantel-piece sobbing as if her heart would break. There was a real convincing ache in the sound—the vibration expressing the sense of loss and defeat and despair which she felt. He was staring at the box wondering why he had been such an idiot as to leave them in his trunk, to have saved them at all.

"Well, I don't know that there is anything to say to that," he observed finally, strolling over to where she was. There wasn't anything that he could say—that he knew. He was terribly sorry—sorry for her, sorry for himself. "Did you read them all?" he asked, curiously.

She nodded her head in the affirmative.

"Well, I didn't care so much for Christina Channing," he observed, deprecatingly. He wanted to say something, anything which would relieve her depressed mood. He knew it couldn't be much. If he could only make her believe that there wasn't anything vital in either of these affairs, that his interests and protestations had been of a light, philandering character. Still the Ruby Kenny letter showed that she cared for him desperately. He could not say anything against Ruby.

Angela caught the name of Christina Channing clearly. It seared itself in her brain. She recalled now that it was she of whom she had heard him speak in a complimentary way from time to time. He had told in studios of what a lovely voice she had, what a charming platform presence she had, how she could sing so feelingly, how intelligently she looked upon life, how good looking she was, how she was coming back to grand opera some day. And he had been in the mountains with her—had made love to her while she, Angela, was out in Blackwood waiting for him patiently. It aroused on the instant all the fighting jealousy that was in her breast; it was the same jealousy that had determined her once before to hold him in spite of the plotting and scheming that appeared to her to be going on about her. They should not have him—these nasty studio superiorities—not any one of them, nor all of them combined, if they were to unite and try to get him. They had treated her shamefully since she had been in the East. They had almost uniformly ignored her. They would come to see Eugene, of course, and now that he was famous they could not be too nice to him, but as for her—well, they had no particular use for her. Hadn't she seen it! Hadn't she watched the critical, hypocritical, examining expressions in their eyes! She wasn't smart enough! She wasn't literary enough or artistic enough. She knew as much about life as they did and more—ten times as much; and yet because she couldn't strut and pose and stare and talk in an affected voice they thought themselves superior. And so did Eugene, the wretched creature! Superior! The cheap, mean, nasty, selfish upstarts! Why, the majority of them had nothing. Their clothes were mere rags and tags, when you came to examine them closely—badly sewed, of poor material, merely slung together, and yet they wore them with such a grand air! She would show them. She would dress herself too, one of these days, when Eugene had the means. She was doing it now—a great deal more than when she first came, and she would do it a great deal more before long. The nasty, mean, cheap, selfish, make-belief things. She would show them! O-oh! how she hated them.

Now as she cried she also thought of the fact that Eugene could write love letters to this horrible Christina Channing—one of the same kind, no doubt; her letters showed it. O-oh! how she hated her! If she could only get at her to poison her. And her sobs sounded much more of the sorrow she felt than of the rage. She was helpless in a way and she knew it. She did not dare to show him exactly what she felt. She was afraid of him. He might possibly leave her. He really did not care for her enough to stand everything from her—or did he? This doubt was the one terrible, discouraging, annihilating feature of the whole thing—if he only cared.

"I wish you wouldn't cry, Angela," said Eugene appealingly, after a time. "It isn't as bad as you think. It looks pretty bad, but I wasn't married then, and I didn't care so very much for these people—not as much as you think; really I didn't. It may look that way to you, but I didn't."

"Didn't care!" sneered Angela, all at once, flaring up. "Didn't care! It looks as though you didn't care, with one of them calling you Honey Boy and Adonis, and the other saying she wishes she were dead. A fine time you'd have convincing anyone that you didn't care. And I out in Blackwood at that very time, longing and waiting for you to come, and you up in the mountains making love to another woman. Oh, I know how much you cared. You showed how much you cared when you could leave me out there to wait for you eating my heart out while you were off in the mountains having a good time with another woman. 'Dear E—,' and 'Precious Honey Boy,' and 'Adonis'! That shows how much you cared, doesn't it!"

Eugene stared before him helplessly. Her bitterness and wrath surprised and irritated him. He did not know that she was capable of such an awful rage as showed itself in her face and words at this moment, and yet he did not know but that she was well justified. Why so bitter though—so almost brutal? He was sick. Had she no consideration for him?

"I tell you it wasn't as bad as you think," he said stolidly, showing for the first time a trace of temper and opposition. "I wasn't married then. I did like Christina Channing; I did like Ruby Kenny. What of it? I can't help it now. What am I going to say about it? What do you want me to say? What do you want me to do?"

"Oh," whimpered Angela, changing her tone at once from helpless accusing rage to pleading, self-commiserating misery. "And you can stand there and say to me 'what of it'? What of it! What of it! What shall you say? What do you think you ought to say? And me believing that you were so honorable and faithful! Oh, if I had only known! If I had only known! I had better have drowned myself a hundred times over than have waked and found that I wasn't loved. Oh, dear, oh, dear! I don't know what I ought to do! I don't know what I can do!"

"But I do love you," protested Eugene soothingly, anxious to say or do anything which would quiet this terrific storm. He could not imagine how he could have been so foolish as to leave these letters lying around. Dear Heaven! What a mess he had made of this! If only he had put them safely outside the home or destroyed them. Still he had wanted to keep Christina's letters; they were so charming.

"Yes, you love me!" flared Angela. "I see how you love me. Those letters show it! Oh, dear! oh, dear! I wish I were dead."

"Listen to me, Angela," replied Eugene desperately, "I know this correspondence looks bad. I did make love to Miss Kenny and to Christina Channing, but you see I didn't care enough to marry either of them. If I had I would have. I cared for you. Believe it or not. I married you. Why did I marry you? Answer me that? I needn't have married you. Why did I? Because I loved you, of course. What other reason could I have?"

"Because you couldn't get Christina Channing," snapped Angela, angrily, with the intuitive sense of one who reasons from one material fact to another, "that's why. If you could have, you would have. I know it. Her letters show it."

"Her letters don't show anything of the sort," returned Eugene angrily. "I couldn't get her? I could have had her, easily enough. I didn't want her. If I had wanted her, I would have married her—you can bet on that."

He hated himself for lying in this way, but he felt for the time being that he had to do it. He did not care to stand in the rôle of a jilted lover. He half-fancied that he could have married Christina if he had really tried.

"Anyhow," he said, "I'm not going to argue that point with you. I didn't marry her, so there you are; and I didn't marry Ruby Kenny either. Well you can think all you want; but I know. I cared for them, but I didn't marry them. I married you instead. I ought to get credit for something on that score. I married you because I loved you, I suppose. That's perfectly plain, isn't it?" He was half convincing himself that he had loved her—in some degree.

"Yes, I see how you love me," persisted Angela, cogitating this very peculiar fact which he was insisting on and which it was very hard intellectually to overcome. "You married me because you couldn't very well get out of it, that's why. Oh, I know. You didn't want to marry me. That's very plain. You wanted to marry someone else. Oh, dear! oh, dear!"

"Oh, how you talk!" replied Eugene defiantly. "Marry someone else! Who did I want to marry? I could have married often enough if I had wanted to. I didn't want to marry, that's all. Believe it or not. I wanted to marry you and I did. I don't think you have any right to stand there and argue so. What you say isn't so, and you know it."

Angela cogitated this argument further. He had married her! Why had he? He might have cared for Christina and Ruby, but he must have cared for her too. Why hadn't she thought of that? There was something in it— something besides a mere desire to deceive her. Perhaps he did care for her a little. Anyway it was plain that she could not get very far by arguing with him—he was getting stubborn, argumentative, contentious. She had not seen him that way before.

"Oh!" she sobbed, taking refuge from this very difficult realm of logic in the safer and more comfortable one of illogical tears. "I don't know what to do! I don't know what to think!"

She was badly treated, no doubt of that. Her life was a failure, but even so there was some charm about him. As he stood there, looking aimlessly around, defiant at one moment, appealing at another, she could not help seeing that he was not wholly bad. He was just weak on this one point.

He loved pretty women. They were always trying to win him to them. He was probably not wholly to blame. If he would only be repentant enough, this thing might be allowed to blow over. It couldn't be forgiven. She never could forgive him for the way he had deceived her. Her ideal of him had been pretty hopelessly shattered—but she might live with him on probation.

"Angela!" he said, while she was still sobbing, and feeling that he ought to apologize to her. "Won't you believe me? Won't you forgive me? I don't like to hear you cry this way. There's no use saying that I didn't do anything. There's no use my saying anything at all, really. You won't believe me. I don't want you to; but I'm sorry. Won't you believe that? Won't you forgive me?"

Angela listened to this curiously, her thoughts going around in a ring for she was at once despairing, regretful, revengeful, critical, sympathetic toward him, desirous of retaining her state, desirous of obtaining and retaining his love, desirous of punishing him, desirous of doing any one of a hundred things. Oh, if he had only never done this! And he was sickly, too. He needed her sympathy.

"Won't you forgive me, Angela?" he pleaded softly, laying his hand on her arm. "I'm not going to do anything like that any more. Won't you believe me? Come on now. Quit crying, won't you?"

Angela hesitated for a while, lingering dolefully. She did not know what to do, what to say. It might be that he would not sin against her any more. He had not thus far, in so far as she knew. Still this was a terrible revelation. All at once, because he manœuvred himself into a suitable position and because she herself was weary of fighting and crying, and because she was longing for sympathy, she allowed herself to be pulled into his arms, her head to his shoulder, and there she cried more copiously than ever. Eugene for the moment felt terribly grieved. He was really sorry for her. It wasn't right. He ought to be ashamed of himself. He should never have done anything like that.

"I'm sorry," he whispered, "really I am. Won't you forgive me?"

"Oh, I don't know what to do! what to think!" moaned Angela after a time.

"Please do, Angela," he urged, holding her questioningly.

There was more of this pleading and emotional badgering until finally out of sheer exhaustion Angela said yes. Eugene's nerves were worn to a thread by the encounter. He was pale, exhausted, distraught. Many scenes like this, he thought, would set him crazy; and still he had to go through a world of petting and love-making even now. It was not easy to bring her back to her normal self. It was bad business, this philandering, he thought. It seemed to lead to all sorts of misery for him, and Angela was jealous. Dear Heaven! what a wrathful, vicious, contentious nature she had when she was aroused. He had never suspected that. How could he truly love her when she acted like that? How could he sympathize with her? He recalled how she sneered at him—how she taunted him with Christina's having discarded him. He was weary, excited, desirous of rest and sleep, but now he must make more love. He fondled her, and by degrees she came out of her blackest mood; but he was not really forgiven even then. He was just understood better. And she was not truly happy again but only hopeful— and watchful.

CHAPTER XII

Spring, summer and fall came and went with Eugene and Angela first in Alexandria and then in Blackwood. In suffering this nervous breakdown and being compelled to leave New York, Eugene missed some of the finest fruits of his artistic efforts, for M. Charles, as well as a number of other people, were interested in him and were prepared to entertain him in an interesting and conspicuous way. He could have gone out a great deal, but his mental state was such that he was poor company for anyone. He was exceedingly morbid, inclined to discuss gloomy subjects, to look on life as exceedingly sad and to believe that people generally were evil. Lust, dishonesty, selfishness, envy, hypocrisy, slander, hate, theft, adultery, murder, dementia, insanity, inanity—these and death and decay occupied his thoughts. There was no light anywhere. Only a storm of evil and death. These ideas coupled with his troubles with Angela, the fact that he could not work, the fact that he felt he had made a matrimonial mistake, the fact that he feared he might die or go crazy, made a terrible and agonizing winter for him.

Angela's attitude, while sympathetic enough, once the first storm of feeling was over, was nevertheless involved with a substratum of criticism. While she said nothing, agreed that she would forget, Eugene had the consciousness all the while that she wasn't forgetting, that she was secretly reproaching him and that she was looking for new manifestations of weakness in this direction, expecting them and on the alert to prevent them.

The spring-time in Alexandria, opening as it did shortly after they reached there, was in a way a source of relief to Eugene. He had decided for the time being to give up trying to work, to give up his idea of going either to London or Chicago, and merely rest. Perhaps it was true that he was tired. He didn't feel that way. He couldn't sleep and he couldn't work, but he felt brisk enough. It was only because he couldn't work that he was miserable. Still he decided to try sheer idleness. Perhaps that would revive his wonderful art for him. Meantime he speculated ceaselessly on the time he was losing, the celebrities he was missing, the places he was not seeing. Oh, London, London! If he could only do that.

Mr. and Mrs. Witla were immensely pleased to have their boy back with them again. Being in their way simple, unsophisticated people, they could not understand how their son's health could have undergone such a sudden reverse.

"I never saw Gene looking so bad in all his life," observed Witla pére to his wife the day Eugene arrived. "His eyes are so sunken. What in the world do you suppose is ailing him?"

"How should I know?" replied his wife, who was greatly distressed over her boy. "I suppose he's just tired out, that's all. He'll probably be all right after he rests awhile. Don't let on that you think he's looking out of sorts. Just pretend that he's all right. What do you think of his wife?"

"She appears to be a very nice little woman," replied Witla. "She's certainly devoted to him. I never thought Eugene would marry just that type, but he's the judge. I suppose people thought that I would never marry anybody like you, either," he added jokingly.

"Yes, you did make a terrible mistake," jested his wife in return. "You worked awfully hard to make it."

"I was young! I was young! You want to remember that," retorted Witla. "I didn't know much in those days."

"You don't appear to know much better yet," she replied, "do you?"

He smiled and patted her on the back. "Well, anyhow I'll have to make the best of it, won't I? It's too late now."

"It certainly is," replied his wife.

Eugene and Angela were given his old room on the second floor, commanding a nice view of the yard and the street corner, and they settled down to spend what the Witla parents hoped would be months of peaceful days. It was a curious sensation to Eugene to find himself back here in Alexandria looking out upon the peaceful neighborhood in which he had been raised, the trees, the lawn, the hammock replaced several times since he had left, but still in its accustomed place. The thought of the little lakes and the small creek winding about the town were a comfort to him. He could go fishing now and boating, and there were some interesting walks here and there. He began to amuse himself by going fishing the first week, but it was still a little cold, and he decided, for the time being, to confine himself to walking.

Days of this kind grow as a rule quickly monotonous. To a man of Eugene's turn of mind there was so little in Alexandria to entertain him. After London and Paris, Chicago and New York, the quiet streets of his old home town were a joke. He visited the office of the *Appeal* but both Jonas Lyle and Caleb Williams had gone, the former to St. Louis, the latter to Bloomington. Old Benjamin Burgess, his sister's husband's father, was unchanged except in the matter of years. He told Eugene that he was thinking of running for Congress in the next campaign—the Republican organization owed it to him. His son Henry, Sylvia's husband, had become a treasurer of the local bank. He was working as patiently and quietly as ever, going to church Sundays, going to Chicago occasionally on business, consulting with farmers and business men about small loans. He was a close student of the several banking journals of the country, and seemed to be doing very well financially. Sylvia had little to say of how he was getting along. Having lived with him for eleven years, she had become somewhat close-mouthed like himself. Eugene could not help smiling at the lean, slippered subtlety of the man, young as he was. He was so quiet, so conservative, so intent on all the little things which make a conventionally successful life. Like a cabinet maker, he was busy inlaying the little pieces which would eventually make the perfect whole.

Angela took up the household work, which Mrs. Witla grudgingly consented to share with her, with a will. She liked to work and would put the house in order while Mrs. Witla was washing the dishes after breakfast. She would make special pies and cakes for Eugene when she could without giving offense, and she tried to conduct herself so that Mrs. Witla would like her. She did not think so much of the Witla household. It wasn't so much better than her own—hardly as good. Still it was Eugene's birthplace and for that reason important. There was a slight divergence of view-point though, between his mother and herself, over the nature of life and how to live it. Mrs. Witla was of an easier, more friendly outlook on life than Angela. She liked to take things as they came without much worry, while Angela was of a naturally worrying disposition. The two had one very human failing in common—they could not work with anyone else at anything. Each preferred to do all that was to be done rather than share it at all. Both being so anxious to be conciliatory for Eugene's sake and for permanent peace in the family, there was small chance for any disagreement, for neither was without tact. But there was just a vague hint of something in the air—that Angela was a little hard and selfish, on Mrs. Witla's part; that Mrs. Witla was just the least bit secretive, or shy or distant—from Angela's point of view. All was serene and lovely on the surface, however, with many won't-you-let-me's and please-do-now's on both sides. Mrs. Witla, being so much older, was, of course, calmer and in the family seat of dignity and peace.

To be able to sit about in a chair, lie in a hammock, stroll in the woods and country fields and be perfectly happy in idle contemplation and loneliness, requires an exceptional talent for just that sort of thing. Eugene once fancied he had it, as did his parents, but since he had heard the call of fame he could never be still any more. And just at this time he was not in need of solitude and idle contemplation but of diversion and entertainment. He needed companionship of the right sort, gayety, sympathy, enthusiasm. Angela had some of this, when she was not troubled about anything, his parents, his sister, his old acquaintances had a little more to offer. They could not, however, be forever talking to him or paying him attention, and beyond them there was nothing. The town had no resources. Eugene would walk the long country roads with Angela or go boating or fishing sometimes, but still he was lonely. He would sit on the porch or in the hammock and think of what he had seen in London and Paris—how he might be at work. St. Paul's in a mist, the Thames Embankment, Piccadilly, Blackfriars Bridge, the muck of Whitechapel and the East End—how he wished he was out of all this and painting them. If he could only paint. He rigged up a studio in his father's barn, using a north loft door for light and essayed certain things from memory, but there was no making anything come out right. He had this fixed belief, which was a notion purely, that there was always something wrong. Angela, his mother, his father, whom he occasionally asked for an opinion, might protest that it was beautiful or wonderful, but he did not believe it. After a few altering ideas of this kind, under the influences of which he would change and change and change things, he would find himself becoming wild in his feelings, enraged at his condition, intensely despondent and sorry for himself.

"Well," he would say, throwing down his brush, "I shall simply have to wait until I come out of this. I can't do anything this way." Then he would walk or read or row on the lakes or play solitaire, or listen to Angela playing on the piano that his father had installed for Myrtle long since. All the time though he was thinking of his condition, what he was missing, how the gay world was surging on rapidly elsewhere, how long it would be before he got well, if ever. He talked of going to Chicago and trying his hand at scenes there, but Angela persuaded him to rest for a while longer. In June she promised him they would go to Blackwood for the summer, coming back here in the fall if he wished, or going on to New York or staying in Chicago, just as he felt about it. Now he needed rest.

"Eugene will probably be all right by then," Angela volunteered to his mother, "and he can make up his mind whether he wants to go to Chicago or London."

She was very proud of her ability to talk of where they would go and what they would do.

CHAPTER XIII

If it had not been for the lurking hope of some fresh exciting experience with a woman, he would have been unconscionably lonely. As it was, this thought with him—quite as the confirmed drunkard's thought of whiskey—buoyed him up, kept him from despairing utterly, gave his mind the only diversion it had from the ever present thought of failure. If by chance he should meet some truly beautiful girl, gay, enticing, who would fall in love with him! that would be happiness. Only, Angela was constantly watching him these days and, besides, more girls would simply mean that his condition would be aggravated. Yet so powerful was the illusion of desire, the sheer animal magnetism of beauty, that when it came near him in the form of a lovely girl of his own temperamental inclinations he could not resist it. One look into an inviting eye, one glance at a face whose outlines were soft and delicate—full of that subtle suggestion of youth and health which is so characteristic of girlhood—and the spell was cast. It was as though the very form of the face, without will or intention on the part of the possessor, acted hypnotically upon its beholder. The Arabians believed in the magic power of the word Abracadabra to cast a spell. For Eugene the form of a woman's face and body was quite as powerful.

While he and Angela were in Alexandria from February to May, he met one night at his sister's house a girl who, from the point of view of the beauty which he admired and to which he was so susceptible, was extremely hypnotic, and who for the ease and convenience of a flirtation was very favorably situated. She was the daughter of a traveling man, George Roth by name, whose wife, the child's mother, was dead, but who lived with his sister in an old tree-shaded house on the edge of Green Lake not far from the spot where Eugene had once attempted to caress his first love, Stella Appleton. Frieda was the girl's name. She was extremely attractive, not more than eighteen years of age, with large, clear, blue eyes, a wealth of yellowish-brown hair and a plump but shapely figure. She was a graduate of the local high school, well developed for her years, bright, rosy-cheeked, vivacious and with a great deal of natural intelligence which attracted the attention of Eugene at once. Normally he was extremely fond of a natural, cheerful, laughing disposition. In his present state he was abnormally so. This girl and her foster mother had heard of him a long time since through his parents and his sister, whom they knew well and whom they visited frequently. George Roth had moved here since Eugene had first left for Chicago, and because he was so much on the road he had not seen him since. Frieda, on all his previous visits, had been too young to take an interest in men, but now at this age, when she was just blossoming into womanhood, her mind was fixed on them. She did not expect to be interested in Eugene because she knew he was married, but because of his reputation as an artist she was curious about him. Everybody knew who he was. The local papers had written up his success and published his portrait. Frieda expected to see a man of about forty, stern and sober. Instead she met a smiling youth of twenty-nine, rather gaunt and hollow-eyed, but none the less attractive for that. Eugene, with Angela's approval, still affected a loose, flowing tie, a soft turn-down collar, brown corduroy suits as a rule, the coat cut with a belt, shooting jacket fashion, a black iron ring of very curious design upon one of his fingers, and a soft hat. His hands were very thin and white, his skin pale. Frieda, rosy, as thoughtless as a butterfly, charmingly clothed in a dress of blue linen, laughing, afraid of him because of his reputation, attracted his attention at once. She was like all the young, healthy, laughing girls he had ever known, delightful. He wished he were single again that he might fall into a jesting conversation with her. She seemed inclined to be friendly from the first.

Angela being present, however, and Frieda's foster mother, it was necessary for him to be circumspect and distant. The latter, Sylvia and Angela, talked of art and listened to Angela's descriptions of Eugene's eccentricities, idiosyncrasies and experiences, which were a never-failing source of interest to the common run of mortals whom they met. Eugene would sit by in a comfortable chair with a weary, genial or indifferent look on his face as his mood happened to be. To-night he was bored and a little indifferent in his manner. No one here interested him save this girl, the beauty of whose face nourished his secret dreams. He longed to have some such spirit of youth near him always. Why could not women remain young?

While they were laughing and talking, Eugene picked up a copy of Howard Pyle's "Knights of the Round Table" with its warm heavy illustrations of the Arthurian heroes and heroines, and began to study the stately and exaggerated characteristics of the various characters. Sylvia had purchased it for her seven-year old boy Jack, asleep upstairs, but Frieda had read it in her girlhood a few years before. She had been moving restlessly about, conscious of an interest in Eugene but not knowing how to find an opportunity for conversation. His smile, which he sometimes directed toward her, was to her entrancing.

"Oh, I read that," she said, when she saw him looking at it. She had drifted to a position not far behind his chair and near one of the windows. She pretended to be looking out at first, but now began to talk to him. "I used to be crazy about every one of the Knights and Ladies—Sir Launcelot, Sir Galahad, Sir Tristram, Sir Gawaine, Queen Guinevere."

"Did you ever hear of Sir Bluff?" he asked teasingly, "or Sir Stuff? or Sir Dub?" He looked at her with a mocking light of humor in his eyes.

"Oh, there aren't such people," laughed Frieda, surprised at the titles but tickled at the thought of them.

"Don't you let him mock you, Frieda," put in Angela, who was pleased at the girl's gayety and glad that Eugene had found someone in whom he could take an interest. She did not fear the simple Western type of girl like Frieda and her own sister Marietta. They were franker, more kindly, better intentioned than the Eastern studio type, and besides they did not consider themselves superior. She was playing the rôle of the condescending leader here.

"Certainly there are," replied Eugene solemnly, addressing Frieda. "They are the new Knights of the Round Table. Haven't you ever heard of that book?"

"No, I haven't," answered Frieda gaily, "and there isn't any such. You're just teasing me."

"Teasing you? Why I wouldn't think of such a thing. And there is such a book. It's published by Harper and Brothers and is called 'The New Knights of the Round Table.' You simply haven't heard of it, that's all."

Frieda was impressed. She didn't know whether to believe him or not. She opened her eyes in a curiously inquiring girlish way which appealed to Eugene strongly. He wished he were free to kiss her pretty, red, thoughtlessly-parted lips. Angela herself was faintly doubtful as to whether he was speaking of a real book or not.

"Sir Stuff is a very famous Knight," he went on, "and so is Sir Bluff. They're inseparable companions in the book. As for Sir Dub and Sir Hack, and the Lady Dope—"

"Oh, hush, Eugene," called Angela gaily. "Just listen to what he's telling Frieda," she remarked to Miss Roth. "You mustn't mind him though. He's always teasing someone. Why didn't you raise him better, Sylvia?" she asked of Eugene's sister.

"Oh, don't ask me. We never could do anything with Gene. I never knew he had much jesting in him until he came back this time."

"They're very wonderful," they heard him telling Frieda, "all fine rosy gentlemen and ladies."

Frieda was impressed by this charming, good-natured man. His spirit was evidently as youthful and gay as her own. She sat before him looking into his smiling eyes while he teased her about this, that and the other foible of youth. Who were her sweethearts? How did she make love? How many boys lined up to see her come out of church on Sunday? He knew. "I'll bet they look like a line of soldiers on dress parade," he volunteered, "all with nice new ties and clean pocket handkerchiefs and their shoes polished and—"

"Oh, ha! ha!" laughed Frieda. The idea appealed to her immensely. She started giggling and bantering with him and their friendship was definitely sealed. She thought he was delightful.

CHAPTER XIV

The opportunity for further meetings seemed to come about quite naturally. The Witla boathouse, where the family kept one small boat, was at the foot of the Roth lawn, reached by a slightly used lane which came down that side of the house; and also by a grape-arbor which concealed the lake from the lower end of the house and made a sheltered walk to the waterside, at the end of which was a weather-beaten wooden bench. Eugene came here sometimes to get the boat to row or to fish. On several occasions Angela had accompanied him, but she did not care much for rowing or fishing and was perfectly willing that he should go alone if he wanted to. There was also the friendship of Miss Roth for Mr. and Mrs. Witla, which occasionally brought her and Frieda to the house. And Frieda came from time to time to his studio in the barn, to see him paint. Because of her youth and innocence Angela thought very little of her presence there, which struck Eugene as extremely fortunate. He was interested in her charms, anxious to make love to her in a philandering sort of way, without intending to do her any harm. It struck him as a little curious that he should find her living so near the spot where once upon a winter's night he had made love to Stella. There was something not unlike Stella about her, though she was softer, more whole souledly genial and pliable to his moods.

He saw her one day, when he went for his boat, standing out in the yard, and she came down to the waterside to greet him.

"Well," he said, smiling at her fresh morning appearance, and addressing her with that easy familiarity with which he knew how to take youth and life generally, "we're looking as bright as a butterfly. I don't suppose we butterflies have to work very hard, do we?"

"Oh, don't we," replied Frieda. "That's all you know."

"Well, I don't know, that's true, but perhaps one of these butterflies will tell me. Now you, for instance."

Frieda smiled. She scarcely knew how to take him, but she thought he was delightful. She hadn't the faintest conception either of the depth and subtlety of his nature or of the genial, kindly inconstancy of it. She only saw him as a handsome, smiling man, not at all too old, witty, good-natured, here by the bright green waters of this lake, pulling out his boat. He looked so cheerful to her, so care free. She had him indissolubly mixed in her impressions with the freshness of the ground, the newness of the grass, the brightness of the sky, the chirping of the birds and even the little scintillating ripples on the water.

"Butterflies never work, that I know," he said, refusing to take her seriously. "They just dance around in the sunlight and have a good time. Did you ever talk to a butterfly about that?"

Frieda merely smiled at him.

He pushed his boat into the water, holding it lightly by a rope, got down a pair of oars from a rack and stepped into it. Then he stood there looking at her.

"Have you lived in Alexandria long?" he asked.

"About eight years now."

"Do you like it?"

"Sometimes, not always. I wish we lived in Chicago. O-oh!" she sniffed, turning up her pretty nose, "isn't that lovely!" She was smelling some odor of flowers blown from a garden.

"Yes, I get it too. Geraniums, isn't it? They're blooming here, I see. A day like this sets me crazy." He sat down in his boat and put his oars in place.

"Well, I have to go and try my luck for whales. Wouldn't you like to go fishing?"

"I would, all right," said Frieda, "only aunt wouldn't let me, I think. I'd just love to go. It's lots of fun, catching fish."

"Yes, *catching* fish," laughed Eugene. "Well, I'll bring you a nice little shark—one that bites. Would you like that? Down in the Atlantic Ocean they have sharks that bite and bark. They come up out of the water at night and bark like a dog."

"O-o-oh, dear! how funny!" giggled Frieda, and Eugene began slowly rowing his boat lakeward.

"Be sure you bring me a nice fish," she called.

"Be sure you're here to get it when I come back," he answered.

He saw her with the lattice of spring leaves behind her, the old house showing pleasantly on its rise of ground, some house-martens turning in the morning sky.

"What a lovely girl," he thought. "She's beautiful—as fresh as a flower. That is the one great thing in the world—the beauty of girlhood."

He came back after a time expecting to find her, but her foster-mother had sent her on an errand. He felt a keen sense of disappointment.

There were other meetings after this, once on a day when he came back practically fishless and she laughed at him; once when he saw her sunning her hair on the back porch after she had washed it and she came down to stand under the trees near the water, looking like a naiad. He wished then he could take her in his arms, but he was a little uncertain of her and of himself. Once she came to his studio in the barn to bring him a piece of left-over dough which his mother had "turned" on the top of the stove.

"Eugene used to be crazy about that when he was a boy," his mother had remarked.

"Oh, let me take it to him," said Frieda gaily, gleeful over the idea of the adventure.

"That's a good idea," said Angela innocently. "Wait, I'll put it on this saucer."

Frieda took it and ran. She found Eugene staring oddly at his canvas, his face curiously dark. When her head came above the loft floor his expression changed immediately. His guileless, kindly smile returned.

"Guess what," she said, pulling a little white apron she had on over the dish.

"Strawberries." They were in season.

"Oh, no."

"Peaches and cream."

"Where would we get peaches now?"

"At the grocery store."

"I'll give you one more guess."

"Angel cake!" He was fond of that, and Angela occasionally made it.

"Your guesses are all gone. You can't have any."

He reached out his hand, but she drew back. He followed and she laughed. "No, no, you can't have any now."

He caught her soft arm and drew her close to him. "Sure I can't?"

Their faces were close together.

She looked into his eyes for a moment, then dropped her lashes. Eugene's brain swirled with the sense of her beauty. It was the old talisman. He covered her sweet lips with his own and she yielded feverishly.

"There now, eat your dough," she exclaimed when he let her go, pushing it shamefacedly toward him. She was flustered—so much so that she failed to jest about it. "What would Mrs. Witla think," she added, "if she could see us?"

Eugene paused solemnly and listened. He was afraid of Angela.

"I've always liked this stuff, ever since I was a boy," he said in an offhand way.

"So your mother said," replied Frieda, somewhat recovered. "Let me see what you're painting." She came round to his side and he took her hand. "I'll have to go now," she said wisely. "They'll be expecting me back."

Eugene speculated on the intelligence of girls—at least on that of those he liked. Somehow they were all wise under these circumstances— cautious. He could see that instinctively Frieda was prepared to protect him and herself. She did not appear to be suffering from any shock from this revelation. Rather she was inclined to make the best of it.

He folded her in his arms again.

"You're the angel cake and the strawberries and the peaches and cream," he said.

"Don't!" she pleaded. "Don't! I have to go now."

And when he released her she ran quickly down the stairs, giving him a swift, parting smile.

So Frieda was added to the list of his conquests and he pondered over it gravely. If Angela could have seen this scene, what a storm there would have been! If she ever became conscious of what was going on, what a period of wrath there would be! It would be terrible. After her recent discovery of his letters he hated to think of that. Still this bliss of caressing youth—was it not worth any price? To have a bright, joyous girl of eighteen put her arms about you—could you risk too much for it? The world said one life, one love. Could he accede to that? Could any one woman satisfy him? Could Frieda if he had her? He did not know. He did not care to think about it. Only this walking in a garden of flowers—how delicious it was. This having a rose to your lips!

Angela saw nothing of this attraction for some time. She was not prepared yet to believe, poor little depender on the conventions as she understood them, that the world was full of plots and counter-plots, snares, pitfalls and gins. The way of the faithful and well-meaning woman in marriage should be simple and easy. She should not be harassed by uncertainty of affection, infelicities of temper, indifference or infidelity. If she worked hard, as Angela was trying to do, trying to be a good wife, saving, serving, making a sacrifice of her time and services and moods and wishes for her husband's sake, why shouldn't he do the same for her? She knew of no double standard of virtue. If she had she would not have believed in it. Her parents had raised her to see marriage in a different light. Her father was faithful to her mother. Eugene's father was faithful to his wife—that was perfectly plain. Her brothers-in-law were faithful to her sisters, Eugene's brothers-in-law were faithful to his sisters. Why should not Eugene be faithful to her?

So far, of course, she had no evidence to the contrary. He probably was faithful and would remain so. He had said so, but this pre-matrimonial philandering of his looked very curious. It was an astonishing thing that he could have deceived her so. She would never forget it. He was a genius to be sure. The world was waiting to hear what he had to say. He was a great man and should associate with great men, or, failing that, should not want to associate with anyone at all. It was ridiculous for him to be running around after silly women. She thought of this and decided to do her best to prevent it. The seat of the mighty was in her estimation the place for Eugene, with her in the foreground as a faithful and conspicuous acolyte, swinging the censer of praise and delight.

The days went on and various little meetings—some accidental, some premeditated—took place between Eugene and Frieda. There was one afternoon when he was at his sister's and she came there to get a pattern for her foster-mother from Sylvia. She lingered for over an hour, during which time Eugene had opportunities to kiss her a dozen times. The beauty of her eyes and her smile haunted him after she was gone. There was another time when he saw her at dusk near his boathouse, and kissed her in the shadow of the sheltering grape-arbor. In his own home there were clandestine moments and in his studio, the barn loft, for Frieda made occasion a few times to come to him—a promise to make a sketch of her being the excuse. Angela resented this, but she could not prevent it. In the main Frieda exhibited that curious patience in love which women so customarily exhibit and which a man can never understand. She could wait for her own to come to her—for him to find her; while he, with that curious avidness of the male in love, burned as a fed fire to see her. He was jealous of the little innocent walks she took with boys she knew. The fact that it was necessary for her to be away from him was a great deprivation. The fact that he was married to Angela was a horrible disaster. He would look at Angela, when she was with him, preventing him from his freedom in love, with almost calculated hate in his eyes. Why had he married her? As for Frieda, when she was near, and he could not draw near her, his eyes followed her movements with a yearning, devouring glance. He was fairly beside himself with anguish under the spell of her beauty. Frieda had no notion of the consuming flame she had engendered.

It was a simple thing to walk home with her from the post-office—quite accidentally on several occasions. It was a fortuitous thing that Anna Roth should invite Angela and himself, as well as his father and mother, to her house to dinner. On one occasion when Frieda was visiting at the Witla homestead, Angela thought Frieda stepped away from Eugene in a curiously disturbed manner when she came into the parlor. She was not sure. Frieda hung round him in a good-natured way most of the time when various members of the family were present. She wondered if by any chance he was making love to her, but she could not prove it. She tried to watch them from then on, but Eugene was so subtle, Frieda so circumspect, that she never did obtain any direct testimony. Nevertheless, before they left Alexandria there was a weeping scene over this, hysterical, tempestuous, in which she accused him of making love to Frieda, he denying it stoutly.

"If it wasn't for your relatives' sake," she declared, "I would accuse her to her face, here before your eyes. She couldn't dare deny it."

"Oh, you're crazy," said Eugene. "You're the most suspicious woman I ever knew. Good Lord! Can't I look at a woman any more? This little girl! Can't I even be nice to her?"

"Nice to her? Nice to her? I know how you're nice to her. I can see! I can feel! Oh, God! Why can't you give me a faithful husband!"

"Oh, cut it out!" demanded Eugene defiantly. "You're always watching. I can't turn around but you have your eye on me. I can tell. Well, you go ahead and watch. That's all the good it will do you. I'll give you some real reason for watching one of these days. You make me tired!"

"Oh, hear how he talks to me," moaned Angela, "and we're only married one year! Oh, Eugene, how can you? Have you no pity, no shame? Here in your own home, too! Oh! oh! oh!"

To Eugene such hysterics were maddening. He could not understand how anyone should want or find it possible to carry on in this fashion. He was lying "out of the whole cloth" about Frieda, but Angela didn't know and he knew she didn't know. All these tantrums were based on suspicion. If she would do this on a mere suspicion, what would she not do when she had a proved cause?

Still by her tears she as yet had the power of rousing his sympathies and awakening his sense of shame. Her sorrow made him slightly ashamed of his conduct or rather sorry, for the tougher nature was constantly presenting itself. Her suspicions made the further pursuit of this love quest practically impossible. Secretly he already cursed the day he had married her, for Frieda's face was ever before him, a haunting lure to love and desire. In this hour life looked terribly sad to him. He couldn't help feeling that all the perfect things one might seek or find were doomed to the searing breath of an inimical fate. Ashes of roses—that was all life had to offer. Dead sea fruit, turning to ashes upon the lips. Oh, Frieda! Frieda! Oh, youth, youth! That there should dance before him for evermore an unattainable desire—the holy grail of beauty. Oh life, oh death! Which was really better, waking or sleeping? If he could only have Frieda now it would be worth living, but without her—

CHAPTER XV

The weakness of Eugene was that he was prone in each of these new conquests to see for the time being the sum and substance of bliss, to rise rapidly in the scale of uncontrollable, exaggerated affection, until he felt that here and nowhere else, now and in this particular form was ideal happiness. He had been in love with Stella, with Margaret, with Ruby, with Angela, with Christina, and now with Frieda, quite in this way, and it had taught him nothing as yet concerning love except that it was utterly delightful. He wondered at times how it was that the formation of a particular face could work this spell. There was plain magic in the curl of a lock of hair, the whiteness or roundness of a forehead, the shapeliness of a nose or ear, the arched redness of full-blown petal lips. The cheek, the chin, the eye—in combination with these things—how did they work this witchery? The tragedies to which he laid himself open by yielding to these spells—he never stopped to think of them.

It is a question whether the human will, of itself alone, ever has cured or ever can cure any human weakness. Tendencies are subtle things. They are involved in the chemistry of one's being, and those who delve in the mysteries of biology frequently find that curious anomaly, a form of minute animal life born to be the prey of another form of animal life—chemically and physically attracted to its own disaster. Thus, to quote Calkins, "some protozoa are apparently limited to special kinds of food. The 'slipper-animal' (Paramecium) and the 'bell-animal' (Vorticella) live on certain kinds of bacteria, and many others, which live upon smaller protozoa, seem to have a marked affinity for certain kinds. I have watched one of these creatures (Actinobolus) lie perfectly quiet while hundreds of bacteria and smaller kinds of protozoa bumped against it, until a certain variety (Halteria grandinella) came near, when a minute dart, or 'trochocyst,' attached to a relatively long thread, was launched. The victim was invariably hit, and after a short struggle was drawn in and devoured. The results of many experiments indicate that the apparently *willful* selection in these cases is the inevitable action of definite chemical and physical laws which the individual organism can no more change than it can change the course of gravitation. The killing dart mentioned above is called out by the particular kind of prey with the irresistible attraction of an iron filing for a magnet."

Eugene did not know of these curious biologic experiments at this time, but he suspected that these attractions were deeper than human will. He thought at times that he ought to resist his impulses. At other times he asked himself why. If his treasure was in this and he lost it by resistance, what had he? A sense of personal purity? It did not appeal to him. The respect of his fellow-citizens? He believed that most of his fellow-citizens were whited sepulchres. What good did their hypocritical respect do him? Justice to others? Others were not concerned, or should not be in the natural affinity which might manifest itself between two people. That was for them to settle. Besides, there was very little justice in the world. As for his wife—well, he had given her his word, but he had not done so willingly. Might one swear eternal fealty and abide by it when the very essence of nature was lack of fealty, inconsiderateness, destruction, change? A gloomy Hamlet to be sure, asking "can honor set a leg?"—a subtle Machiavelli believing that might made right, sure that it was a matter of careful planning, not ethics which brought success in this world, and yet one of the poorest planners in it. An anarchistic manifestation of selfishness surely; but his additional plea was that he did not make his own mind, nor his emotions, nor anything else. And worst of all, he counselled himself that he was not seizing anything ruthlessly. He was merely accepting that which was thrust temptingly before him by fate.

Hypnotic spells of this character like contagion and fever have their period of duration, their beginning, climax and end. It is written that love is deathless, but this was not written of the body nor does it concern the fevers of desire. The marriage of true minds to which Shakespeare would admit no impediment is of a different texture and has little sex in it. The friendship of Damon and Pythias was a marriage in the best sense, though it concerned two men. The possibilities of intellectual union between a man and a woman are quite the same. This is deathless in so far as it reflects the spiritual ideals of the universe—not more so. All else is illusion of short duration and vanishes in thin air.

When the time came for Eugene to leave Alexandria as he had originally wanted to do, he was not at all anxious to depart; rather it was an occasion of great suffering for him. He could not see any solution to the problem which confronted him in connection with Frieda's love for him. As a matter of fact, when he thought about it at all he was quite sure that she did not understand or appreciate the nature of her affection for him or his for her. It had no basis in responsibility. It was one of those things born of thin air—sunlight, bright waters, the reflection of a bright room—

things which are intangible and insubstantial. Eugene was not one who, if he thought anything at all about it, would persuade a girl to immorality for the mere sake of indulgence. His feelings were invariably compounded of finer things, love of companionship, love of beauty, a variable sense of the consequences which must ensue, not so much to him as to her, though he took himself into consideration. If she were not already experienced and he had no method of protecting her, if he could not take her as his wife or give her the advantages of his presence and financial support, secretly or openly, if he could not keep all their transactions a secret from the world, he was inclined to hesitate. He did not want to do anything rash—as much for her sake as for his. In this case, the fact that he could not marry her, that he could not reasonably run away with her, seeing that he was mentally sick and of uncertain financial condition, the fact that he was surrounded by home conditions which made it of the greatest importance that he should conduct himself circumspectly, weighed greatly with him. Nevertheless a tragedy could easily have resulted here. If Frieda had been of a headstrong, unthinking nature; if Angela had been less watchful, morbid, appealing in her mood; if the family and town conditions had been less weighty; if Eugene had had health and ample means, he would probably have deserted Angela, taken Frieda to some European city—he dreamed of Paris in this connection—and found himself confronted later by an angry father or a growing realization that Frieda's personal charms were not the sum and substance of his existence, or both. George Roth, for all he was a traveling salesman, was a man of considerable determination. He might readily have ended the life of his daughter's betrayer—art reputation or no. He worshiped Frieda as the living image of his dead wife, and at best he would have been heartbroken.

As it was, there was not much chance of this, for Eugene was not rash. He was too philosophic. Conditions might have arisen in which he would have shown the most foolhardy bravado, but not in his present state. There was not sufficient anguish in his own existence to drive him to action. He saw no clear way. So, in June, with Angela he took his departure for Blackwood, pretending, to her, outward indifference as to his departure, but inwardly feeling as though his whole life were coming to nothing.

When he reached Blackwood he was now, naturally, disgusted with the whole atmosphere of it. Frieda was not there. Alexandria, from having been the most wearisome sidepool of aimless inactivity, had suddenly taken on all the characteristics of paradise. The little lakes, the quiet streets, the court house square, his sister's home, Frieda's home, his own home, had been once more invested for him with the radiance of romance—that intangible glory of feeling which can have no existence outside the illusion of love. Frieda's face was everywhere in it, her form, the look of her eyes. He could see nothing there now save the glory of Frieda. It was as though the hard, weary face of a barren landscape were suddenly bathed in the soft effulgence of a midnight moon.

As for Blackwood, it was as lovely as ever but he could not see it. The fact that his attitude had changed toward Angela for the time being made all the difference. He did not really hate her—he told himself that. She was not any different from that she had been, that was perfectly plain. The difference was in him. He really could not be madly in love with two people at once. He had entertained joint affections for Angela and Ruby, and Angela and Christina, but those were not the dominating fevers which this seemed to be. He could not for the time get the face of this girl out of his mind. He was sorry for Angela at moments. Then, because of her insistence on his presence with her—on her being in his company, "following him around" as he put it, he hated her. Dear Heaven! if he could only be free without injuring her. If he could only get loose. Think, at this moment he might be with Frieda walking in the sun somewhere, rowing on the lake at Alexandria, holding her in his arms. He would never forget how she looked the first morning she came into his barn studio at home—how enticing she was the first night he saw her at Sylvia's. What a rotten mess living was, anyhow. And so he sat about in the hammock at the Blue homestead, or swung in a swing that old Jotham had since put up for Marietta's beaux, or dreamed in a chair in the shade of the house, reading. He was dreary and lonely with just one ambition in the world—Frieda.

Meanwhile, as might be expected, his health was not getting any better. Instead of curing himself of those purely carnal expressions of passion which characterized his life with Angela, the latter went on unbroken. One would have thought that his passion for Frieda would have interrupted this, but the presence of Angela, the comparatively enforced contact, her insistence on his attentions, broke down again and again the protecting barrier of distaste. Had he been alone, he would have led a chaste life until some new and available infatuation seized him. As it was there was no refuge either from himself or Angela, and the at times almost nauseating relationship went on and on.

Those of the Blue family, who were in the home or near it, were delighted to see him. The fact that he had achieved such a great success, as the papers had reported, with his first exhibition and had not lost ground with the second—a very interesting letter had come from M. Charles saying that the Paris pictures would be shown in Paris in July—gave them a great estimate of him. Angela was a veritable queen in this home atmosphere; and as for Eugene, he was given the privilege of all geniuses to do as he pleased. On this occasion Eugene was the centre of interest, though he appeared not to be, for his four solid Western brothers-in-law gave no indication that they thought he was unusual. He was not their type—banker, lawyer, grain merchant and real estate dealer—but they felt proud of him just the same. He was different, and at the same time natural, genial, modest, inclined to appear far more interested in their affairs than he really was. He would listen by the hour to the details of their affairs, political, financial, agricultural, social. The world was a curious compost to Eugene and he was always anxious to find out how other people lived. He loved a good story, and while he rarely told one he made a splendid audience for those who did. His eyes would sparkle and his whole face light with the joy of the humor he felt.

Through all this—the attention he was receiving, the welcome he was made to feel, the fact that his art interests were not yet dead (the Paris exhibition being the expiring breath of his original burst of force), he was nevertheless feeling the downward trend of his affairs most keenly. His mind was not right. That was surely true. His money affairs were getting worse, not better, for while he could hope for a few sales yet (the Paris pictures did not sell in New York) he was not certain that this would be the case. This homeward trip had cost him two hundred of his seventeen hundred dollars and there would be additional expenses if he went to Chicago, as he planned in the fall. He could not live a single year on fifteen hundred dollars—scarcely more than six months, and he could not paint or illustrate anything new in his present state. Additional sales of the pictures of the two original exhibitions must be effected in a reasonable length of time or he would find himself in hard straits.

Meanwhile, Angela, who had obtained such a high estimate of his future by her experience in New York and Paris, was beginning to enjoy herself again, for after all, in her judgment, she seemed to be able to manage Eugene very well. He might have had some slight understanding with Frieda Roth— it couldn't have been much or she would have seen it, she thought—but she had managed to break it up. Eugene was cross, naturally, but that was due more to her quarreling than anything else. These storms of feeling on her part—not always premeditated—seemed very essential. Eugene must be made to understand that he was married now; that he could not look upon or run after girls as he had in the old days. She was well aware that he was considerably younger than she was in temperament, inclined to be exceedingly boyish, and this was apt to cause trouble anywhere. But if she watched over him, kept his attention fixed on her, everything would come out all right. And then there were all these other delightful qualities—his looks, his genial manner, his reputation, his talent. What a delightful thing it had become to announce herself as Mrs. Eugene Witla and how those who knew about him sat up. Big people were his friends, artists admired him, common, homely, everyday people thought he was nice and considerate and able and very worth while. He was generally liked everywhere. What more could one want?

Angela knew nothing of his real thoughts, for because of sympathy, a secret sense of injustice toward her on his part, a vigorous, morbid impression of the injustice of life as a whole, a desire to do things in a kindly or at least a secret and not brutal way, he was led to pretend at all times that he really cared for her; to pose as being comfortable and happy; to lay all his moods to his inability to work. Angela, who could not read him clearly, saw nothing of this. He was too subtle for her understanding at times. She was living in a fool's paradise; playing over a sleeping volcano.

He grew no better and by fall began to get the notion that he could do better by living in Chicago. His health would come back to him there perhaps. He was terribly tired of Blackwood. The long tree-shaded lawn was nothing to him now. The little lake, the stream, the fields that he had rejoiced in at first were to a great extent a commonplace. Old Jotham was a perpetual source of delight to him with his kindly, stable, enduring attitude toward things and his interesting comment on life, and Marietta entertained him with her wit, her good nature, her intuitive understanding; but he could not be happy just talking to everyday, normal, stable people, interesting and worthwhile as they might be. The doing of simple things, living a simple life, was just now becoming irritating. He must go to London, Paris—do things. He couldn't loaf this way. It mattered little that he could not work. He must try. This isolation was terrible.

There followed six months spent in Chicago in which he painted not one picture that was satisfactory to him, that was not messed into nothingness by changes and changes and changes. There were then three months in the mountains of Tennessee because someone told him of a wonderfully curative spring in a delightful valley where the spring came as a dream of color and the expense of living was next to nothing. There were four months of summer in southern Kentucky on a ridge where the air was cool, and after that five months on the Gulf of Mexico, at Biloxi, in Mississippi, because some comfortable people in Kentucky and Tennessee told Angela of this delightful winter resort farther South. All this time Eugene's money, the fifteen hundred dollars he had when he left Blackwood, several sums of two hundred, one hundred and fifty and two hundred and fifty, realized from pictures sold in New York and Paris during the fall and winter following his Paris exhibition, and two hundred which had come some months afterward from a fortuitous sale by M. Charles of one of his old New York views, had been largely dissipated. He still had five hundred dollars, but with no pictures being sold and none painted he was in a bad way financially in so far as the future was concerned. He could possibly return to Alexandria with Angela and live cheaply there for another six months, but because of the Frieda incident both he and she objected to it. Angela was afraid of Frieda and was resolved that she would not go there so long as Frieda was in the town, and Eugene was ashamed because of the light a return would throw on his fading art prospects. Blackwood was out of the question to him. They had lived on her parents long enough. If he did not get better he must soon give up this art idea entirely, for he could not live on trying to paint.

He began to think that he was possessed—obsessed of a devil—and that some people were pursued by evil spirits, fated by stars, doomed from their birth to failure or accident. How did the astrologer in New York know that he was to have four years of bad luck? He had seen three of them already. Why did a man who read his palm in Chicago once say that his hand showed two periods of disaster, just as the New York astrologer had and that he was likely to alter the course of his life radically in the middle portion of it? Were there any fixed laws of being? Did any of the so-called naturalistic school of philosophers and scientists whom he had read know anything at all? They were always talking about the fixed laws of the universe—the unalterable laws of chemistry and physics. Why didn't chemistry or physics throw some light on his peculiar physical condition, on the truthful prediction of the astrologer, on the signs and portents which he had come to observe for himself as foretelling trouble or good fortune for himself. If his left eye twitched he had observed of late he was going to have a quarrel with someone—invariably Angela. If he found a penny or any money, he was going to get money; for every notification of a sale of a picture with the accompanying check had been preceded by the discovery of a coin somewhere: once a penny in State Street, Chicago, on a rainy day—M. Charles wrote that a picture had been sold in Paris for two hundred; once a three-cent piece of the old American issue in the dust of a road in Tennessee—M. Charles wrote that one of his old American views had brought one hundred and fifty; once a penny in sands by the Gulf in Biloxi—another notification of a sale. So it went. He found that when doors squeaked, people were apt to get sick in the houses where they were; and a black dog howling in front of a house was a sure sign of death. He had seen this with his own eyes, this sign which his mother had once told him of as having been verified in her experience, in connection with the case of a man who was sick in Biloxi. He was sick, and a dog came running along the street and stopped in front of this place—a black dog—and the man died. Eugene saw this with his own eyes,—that is, the dog and the sick man's death notice. The dog howled at four o'clock in the afternoon and the next morning the man was dead. He saw the crape on the door. Angela mocked at his superstition, but he was convinced. "There are more things in heaven and earth, Horatio, than are dreamt of in your philosophy."

CHAPTER XVI

Eugene was reaching the point where he had no more money and was compelled to think by what process he would continue to make a living in the future. Worry and a hypochondriacal despair had reduced his body to a comparatively gaunt condition. His eyes had a nervous, apprehensive look. He would walk about speculating upon the mysteries of nature, wondering how he was to get out of this, what was to become of him, how soon, if ever, another picture would be sold, when? Angela, from having fancied that his illness was a mere temporary indisposition, had come to feel that he might be seriously affected for some time. He was not sick physically: he could walk and eat and talk vigorously enough, but he could not work and he was worrying, worrying, worrying.

Angela was quite as well aware as Eugene that their finances were in a bad way or threatening to become so, though he said nothing at all about them. He was ashamed to confess at this day, after their very conspicuous beginning in New York, that he was in fear of not doing well. How silly—he with all his ability! Surely he would get over this, and soon.

Angela's economical upbringing and naturally saving instinct stood her in good stead now, for she could market with the greatest care, purchase to the best advantage, make every scrap and penny count. She knew how to make her own clothes, as Eugene had found out when he first visited Blackwood, and was good at designing hats. Although she had thought in New York, when Eugene first began to make money, that now she would indulge in tailor-made garments and the art of an excellent dressmaker, she had never done so. With true frugality she had decided to wait a little while, and then Eugene's health having failed she had not the chance any more. Fearing the possible long duration of this storm she had begun to mend and clean and press and make over whatever seemed to require it. Even when Eugene suggested that she get something new she would not do it. Her consideration for their future—the difficulty he might have in making a living, deterred her.

Eugene noted this, though he said nothing. He was not unaware of the fear that she felt, the patience she exhibited, the sacrifice she made of her own whims and desires to his, and he was not entirely unappreciative. It was becoming very apparent to him that she had no life outside his own—no interests. She was his shadow, his alter ego, his servant, his anything he wanted her to be. "Little Pigtail" was one of his jesting pet names for her because in the West as a boy they had always called anyone who ran errands for others a pigtailer. In playing "one old cat," if one wanted another to chase the struck balls he would say: "You pig-tail for me, Willie, will you?" And Angela was his "little pigtail."

There were no further grounds for jealousy during the time, almost two years, in which they were wandering around together, for the reason that she was always with him, almost his sole companion, and that they did not stay long enough in any one place and under sufficiently free social conditions to permit him to form those intimacies which might have resulted disastrously. Some girls did take his eye—the exceptional in youth and physical perfection were always doing that, but he had no chance or very little of meeting them socially. They were not living with people they knew, were not introduced in the local social worlds, which they visited. Eugene could only look at these maidens whom he chanced to spy from time to time, and wish that he might know them better. It was hard to be tied down to a conventional acceptance of matrimony—to pretend that he was interested in beauty only in a sociological way. He had to do it before Angela though (and all conventional people for that matter), for she objected strenuously to the least interest he might manifest in any particular woman. All his remarks had to be general and guarded in their character. At the least show of feeling or admiration Angela would begin to criticize his choice and to show him wherein his admiration was ill-founded. If he were especially interested she would attempt to tear his latest ideal to pieces. She had no mercy, and he could see plainly enough on what her criticism was based. It made him smile but he said nothing. He even admired her for her heroic efforts to hold her own, though every victory she seemed to win served only to strengthen the bars of his own cage.

It was during this time that he could not help learning and appreciating just how eager, patient and genuine was her regard for his material welfare. To her he was obviously the greatest man in the world, a great painter, a great thinker, a great lover, a great personality every way. It didn't make so much difference to her at this time that he wasn't making any money. He would sometime, surely, and wasn't she getting it all in fame anyhow, now? Why, to be Mrs. Eugene Witla, after what she had seen of him in New York and Paris, what more could she want? Wasn't it all right for her to rake and scrape now, to make her own clothes and hats, save, mend, press and patch? He would come out of all this silly feeling about other women once he became a little older, and then he would be all right. Anyhow he appeared to love her now; and that was something. Because he was lonely, fearsome, uncertain of himself, uncertain of the future, he welcomed these unsparing attentions on her part, and this deceived her. Who else would give them to him, he thought; who else would be so faithful in times like these? He almost came to believe that he could love her again, be faithful to her, if he could keep out of the range of these other enticing personalities. If only he could stamp out this eager desire for other women, their praise and their beauty!

But this was more because he was sick and lonely than anything else. If he had been restored to health then and there, if prosperity had descended on him as he so eagerly dreamed, it would have been the same as ever. He was as subtle as nature itself; as changeable as a chameleon. But two things were significant and real—two things to which he was as true and unvarying as the needle to the pole—his love of the beauty of life which was coupled with his desire to express it in color, and his love of beauty in the form of the face of a woman, or rather that of a girl of eighteen. That blossoming of life in womanhood at eighteen!—there was no other thing under the sun like it to him. It was like the budding of the trees in spring; the blossoming of flowers in the early morning; the odor of roses and dew, the color of bright waters and clear jewels. He could not be faithless to that. He could not get away from it. It haunted him like a joyous vision, and the fact that the charms of Stella and Ruby and Angela and Christina and Frieda in whom it had been partially or wholly shadowed forth at one time or another had come and gone, made little difference. It remained clear and demanding. He could not escape it—the thought; he could not deny it. He was haunted by this, day after day, and hour after hour; and when he said to himself that he was a fool, and that it would lure him as a will-o'-the-wisp to his destruction and that he could find no profit in it ultimately, still it would not down. The beauty of youth; the beauty of eighteen! To him life without it was a joke, a shabby scramble, a work-horse job, with only silly material details like furniture and houses and steel cars and stores all involved in a struggle for what? To make a habitation for more shabby humanity? Never! To make a habitation for beauty? Certainly! What beauty? The beauty of old age?—How silly! The beauty of middle age? Nonsense! The beauty of maturity? No! The beauty of youth? Yes. The beauty of eighteen. No more and no less. That was the standard, and the history of the world proved it. Art, literature, romance, history, poetry—if they did not turn on this and the lure of this and the wars and sins because of this, what did they turn on? He was for beauty. The history of the world justified him. Who could deny it?

CHAPTER XVII

From Biloxi, because of the approach of summer when it would be unbearably warm there, and because his funds were so low that it was necessary to make a decisive move of some kind whether it led to complete disaster or not, he decided to return to New York. In storage with Kellners (M. Charles had kindly volunteered to take care of them for him) were a number of the pictures left over from the original show, and nearly all the paintings of the Paris exhibition. The latter had not sold well. Eugene's idea was that he could slip into New York quietly, take a room in some side street or in Jersey City or Brooklyn where he would not be seen, have the pictures in the possession of M. Charles returned to him, and see if he could not get some of the minor art dealers or speculators of whom he had heard to come and look at them and buy them outright. Failing that, he might take them himself, one by one, to different dealers here and there and dispose of them. He remembered now that Eberhard Zang had, through Norma Whitmore, asked him to come and see him. He fancied that, as Kellners had been so interested, and the newspaper critics had spoken of him so kindly the smaller dealers would be eager to take up with him. Surely they would buy this material. It was exceptional—very. Why not?

Eugene forgot or did not know the metaphysical side of prosperity and failure. He did not realize that "as a man thinketh so is he," and so also is the estimate of the whole world at the time he is thinking of himself thus—not as he is but as he thinks he is. The sense of it is abroad—by what processes we know not, but so it is.

Eugene's mental state, so depressed, so helpless, so fearsome—a rudderless boat in the dark, transmitted itself as an impression, a wireless message to all those who knew him or knew of him. His breakdown, which had first astonished M. Charles, depressed and then weakened the latter's interest in him. Like all other capable, successful men in the commercial world M. Charles was for strong men—men in the heyday of their success, the zenith of their ability. The least variation from this standard of force and interest was noticeable to him. If a man was going to fail—going to get sick and lose his interest in life or have his viewpoint affected, it might be very sad, but there was just one thing to do under such circumstances—get away from him. Failures of any kind were dangerous things to countenance. One must not have anything to do with them. They were very unprofitable. Such people as Temple Boyle and Vincent Beers, who had been his instructors in the past and who had heard of him in Chicago at the time of his success, Luke Severas, William McConnell, Oren Benedict, Hudson Dula, and others wondered what had become of him. Why did he not paint any more? He was never seen in the New York haunts of art! It was rumored at the time of the Paris exhibition that he was going to London to do a similar group of views, but the London exhibition never came off. He had told Smite and MacHugh the spring he left that he might do Chicago next, but that came to nothing. There was no evidence of it. There were rumors that he was very rich, that his art had failed him, that he had lost his mind even, and so the art world that knew him and was so interested in him no longer cared very much. It was too bad but—so thought the rival artists—there was one less difficult star to contend with. As for his friends, they were sorry, but such was life. He might recover. If not,—well—.

As time went on, one year, another year, another year, the strangeness of his suddenly brilliant burst and disappearance became to the talented in this field a form of classic memory. He was a man of such promise! Why did he not go on painting? There was an occasional mention in conversation or in print, but Eugene to all intents and purposes was dead.

When he came to New York it was after his capital had been reduced to three hundred dollars and he had given Angela one hundred and twenty-five of this to take her back to Blackwood and keep her there until he could make such arrangements as would permit her to join him. After a long discussion they had finally agreed that this would be best, for, seeing that he could neither paint nor illustrate, there was no certainty as to what he would do. To come here on so little money with her was not advisable. She had her home where she was welcome to stay for a while anyhow. Meanwhile he figured he could weather any storm alone.

The appearance of the metropolis, after somewhat over two years of absence during which he had wandered everywhere, was most impressive to Eugene. It was a relief after the mountains of Kentucky and Tennessee and the loneliness of the Biloxi coast, to get back to this swarming city where millions were hurrying to and fro, and where one's misery as well as one's prosperity was apparently swallowed up in an inconceivable mass of life. A subway was being built. The automobile, which only a few years before was having a vague, uncertain beginning, was now attaining a tremendous vogue. Magnificent cars of new design were everywhere. From the ferry-house in Jersey City he could see notable changes in the skyline, and a single walk across Twenty-third Street and up Seventh Avenue showed him a changing world—great hotels, great apartment houses, a tremendous crush of vainglorious life which was moulding the city to its desires. It depressed him greatly, for he had always hoped to be an integral part of this magnificence and display and now he was not—might never be again.

It was still raw and cold, for the spring was just beginning to break, and Eugene was compelled to buy a light overcoat, his own imperishable great coat having been left behind, and he had no other fit to wear. Appearances, he thought, demanded this. He had spent forty of his closely-guarded one hundred and seventy-five dollars coming from Biloxi to New York, and now an additional fifteen was required for this coat, leaving him one hundred and twenty-five dollars with which to begin his career anew. He was greatly worried as to the outcome, but curiously also he had an abiding subconscious feeling that it could not be utterly destructive to him.

He rented a cheap room in a semi-respectable neighborhood in West Twenty-fourth Street near Eleventh Avenue solely because he wanted to keep out of the run of intellectual life and hide until he could get on his feet. It was an old and shabby residence in an old and shabby red brick neighborhood such as he had drawn in one of his views, but it was not utterly bad. The people were poor but fairly intellectual. He chose this particular neighborhood with all its poverty because it was near the North River where the great river traffic could be seen, and where, because of some open lots in which were stored wagons, his one single west window gave him a view of all this life. About the corner in Twenty-third Street, in another somewhat decayed residence, was a moderate priced restaurant and boarding house. Here he could get a meal for twenty-five cents. He cared nothing for the life that was about him. It was cheap, poor, from a money point of view, dingy, but he would not be here forever he hoped. These people did not know him. Besides the number 552 West 24th Street did not sound bad. It might be one of the old neighborhoods with which New York was dotted, and which artists were inclined to find and occupy.

After he had secured this room from a semi-respectable Irish landlady, a dock weigher's wife, he decided to call upon M. Charles. He knew that he looked quite respectable as yet, despite his poverty and decline. His clothes were good, his overcoat new, his manner brisk and determined. But what he could not see was that his face in its thin sallowness, and his eyes with their semi-feverish lustre bespoke a mind that was harassed by trouble of some kind. He stood outside the office of Kellner and Son in Fifth Avenue—a half block from the door, wondering whether he should go in, and just what he should say. He had written to M. Charles from time to time that his health was bad and that he couldn't work—always that he hoped to be better soon. He had always hoped that a reply would come that another of his pictures had been sold. One year had gone and then two, and now a third was under way and still he was not any better. M. Charles would look at him searchingly. He would have to bear his gaze unflinchingly. In his present nervous state this was difficult and yet he was not without a kind of defiance even now. He would force himself back into favor with life sometime.

He finally mustered up his courage and entered and M. Charles greeted him warmly.

"This certainly is good,—to see you again. I had almost given up hope that you would ever come back to New York. How is your health now? And how is Mrs. Witla? It doesn't seem as though it had been three years. You're looking excellent. And how is painting going now? Getting to the point where you can do something again?"

Eugene felt for the moment as though M. Charles believed him to be in excellent condition, whereas that shrewd observer of men was wondering what could have worked so great a change. Eugene appeared to be eight years older. There were marked wrinkles between his eyes and an air of lassitude and weariness. He thought to himself, "Why, this man may possibly be done for artistically. Something has gone from him which I noted the first time I met him: that fire and intense enthusiasm which radiated force after the fashion of an arclight. Now he seems to be seeking to draw something in,—to save himself from drowning as it were. He is making a voiceless appeal for consideration. What a pity!"

The worst of it all was that in his estimation nothing could be done in such a case. You couldn't do anything for an artist who could do nothing for himself. His art was gone. The sanest thing for him to do would be to quit trying, go at some other form of labor and forget all about it. It might be that he would recover, but it was a question. Nervous breakdowns were not infrequently permanent.

Eugene noticed something of this in his manner. He couldn't tell exactly what it was, but M. Charles seemed more than ordinarily preoccupied, careful and distant. He wasn't exactly chilly in his manner, but reserved, as though he were afraid he might be asked to do something which he could not very well do.

"I noticed that the Paris scenes did not do very well either here or in Paris," observed Eugene with an air of nonchalance, as though it were a matter of small importance, at the same time hoping that he would have some favorable word. "I had the idea that they would take better than they did. Still I don't suppose I ought to expect everything to sell. The New York ones did all right."

"They did very well indeed, much better than I expected. I didn't think as many would be sold as were. They were very new and considerably outside the lines of current interest. The Paris pictures, on the other hand, were foreign to Americans in the wrong sense. By that I mean they weren't to be included in that genre art which comes from abroad, but is not based on any locality and is universal in its appeal—thematically speaking. Your Paris pictures were, of course, pictures in the best sense to those who see art as color and composition and idea, but to the ordinary lay mind they were, I take it, merely Paris scenes. You get what I mean. In that sense they were foreign, and Paris has been done illustratively anyhow. You might have done better with London or Chicago. Still you have every reason to congratulate yourself. Your work made a distinct impression both here and in France. When you feel able to return to it I have no doubt you will find that time has done you no harm."

He tried to be polite and entertaining, but he was glad when Eugene went away again.

The latter turned out into the street disconsolate. He could see how things were. He was down and out for the present and would have to wait.

CHAPTER XVIII

The next thing was to see what could be done with the other art dealers and the paintings that were left. There were quite a number of them. If he could get any reasonable price at all he ought to be able to live quite awhile—long enough anyhow to get on his feet again. When they came to his quiet room and were unpacked by him in a rather shamefaced and disturbed manner and distributed about, they seemed wonderful things. Why, if the critics had raved over them and M. Charles had thought they were so fine, could they not be sold? Art dealers would surely buy them! Still, now that he was on the ground again and could see the distinctive art shops from the sidewalks his courage failed him. They were not running after pictures. Exceptional as he might be, there were artists in plenty—good ones. He could not run to other well known art dealers very well for his work had become identified with the house of Kellner and Son. Some of the small dealers might buy them but they would not buy them all—probably one or two at the most, and that at a sacrifice. What a pass to come to!—he, Eugene Witla, who three years before had been in the heyday of his approaching prosperity, wondering as he stood in the room of a gloomy side-street house how he was going to raise money to live through the summer, and how he was going to sell the paintings which had seemed the substance of his fortune but two years before. He decided that he would ask several of the middle class dealers whether they would not come and look at what he had to show. To a number of the smaller dealers in Fourth, Sixth, Eighth Avenues and elsewhere he would offer to sell several outright when necessity pinched. Still he had to raise money soon. Angela could not be left at Blackwood indefinitely.

He went to Jacob Bergman, Henry LaRue, Pottle Frères and asked if they would be interested to see what he had. Henry Bergman, who was his own manager, recalled his name at once. He had seen the exhibition but was not eager. He asked curiously how the pictures of the first and second exhibitions had sold, how many there were of them, what prices they brought. Eugene told him.

"You might bring one or two here and leave them on sale. You know how that is. Someone might take a fancy to them. You never can tell."

He explained that his commission was twenty-five per cent, and that he would report when a sale was made. He was not interested to come and see them. Eugene could select any two pictures he pleased. It was the same with Henry LaRue and Pottle Frères, though the latter had never heard of him. They asked him to show them one of his pictures. Eugene's pride was touched the least bit by this lack of knowledge on their part, though seeing how things were going with him he felt as though he might expect as much and more.

Other art dealers he did not care to trust with his paintings on sale, and he was now ashamed to start carrying them about to the magazines, where at least one hundred and twenty-five to one hundred and fifty per picture might be expected for them, if they were sold at all. He did not want the magazine art world to think that he had come to this. His best friend was Hudson Dula, and he might no longer be Art Director of *Truth*. As a matter of fact Dula was no longer there. Then there were Jan Jansen and several others, but they were no doubt thinking of him now as a successful painter. It seemed as though his natural pride were building insurmountable barriers for him. How was he to live if he could not do this and could not paint? He decided on trying the small art dealers with a single picture, offering to sell it outright. They might not recognize him and so might buy it direct. He could accept, in such cases, without much shock to his pride, anything which they might offer, if it were not too little.

He tried this one bright morning in May, and though it was not without result it spoiled the beautiful day for him. He took one picture, a New York scene, and carried it to a third rate art dealer whose place he had seen in upper Sixth Avenue, and without saying anything about himself asked if he would like to buy it. The proprietor, a small, dark individual of Semitic extraction, looked at him curiously and at his picture. He could tell from a single look that Eugene was in trouble, that he needed money and that he was anxious to sell his picture. He thought of course that he would take anything for it and he was not sure that he wanted the picture at that. It was not very popular in theme, a view of a famous Sixth Avenue restaurant showing behind the track of the L road, with a driving rain pouring in between the interstices of light. Years after this picture was picked up by a collector from Kansas City at an old furniture sale and hung among his gems, but this morning its merits were not very much in evidence.

"I see that you occasionally exhibit a painting in your window for sale. Do you buy originals?"

"Now and again," said the man indifferently—"not often. What have you?"

"I have an oil here that I painted not so long ago. I occasionally do these things. I thought maybe you would like to buy it."

The proprietor stood by indifferently while Eugene untied the string, took off the paper and stood the picture up for inspection. It was striking enough in its way but it did not appeal to him as being popular. "I don't think it's anything that I could sell here," he remarked, shrugging his shoulders. "It's good, but we don't have much call for pictures of any kind. If it were a straight landscape or a marine or a figure of some kind—. Figures sell best. But this—I doubt if I could get rid of it. You might leave it on sale if you want to. Somebody might like it. I don't think I'd care to buy it."

"I don't care to leave it on sale," replied Eugene irritably. Leave one of his pictures in a cheap side-street art store—and that on sale! He would not. He wanted to say something cutting in reply but he curbed his welling wrath to ask,

"How much do you think it would be worth if you did want it?"

"Oh," replied the proprietor, pursing his lips reflectively, "not more than ten dollars. We can't ask much for anything we have on view here. The Fifth Avenue stores take all the good trade."

Eugene winced. Ten dollars! Why, what a ridiculous sum! What was the use of coming to a place like this anyhow? He could do better dealing with the art directors or the better stores. But where were they? Whom could he deal with? Where were there any stores much better than this outside the large ones which he had already canvassed. He had better keep his pictures and go to work now at something else. He only had thirty-five of them all told and at this rate he would have just three hundred and fifty dollars when they were all gone. What good would that do him? His mood and this preliminary experience convinced him that they could not be sold for any much greater sum. Fifteen dollars or less would probably be offered and he would be no better off at the end. His pictures would be gone and he would have nothing. He ought to get something to do and save his pictures. But what?

To a man in Eugene's position—he was now thirty-one years of age, with no training outside what he had acquired in developing his artistic judgment and ability—this proposition of finding something else which he could do was very difficult. His mental sickness was, of course, the first great bar. It made him appear nervous and discouraged and so more or less objectionable to anyone who was looking for vigorous healthy manhood in the shape of an employee. In the next place, his look and manner had become decidedly that of the artist—refined, retiring, subtle. He also had an air at times of finicky standoffishness, particularly in the presence of those who appeared to him commonplace or who by their look or manner appeared to be attempting to set themselves over him. In the last place, he could think of nothing that he really wanted to do—the idea that his art ability would come back to him or that it ought to serve him in this crisis, haunting him all the time. Once he had thought he might like to be an art director; he was convinced that he would be a good one. And another time he had thought he would like to write, but that was long ago. He had never written anything since the Chicago newspaper specials, and several efforts at concentrating his mind for this quickly proved to him that writing was not for him now. It was hard for him to formulate an intelligent consecutive-idea'd letter to Angela. He harked back to his old Chicago days and remembering that he had been a collector and a driver of a laundry wagon, he decided that he might do something of that sort. Getting a position as a street-car conductor or a drygoods clerk appealed to him as possibilities. The necessity of doing something within regular hours and in a routine way appealed to him as having curative properties. How should he get such a thing?

If it had not been for the bedeviled state of his mind this would not have been such a difficult matter, for he was physically active enough to hold any ordinary position. He might have appealed frankly and simply to M. Charles or Isaac Wertheim and through influence obtained something which would have tided him over, but he was too sensitive to begin with and his present weakness made him all the more fearful and retiring. He had but one desire when he thought of doing anything outside his creative gift, and that was to slink away from the gaze of men. How could he, with his appearance, his reputation, his tastes and refinement, hobnob with conductors, drygoods clerks, railroad hands or drivers? It wasn't possible— he hadn't the strength. Besides all that was a thing of the past, or he thought it was. He had put it behind him in his art student days. Now to have to get out and look for a job! How could he? He walked the streets for days and days, coming back to his room to see if by any chance he could paint yet, writing long, rambling, emotional letters to Angela. It was pitiful. In fits of gloom he would take out an occasional picture and sell it, parting with it for ten or fifteen dollars after he had carried it sometimes for miles. His one refuge was in walking, for somehow he could not walk and feel very, very bad. The beauty of nature, the activity of people entertained and diverted his mind. He would come back to his room some evenings feeling as though a great change had come over him, as though he were going to do better now; but this did not last long. A little while and he would be back in his old mood again. He spent three months this way, drifting, before he realized that he must do something—that fall and winter would be coming on again in a little while and he would have nothing at all.

In his desperation he first attempted to get an art directorship, but two or three interviews with publishers of magazines proved to him pretty quickly that positions of this character were not handed out to the inexperienced. It required an apprenticeship, just as anything else did, and those who had positions in this field elsewhere had the first call. His name or appearance did not appear to strike any of these gentlemen as either familiar or important in any way. They had heard of him as an illustrator and a painter, but his present appearance indicated that this was a refuge in ill health which he was seeking, not a vigorous, constructive position, and so they would have none of him. He next tried at three of the principal publishing houses, but they did not require anyone in that capacity. Truth to tell he knew very little of the details and responsibilities of the position, though he thought he did. After that there was nothing save drygoods stores, street-car registration offices, the employment offices of the great railroads and factories. He looked at sugar refineries, tobacco factories, express offices, railroad freight offices, wondering whether in any of these it would be possible for him to obtain a position which would give him a salary of ten dollars a week. If he could get that, and any of the pictures now on show with Jacob Bergman, Henry LaRue and Pottle Frères should be sold, he could get along. He might even live on this with Angela if he could sell an occasional picture for ten or fifteen dollars. But he was paying seven dollars a week for nothing save food and room, and scarcely managing to cling to the one hundred dollars which had remained of his original traveling fund after he had paid all his opening expenses here in New York. He was afraid to part with all his pictures in this way for fear he would be sorry for it after a while.

Work is hard to get under the most favorable conditions of health and youth and ambition, and the difficulties of obtaining it under unfavorable ones need not be insisted on. Imagine if you can the crowds of men, forty, fifty, one hundred strong, that wait at the door of every drygoods employment office, every street-car registration bureau, on the special days set aside for considering applications, at every factory, shop or office where an advertisement calling for a certain type of man or woman was inserted in the newspapers. On a few occasions that Eugene tried or attempted to try, he found himself preceded by peculiar groups of individuals who eyed him curiously as he approached, wondering, as he thought, whether a man of his type could be coming to apply for a job. They seemed radically different from himself to his mind, men with little education and a grim consciousness of the difficulties of life; young men, vapid looking men, shabby, stale, discouraged types—men who, like himself, looked as though they had seen something very much better, and men who looked as though they had seen things a great deal worse. The evidence which frightened him was the presence of a group of bright, healthy, eager looking boys of nineteen, twenty, twenty-one and twenty-two who, like himself when he first went to Chicago years before, were everywhere he went. When he drew near he invariably found it impossible to indicate in any way that he was looking for anything. He couldn't. His courage failed him; he felt that he looked too superior; self-consciousness and shame overcame him.

He learned now that men rose as early as four o'clock in the morning to buy a newspaper and ran quickly to the address mentioned in order to get the place at the head of the line, thus getting the first consideration as an applicant. He learned that some other men, such as waiters, cooks, hotel employees and so on, frequently stayed up all night in order to buy a paper at two in the morning, winter or summer, rain or snow, heat or cold, and hurry to the promising addresses they might find. He learned that the crowds of applicants were apt to become surly or sarcastic or contentious as their individual chances were jeopardized by ever-increasing numbers. And all this was going on all the time, in winter or summer, heat or cold, rain or snow. Pretending interest as a spectator, he would sometimes stand and watch, hearing the ribald jests, the slurs cast upon life, fortune, individuals in particular and in general by those who were wearily or hopelessly waiting. It was a horrible picture to him in his present condition. It was like the grinding of the millstones, upper and nether. These were the chaff. He was a part of the chaff at present, or in danger of becoming so. Life was winnowing him out. He might go down, down, and there might never be an opportunity for him to rise any more.

Few, if any of us, understand thoroughly the nature of the unconscious stratification which takes place in life, the layers and types and classes into which it assorts itself and the barriers which these offer to a free migration of individuals from one class to another. We take on so naturally the material habiliments of our temperaments, necessities and opportunities. Priests, doctors, lawyers, merchants, appear to be born with their particular mental attitude and likewise the clerk, the ditch-digger, the janitor. They have their codes, their guilds and their class feelings. And while they may be spiritually closely related, they are physically far apart. Eugene, after hunting for a place for a month, knew a great deal more about this stratification than he had ever dreamed of knowing. He found that he was naturally barred by temperament from some things, from others by strength and weight, or rather the lack of them; from others, by inexperience; from others, by age; and so on. And those who were different from him in any or all of these respects were inclined to look at him askance. "You are not as we are," their eyes seemed to say; "why do you come here?"

One day he approached a gang of men who were waiting outside a car barn and sought to find out where the registration office was. He did not lay off his natural manner of superiority—could not, but asked a man near him if he knew. It had taken all his courage to do this.

"He wouldn't be after lookin' fer a place as a conductor now, would he?" he heard someone say within his hearing. For some reason this remark took all his courage away. He went up the wooden stairs to the little office where the application blanks were handed out, but did not even have the courage to apply for one. He pretended to be looking for someone and went out again. Later, before a drygoods superintendent's office, he heard a youth remark, "Look what wants to be a clerk." It froze him.

It is a question how long this aimless, nervous wandering would have continued if it had not been for the accidental recollection of an experience which a fellow artist once related to him of a writer who had found himself nervously depressed and who, by application to the president of a railroad, had secured as a courtesy to the profession which he represented so ably a position as an apprentice in a surveying corps, being given transportation to a distant section of the country and employed at a laborer's wages until he was well. Eugene now thought of this as quite an idea for himself. Why it had not occurred to him before he did not know. He could apply as an artist—his appearance would bear him out, and being able to speak from the vantage point of personal ability temporarily embarrassed by ill health, his chances of getting something would be so much better. It would not be the same as a position which he had secured for himself without fear or favor, but it would be a position, different from farming with Angela's father because it would command a salary.

CHAPTER XIX

This idea of appealing to the president of one of the great railroads that entered New York was not so difficult to execute. Eugene dressed himself very carefully the next morning, and going to the office of the company in Forty-second Street, consulted the list of officers posted in one of the halls, and finding the president to be on the third floor, ascended. He discovered, after compelling himself by sheer will power to enter, that this so-called office was a mere anteroom to a force of assistants serving the president, and that no one could see him except by appointment.

"You might see his secretary if he isn't busy," suggested the clerk who handled his card gingerly.

Eugene was for the moment undetermined what to do but decided that maybe the secretary could help him. He asked that his card might be taken to him and that no explanation be demanded of him except by the secretary in person. The latter came out after a while, an under secretary of perhaps twenty-eight years of age, short and stout. He was bland and apparently good natured.

"What is it I can do for you?" he asked.

Eugene had been formulating his request in his mind—some method of putting it briefly and simply.

"I came up to see Mr. Wilson," he said, "to see if he would not send me out as a day-laborer of some kind in connection with some department of the road. I am an artist by profession and I am suffering from neurasthenia. All the doctors I have consulted have recommended that I get a simple, manual position of some kind and work at it until I am well. I know of an instance in which Mr. Wilson, assisted, in this way, Mr. Savin the author, and I thought he might be willing to interest himself in my case."

At the sound of Henry Savin's name the under-secretary pricked up his ears. He had, fortunately, read one of his books, and this together with Eugene's knowledge of the case, his personal appearance, a certain ring of sincerity in what he was saying, caused him to be momentarily interested.

"There is no position in connection with any clerical work which the president could give you, I am sure," he replied. "All of these things are subject to a system of promotion. It might be that he could place you with one of the construction gangs in one of the departments under a foreman. I don't know. It's very hard work, though. He might consider your case." He smiled commiseratingly. "I question whether you're strong enough to do anything of that sort. It takes a pretty good man to wield a pick or a shovel."

"I don't think I had better worry about that now," replied Eugene in return, smiling wearily. "I'll take the work and see if it won't help me. I think I need it badly enough."

He was afraid the under-secretary would repent of his suggestion and refuse him entirely.

"Can you wait a little while?" asked the latter curiously. He had the idea that Eugene was someone of importance, for he had suggested as a parting argument that he could give a number of exceptional references.

"Certainly," said Eugene, and the secretary went his way, coming back in half an hour to hand him an enveloped letter.

"We have the idea," he said quite frankly waiving any suggestion of the president's influence in the matter and speaking for himself and the secretary-in-chief, with whom he had agreed that Eugene ought to be assisted, "that you had best apply to the engineering department. Mr. Hobsen, the chief-engineer, can arrange for you. This letter I think will get you what you want."

Eugene's heart bounded. He looked at the superscription and saw it addressed to Mr. Woodruff Hobsen, Chief Engineer, and putting it in his pocket without stopping to read it, but thanking the under-secretary profusely, went out. In the hall at a safe distance he stopped and opened it, finding that it spoke of him familiarly as "Mr. Eugene Witla, an artist, temporarily incapacitated by neurasthenia," and went on to say that he was "desirous of being appointed to some manual toil in some construction corps. The president's office recommends this request to your favor."

When he read this he knew it meant a position. It roused curious feelings as to the nature and value of stratification. As a laborer he was nothing: as an artist he could get a position as a laborer. After all, his ability as an artist was worth something. It obtained him this refuge. He hugged it joyously, and a few moments later handed it to an under-secretary in the Chief-Engineer's office. Without being seen by anyone in authority he was in return given a letter to Mr. William Haverford, "Engineer of Maintenance of Way," a pale, anæmic gentleman of perhaps forty years of age, who, as

Eugene learned from him when he was eventually ushered into his presence a half hour later, was a captain of thirteen thousand men. The latter read the letter from the Engineer's office curiously. He was struck by Eugene's odd mission and his appearance as a man. Artists were queer. This was like one. Eugene reminded him of himself a little in his appearance.

"An artist," he said interestedly. "So you want to work as a day laborer?" He fixed Eugene with clear, coal-black eyes looking out of a long, pear-shaped face. Eugene noticed that his hands were long and thin and white and that his high, pale forehead was crowned by a mop of black hair.

"Neurasthenia. I've heard a great deal about that of late, but have never been troubled that way myself. I find that I derive considerable benefit when I am nervous from the use of a rubber exerciser. You have seen them perhaps?"

"Yes," Eugene replied, "I have. My case is much too grave for that, I think. I have traveled a great deal. But it doesn't seem to do me any good. I want work at something manual, I fancy—something at which I have to work. Exercise in a room would not help me. I think I need a complete change of environment. I will be much obliged if you will place me in some capacity."

"Well, this will very likely be it," suggested Mr. Haverford blandly. "Working as a day-laborer will certainly not strike you as play. To tell you the truth, I don't think you can stand it." He reached for a glass-framed map showing the various divisions of the railroad stretching from New England to Chicago and St. Louis, and observed quietly. "I could send you to a great many places, Pennsylvania, New York, Ohio, Michigan, Canada." His finger roved idly about. "I have thirteen thousand men in my department and they are scattered far and wide."

Eugene marveled. Such a position! Such authority! This pale, dark man sitting as an engineer at a switch board directing so large a machine.

"You have a large force," he said simply. Mr. Haverford smiled wanly.

"I think, if you will take my advice, you will not go in a construction corps right away. You can hardly do manual labor. There is a little carpenter shop which we have at Speonk, not very far outside the city, which I should think would answer your needs admirably. A little creek joins the Hudson there and it's out on a point of land, the shop is. It's summer now, and to put you in a broiling sun with a gang of Italians would be a little rough. Take my advice and go here. It will be hard enough. After you are broken in and you think you want a change I can easily arrange it for you. The money may not make so much difference to you but you may as well have it. It will be fifteen cents an hour. I will give you a letter to Mr. Litlebrown, our division engineer, and he will see that you are properly provided for."

Eugene bowed. Inwardly he smiled at the thought that the money would not be acceptable to him. Anything would be acceptable. Perhaps this would be best. It was near the city. The description of the little carpenter shop out on the neck of land appealed to him. It was, as he found when he looked at the map of the immediate division to which this belonged, almost within the city limits. He could live in New York—the upper portion of it anyhow.

Again there was a letter, this time to Mr. Henry C. Litlebrown, a tall, meditative, philosophic man whom Eugene found two days later in the division offices at Yonkers, who in turn wrote a letter to Mr. Joseph Brooks, Superintendent of Buildings, at Mott Haven, whose secretary finally gave Eugene a letter to Mr. Jack Stix, foreman carpenter at Speonk. This letter, when presented on a bright Friday afternoon, brought him the advice to come Monday at seven A. M., and so Eugene saw a career as a day laborer stretching very conspicuously before him.

The "little shop" in question was located in the most charming manner possible. If it had been set as a stage scene for his especial artistic benefit it could not have been better. On a point of land between the river and the main line of the railroad and a little creek, which was east of the railroad and which the latter crossed on a trestle to get back to the mainland again, it stood, a long, low two-storey structure, green as to its roof, red as to its body, full of windows which commanded picturesque views of passing yachts and steamers and little launches and row-boats anchored safely in the waters of the cove which the creek formed. There was a veritable song of labor which arose from this shop, for it was filled with planes, lathes and wood-turning instruments of various kinds, to say nothing of a great group of carpenters who could make desks, chairs, tables, in short, office furniture of various kinds, and who kept the company's needs of these fittings for its depots and offices well supplied. Each carpenter had a bench before a window on the second floor, and in the centre were the few necessary machines they were always using, small jig, cross cut, band and rip saws, a plane, and four or five lathes. On the ground floor was the engine room, the blacksmith's shop, the giant plane, the great jig and cross cut saws, and the store room and supply closets. Out in the yard were piles of lumber, with tracks in between, and twice every day a local freight called "The Dinky" stopped to switch in or take out loaded cars of lumber or finished furniture and supplies. Eugene, as he approached on the day he presented his letter, stopped to admire the neatness of the low board fence which surrounded it all, the beauty of the water, the droning sweetness of the saws.

"Why, the work here couldn't be very hard," he thought. He saw carpenters looking out of the upper windows, and a couple of men in brown overalls and jumpers unloading a car. They were carrying great three-by-six joists on their shoulders. Would he be asked to do anything like that. He scarcely thought so. Mr. Haverford had distinctly indicated in his letter to Mr. Litlebrown that he was to be built up by degrees. Carrying great joists did not appeal to him as the right way, but he presented his letter. He had previously looked about on the high ground which lay to the back of the river and which commanded this point of land, to see if he could find a place to board and lodge, but had seen nothing. The section was very exclusive, occupied by suburban New Yorkers of wealth, and they were not interested in the proposition which he had formulated in his own mind, namely his temporary reception somewhere as a paying guest. He had visions of a comfortable home somewhere now with nice people, for strangely enough the securing of this very minor position had impressed him as the beginning of the end of his bad luck. He was probably going to get well now, in the course of time. If he could only live with some nice family for the summer. In the fall if he were improving, and he thought he might be, Angela could come on. It might be that one of the dealers, Pottle Frères or Jacob Bergman or Henry LaRue would have sold a picture. One hundred and fifty or two hundred dollars joined to his salary would go a long way towards making their living moderately comfortable. Besides Angela's taste and economy, coupled with his own art judgment, could make any little place look respectable and attractive.

The problem of finding a room was not so easy. He followed the track south to a settlement which was visible from the shop windows a quarter of a mile away, and finding nothing which suited his taste as to location, returned to Speonk proper and followed the little creek inland half a mile. This adventure delighted him for it revealed a semi-circle of charming cottages ranged upon a hill slope which had for its footstool the little silvery-bosomed stream. Between the stream and the hill slope ran a semi-circular road and above that another road. Eugene could see at a glance that here was middle class prosperity, smooth lawns, bright awnings, flower pots of blue and yellow and green upon the porches, doorsteps and verandas. An auto standing in front of one house indicated a certain familiarity with the ways of the rich, and a summer road house, situated at the intersection of a road leading out from New York and the little stream where it was crossed by a bridge, indicated that the charms of this village were not unknown to those who came touring and seeking for pleasure. The road house itself was hung with awnings and one dining balcony out over the water. Eugene's desire was fixed on this village at once. He wanted to live here—anywhere in it. He walked about under the cool shade of the trees looking at first one door yard and then another wishing that he might introduce himself by letter and be received. They ought to welcome an artist of his ability and refinement and would, he thought, if they knew. His working in a furniture factory or for the railroad as a day laborer for his health simply added to his picturesque character. In his wanderings he finally came upon a Methodist church quaintly built of red brick and grey stone trimmings, and the sight of its tall, stained glass windows and square fortress-like bell-tower gave him an idea. Why not appeal to the minister? He could explain to him what he wanted, show him his credentials—for he had with him old letters from editors, publishers and art houses—and give him a clear understanding as to why he wanted to come here at all. His ill health and distinction ought to appeal to this man, and he would probably direct him to some one who would gladly have him. At five in the afternoon he knocked at the door and was received in the pastor's study—a large still room in which a few flies were buzzing in the shaded light. In a few moments the minister himself came in—a tall, grey-headed man, severely simple in his attire and with the easy air of one who is used to public address. He was about to ask what he could do for him when Eugene began with his explanation.

"You don't know me at all. I am a stranger in this section. I am an artist by profession and I am coming to Speonk on Monday to work in the railroad shop there for my health. I have been suffering from a nervous breakdown and am going to try day labor for awhile. I want to find a convenient, pleasant place to live, and I thought you might know of someone here, or near here, who might be willing to take me in for a little while. I can give excellent references. There doesn't appear to be anything in the immediate neighborhood of the shop."

"It is rather isolated there," replied the old minister, studying Eugene carefully. "I have often wondered how all those men like it, traveling so far. None of them live about here." He looked at Eugene solemnly, taking in his various characteristics. He was not badly impressed. He seemed to be a reserved, thoughtful, dignified young man and decidedly artistic. It struck him as very interesting that he should be trying so radical a thing as day labor for his nerves.

"Let me see," he said thoughtfully. He sat down in his chair near his table and put his hand over his eyes. "I don't think of anyone just at the moment. There are plenty of families who have room to take you if they would, but I question very much whether they would. In fact I'm rather sure they wouldn't. Let me see now."

He thought again.

Eugene studied his big aquiline nose, his shaggy grey eyebrows, his thick, crisp, grey hair. Already his mind was sketching him, the desk, the dim walls, the whole atmosphere of the room.

"No, no," he said slowly. "I don't think of anyone. There is one family—Mrs. Hibberdell. She lives in the—let me see—first, second, third, tenth house above here. She has one nephew with her at present, a young man of about your age, and I don't think anyone else. I don't know that she would consider taking you in, but she might. Her house is quite large. She did have her daughter with her at one time, but I'm not sure that she's there now. I think not."

He talked as though he were reporting his own thoughts to himself audibly.

Eugene pricked up his ears at the mention of a daughter. During all the time he had been out of New York he had not, with the exception of Frieda, had a single opportunity to talk intimately with any girl. Angela had been with him all the time. Here in New York since he had been back he had been living under such distressing conditions that he had not thought of either youth or love. He had no business to be thinking of it now, but this summer air, this tree-shaded village, the fact that he had a position, small as it was, on which he could depend and which would no doubt benefit him mentally, and that he was somehow feeling better about himself because he was going to work, made him feel that he might look more interestedly on life again. He was not going to die; he was going to get well. Finding this position proved it. And he might go to the house now and find some charming girl who would like him very much. Angela was away. He was alone. He had again the freedom of his youth. If he were only well and working!

He thanked the old minister very politely and went his way, recognizing the house by certain details given him by the minister, a double balconied veranda, some red rockers, two yellow jardinières at the doorstep, a greyish white picket fence and gate. He walked up smartly and rang the bell. A very intelligent woman of perhaps fifty-five or sixty with bright grey hair and clear light blue eyes was coming out with a book in her hand. Eugene stated his case. She listened with keen interest, looking him over the while. His appearance took her fancy, for she was of a strong intellectual and literary turn of mind.

"I wouldn't ordinarily consider anything of the kind, but I am alone here with my nephew and the house could easily accommodate a dozen. I don't want to do anything which will irritate him, but if you will come back in the morning I will let you know. It would not disturb me to have you about. Do you happen to know of an artist by the name of Deesa?"

"I know him well," replied Eugene. "He's an old friend of mine."

"He is a friend of my daughter's, I think. Have you enquired anywhere else here in the village?"

"No," said Eugene.

"That is just as well," she replied.

He took the hint.

So there was no daughter here. Well, what matter? The view was beautiful. Of an evening he could sit out here in one of the rocking chairs and look at the water. The evening sun, already low in the west was burnishing it a bright gold. The outline of the hill on the other side was dignified and peaceful. He could sleep and work as a day laborer and take life easy for a while. He could get well now and this was the way to do it. Day laborer! How fine, how original, how interesting. He felt somewhat like a knight-errant reconnoitring a new and very strange world.

CHAPTER XX

The matter of securing admission to this house was quickly settled. The nephew, a genial, intelligent man of thirty-four, as Eugene discovered later, had no objection. It appeared to Eugene that in some way he contributed to the support of this house, though Mrs. Hibberdell obviously had some money of her own. A charmingly furnished room on the second floor adjoining one of the several baths was assigned him, and he was at once admitted to the freedom of the house. There were books, a piano (but no one to play it), a hammock, a maid-of-all-work, and an atmosphere of content and peace. Mrs. Hibberdell, a widow, presumably of some years of widowhood, was of that experience and judgment in life which gave her intellectual poise. She was not particularly inquisitive about anything in connection with him, and so far as he could see from surface indications was refined, silent, conservative. She could jest, and did, in a subtle understanding way. He told her quite frankly at the time he applied that he was married, that his wife was in the West and that he expected her to return after his health was somewhat improved. She talked with him about art and books and life in general. Music appeared to be to her a thing apart. She did not care much for it. The nephew, Davis Simpson, was neither literary nor artistic, and apparently cared little for music. He was a buyer for one of the larger department stores, a slight, dapper, rather dandified type of man, with a lean, not thin but tight-muscled face, and a short black mustache, and he appeared to be interested only in the humors of character, trade, baseball and methods of entertaining himself. The things that pleased Eugene about him were that he was clean, simple, direct, good-natured and courteous. He had apparently no desire to infringe on anybody's privacy, but was fond of stirring up light discussions and interpolating witty remarks. He liked also to grow flowers and to fish. The care of a border of flowers which glorified a short gravel path in the back yard received his especial attention evenings and mornings.

It was a great pleasure for Eugene to come into this atmosphere after the storm which had been assailing him for the past three years, and particularly for the past ninety days. He was only asked to pay eight dollars a week by Mrs. Hibberdell, though he realized that what he was obtaining in home atmosphere here was not ordinarily purchasable at any price in the public market. The maid saw to it that a little bouquet of flowers was put on his dressing table daily. He was given fresh towels and linen in ample quantities. The bath was his own. He could sit out on the porch of an evening and look at the water uninterrupted or he could stay in the library and read. Breakfast and dinner were invariably delightful occasions, for though he rose at five-forty-five in order to have his bath, breakfast, and be able to walk to the factory and reach it by seven, Mrs. Hibberdell was invariably up, as it was her habit to rise thus early, had been so for years. She liked it. Eugene in his weary mood could scarcely understand this. Davis came to the table some few moments before he would be leaving. He invariably had some cheery remark to offer, for he was never sullen or gloomy. His affairs, whatever they were, did not appear to oppress him. Mrs. Hibberdell would talk to Eugene genially about his work, this small, social centre of which they were a part and which was called Riverwood, the current movements in politics, religion, science and so forth. There were references sometimes to her one daughter, who was married and living in New York. It appeared that she occasionally visited her mother here. Eugene was delighted to think he had been so fortunate as to find this place. He hoped to make himself so agreeable that there would be no question as to his welcome, and he was not disappointed.

Between themselves Mrs. Hibberdell and Davis discussed him, agreeing that he was entirely charming, a good fellow, and well worth having about. At the factory where Eugene worked and where the conditions were radically different, he made for himself an atmosphere which was almost entirely agreeable to him, though he quarreled at times with specific details. On the first morning, for instance, he was put to work with two men, heavy clods of souls he thought at first, familiarly known about the yard as John and Bill. These two, to his artistic eye, appeared machines, more mechanical than humanly self-directive. They were of medium height, not more than five feet, nine inches tall and weighed about one hundred and eighty pounds each. One had a round, poorly modeled face very much the shape of an egg, to which was attached a heavy yellowish mustache. He had a glass eye, complicated in addition by a pair of spectacles which were fastened over his large, protruding red ears with steel hooks. He wore a battered brown hat, now a limp shapeless mass. His name was Bill Jeffords and he responded sometimes to the sobriquet of "One Eye."

The other man was John alias "Jack" Duncan, an individual of the same height and build with but slightly more modeling to his face and with little if any greater intelligence. He looked somewhat the shrewder—Eugene fancied there might be lurking in him somewhere a spark of humor, but he was mistaken. Unquestionably in Jeffords there was none. Jack Stix, the foreman-carpenter, a tall, angular, ambling man with red hair, a red mustache, shifty, uncertain blue eyes and noticeably big hands and feet, had suggested to Eugene that he work with these men for a little while. It was his idea to "try him out," as he told one of the associate foremen who was in charge of a gang of Italians working in the yard for the morning, and he was quite equal to doing it. He thought Eugene had no business here and might possibly be scared off by a little rough work.

"He's up here for his health," he told him. "I don't know where he comes from. Mr. Brooks sent him up here with orders to put him on. I want to see how he takes to real work for awhile."

"Look out you don't hurt him," suggested the other. "He don't look very strong to me."

"He's strong enough to carry a few spiles, I guess. If Jimmy can carry 'em, he can. I don't intend to keep him at it long."

Eugene knew nothing of this, but when he was told to "come along, new man" and shown a pile of round, rough ash trunk cutting six inches in diameter and eight feet long, his courage failed him. He was suffered to carry some of these to the second floor, how many he did not know.

"Take 'em to Thompson up there in the corner," said Jeffords dully.

Eugene grasped one uncertainly in the middle with his thin, artistic hands. He did not know that there were ways of handling lumber just as there were ways of handling a brush. He tried to lift it but could not. The rough bark scratched his fingers cruelly.

"Yah gotta learn somepin about that before yuh begin, I guess," said Jack Duncan, who had been standing by eyeing him narrowly.

Jeffords had gone about some other work.

"I suppose I don't know very much about it," replied Eugene shamefacedly stopping and waiting for further instructions.

"Lemme show you a trick," said his associate. "There's tricks in all these here trades. Take it by the end this-a-way, and push it along until you can stand it up. Stoop down now and put your shoulder right next the middle. Gotta pad under your shirt? You oughtta have one. Now put your right arm out ahead o'yuh, on the spile. Now you're all right."

Eugene straightened up and the rough post balanced itself evenly but crushingly on his shoulder. It appeared to grind his muscles and his back and legs ached instantly. He started bravely forward straining to appear at ease but within fifty feet he was suffering agony. He walked the length of the shop, however, up the stairs and back again to the window where

Thompson was, his forehead bursting with perspiration and his ears red with blood. He fairly staggered as he neared the machine and dropped the post heavily.

"Look what you're doin'," said a voice behind him. It was Thompson, the lathe worker. "Can't you put that down easy?"

"No, I can't," replied Eugene angrily, his face tinged with a faint blush from his extreme exertion. He was astonished and enraged to think they should put him to doing work like this, especially since Mr. Haverford had told him it would be easy. He suspected at once a plot to drive him away. He would have added "these are too damn heavy for me," but he restrained himself. He went down stairs wondering how he was to get up the others. He fingered about the pole gingerly hoping that the time taken this way would ease his pain and give him strength for the next one. Finally he picked up another and staggered painfully to the loft again. The foreman had his eye on him but said nothing. It amused him a little to think Eugene was having such a hard time. It wouldn't hurt him for a change, would do him good. "When he gets four carried up let him go," he said to Thompson, however, feeling that he had best lighten the situation a little. The latter watched Eugene out of the tail of his eye noting the grimaces he made and the strain he was undergoing, but he merely smiled. When four had been dropped on the floor he said: "That'll do for the present," and Eugene, heaving a groan of relief, went angrily away. In his nervous, fantastic, imaginative and apprehensive frame of mind, he imagined he had been injured for life. He feared he had strained a muscle or broken a blood vessel somewhere.

"Good heavens, I can't stand anything like this," he thought. "If the work is going to be this hard I'll have to quit. I wonder what they mean by treating me this way. I didn't come here to do this."

Visions of days and weeks of back-breaking toil stretched before him. It would never do. He couldn't stand it. He saw his old search for work coming back, and this frightened him in another direction. "I mustn't give up so easily," he counseled himself in spite of his distress. "I have to stick this out a little while anyhow." It seemed in this first trying hour as though he were between the devil and the deep sea. He went slowly down into the yard to find Jeffords and Duncan. They were working at a car, one inside receiving lumber to be piled, the other bringing it to him.

"Get down, Bill," said John, who was on the ground looking up at his partner indifferently. "You get up there, new man. What's your name?"

"Witla," said Eugene.

"Well, my name's Duncan. We'll bring this stuff to you and you pile it."

It was more heavy lumber, as Eugene apprehensively observed, quarter cut joists for some building—"four by fours" they called them—but after he was shown the art of handling them they were not unmanageable. There were methods of sliding and balancing them which relieved him of a great quantity of labor. Eugene had not thought to provide himself with gloves though, and his hands were being cruelly torn. He stopped once to pick a splinter out of his thumb and Jeffords, who was coming up, asked, "Ain't cha got no gloves?"

"No," said Eugene, "I didn't think to get any."

"Your hands'll get pretty well bunged up, I'm afraid. Maybe Joseph'll let you have his for to-day, you might go in and ask him."

"Where's Joseph?" asked Eugene.

"He's inside there. He's taking from the plane."

Eugene did not understand this quite. He knew what a plane was, had been listening to it sing mightily all the morning, the shavings flying as it smoothed the boards, but *taking*?

"Where's Joseph?" he asked of the plane driver.

He nodded his head to a tall hump-shouldered boy of perhaps twenty-two. He was a big, simple, innocent looking fellow. His face was long and narrow, his mouth wide, his eyes a watery blue, his hair a shock of brown, loose and wavy, with a good sprinkling of sawdust in it. About his waist was a big piece of hemp bagging tied by a grass rope. He wore an old faded wool cap with a long visor in order to shield his eyes from the flying chips and dust, and when Eugene came in one hand was lifted protectingly to shield his eyes. Eugene approached him deprecatingly.

"One of the men out in the yard said that you might have a pair of gloves you would lend me for to-day. I'm piling lumber and it's tearing my hands. I forgot to get a pair."

"Sure," said Joseph genially waving his hand to the driver to stop. "They're over here in my locker. I know what that is. I been there. When I come here they rubbed it into me jist as they're doin' to you. Doncher mind. You'll come out all right. Up here for your health, are you? It ain't always like that. Somedays there ain't most nothin' to do here. Then somedays ag'in there's a whole lot. Well, it's good healthy work, I can say that. I ain't most never sick. Nice fresh air we git here and all that."

He rambled on, fumbling under his bagging apron for his keys, unlocking his locker and producing a great pair of old yellow lumber gloves. He gave them to Eugene cheerfully and the latter thanked him. He liked Eugene at once and Eugene liked him. "A nice fellow that," he said, as he went back to his car. "Think of how genially he gave me these. Lovely! If only all men were as genial and kindly disposed as this boy, how nice the world would be." He put on the gloves and found his work instantly easier for he could grasp the joists firmly and without pain. He worked on until noon when the whistle blew and he ate a dreary lunch sitting by himself on one side, pondering. After one he was called to carry shavings, one basket after another back through the blacksmith shop to the engine room in the rear where was a big shaving bin. By four o'clock he had seen almost all the characters he was going to associate with for the time that he stayed there. Harry Fornes, the blacksmith or "the village smith," as Eugene came to call him later on, Jimmy Sudds, the blacksmith's helper or "maid-of-all-work" as he promptly named him; John Peters, the engineer, Malachi Dempsey, the driver of the great plane, Joseph Mews and, in addition, carpenters, tin-smiths, plumbers, painters, and those few exceptional cabinet makers who passed through the lower floor now and then, men who were about the place from time to time and away from it at others all of whom took note of Eugene at first as a curiosity.

Eugene was himself intensely interested in the men. Harry Fornes and Jimmy Sudds attracted him especially. The former was an undersized American of distant Irish extraction who was so broad chested, swollen armed, square-jawed and generally self-reliant and forceful as to seem a minor Titan. He was remarkably industrious, turning out a great deal of work and beating a piece of iron with a resounding lick which could be heard all about the hills and hollows outside. Jimmy Sudds, his assistant, was like his master equally undersized, dirty, gnarled, twisted, his teeth showing like a row of yellow snags, his ears standing out like small fans, his eye askew, but nevertheless with so genial a look in his face as to disarm criticism at once. Every body liked Jimmy Sudds because he was honest, single-minded and free of malicious intent. His coat was three and his trousers two times too large for him, and his shoes were obviously bought at a second-hand store, but he had the vast merit of being a picture. Eugene was fascinated with him. He learned shortly that Jimmy Sudds truly believed that buffaloes were to be shot around Buffalo, New York.

John Peters, the engineer, was another character who fixed his attention. John was almost helplessly fat and was known for this reason as "Big John." He was a veritable whale of a man. Six feet tall, weighing over three hundred pounds and standing these summer days in his hot engine room, his shirt off, his suspenders down, his great welts of fat showing through his thin cotton undershirt, he looked as though he might be suffering, but he was not. John, as Eugene soon found out, did not take life emotionally. He stood mostly in his engine room door when the shade was there staring out on the glistening water of the river, occasionally wishing that he didn't need to work but could lie and sleep indefinitely instead.

"Wouldja think them fellers would feel purty good sittin' out there on the poop deck of them there yachts smokin' their perfectos?" he once asked Eugene, apropos of the magnificent private vessels that passed up and down the river.

"I certainly would," laughed Eugene.

"Aw! Haw! That's the life fer yer uncle Dudley. I could do that there with any of 'em. Aw! Haw!"

Eugene laughed joyously.

"Yes, that's the life," he said. "We all could stand our share."

Malachi Dempsey, the driver of the great plane, was dull, tight-mouthed, silent, more from lack of ideas than anything else, though oyster-wise he had learned to recede from all manner of harm by closing his shell tightly. He knew no way to avoid earthly harm save by being preternaturally silent, and Eugene saw this quickly. He used to stare at him for long periods at a time, marvelling at the curiosity his attitude presented. Eugene himself, though, was a curiosity to the others, even more so than they to him. He did not look like a workingman and could not be made to do so. His spirit was too high, his eye too flashing and incisive. He smiled at himself carrying basketful after basketful of shavings from the planing room, where it rained shavings and from which, because of the lack of a shaving blower, they had to be removed back to the hot engine room where Big John presided. The latter took a great fancy to Eugene, but something after the fashion of a dog for a master. He did not have a single idea above his engine, his garden at home, his wife, his children and his pipe. These and sleep—lots of it—were his joys, his recreations, the totality of his world.

CHAPTER XXI

There were many days now, three months all told, in which Eugene obtained insight into the workaday world such as he had not previously had. It is true he had worked before in somewhat this fashion, but his Chicago experience was without the broad philosophic insight which had come to him since. Formerly the hierarchies of power in the universe and on earth were inexplicable to him—all out of order; but here, where he saw by degrees ignorant, almost animal intelligence, being directed by greater, shrewder, and at times it seemed to him possibly malicious intelligences— he was not quite sure about that—who were so strong that the weaker ones must obey them, he began to imagine that in a rough way life might possibly be ordered to the best advantage even under this system. It was true that men quarreled here with each other as to who should be allowed to lead. There was here as elsewhere great seeking for the privileges and honors of direction and leadership in such petty things as the proper piling of lumber, the planing of boards, the making of desks and chairs, and men were grimly jealous of their talents and abilities in these respects, but in the main it was the jealousy that makes for ordered, intelligent control. All were striving to do the work of intelligence, not of unintelligence. Their pride, however ignorant it might be, was in the superior, not the inferior. They might complain of their work, snarl at each other, snarl at their bosses, but after all it was because they were not able or permitted to do the higher work and carry out the orders of the higher mind. All were striving to do something in a better way, a superior way, and to obtain the honors and emoluments that come from doing anything in a superior way. If they were not rewarded according to their estimate of their work there was wrath and opposition and complaint and self-pity, but the work of the superior intelligence was the thing which each in his blind, self-seeking way was apparently trying to do.

Because he was not so far out of his troubles that he could be forgetful of them, and because he was not at all certain that his talent to paint was ever coming back to him, he was not as cheerful at times as he might have been; but he managed to conceal it pretty well. This one thought with its attendant ills of probable poverty and obscurity were terrible to him. Time was slipping away and youth. But when he was not thinking of this he was cheerful enough. Besides he had the ability to simulate cheerfulness even when he did not feel it. Because he did not permanently belong to this world of day labor and because his position which had been given him as a favor was moderately secure, he felt superior to everything about him. He did not wish to show this feeling in any way—was very anxious as a matter of fact to conceal it, but his sense of superiority and ultimate indifference to all these petty details was an abiding thought with him. He went to and fro carrying a basket of shavings, jesting with "the village smith," making friends with "Big John," the engineer, with Joseph, Malachi Dempsey, little Jimmy Sudds, in fact anyone and everyone who came near him who would be friends. He took a pencil one day at the noon hour and made a sketch of Harry Fornes, the blacksmith, his arm upraised at the anvil, his helper, Jimmy Sudds, standing behind him, the fire glowing in the forge. Fornes, who was standing beside him, looking over his shoulder, could scarcely believe his eyes.

"Wotcha doin'?" he asked Eugene curiously, looking over his shoulder, for it was at the blacksmith's table, in the sun of his window that he was sitting, looking out at the water. Eugene had bought a lunch box and was carrying with him daily a delectable lunch put up under Mrs. Hibberdell's direction. He had eaten his noonday meal and was idling, thinking over the beauty of the scene, his peculiar position, the curiosities of this shop—anything and everything that came into his head.

"Wait a minute," he said genially, for he and the smith were already as thick as thieves.

The latter gazed interestedly and finally exclaimed:

"W'y that's me, ain't it?"

"Yep!" said Eugene.

"Wat are you goin' to do with that wen you get through with it?" asked the latter avariciously.

"I'm going to give it to you, of course."

"Say, I'm much obliged fer that," replied the smith delightedly. "Gee, the wife'll be tickled to see that. You're a artist, ain't cher? I hearda them fellers. I never saw one. Gee, that's good, that looks just like me, don't it?"

"Something," said Eugene quietly, still working.

The helper came in.

"Watcha' doin'?" he asked.

"He's drawin' a pitcher, ya rube, watchye suppose he's doin'," informed the blacksmith authoritatively. "Don't git too close. He's gotta have room."

"Aw, whose crowdin'?" asked the helper irritably. He realized at once that his superior was trying to shove him in the background, this being a momentous occasion. He did not propose that any such thing should happen. The blacksmith glared at him irritably but the progress of the art work was too exciting to permit of any immediate opportunities for hostilities, so Jimmy was allowed to crowd close and see.

"Ho, ho! that's you, ain't it," he asked the smith curiously, indicating with a grimy thumb the exact position of that dignitary on the drawing.

"Don't," said the latter, loftily—"sure! He's gotta have room."

"An' there's me. Ho! Ho! Gee, I look swell, don't I? Ho! ho!"

The little helper's tushes were showing joyously—a smile that extended far about either side of his face. He was entirely unconscious of the rebuke administered by the smith.

"If you're perfectly good, Jimmy," observed Eugene cheerfully still working, "I may make a sketch of you, sometime!"

"Na! Will you? Go on! Say, hully chee. Dat'll be fine, won't it? Say, ho! ho! De folks at home won't know me. I'd like to have a ting like dat, say!"

Eugene smiled. The smith was regretful. This dividing of honors was not quite all that it might be. Still his own picture was delightful. It looked exactly like the shop. Eugene worked until the whistle blew and the belts began to slap and the wheels to whirr. Then he got up.

"There you are, Fornes," he said. "Like it?"

"Gee, it's swell," said the latter and carried it to the locker. He took it out after a bit though and hung it up over his bench on the wall opposite his forge, for he wanted everyone to see. It was one of the most significant events in his life. This sketch was the subject immediately of a perfect storm of discussion. Eugene was an artist—could draw pictures—that was a revelation in itself. Then this picture was so life-like. It looked like Fornes and Sudds and the shop. Everyone was interested. Everyone jealous. They could not understand how God had favored the smith in this manner. Why hadn't Eugene sketched them before he did him? Why didn't he immediately offer to sketch them now? Big John came first, tipped off and piloted by Jimmy Sudds.

"Say!" he said his big round eyes popping with surprise. "There's some class to that, what? That looks like you, Fornes. Jinged if it don't! An'

Suddsy! Bless me if there ain't Suddsy. Say, there you are, kid, natural as life, damned if you ain't. That's fine. You oughta keep that, smith."

"I intend to," said the latter proudly.

Big John went back to his engine room regretfully. Next came Joseph Mews, his shoulders humped, his head bobbing like a duck, for he had this habit of nodding when he walked.

"Say, wot d'ye thinka that?" he asked. "Ain't that fine. He kin drawr jist as good as they do in them there magazines. I see them there things in them, now an' then. Ain't that swell? Lookit Suddsy back in there. Eh, Suddsy, you're in right, all right. I wisht he'd make a picture o' us out there. We're just as good as you people. Wats the matter with us, eh?"

"Oh, he ain't goin' to be bothered makin' pitchers of you mokes," replied the smith jestingly. "He only draws real ones. You want to remember that, Mews. He's gotta have good people to make sketches of. None o' your half-class plane-drivers and jig-saw operators."

"Is that so? Is that so?" replied Joseph contemptuously, his love of humor spurred by the slight cast upon his ability. "Well if he was lookin' for real ones he made a mistake wen he come here. They're all up front. You don't want to forget that, smith. They don't live in no blacksmith's shop as I ever seen it."

"Cut it out! Cut it out!" called little Sudds from a position of vantage near the door. "Here comes the boss," and Joseph immediately pretended to be going to the engine room for a drink. The smith blew up his fire as though it were necessary to heat the iron he had laid in the coals. Jack Stix came ambling by.

"Who did that?" he asked, stopping after a single general, glance and looking at the sketch on the wall.

"Mr. Witla, the new man," replied the smith, reverently.

"Say, that's pretty good, ain't it?" the foreman replied pleasantly. "He did that well. He must be an artist."

"I think he is," replied the smith, cautiously. He was always eager to curry favor with the boss. He came near to his side and looked over his arm. "He done it here today at noon in about a half an hour."

"Say, that's pretty good now," and the foreman went on his way, thinking.

If Eugene could do that, why was he here? It must be his run down condition, sure enough. And he must be the friend of someone high in authority. He had better be civil. Hitherto he had stood in suspicious awe of Eugene, not knowing what to make of him. He could not figure out just why he was here—a spy possibly. Now he thought that he might be mistaken.

"Don't let him work too hard," he told Bill and John. "He ain't any too strong yet. He came up here for his health."

He was obeyed in this respect, for there was no gain-saying the wishes of a foreman, but this open plea for consideration was the one thing if any which could have weakened Eugene's popularity. The men did not like the foreman. He would have been stronger at any time in the affections of the men if the foreman had been less markedly considerate or against him entirely.

The days which followed were restful enough though hard, for Eugene found that the constant whirl of work which went on here, and of which he had naturally to do his share, was beneficial to him. For the first time in several years he slept soundly. He would don his suit of blue overalls and jumper in the morning a few minutes before the whistle blew at seven and from then on until noon, and from one o'clock until six he would carry shavings, pile lumber for one or several of the men in the yard, load or unload cars, help Big John stoke his boilers, or carry chips and shavings from the second floor. He wore an old hat which he had found in a closet at Mrs. Hibberdell's, a faded, crumpled memory of a soft tan-colored sombrero which he punched jauntily to a peak and wore over one ear. He had big new yellow gloves which he kept on his hands all day, which were creased and frayed, but plenty good enough for this shop and yard. He learned to handle lumber nicely, to pile with skill, to "take" for Malachi Dempsey from the plane, to drive the jig-saw, and other curious bits. He was tireless in his energy because he was weary of thinking and hoped by sheer activity to beat down and overcome his notion of artistic inability—to forget that he believed that he couldn't paint and so be able to paint again. He had surprised himself in these sketches he had made, for his first feeling under the old régime would have been that he could not make them. Here, because the men were so eager and he was so much applauded, he found it rather easy and, strange to say, he thought they were good.

At the home of Mrs. Hibberdell at night he would lay off all his working clothes before dinner, take a cold bath and don a new brown suit, which because of the assurance of this position he had bought for eighteen dollars, ready made. He found it hard to get off to buy anything, for his pay ceased (fifteen cents an hour) the moment he left the shop. He had put his pictures in storage in New York and could not get off (or at least did not want to take the time off) to go and sell any. He found that he could leave without question if he wanted no pay, but if he wanted pay and had a good reason he could sometimes be excused. His appearance about the house and yard after six-thirty in the evening and on Sundays was attractive enough. He looked delicate, refined, conservative, and, when not talking to someone, rather wistful. He was lonely and restless, for he felt terribly out of it. This house was lonely. As at Alexandria, before he met Frieda, he was wishing there were some girls about. He wondered where Frieda was, what she was doing, whether she had married. He hoped not. If life had only given him a girl like Frieda—so young, so beautiful! He would sit and gaze at the water after dark in the moonlight, for this was his one consolation—the beauty of nature—thinking. How lovely it all was! How lovely life was,—this village, the summer trees, the shop where he worked, the water, Joseph, little Jimmy, Big John, the stars. If he could paint again, if he could be in love again. In love! In love! Was there any other sensation in the world like that of being in love?

A spring evening, say, some soft sweet odours blowing as they were tonight, the dark trees bending down, or the twilight angelically silver, hyacinth, orange, some soothing murmurs of the wind; some faint chirping of the tree-toads or frogs and then your girl. Dear God! Could anything be finer than that? Was anything else in life worth while? Your girl, her soft young arms about your neck, her lips to yours in pure love, her eyes speaking like twin pools of color here in the night.

So had it been only a little while ago with Frieda. So had it been once with Angela. So long ago with Stella! Dear, sweet Stella, how nice she was. And now here he was sick and lonely and married and Angela would be coming back soon—and—He would get up frequently to shut out these thoughts, and either read or walk or go to bed. But he was lonely, almost irritably so. There was only one true place of comfort for Eugene anywhere and that was in the spring time in love.

CHAPTER XXII

It was while he was mooning along in this mood, working, dreaming, wishing, that there came, one day to her mother's house at Riverwood, Carlotta Wilson—Mrs. Norman Wilson, in the world in which she moved—a tall brunette of thirty-two, handsome after the English fashion, shapely, graceful, with a knowledge of the world which was not only compounded of natural intelligence and a sense of humor, but experiences fortunate and unfortunate which had shown her both the showy and the seamy sides of life. To begin with she was the wife of a gambler—a professional gambler—of that peculiar order which essays the rôle of a gentleman, looks the part, and fleeces unmercifully the unwary partakers of their companionship. Carlotta Hibberdell, living with her mother at that time in Springfield, Massachusetts, had met him at a local series of races, which she was attending with her father and mother, where Wilson happened to be accidentally upon another mission. Her father, a real estate dealer, and fairly successful at one time, was very much interested in racing horses, and owned several of worthy records though of no great fame. Norman Wilson had posed as a real estate speculator himself, and had handled several fairly successful deals in land, but his principal skill and reliance was in gambling. He was familiar with all the gambling opportunities of the city, knew a large circle of those who liked to gamble, men and women in New York and elsewhere, and his luck or skill at times was phenomenal. At other times it was very bad. There were periods when he could afford to live in the most expensive apartment houses, dine at the best restaurants, visit the most expensive country pleasure resorts and otherwise disport himself in the companionship of friends. At other times, because of bad luck, he could not afford any of these things and though he held to his estate grimly had to borrow money to do it. He was somewhat of a fatalist in his interpretation of affairs and would hang on with the faith that his luck would turn. It did turn invariably, of course, for when difficulties began to swarm thick and fast he would think vigorously and would usually evolve some idea which served to help him out. His plan was always to spin a web like a spider and await the blundering flight of some unwary fly.

At the time she married him Carlotta Hibberdell did not know of the peculiar tendencies and subtle obsession of her ardent lover. Like all men of his type he was suave, persuasive, passionate, eager. There was a certain cat-like magnetism about him also which fascinated her. She could not understand him at that time and she never did afterwards. The license which he subsequently manifested not only with her but with others astonished and disgusted her. She found him selfish, domineering, outside his own particular field shallow, not at all artistic, emotional, or poetic. He was inclined to insist on the last touch of material refinement in surroundings (so far as he understood them) when he had money, but she found to her regret that he did not understand them. In his manner with her and everyone else he was top-lofty, superior, condescending. His stilted language at times enraged and at other times amused her, and when her original passion passed and she began to see through his pretence to his motives and actions she became indifferent and then weary. She was too big a woman mentally to quarrel with him much. She was too indifferent to life in its totality to really care. Her one passion was for an ideal lover of some type, and having been thoroughly mistaken in him she looked abroad wondering whether there were any ideal men.

Various individuals came to their apartments. There were gamblers, blasé society men, mining experts, speculators, sometimes with, sometimes without a wife. From these and from her husband and her own observation she learned of all sorts of scoundrels, mes-alliances, [sic] queer manifestations of incompatibility of temper, queer freaks of sex desire. Because she was good looking, graceful, easy in her manners, there were no end of proposals, overtures, hints and luring innuendos cast in her direction. She had long been accustomed to them. Because her husband deserted her openly for other women and confessed it in a blasé way she saw no valid reason for keeping herself from other men. She chose her lovers guardedly and with subtle taste, beginning after mature deliberation with one who pleased her greatly. She was seeking refinement, emotion, understanding coupled with some ability and they were not so easy to find. The long record of her liaisons is not for this story, but their impress on her character was important.

She was indifferent in her manner at most times and to most people. A good jest or story drew from her a hearty laugh. She was not interested in books except those of a very exceptional character—the realistic school—and these she thought ought not to be permitted except to private subscribers, nevertheless she cared for no others. Art was fascinating—really great art. She loved the pictures of Rembrandt, Frans Hals, Correggio, Titian. And with less discrimination, and more from a sensual point of view the nudes of Cabanel, Bouguereau and Gerome. To her there was reality in the works of these men, lightened by great imagination. Mostly people interested her, the vagaries of their minds, the idiosyncrasies of their characters, their lies, their subterfuges, their pretences, their fears. She knew that she was a dangerous woman and went softly, like a cat, wearing a half-smile not unlike that seen on the lips of Monna Lisa, but she did not worry about herself. She had too much courage. At the same time she was tolerant, generous to a fault, charitable. When someone suggested that she overdid the tolerance, she replied, "Why shouldn't I? I live in such a magnificent glass house."

The reason for her visit home on this occasion was that her husband had practically deserted her for the time being. He was in Chicago for some reason principally because the atmosphere in New York was getting too hot for him, as she suspected. Because she hated Chicago and was weary of his company she refused to go with him. He was furious for he suspected her of liaisons, but he could not help himself. She was indifferent. Besides she had other resources than those he represented, or could get them.

A certain wealthy Jew had been importuning her for years to get a divorce in order that he might marry her. His car and his resources were at her command but she condescended only the vaguest courtesies. It was within the ordinary possibilities of the day for him to call her up and ask if he could not come with his car. He had three. She waved most of this aside indifferently. "What's the use?" was her pet inquiry. Her husband was not without his car at times. She had means to drive when she pleased, dress as she liked, and was invited to many interesting outings. Her mother knew well of her peculiar attitude, her marital troubles, her quarrels and her tendency to flirt. She did her best to keep her in check, for she wanted to retain for her the privilege of obtaining a divorce and marrying again, the next time successfully. Norman Wilson, however, would not readily give her a legal separation even though the preponderance of evidence was against him and, if she compromised herself, there would be no hope. She half suspected that her daughter might already have compromised herself, but she could not be sure. Carlotta was too subtle. Norman made open charges in their family quarrels, but they were based largely on jealousy. He did not know for sure.

Carlotta Wilson had heard of Eugene. She did not know of him by reputation, but her mother's guarded remarks in regard to him and his presence, the fact that he was an artist, that he was sick and working as a laborer for his health aroused her interest. She had intended to spend the period of her husband's absence at Narragansett with some friends, but before doing so she decided to come home for a few days just to see for herself. Instinctively her mother suspected curiosity on her part in regard to Eugene. She threw out the remark that he might not stay long, in the hope that her daughter might lose interest. His wife was coming back. Carlotta discerned this opposition—this desire to keep her away. She decided that she would come.

"I don't know that I want to go to Narragansett just now," she told her mother. "I'm tired. Norman has just worn my nerves to a frazzle. I think I'll come up home for a week or so."

"All right," said her mother, "but do be careful how you act now. This Mr. Witla appears to be a very nice man and he's happily married. Don't you go casting any looks in his direction. If you do I won't let him stay here at all."

"Oh, how you talk," replied Carlotta irritably. "Do give me a little credit for something. I'm not going up there to see him. I'm tired, I tell you. If you don't want me to come I won't."

"It isn't that, I do want you. But you know how you are. How do you ever expect to get free if you don't conduct yourself circumspectly? You know that you—"

"Oh, for heaven's sake, I hope you're not going to start that old argument again," exclaimed Carlotta defensively. "What's the use beginning on that? We've been all over it a thousand times. I can't go anywhere or do anything but what you want to fuss. Now I'm not coming up there to do anything but rest. Why will you always start in to spoil everything?"

"Well now, you know well enough, Carlotta—" reiterated her mother.

"Oh, chuck it. I'll not come. To hell with the house. I'll go to Narragansett. You make me tired!"

Her mother looked at her tall daughter, graceful, handsome, her black hair parted in rich folds, irritated and yet pleased with her force and ability. If she would only be prudent and careful, what a figure she might yet become! Her complexion was like old rose-tinted ivory, her lips the color of dark raspberries, her eyes bluish grey, wide set, large, sympathetic, kindly. What a pity she had not married some big, worthy man to begin with. To be tied up to this gambler, even though they did live in Central Park West and had a comparatively sumptuous apartment, was a wretched thing. Still it was better than poverty or scandal, though if she did not take care of herself both might ensue. She wanted her to come to Riverwood for she liked her company, but she wanted her to behave herself. Perhaps Eugene would save the day. He was certainly restrained enough in his manner and remarks. She went back to Riverwood, and Carlotta, the quarrel smoothed over, followed her.

Eugene did not see her during the day she arrived, for he was at work; and she did not see him as he came in at night. He had on his old peaked hat and carried his handsome leather lunch box jauntily in one hand. He went to his room, bathed, dressed and then out on the porch to await the call of the dinner gong. Mrs. Hibberdell was in her room on the second floor and "Cousin Dave," as Carlotta called Simpson, was in the back yard. It was a lovely twilight. He was in the midst of deep thoughts about the beauty of the scene, his own loneliness, the characters at the shop-work, Angela and what not, when the screen door opened and she stepped out. She had on a short-sleeved house dress of spotted blue silk with yellow lace set about the neck and the ends of the sleeves. Her shapely figure, beautifully proportioned to her height, was set in a smooth, close fitting corset. Her hair, laid in great braids at the back, was caught in a brown spangled net. She carried herself with thoughtfulness and simplicity, seeming naturally indifferent.

Eugene rose. "I'm in your way, I think. Won't you have this chair?"

"No, thanks. The one in the corner will do. But I might as well introduce myself, since there isn't anyone here to do it. I'm Mrs. Wilson, Mrs. Hibberdell's daughter. You're Mr. Witla?"

"Yes, I answer to that," said Eugene, smiling. He was not very much impressed at first. She seemed nice and he fancied intelligent—a little older than he would have preferred any woman to be who was to interest him. She sat down and looked at the water. He took his chair and held his peace. He was not even interested to talk to her. She was nice to look at, however. Her presence lightened the scene for him.

"I always like to come up here," she volunteered finally. "It's so warm in the city these days. I don't think many people know of this place. It's out of the beaten track."

"I enjoy it," said Eugene. "It's such a rest for me. I don't know what I would have done if your mother hadn't taken me in. It's rather hard to find any place, doing what I am."

"You've taken a pretty strenuous way to get health, I should say," she observed. "Day labor sounds rough to me. Do you mind it?"

"Not at all. I like it. The work is interesting and not so very hard. It's all so new to me, that's what makes it easy. I like the idea of being a day laborer and associating with laborers. It's only because I'm run down in health that I worry. I don't like to be sick."

"It is bad," she replied, "but this will probably put you on your feet. I think we're always inclined to look on our present troubles as the worst. I know I am."

"Thanks for the consolation," he said.

She did not look at him and he rocked to and fro silently. Finally the dinner gong struck. Mrs. Hibberdell came down stairs and they went in.

The conversation at dinner turned on his work for a few moments and he described accurately the personalities of John and Bill and Big John the engineer, and little Suddsy and Harry Fornes, the blacksmith. Carlotta listened attentively without appearing to, for everything about Eugene seemed singular and exceptional to her. She liked his tall, spare body, his lean hands, his dark hair and eyes. She liked the idea of his dressing as a laboring man in the morning, working all day in the shop, and yet appearing so neat and trim at dinner. He was easy in his manner, apparently lethargic in his movements and yet she could feel a certain swift force that filled the room. It was richer for his presence. She understood at a glance that he was an artist, in all probability a good one. He said nothing of that, avoided carefully all reference to his art, and listened attentively. She felt though as if he were studying her and everyone else, and it made her gayer. At the same time she had a strong leaning toward him. "What an ideal man to be associated with," was one of her repeated thoughts.

Although she was about the house for ten days and he met her after the third morning not only at dinner, which was natural enough, but at breakfast (which surprised him a little), he paid not so very much attention to her. She was nice, very, but Eugene was thinking of another type. He thought she was uncommonly pleasant and considerate and he admired her style of dressing and her beauty, studying her with interest, wondering what sort of a life she led, for from various bits of conversation he overheard not only at table but at other times he judged she was fairly well to do. There was an apartment in Central Park West, card parties, automobile parties, theatre parties and a general sense of people—acquaintances anyhow, who were making money. He heard her tell of a mining engineer, Dr. Rowland; of a successful coal-mining speculator, Gerald Woods; of a Mrs. Hale who was heavily interested in copper mines and apparently very wealthy. "It's a pity Norman couldn't connect with something like that and make some real money," he heard her say to her mother one evening. He understood that Norman was her husband and that he probably would be back soon. So he kept his distance—interested and curious but hardly more.

Mrs. Wilson was not so easily baffled, however. A car appeared one evening at the door immediately after dinner, a great red touring car, and Mrs. Wilson announced easily, "We're going for a little spin after dinner, Mr. Witla. Don't you want to come along?"

Eugene had never ridden in an automobile at that time. "I'd be very pleased," he said, for the thought of a lonely evening in an empty house had sprung up when he saw it appear.

There was a chauffeur in charge—a gallant figure in a brown straw cap and tan duster, but Mrs. Wilson manœuvred for place.

"You sit with the driver, coz," she said to Simpson, and when her mother stepped in she followed after, leaving Eugene the place to the right of her.

"There must be a coat and cap in the locker," she said to the chauffeur; "let Mr. Witla have it."

The latter extracted a spare linen coat and straw cap which Eugene put on.

"I like automobiling, don't you?" she said to Eugene good-naturedly. "It's so refreshing. If there is any rest from care on this earth it's in traveling fast."

"I've never ridden before," replied Eugene simply. Something about the way he said it touched her. She felt sorry for him because he appeared lonely and gloomy. His indifference to her piqued her curiosity and irritated her pride. Why shouldn't he take an interest in her? As they sped under leafy lanes, up hill and down dale, she made out his face in the starlight. It was pale, reflective, indifferent. "These deep thinkers!" she chided him. "It's terrible to be a philosopher." Eugene smiled.

When they reached home he went to his room as did all the others to theirs. He stepped out into the hall a few minutes later to go to the library for a book, and found that her door which he had to pass was wide open. She was sitting back in a Morris chair, her feet upon another chair, her skirts slightly drawn up revealing a trim foot and ankle. She did not stir but looked up and smiled winningly.

"Aren't you tired enough to sleep?" he asked.

"Not quite yet," she smiled.

He went down stairs and turning on a light in the library stood looking at a row of books reading the titles. He heard a step and there she was looking at the books also.

"Don't you want a bottle of beer?" she asked. "I think there is some in the ice box. I forgot that you might be thirsty."

"I really don't care," he said. "I'm not much for drinks of any kind."

"That's not very sociable," she laughed.

"Let's have the beer then," he said.

She threw herself back languidly in one of the big dining room chairs when she had brought the drinks and some Swiss cheese and crackers, and said: "I think you'll find some cigarettes on the table in the corner if you like."

He struck her a match and she puffed her cigarette comfortably. "I suppose you find it lonely up here away from all your friends and companions," she volunteered.

"Oh, I've been sick so long I scarcely know whether I have any."

He described some of his imaginary ailments and experiences and she listened to him attentively. When the beer was gone she asked him if he would have more but he said no. After a time because he stirred wearily, she got up.

"Your mother will think we're running some sort of a midnight game down here," he volunteered.

"Mother can't hear," she said. "Her room is on the third floor and besides she doesn't hear very well. Dave don't mind. He knows me well enough by now to know that I do as I please."

She stood closer to Eugene but still he did not see. When he moved away she put out the lights and followed him to the stairs.

"He's either the most bashful or the most indifferent of men," she thought, but she said softly, "Good-night. Pleasant dreams to you," and went her way.

Eugene thought of her now as a good fellow, a little gay for a married woman, but probably circumspect withal. She was simply being nice to him. All this was simply because, as yet, he was not very much interested.

There were other incidents. One morning he passed her door. Her mother had already gone down to breakfast and there was the spectacle of a smooth, shapely arm and shoulder quite bare to his gaze as she lay on her pillow apparently unconscious that her door was open. It thrilled him as something sensuously beautiful for it was a perfect arm. Another time he saw her of an evening just before dinner buttoning her shoes. Her dress was pulled three-quarters of the way to her knees and her shoulders and arms were bare, for she was still in her corset and short skirts. She seemed not to know that he was near. One night after dinner he started to whistle something and she went to the piano to keep him company. Another time he hummed on the porch and she started the same song, singing with him. He drew his chair near the window where there was a couch after her mother had retired for the night, and she came and threw herself on it. "You don't mind if I lie here?" she said, "I'm tired tonight."

"Not at all. I'm glad of your company. I'm lonely."

She lay and stared at him, smiling. He hummed and she sang. "Let me see your palm," she said, "I want to learn something." He held it out. She fingered it temptingly. Even this did not wake him.

She left for five days because of some necessity in connection with her engagements and when she returned he was glad to see her. He had been lonesome, and he knew now that she made the house gayer. He greeted her genially.

"I'm glad to see you back," he said.

"Are you really?" she replied. "I don't believe it."

"Why not?" he asked.

"Oh, signs, omens and portents. You don't like women very well I fancy."

"Don't I!"

"No, I think not," she replied.

She was charming in a soft grayish green satin. He noticed that her neck was beautiful and that her hair looped itself gracefully upon the back of it. Her nose was straight and fine, sensitive because of its thin partitioning walls. He followed her into the library and they went out on the porch. Presently he returned—it was ten o'clock—and she came also. Davis had gone to his room, Mrs. Hibberdell to hers.

"I think I'll read," he said, aimlessly.

"Why anything like that?" she jested. "Never read when you can do anything else."

"What else can I do?"

"Oh, lots of things. Play cards, tell fortunes, read palms, drink beer—" She looked at him wilfully.

He went to his favorite chair near the window, side by side with the window-seat couch. She came and threw herself on it.

"Be gallant and fix my pillows for me, will you?" she asked.

"Of course I will," he said.

He took a pillow and raised her head, for she did not deign to move.

"Is that enough?" he inquired.

"One more."

He put his hand under the first pillow and lifted it up. She took hold of his free hand to raise herself. When she had it she held it and laughed a curious excited laugh. It came over him all at once, the full meaning of all the things she had been doing. He dropped the pillow he was holding and looked at her steadfastly. She relaxed her hold and leaned back, languorous, smiling. He took her left hand, then her right and sat down beside her. In a moment he slipped one arm under her waist and bending over put his lips to hers. She twined her arms about his neck tightly and hugged him close; then looking in his eyes she heaved a great sigh.

"You love me, don't you?" he asked.

"I thought you never would," she sighed, and clasped him to her again.

CHAPTER XXIII

The form of Carlotta Wilson was perfect, her passion eager, her subtlety a match for almost any situation. She had deliberately set out to win Eugene because he was attractive to her and because, by his early indifference, he had piqued her vanity and self-love. She liked him though, liked every one of his characteristics, and was as proud of her triumph as a child with a new toy. When he had finally slipped his arm under her waist she had thrilled with a burning, vibrating thrill throughout her frame and when she came to him it was with the eagerness of one wild for his caresses. She threw herself on him, kissed him sensuously scores of times, whispered her desire and her affection. Eugene thought, now that he saw her through the medium of an awakened passion, that he had never seen anything more lovely. For the time being he forgot Frieda, Angela, his loneliness, the fact that he was working in supposed prudent self-restraint to effect his recovery, and gave himself up to the full enjoyment of this situation.

Carlotta was tireless in her attentions. Once she saw that he really cared, or imagined he did, she dwelt in the atmosphere of her passion and affection. There was not a moment that she was not with or thinking of Eugene when either was possible. She lay in wait for him at every turn, gave him every opportunity which her skill could command. She knew the movements of her mother and cousin to the least fraction—could tell exactly where they were, how long they were likely to remain, how long it would take them to reach a certain door or spot from where they were standing. Her step was noiseless, her motions and glances significant and interpretative. For a month or thereabouts she guided Eugene through the most perilous situations, keeping her arms about him to the last possible moment, kissing him silently and swiftly at the most unexpected times and in the most unexpected surroundings. Her weary languor, her seeming indifference, disappeared, and she was very much alive—except in the presence of others. There her old manner remained, intensified even, for she was determined to throw a veil of darkness over her mother and her cousin's eyes. She succeeded admirably for the time being, for she lied to her mother out of the whole cloth, pretending that Eugene was nice but a little slow so far as the ways of the world were concerned. "He may be a good artist," she volunteered, "but he isn't very much of a ladies' man. He hasn't the first trace of gallantry."

Mrs. Hibberdell was glad. At least there would be no disturbance here. She feared Carlotta, feared Eugene, but she saw no reason for complaint. In her presence all was seemingly formal and at times almost distant. She did not like to say to her daughter that she should not come to her own home now that Eugene was here, and she did not like to tell him to leave. Carlotta said she liked him fairly well, but that was nothing. Any married woman might do that. Yet under her very eyes was going forward the most disconcerting license. She would have been astounded if she had known the manner in which the bath, Carlotta's chamber and Eugene's room were being used. The hour never struck when they were beyond surveillance but what they were together.

Eugene grew very indifferent in the matter of his work. From getting to the point where he was enjoying it because he looked upon it as a form of exercise which was benefiting him, and feeling that he might not have to work indefinitely if he kept up physical rehabilitation at this pace, he grew languid about it and moody over the time he had to give to it. Carlotta had the privilege of a certain automobile and besides she could afford to hire one of her own. She began by suggesting that he meet her at certain places and times for a little spin and this took him away from his work a good portion of the time.

"You don't have to work every day, do you?" she asked him one Sunday afternoon when they were alone. Simpson and Mrs. Hibberdell had gone out for a walk and they were in her room on the second floor. Her mother's was on the third.

"I don't have to," he said, "if I don't mind losing the money they pay. It's fifteen cents an hour and I need that. I'm not working at my regular profession, you must remember."

"Oh, chuck that," she said. "What's fifteen cents an hour? I'll give you ten times that to come and be with me."

"No, you won't," he said. "You won't give me anything. We won't go anywhere on that basis."

"Oh, Eugene, how you talk. Why won't you?" she asked. "I have lots of it—at least lots more than you have just now. And it might as well be spent this way as some other. It won't be spent right anyhow—that is not for any exceptional purpose. Why shouldn't you have some of it? You can pay it back to me."

"I won't do it," said Eugene. "We won't go anywhere on that basis. I'd rather go and work. It's all right, though. I can sell a picture maybe. I expect to hear any day of something being sold. What is it you want to do?"

"I want you to come automobiling with me tomorrow. Ma is going over to her sister Ella's in Brooklyn. Has that shop of yours a phone?"

"Sure it has. I don't think you'd better call me up there though."

"Once wouldn't hurt."

"Well, perhaps not. But we'd better not begin that, or at least not make a practice of it. These people are very strict. They have to be."

"I know," said Carlotta. "I won't. I was just thinking. I'll let you know. You know that river road that runs on the top of the hill over there?"

"Yes."

"You be walking along there tomorrow at one o'clock and I'll pick you up. You can come this once, can't you?"

"Sure," said Eugene. "I can come. I was just joking. I can get some money." He had still his hundred dollars which he had not used when he first started looking for work. He had been clinging to it grimly, but now in this lightened atmosphere he thought he might spend some of it. He was going to get well. Everything was pointing that way. His luck was with him.

"Well, I'll get the car. You don't mind riding in that, do you?"

"No," he said. "I'll wear a good suit to the shop and change over there."

She laughed gaily, for his scruples and simplicity amused her.

"You're a prince—my Prince Charming," she said and she flung herself in his lap. "Oh, you angel man, heaven-born! I've been waiting for you I don't know how long. Wise man! Prince Charming! I love you! I love you! I think you're the nicest thing that ever was."

Eugene caressed her gently.

"And you're my wise girl. But we are no good, neither you nor I. You're a wastrel and a stray. And I—I hesitate to think what I am."

"What is a wastrel?" she asked. "That's a new one on me. I don't remember."

"Something or someone that can be thrown away as useless. A stray is a pigeon that won't stay with the flock."

"That's me," said Carlotta, holding out her firm, smooth arms before her and grinning mischievously. "I won't stay with any flock. Nix for the flocks. I'd rather be off with my wise man. He is nice enough for me. He's better nor nine or ten flocks." She was using corrupt English for the joy of it. "Just me and you, Prince Charming. Am I your lovely wastrel? Do you like strays? Say you do. Listen! Do you like strays?"

Eugene had been turning his head away, saying "scandalous! terrible, you're the worst ever," but she stopped his mouth with her lips.

"Do you?"

"This wastrel, yes. This stray," he replied, smoothing her cheek. "Ah, you're lovely, Carlotta, you're beautiful. What a wonderful woman you are."

She gave herself to him completely.

"Whatever I am, I'm yours, wise man," she went on. "You can have anything you want of me, do anything you please with me. You're like an opiate to me, Eugene, sweet! You stop my mouth and close my eyes and seal my ears. You make me forget everything I suppose I might think now and then but I don't want to. I don't want to! And I don't care. I wish you were single. I wish I were free. I wish we had an island somewhere together. Oh, hell! Life is a wearisome tangle, isn't it? 'Take the cash and let the credit go.'"

By this time Carlotta had heard enough of Eugene's life to understand what his present condition was. She knew he was sick though not exactly why. She thought it was due to overwork. She knew he was out of funds except for certain pictures he had on sale, but that he would regain his art ability and re-establish himself she did not doubt. She knew something of Angela and thought it was all right that she should be away from him, but now she wished the separation might be permanent. She went into the city and asking about at various art stores learned something of Eugene's art history and his great promise. It made him all the more fascinating in her eyes. One of his pictures on exhibition at Pottle Frères was bought by her after a little while and the money sent to Eugene, for she had learned from him how these pictures, any pictures, were exhibited on sale and the painter paid, minus the commission, when the sale was made. She took good care to make it clear to the manager at Pottle Frères that she was doing this so that Eugene could have the money and saw to it that the check reached him promptly. If Eugene had been alone this check of three hundred dollars would have served to bring Angela to him. As it was it gave him funds to disport himself with in her company. He did not know that she had been the means of his getting it, or to whom the picture had been sold. A fictitious name was given. This sale somewhat restored Eugene's faith in his future, for if one of his pictures would sell so late in the day for this price, others would.

There were days thereafter of the most curious composition. In the morning he would leave dressed in his old working suit and carrying his lunch box, Carlotta waving him a farewell from her window, or, if he had an engagement outside with Carlotta, wearing a good suit, and trusting to his overalls and jumper to protect it, working all day with John and Bill, or Malachi Dempsey and Joseph—for there was rivalry between these two groups as to which should have his company—or leaving the shop early and riding with her a part of the time, coming home at night to be greeted by Carlotta as though she had not seen him at all. She watched for his coming as patiently as a wife and was as eager to see if there was anything she could do for him. In the shop Malachi and Joseph or John and Bill and sometimes some of the carpenters up stairs would complain of a rush of work in order that they might have his assistance or presence. Malachi and Joseph could always enter the complaint that they were in danger of being hampered by shavings, for the latter were constantly piling up in great heaps, beautiful shavings of ash and yellow pine and walnut which smelled like resin and frankincense and had the shape of girl's curls or dry breakfast food, or rich damp sawdust. Or John and Bill would complain that they were being overworked and needed someone in the car to receive. Even Big John, the engineer, tried to figure out some scheme by which he could utilize Eugene as a fireman, but that was impossible; there was no call for any such person. The foreman understood well enough what the point was but said nothing, placing Eugene with the particular group which seemed to need him most. Eugene was genial enough about the matter. Wherever he was was right. He liked to be in the cars or on a lumber pile or in the plane room. He also liked to stand and talk to Big John or Harry Fornes, his basket under his arm—"kidding," as he called it. His progress to and fro was marked by endless quips and jests and he was never weary.

When his work was done at night he would hurry home, following the right bank of the little stream until he reached a path which led up to the street whereon was the Hibberdell house. On his way he would sometimes stop and study the water, its peaceful current bearing an occasional stick or straw upon its bosom, and contrasting the seeming peace of its movement with his own troubled life. The subtlety of nature as expressed in water appealed to him. The difference between this idyllic stream bank and his shop and all who were of it, struck him forcefully. Malachi Dempsey had only the vaguest conception of the beauty of nature. Jack Stix was scarcely more artistic than the raw piles of lumber with which he dealt. Big John had no knowledge of the rich emotions of love or of beauty which troubled Eugene's brain. They lived on another plane, apparently.

And at the other end of the stream awaiting him was Carlotta, graceful, sophisticated, eager in her regard for him, lukewarm in her interest in morals, sybaritic in her moods, representing in a way a world which lived upon the fruits of this exploited toil and caring nothing about it. If he said anything to Carlotta about the condition of Joseph Mews, who carried bundles of wood home to his sister of an evening to help save the expense of fuel, she merely smiled. If he talked of the poverty of the masses she said, "Don't be doleful, Eugene." She wanted to talk of art and luxury and love, or think of them at least. Her love of the beauty of nature was keen. There were certain inns they could reach by automobile where they could sit and dine and drink a bottle of wine or a pitcher of claret cup, and here she would muse on what they would do if they were only free. Angela was frequently in Carlotta's thoughts, persistently in Eugene's, for he could not help feeling that he was doing her a rank injustice.

She had been so patient and affectionate all this long time past, had tended him as a mother, waited on him as a servant. Only recently he had been writing in most affectionate terms, wishing she were with him. Now all that was dead again. It was hard work to write. Everything he said seemed a lie and he did not want to say it. He hated to pretend. Still, if he did not write Angela would be in a state of mortal agony, he thought, and would shortly come to look him up. It was only by writing, protesting his affection, explaining why in his judgment it was unadvisable for her to come at present, that she could be made to stay where she was. And now that he was so infatuated with Carlotta this seemed very desirable. He did not delude himself that he would ever be able to marry her. He knew that he could not get a divorce, there being no grounds, and the injustice to Angela being such a bar to his conscience; and as for Carlotta, her future was very uncertain. Norman Wilson, for all that he disregarded her at times, did not want to give her up. He was writing, threatening to come back to New York if she did not come to him, though the fact that she was in her mother's home, where he considered her safe, was some consolation to him. Angela was begging Eugene to let her come. They would get along, she argued, on whatever he got and he would be better off with her than alone. She pictured him living in some uncomfortable boarding house where he was not half attended to and intensely lonely. Her return meant the leaving of this lovely home—for Mrs. Hibberdell had indicated that she would not like to keep him and his wife—and so the end of this perfect romance with Carlotta. An end to lovely country inns and summer balconies where they were dining together! An end to swift tours in her automobile, which she guided skilfully herself, avoiding the presence of a chauffeur. An end to lovely trysts under trees and by pretty streams where he kissed and fondled her and where she lingered joyously in his arms!

"If ma could only see us now," she would jest; or,

"Do you suppose Bill and John would recognize you here if they saw you?"

Once she said: "This is better than the engine room, isn't it?"

"You're a bad lot, Carlotta," he would declare, and then would come to her lips the enigmatic smile of Monna Lisa.

"You like bad lots, don't you? Strays make fine hunting."

In her own philosophy she was taking the cash and letting the credit go.

CHAPTER XXIV

Days like this could not go on forever. The seed of their destruction was in their beginning. Eugene was sad. He used to show his mood at times and if she asked him what was the matter, would say: "We can't keep this thing up much longer. It must come to an end soon."

"You're certainly a gloomy philosopher, Genie," she would say, reproachfully, for she had hopes that it could be made to last a long while under any circumstances. Eugene had the feeling that no pretence would escape Angela's psychology. She was too sensitive to his unspoken moods and feelings. She would come soon, willynilly, and then all this would be ended. As a matter of fact several things combined to bring about change and conclusion.

For one thing Mrs. Hibberdell had been more and more impressed with the fact that Carlotta was not merely content to stay but that once having come she was fairly determined to remain. She had her own apartment in the city, ostensibly closed for the summer, for she had protested that it was too hot to live in town when she first proposed going to Narragansett. After seeing Eugene she figured out a possible use for it, though that use was dangerous, for Norman Wilson might return at any time. Nevertheless, they had been there on occasions—this with the double effect of deceiving her mother and entertaining Eugene. If she could remain away from Riverwood a percentage of the time, she argued with Eugene, it would make her stay less suspicious and would not jeopardize their joy in companionship. So she did this. At the same time she could not stay away from Riverwood entirely, for Eugene was there necessarily morning and evening.

Nevertheless, toward the end of August Mrs. Hibberdell was growing suspicious. She had seen an automobile entering Central Park once when Carlotta had phoned her that she had a sick headache and could not come up. It looked to Mrs. Hibberdell, who had gone down town shopping on the strength of this ailment and who had phoned Carlotta that she was going to call at her apartment in the evening, as though Eugene and Carlotta were in it. Eugene had gone to work that morning, which made it seem doubtful, but it certainly looked very much like him. Still she did not feel sure it was he or Carlotta either. When she came to the latter's apartment Carlotta was there, feeling better, but stating that she had not been out. Mrs. Hibberdell concluded thoughtfully that she must have been mistaken.

Her own room was on the third floor, and several times after all had retired and she had come down to the kitchen or dining room or library for something, she had heard a peculiar noise as of someone walking lightly. She thought it was fancy on her part, for invariably when she reached the second floor all was dark and still. Nevertheless she wondered whether Eugene and Carlotta could be visiting. Twice, between breakfast and the time Eugene departed, she thought she heard Eugene and Carlotta whispering on the second floor, but there was no proof. Carlotta's readiness to rise for breakfast at six-thirty in order to be at the same table with Eugene was peculiar, and her giving up Narragansett for Riverwood was most significant. It remained for one real discovery to resolve all her suspicions into the substance of fact and convict Carlotta of being the most conscienceless of deceivers.

It came about in this fashion. One Sunday morning Davis and Mrs. Hibberdell had decided to go automobiling. Eugene and Carlotta were invited but had refused, for Carlotta on hearing the discussion several days before had warned Eugene and planned to have the day for herself and her lover. She cautioned him to pretend the need of making visits down town. As for herself she had said she would go, but on the day in question did not feel well enough. Davis and Mrs. Hibberdell departed, their destination being Long Island. It was an all day tour. After an hour their machine broke, however, and after sitting in it two hours waiting for repairs—long enough to spoil their plans—they came back by trolley. Eugene had not gone down town. He was not even dressed when the door opened on the ground floor and Mrs. Hibberdell came in.

"Oh, Carlotta," she called, standing at the foot of the stairs and expecting Carlotta to appear from her own room or a sort of lounging and sewing room which occupied the front of the house on the second floor and where she frequently stayed. Carlotta unfortunately was with Eugene and the door to this room was commanded from where Mrs. Hibberdell was standing. She did not dare to answer.

"Oh, Carlotta," called her mother again.

The latter's first thought was to go back in the kitchen and look there, but on second thoughts she ascended the steps and started for the sewing room. Carlotta thought she had entered. In an instant she had seized the opportunity to step into the bath which was next to Eugene's room but she was scarcely quick enough. Her mother had not gone into the room—only opened the door and looked in. She did not see Carlotta step out of Eugene's room, but she did see her entering the bath, in negligee, and she could scarcely have come from anywhere else. Her own door which was between Eugene's room and the sewing room was ten feet away. It did not seem possible that she could have come from there: she had not had time enough, and anyhow why had she not answered?

The first impulse of Mrs. Hibberdell was to call to her. Her second thought was to let the ruse seem successful. She was convinced that Eugene was in his room, and a few moments later a monitory cough on his part—coughed for a purpose—convinced her.

"Are you in the bath, Carlotta?" she called quietly, after looking into Carlotta's room.

"Yes," came the reply, easily enough now. "Did your machine break down?"

A few remarks were exchanged through the door and then Mrs. Hibberdell went to her room. She thought over the situation steadily for it greatly irritated her. It was not the same as the discovered irregularity of a trusted and virtuous daughter. Carlotta had not been led astray. She was a grown woman, married, experienced. In every way she knew as much about life as her mother—in some respects more. The difference between them was in ethical standards and the policy that aligns itself with common sense, decency, self preservation, as against its opposite. Carlotta had so much to look out for. Her future was in her own hands. Besides, Eugene's future, his wife's rights and interests, her mother's home, her mother's standards, were things which she ought to respect—ought to want to respect. To find her lying as she had been this long time, pretending indifference, pretending absence, and no doubt associating with Eugene all the while, was disgusting. She was very angry, not so much at Eugene, though her respect for him was greatly lowered, artist though he was, as at Carlotta. She ought to do better. She ought to be ashamed not to guard herself against a man like Eugene, instead of luring him on. It was Carlotta's fault, and she determined to reproach her bitterly and to break up this wretched alliance at once.

There was an intense and bitter quarrel the next morning, for Mrs. Hibberdell decided to hold her peace until Eugene and Davis should be out of the house. She wanted to have this out with Carlotta alone, and the clash came shortly after breakfast when both the others had left. Carlotta had already warned Eugene that something might happen on account of this, but under no circumstances was he to admit anything unless she told him to. The maid was in the kitchen out of ear shot, and Mrs. Hibberdell and Carlotta were in the library when the opening gun was fired. In a way Carlotta was prepared, for she fancied her mother might have seen other things—what or how much she could not guess. She was not without the dignity of a Circe, for she had been through scenes like this before. Her own husband had charged her with infidelity more than once, and she had been threatened with physical violence by him. Her face was pale but calm.

"Now, Carlotta," observed her mother vigorously, "I saw what was going on yesterday morning when I came home. You were in Mr. Witla's room with your clothes off. I saw you come out. Please don't deny it. I saw you come out. Aren't you ashamed of yourself? How can you treat me that way after your promise not to do anything out of the way here?"

"You didn't see me come out of his room and I wasn't in there," said Carlotta brazenly. Her face was pale, but she was giving a fair imitation of righteous surprise. "Why do you make any such statement as that?"

"Why, Carlotta Hibberdell, how dare you contradict me; how dare you lie! You came out of that room. You know you did. You know that you were in there. You know that I saw you. I should think you would be ashamed of yourself, slipping about this house like a street girl and your own mother in it. Aren't you ashamed of yourself? Have you no sense of decency left? Oh, Carlotta, I know you are bad, but why will you come here to be so? Why couldn't you let this man alone? He was doing well enough. It's a shame, the thing you have done. It's an outrage. Mrs. Witla ought to come here and whip you within an inch of your life."

"Oh, how you talk," said Carlotta, irritably. "You make me tired. You didn't see me. It's the old story—suspicion. You're always full of suspicion. You didn't see me and I wasn't in there. Why do you start a fuss for nothing!"

"A fuss! A fuss for nothing—the idea, you evil woman. A fuss for nothing. How can you talk that way! I can hardly believe my senses. I can hardly believe you would dare to brazenly face me in this way. I saw you and now you deny it."

Mrs. Hibberdell had not seen her, but she was convinced that what she said was true.

Carlotta brazened it out. "You didn't," she insisted.

Mrs. Hibberdell stared. The effrontery of it took her breath away.

"Carlotta," she exclaimed, "I honestly think you are the worst woman in the world. I can't think of you as my daughter—you are too brazen. You're the worst because you're calculating. You know what you're doing, and you are deliberate in your method of doing it. You're evil-minded. You know exactly what you want and you set out deliberately to get it. You have done it in this case. You started out to get this man and you have succeeded in doing it. You have no sense of shame, no pride, no honesty, no honor, no respect for me or anyone else. You do not love this man. You know you don't. If you did you would never degrade him and yourself and me as you have done. You've simply indulged in another vile relationship because you wanted to, and now when you're caught you brazen it out. You're evil, Carlotta. You're as low as a woman can be, even if you are my daughter."

"It isn't true," said Carlotta. "You're just talking to hear yourself talk."

"It is true and you know it," reproved her mother. "You talk about Norman. He never did a thing worse in his life than you have done. He may be a gambler and immoral and inconsiderate and selfish. What are you? Can you stand there and tell me you're any better? Pah! If you only had a sense of shame something could be done for you, but you haven't any. You're just vile, that's all."

"How you talk, ma," she observed, calmly; "how you carry on, and that on a mere suspicion. You didn't see me. I might have been in there but you didn't see me and I wasn't. You're making a storm just because you want to. I like Mr. Witla. I think he's very nice, but I'm not interested in him and I haven't done anything to harm him. You can turn him out if you want to. That's none of my affairs. You're simply raging about as usual without any facts to go upon."

Carlotta stared at her mother, thinking. She was not greatly disturbed. It was pretty bad, no doubt of that, but she was not thinking so much of that as of the folly of being found out. Her mother knew for certain, though she would not admit to her that she knew. Now all this fine summer romance would end—the pleasant convenience of it, anyhow. Eugene would be put to the trouble of moving. Her mother might say something disagreeable to him. Besides, she knew she was better than Norman because she did not associate with the same evil type of people. She was not coarse, she was not thick-witted, she was not cruel, she was not a user of vile language or an expresser of vile ideas, and Norman was at times. She might lie and she might be calculating, but not to anyone's disadvantage—she was simply passion driven—boldly so and only toward love or romance. "Am I evil?" she often asked herself. Her mother said she was evil. Well, she was in one way; but her mother was angry, that was all. She did not mean all she said. She would come round. Still Carlotta did not propose to admit the truth of her mother's charges or to go through this situation without some argument. There were charges which her mother was making which were untenable—points which were inexcusable.

"Carlotta Hibberdell, you're the most brazen creature I ever knew! You're a terrible liar. How can you stand there and look me in the eye and say that, when you know that I know? Why lie in addition to everything else? Oh! Carlotta, the shame of it. If you only had some sense of honor! How can you lie like that? How can you?"

"I'm not lying," declared Carlotta, "and I wish you would quit fussing. You didn't see me. You know you didn't. I came out of my room and you were in the front room. Why do you say you weren't. You didn't see me. Supposing I am a liar. I'm your daughter. I may be vile. I didn't make myself so. Certainly I'm not in this instance. Whatever I am I come by it honestly. My life hasn't been a bed of roses. Why do you start a silly fight? You haven't a thing to go on except suspicion and now you want to raise a row. I don't care what you think of me. I'm not guilty in this case and you can think what you please. You ought to be ashamed to charge me with something of which you are not sure."

She walked to the window and stared out. Her mother shook her head. Such effrontery was beyond her. It was like her daughter, though. She took after her father and herself. Both were self-willed and determined when aroused. At the same time she was sorry for her girl, for Carlotta was a capable woman in her way and very much dissatisfied with life.

"I should think you would be ashamed of yourself, Carlotta, whether you admit it to me or not," she went on. "The truth is the truth and it must hurt you a little. You were in that room. We won't argue that, though. You set out deliberately to do this and you have done it. Now what I have to say is this: You are going back to your apartment today, and Mr. Witla is going to leave here as quick as he can get a room somewhere else. You're not going to continue this wretched relationship any longer if I can help it. I'm going to write to his wife and to Norman too, if I can't do anything else to break this up. You're going to let this man alone. You have no right to come between him and Mrs. Witla. It's an outrage, and no one but a vile, conscienceless woman would do it. I'm not going to say anything to him now, but he's going to leave here and so are you. When it's all over you can come back if you want to. I'm ashamed for you. I'm ashamed for myself. If it hadn't been for my own feelings and those of Davis, I would have ordered you both out of the house yesterday and you know it. It's consideration for myself that's made me smooth it over as much as I have. He, the vile thing, after all the courtesy I have shown him. Still I don't blame him as much as I do you, for he would never have looked at you if you hadn't made him. My own daughter! My own house! Tch! Tch! Tch!"

There was more conversation—that fulgurous, coruscating reiteration of charges. Eugene was no good. Carlotta was vile. Mrs. Hibberdell wouldn't have believed it possible if she hadn't seen it with her own eyes. She was going to tell Norman if Carlotta didn't reform—over and over, one threat after another.

"Well," she said, finally, "you're going to get your things ready and go into the city this afternoon. I'm not going to have you here another day."

"No I'm not," said Carlotta boldly, pondering over all that had been said. It was a terrible ordeal, but she would not go today. "I'm going in the morning. I'm not going to pack that fast. It's too late. I'm not going to be ordered out of here like a servant."

Her mother groaned, but she gave in. Carlotta could not be made to do anything she did not want to do. She went to her room, and presently Mrs. Hibberdell heard her singing. She shook her head. Such a personality. No wonder Eugene succumbed to her blandishments. What man wouldn't?

CHAPTER XXV

The sequel of this scene was not to be waited for. At dinner time Mrs. Hibberdell announced in the presence of Carlotta and Davis that the house was going to be closed up for the present, and very quickly. She and Carlotta were going to Narragansett for the month of September and a part of October. Eugene, having been forewarned by Carlotta, took it with a show of polite surprise. He was sorry. He had spent such a pleasant time here. Mrs. Hibberdell could not be sure whether Carlotta had told him or not, he seemed so innocent, but she assumed that she had and that he like Carlotta was "putting on." She had informed Davis that for reasons of her own she wanted to do this. He suspected what they were, for he had seen signs and slight demonstrations which convinced him that Carlotta and Eugene had reached an understanding. He did not consider it anything very much amiss, for Carlotta was a woman of the world, her own boss and a "good fellow." She had always been nice to him. He did not want to put any obstacles in her way. In addition, he liked Eugene. Once he had said to Carlotta jestingly, "Well, his arms are almost as long as Norman's—not quite maybe."

"You go to the devil," was her polite reply.

Tonight a storm came up, a brilliant, flashing summer storm. Eugene went out on the porch to watch it. Carlotta came also.

"Well, wise man," she said, as the thunder rolled. "It's all over up here. Don't let on. I'll see you wherever you go, but this was so nice. It was fine to have you near me. Don't get blue, will you? She says she may write your wife, but I don't think she will. If she thinks I'm behaving, she won't. I'll try and fool her. It's too bad, though. I'm crazy about you, Genie."

Now that he was in danger of losing Carlotta, her beauty took on a special significance for Eugene. He had come into such close contact with her, had seen her under such varied conditions, that he had come to feel a profound admiration for not only her beauty but her intellect and ability as well. One of his weaknesses was that he was inclined to see much more in those he admired than was really there. He endowed them with the romance of his own moods—saw in them the ability to do things which he only could do. In doing this of course he flattered their vanity, aroused their self-confidence, made them feel themselves the possessors of latent powers and forces which before him they had only dreamed of. Margaret, Ruby, Angela, Christina and Carlotta had all gained this feeling from him. They had a better opinion of themselves for having known him. Now as he looked at Carlotta he was intensely sorry, for she was so calm, so affable, so seemingly efficient and self reliant, and such a comfort to him in these days.

"Circe!" he said, "this is too bad. I'm sorry. I'm going to hate to lose you."

"You won't lose me," she replied. "You can't. I won't let you. I've found you now and I'm going to keep you. This don't mean anything. We can find places to meet. Get a place where they have a phone if you can. When do you think you'll go?"

"Right away," said Eugene. "I'll take tomorrow morning off and look."

"Poor Eugene," she said sympathetically. "It's too bad. Never mind though. Everything will come out right."

She was still not counting on Angela. She thought that even if Angela came back, as Eugene told her she would soon, a joint arrangement might possibly be made. Angela could be here, but she, Carlotta, could share Eugene in some way. She thought she would rather live with him than any other man on earth.

It was only about noon the next morning when Eugene had found another room, for, in living here so long, he had thought of several methods by which he might have obtained a room in the first place. There was another church, a library, the postmaster and the ticket agent at Speonk who lived in the village. He went first to the postmaster and learned of two families, one the home of a civil engineer, where he might be welcome, and it was here that he eventually settled. The view was not quite so attractive, but it was charming, and he had a good room and good meals. He told them that he might not stay long, for his wife was coming back soon. The letters from Angela were becoming most importunate.

He gathered up his belongings at Mrs. Hibberdell's and took a polite departure. After he was gone Mrs. Hibberdell of course changed her mind, and Carlotta returned to her apartment in New York. She communicated with Eugene not only by phone but by special delivery, and had him meet her at a convenient inn the second evening of his departure. She was planning some sort of a separate apartment for them, when Eugene informed her that Angela was already on her way to New York and that nothing could be done at present.

Since Eugene had left her at Biloxi, Angela had spent a most miserable period of seven months. She had been grieving her heart out, for she imagined him to be most lonely, and at the same time she was regretful that she had ever left him. She might as well have been with him. She figured afterward that she might have borrowed several hundred dollars from one of her brothers, and carried out the fight for his mental recovery by his side. Once he had gone she fancied she might have made a mistake matrimonially, for he was so impressionable—but his condition was such that she did not deem him to be interested in anything save his recovery. Besides, his attitude toward her of late had been so affectionate and in a way dependent. All her letters since he had left had been most tender, speaking of his sorrow at this necessary absence and hoping that the time would soon come when they could be together. The fact that he was lonely finally decided her and she wrote that she was coming whether he wanted her to or not.

Her arrival would have made little difference except that by now he was thoroughly weaned away from her again, had obtained a new ideal and was interested only to see and be with Carlotta. The latter's easy financial state, her nice clothes, her familiarity with comfortable and luxurious things— better things than Eugene had ever dreamed of enjoying—her use of the automobile, her freedom in the matter of expenditures—taking the purchase of champagne and expensive meals as a matter of course—dazzled and fascinated him. It was rather an astonishing thing, he thought, to have so fine a woman fall in love with him. Besides, her tolerance, her indifference to petty conventions, her knowledge of life and literature and art—set her in marked contrast to Angela, and in all ways she seemed rare and forceful to him. He wished from his heart that he could be free and could have her.

Into this peculiar situation Angela precipitated herself one bright Saturday afternoon in September. She was dying to see Eugene again. Full of grave thoughts for his future, she had come to share it whatever it might be. Her one idea was that he was sick and depressed and lonely. None of his letters had been cheerful or optimistic, for of course he did not dare to confess the pleasure he was having in Carlotta's company. In order to keep her away he had to pretend that lack of funds made it inadmissible for her to be here. The fact that he was spending, and by the time she arrived had spent, nearly the whole of the three hundred dollars his picture sold to Carlotta had brought him, had troubled him—not unduly, of course, or he would not have done it. He had qualms of conscience, severe ones, but they passed with the presence of Carlotta or the reading of his letters from Angela.

"I don't know what's the matter with me," he said to himself from time to time. "I guess I'm no good." He thought it was a blessing that the world could not see him as he was.

One of the particular weaknesses of Eugene's which should be set forth here and which will help to illuminate the bases of his conduct was that he was troubled with a dual point of view—a condition based upon a peculiar power of analysis—self-analysis in particular, which was constantly permitting him to tear himself up by the roots in order to see how he was getting along. He would daily and hourly when not otherwise employed lift the veil from his inner mental processes as he might lift the covering from a well, and peer into its depths. What he saw was not very inviting and vastly disconcerting, a piece of machinery that was not going as a true man should, clock fashion, and corresponding in none of its moral characteristics to the recognized standard of a man. He had concluded by now, from watching various specimens, that sane men were honest, some inherently moral, some regulated by a keen sense of duty, and occasionally all of these virtues and others were bound up in one man. Angela's father was such an one. M. Charles appeared to be another. He had concluded from his association with Jerry Mathews, Philip Shotmeyer, Peter MacHugh and Joseph Smite that they were all rather decent in respect to morals. He had never seen them under temptation but he imagined they were. Such a man as William Haverford, the Engineer of Maintenance of Way, and Henry C. Litlebrown, the Division Engineer of this immense road, struck him as men who must have stuck close to a sense of duty and the conventions of the life they represented, working hard all the time, to have attained the positions they had. All this whole railroad system which he was watching closely from day to day from his little vantage point of connection with it, seemed a clear illustration of the need of a sense of duty and reliability. All of these men who worked for this company had to be in good health, all had to appear at their posts on the tick of the clock, all had to perform faithfully the duties assigned them, or there would be disasters. Most of them had climbed by long, arduous years of work to very modest positions of prominence, as conductors, engineers, foremen, division superintendents. Others more gifted or more blessed by fortune became division engineers, superintendents, vice-presidents and presidents. They were all slow climbers, rigid in their sense of duty, tireless in their energy, exact, thoughtful. What was he?

He looked into the well of his being and there he saw nothing but shifty and uncertain currents. It was very dark down there. He was not honest, he said to himself, except in money matters—he often wondered why. He was not truthful. He was not moral. This love of beauty which haunted him seemed much more important than anything else in the world, and his pursuit of that seemed to fly in the face of everything else which was established and important. He found that men everywhere did not think much of a man who was crazy after women. They might joke about an occasional lapse as an amiable vice or one which could be condoned, but they wanted little to do with a man who was overpowered by it. There was a case over in the railroad yard at Speonk recently which he had noted, of a foreman who had left his wife and gone after some hoyden in White Plains, and because of this offense he was promptly discharged. It appeared, though, that before this he had occasionally had such lapses and that each time he had been discharged, but had been subsequently forgiven. This one weakness, and no other, had given him a bad reputation among his fellow railroad men—much as that a drunkard might have. Big John Peters, the engineer, had expressed it aptly to Eugene one day when he told him in confidence that "Ed Bowers would go to hell for his hide," the latter being the local expression for women. Everybody seemed to pity him, and the man seemed in a way to pity himself. He had a hang-dog look when he was re-instated, and yet everybody knew that apart from this he was a fairly competent foreman. Still it was generally understood that he would never get anywhere.

From that Eugene argued to himself that a man who was cursed with this peculiar vice could not get anywhere; that he, if he kept it up, would not. It was like drinking and stealing, and the face of the world was against it. Very frequently it went hand in hand with those things—"birds of a feather" he thought. Still he was cursed with it, and he no more than Ed Bowers appeared to be able to conquer it. At least he was yielding to it now as he had before. It mattered not that the women he chose were exceptionally beautiful and fascinating. They were women, and ought he to want them? He had one. He had taken a solemn vow to love and cherish her, or at least had gone through the formality of such a vow, and here he was running about with Carlotta, as he had with Christina and Ruby before her. Was he not always looking for some such woman as this? Certainly he was. Had he not far better be seeking for wealth, distinction, a reputation for probity, chastity, impeccable moral honor? Certainly he had. It was the way to distinction apparently, assuming the talent, and here he was doing anything but take that way. Conscience was his barrier, a conscience unmodified by cold self-interest. Shame upon himself! Shame upon his weak-kneed disposition, not to be able to recover from this illusion of beauty. Such were some of the thoughts which his moments of introspection brought him.

On the other hand, there came over him that other phase of his duality—the ability to turn his terrible searchlight of intelligence which swept the heavens and the deep as with a great white ray—upon the other side of the question. It revealed constantly the inexplicable subtleties and seeming injustices of nature. He could not help seeing how the big fish fed upon the little ones, the strong were constantly using the weak as pawns; the thieves, the grafters, the murderers were sometimes allowed to prey on society without let or hindrance. Good was not always rewarded—frequently terribly ill-rewarded. Evil was seen to flourish beautifully at times. It was all right to say that it would be punished, but would it? Carlotta did not think so. She did not think the thing she was doing with him was very evil. She had said to him over and over that it was an open question, that he was troubled with an ingrowing conscience. "I don't think it's so bad," she once told him. "It depends somewhat on how you were raised." There was a system apparently in society, but also apparently it did not work very well. Only fools were held by religion, which in the main was an imposition, a graft and a lie. The honest man might be very fine but he wasn't very successful. There was a great to-do about morals, but most people were immoral or unmoral. Why worry? Look to your health! Don't let a morbid conscience get the better of you. Thus she counselled, and he agreed with her. For the rest the survival of the fittest was the best. Why should he worry? He had talent.

It was thus that Eugene floundered to and fro, and it was in this state, brooding and melancholy, that Angela found him on her arrival. He was as gay as ever at times, when he was not thinking, but he was very thin and hollow-eyed, and Angela fancied that it was overwork and worry which kept in this state. Why had she left him? Poor Eugene! She had clung desperately to the money he had given her, and had most of it with her ready to be expended now for his care. She was so anxious for his recovery and his peace of mind that she was ready to go to work herself at anything she could find, in order to make his path more easy. She was thinking that fate was terribly unjust to him, and when he had gone to sleep beside her the first night she lay awake and cried. Poor Eugene! To think he should be tried so by fate. Nevertheless, he should not be tortured by anything which she could prevent. She was going to make him as comfortable and happy as she could. She set about to find some nice little apartment or rooms where they could live in peace and where she could cook Eugene's meals for him. She fancied that maybe his food had not been exactly right, and when she got him where she could manifest a pretence of self-confidence and courage that he would take courage from her and grow better. So she set briskly about her task, honeying Eugene the while, for she was confident that this above all things was the thing he needed. She little suspected what a farce it all appeared to him, how mean and contemptible he appeared to himself. He did not care to be mean—to rapidly disillusion her and go his way; and yet this dual existence sickened him. He could not help but feel that from a great many points of view Angela was better than Carlotta. Yet the other woman was wider in her outlook, more gracious in her appearance, more commanding, more subtle. She was a princess of the world, subtle, deadly Machiavellian, but a princess nevertheless. Angela was better described by the current and acceptable phrase of the time—a "thoroughly good woman," honest, energetic, resourceful, in all things obedient to the race spirit and the conventional feelings of the time. He knew that society would support her thoroughly and condemn Carlotta, and yet Carlotta interested him more. He wished that he might have both and no fussing. Then all would be beautiful. So he thought.

CHAPTER XXVI

The situation which here presented itself was subject to no such gracious and generous development. Angela was the soul of watchfulness, insistence on duty, consideration for right conduct and for the privileges, opportunities and emoluments which belonged to her as the wife of a talented artist, temporarily disabled, it is true, but certain to be distinguished in the future. She was deluding herself that this recent experience of reverses had probably hardened and sharpened Eugene's practical instincts, made him less indifferent to the necessity of looking out for himself, given him keener instincts of self-protection and economy. He had done very well to live on so little she thought, but they were going to do better—they were going to save. She was going to give up those silly dreams she had entertained of a magnificent studio and hosts of friends, and she was going to start now saving a fraction of whatever they made, however small it might be, if it were only ten cents a week. If Eugene could only make nine dollars a week by working every day, they were going to live on that. He still had ninety-seven of the hundred dollars he had brought with him, he told her, and this was going in the bank. He did not tell her of the sale of one of his pictures and of the subsequent dissipation of the proceeds. In the bank, too, they were going to put any money from subsequent sales until he was on his feet again. One of these days if they ever made any money, they were going to buy a house somewhere in which they could live without paying rent. Some of the money in the bank, a very little of it, might go for clothes if worst came to worst, but it would not be touched unless it was absolutely necessary. She needed clothes now, but that did not matter. To Eugene's ninety-seven was added Angela's two hundred and twenty-eight which she brought with her, and this total sum of three hundred and twenty-five dollars was promptly deposited in the Bank of Riverwood.

Angela by personal energy and explanation found four rooms in the house of a furniture manufacturer; it had been vacated by a daughter who had married, and they were glad to let it to an artist and his wife for practically nothing so far as real worth was concerned, for this was a private house in a lovely lawn. Twelve dollars per month was the charge. Mrs. Witla seemed very charming to Mrs. Desenas, who was the wife of the manufacturer, and for her especial benefit a little bedroom on the second floor adjoining a bath was turned into a kitchen, with a small gas stove, and Angela at once began housekeeping operations on the tiny basis necessitated by their income. Some furniture had to be secured, for the room was not completely furnished, but Angela by haunting the second-hand stores in New York, looking through all the department stores, and visiting certain private sales, managed to find a few things which she could buy cheaply and which would fit in with the dressing table, library table, dining table and one bed which were already provided. The necessary curtains for the bath and kitchen windows she cut, decorated and hung for herself. She went down to the storage company where the unsold and undisplayed portion of Eugene's pictures were and brought back seven, which she placed in the general living-room and dining-room. All Eugene's clothes, his underwear and socks particularly, received her immediate attention, and she soon had his rather attenuated wardrobe in good condition. From the local market she bought good vegetables and a little meat and made delightful stews, ragouts, combinations of eggs and tasty meat juices after the French fashion. All her housekeeping art was employed to the utmost to make everything look clean and neat, to maintain a bountiful supply of varied food on the table and yet to keep the cost down, so that they could not only live on nine dollars a week, but set aside a dollar or more of that for what Angela called their private bank account. She had a little hollow brown jug, calculated to hold fifteen dollars in change, which could be opened when full, which she conscientiously endeavored to fill and refill. Her one desire was to rehabilitate her husband in the eyes of the world—this time to stay—and she was determined to do it.

For another thing, reflection and conversation with one person and another had taught her that it was not well for herself or for Eugene for her to encourage him in his animal passions. Some woman in Blackwood had pointed out a local case of locomotor-ataxia which had resulted from lack of self-control, and she had learned that it was believed that many other nervous troubles sprang from the same source. Perhaps Eugene's had. She had resolved to protect him from himself. She did not believe she could be injured, but Eugene was so sensitive, so emotional.

The trouble with the situation was that it was such a sharp change from his recent free and to him delightful mode of existence that it was almost painful. He could see that everything appeared to be satisfactory to her, that she thought all his days had been moral and full of hard work. Carlotta's presence in the background was not suspected. Her idea was that they would work hard together now along simple, idealistic lines to the one end—success for him, and of course, by reflection, for her.

Eugene saw the charm of it well enough, but it was only as something quite suitable for others. He was an artist. The common laws of existence could not reasonably apply to an artist. The latter should have intellectual freedom, the privilege of going where he pleased, associating with whom he chose. This marriage business was a galling yoke, cutting off all rational opportunity for enjoyment, and he was now after a brief period of freedom having that yoke heavily adjusted to his neck again. Gone were all the fine dreams of pleasure and happiness which so recently had been so real— the hope of living with Carlotta—the hope of associating with her on easy and natural terms in that superior world which she represented. Angela's insistence on the thought that he should work every day and bring home nine dollars a week, or rather its monthly equivalent, made it necessary for him to take sharp care of the little money he had kept out of the remainder of the three hundred in order to supply any deficiency which might occur from his taking time off. For there was no opportunity now of seeing Carlotta of an evening, and it was necessary to take a regular number of afternoons or mornings off each week, in order to meet her. He would leave the little apartment as usual at a quarter to seven in the morning, dressed suitably for possible out-door expeditions, for in anticipation of difficulty he had told Angela that it was his custom to do this, and sometimes he would go to the factory and sometimes he would not. There was a car line which carried him rapidly cityward to a rendezvous, and he would either ride or walk with her as the case might be. There was constant thought on his and her part of the risk involved, but still they persisted. By some stroke of ill or good fortune Norman Wilson returned from Chicago, so that Carlotta's movements had to be calculated to a nicety, but she did not care. She trusted most to the automobiles which she could hire at convenient garages and which would carry them rapidly away from the vicinity where they might be seen and recognized.

It was a tangled life, difficult and dangerous. There was no peace in it, for there is neither peace nor happiness in deception. A burning joy at one time was invariably followed by a disturbing remorse afterward. There was Carlotta's mother, Norman Wilson, and Angela, to guard against, to say nothing of the constant pricking of his own conscience.

It is almost a foregone conclusion in any situation of this kind that it cannot endure. The seed of its undoing is in itself. We think that our actions when unseen of mortal eyes resolve themselves into nothingness, but this is not true. They are woven indefinably into our being, and shine forth ultimately as the real self, in spite of all our pretences. One could almost accept the Brahmanistic dogma of a psychic body which sees and is seen where we dream all to be darkness. There is no other supposition on which to explain the facts of intuition. So many individuals have it. They know so well without knowing why they know.

Angela had this intuitive power in connection with Eugene. Because of her great affection for him she divined or apprehended many things in connection with him long before they occurred. Throughout her absence from him she had been haunted by the idea that she ought to be with him, and now that she was here and the first excitement of contact and adjustment was over, she was beginning to be aware of something. Eugene was not the same as he had been a little while before he had left her. His attitude, in spite of a kindly show of affection, was distant and preoccupied. He had no real power of concealing anything. He appeared at times—at most times when he was with her—to be lost in a mist of speculation. He was lonely and a little love-sick, because under the pressure of home affairs Carlotta was not able to see him quite so much. At the same time, now that the fall was coming on, he was growing weary of the shop at Speonk, for the gray days and slight chill which settled upon the earth at times caused the shop windows to be closed and robbed the yard of that air of romance which had characterized it when he first came there. He could not take his way of an evening along the banks of the stream to the arms of Carlotta. The novelty of Big John and Joseph Mews and Malachi Dempsey and Little Suddsy had worn off. He was beginning now to see also that they were nothing but plain workingmen after all, worrying over the fact that they were not getting more than fifteen or seventeen and a half cents an hour; jealous of each other and their superiors, full of all the frailties and weaknesses to which the flesh is heir.

His coming had created a slight diversion for them, for he was very strange, but his strangeness was no longer a novelty. They were beginning to see him also as a relatively commonplace human being. He was an artist, to be sure, but his actions and intentions were not so vastly different from those of other men.

A shop of this kind, like any other institution where people are compelled by force of circumstances to work together whether the weather be fair or foul, or the mood grave or gay, can readily become and frequently does become a veritable hell. Human nature is a subtle, irritable, irrational thing. It is not so much governed by rules of ethics and conditions of understanding as a thing of moods and temperament. Eugene could easily see, philosopher that he was, that these people would come here enveloped in some mist of home trouble or secret illness or grief and would conceive that somehow it was not their state of mind but the things around them which were the cause of all their woe. Sour looks would breed sour looks in return; a gruff question would beget a gruff answer; there were long-standing grudges between one man and another, based on nothing more than a grouchy observation at one time in the past. He thought by introducing gaiety and persistent, if make-believe, geniality that he was tending to obviate and overcome the general condition, but this was only relatively true. His own gaiety was capable of becoming as much of a weariness to those who were out of the spirit of it, as was the sour brutality with which at times he was compelled to contend. So he wished that he might arrange to get well and get out of here, or at least change his form of work, for it was plain to be seen that this condition would not readily improve. His presence was a commonplace. His power to entertain and charm was practically gone.

This situation, coupled with Angela's spirit of honest conservatism was bad, but it was destined to be much worse. From watching him and endeavoring to decipher his moods, Angela came to suspect something—she could not say what. He did not love her as much as he had. There was a coolness in his caresses which was not there when he left her. What could have happened, she asked herself. Was it just absence, or what? One day when he had returned from an afternoon's outing with Carlotta and was holding her in his arms in greeting, she asked him solemnly:

"Do you love me, Honeybun?"

"You know I do," he asseverated, but without any energy, for he could not regain his old original feeling for her. There was no trace of it, only sympathy, pity, and a kind of sorrow that she was being so badly treated after all her efforts.

"No, you don't," she replied, detecting the hollow ring in what he said. Her voice was sad, and her eyes showed traces of that wistful despair into which she could so readily sink at times.

"Why, yes I do, Angelface," he insisted. "What makes you ask? What's come over you?" He was wondering whether she had heard anything or seen anything and was concealing her knowledge behind this preliminary inquiry.

"Nothing," she replied. "Only you don't love me. I don't know what it is. I don't know why. But I can feel it right here," and she laid her hand on her heart.

The action was sincere, unstudied. It hurt him, for it was like that of a little child.

"Oh, hush! Don't say that," he pleaded. "You know I do. Don't look so gloomy. I love you—don't you know I do?" and he kissed her.

"No, no!" said Angela. "I know! You don't. Oh, dear; oh, dear; I feel so bad!"

Eugene was dreading another display of the hysteria with which he was familiar, but it did not come. She conquered her mood, inasmuch as she had no real basis for suspicion, and went about the work of getting him his dinner. She was depressed, though, and he was fearful. What if she should ever find out!

More days passed. Carlotta called him up at the shop occasionally, for there was no phone where he lived, and she would not have risked it if there had been. She sent him registered notes to be signed for, addressed to Henry Kingsland and directed to the post office at Speonk. Eugene was not known there as Witla and easily secured these missives, which were usually very guarded in their expressions and concerned appointments — the vaguest, most mysterious directions, which he understood. They made arrangements largely from meeting to meeting, saying, "If I can't keep it Thursday at two it will be Friday at the same time; and if not then, Saturday. If anything happens I'll send you a registered special." So it went on.

One noontime Eugene walked down to the little post office at Speonk to look for a letter, for Carlotta had not been able to meet him the previous day and had phoned instead that she would write the following day. He found it safely enough, and after glancing at it—it contained but few words—decided to tear it up as usual and throw the pieces away. A mere expression, "Ashes of Roses," which she sometimes used to designate herself, and the superscription, "Oh, Genie!" made it, however, inexpressibly dear to him. He thought he would hold it in his possession just a little while—a few hours longer. It was enigmatic enough to anyone but himself, he thought, even if found. "The bridge, two, Wednesday." The bridge referred to was one over the Harlem at Morris Heights. He kept the appointment that day as requested, but by some necromancy of fate he forgot the letter until he was within his own door. Then he took it out, tore it up into four or five pieces quickly, put it in his vest pocket, and went upstairs intending at the first opportunity to dispose of it.

Meanwhile, Angela, for the first time since they had been living at Riverwood, had decided to walk over toward the factory about six o'clock and meet Eugene on his way home. She heard him discourse on the loveliness of this stream and what a pleasure it was to stroll along its banks morning and evening. He was so fond of the smooth water and the overhanging leaves! She had walked with him there already on several Sundays. When she went this evening she thought what a pleasant surprise it would be for him, for she had prepared everything on leaving so that his supper would not be delayed when they reached home. She heard the whistle blow as she neared the shop, and, standing behind a clump of bushes on the thither side of the stream, she waited, expecting to pounce out on Eugene with a loving "Boo!" He did not come.

The forty or fifty men who worked here trickled out like a little stream of black ants, and then, Eugene not appearing, Angela went over to the gate which Joseph Mews in the official capacity of gateman, after the whistle blew, was closing.

"Is Mr. Witla here?" asked Angela, peering through the bars at him. Eugene had described Joseph so accurately to her that she recognized him at sight.

"No, ma'am," replied Joseph, quite taken back by this attractive arrival, for good-looking women were not common at the shop gate of the factory. "He left four or five hours ago. I think he left at one o'clock, if I remember right. He wasn't working with us today. He was working out in the yard."

"You don't know where he went, do you?" asked Angela, who was surprised at this novel information. Eugene had not said anything about going anywhere. Where could he have gone?

"No'm, I don't," replied Joseph volubly. "He sometimes goes off this way—quite frequent, ma'am. His wife calls him up—er—now, maybe you're his wife."

"I am," said Angela; but she was no longer thinking of what she was saying, her words on the instant were becoming mechanical. Eugene going away frequently? He had never said anything to her! His wife calling him up! Could there be another woman! Instantly all her old suspicions, jealousies, fears, awoke, and she was wondering why she had not fixed on this fact before. That explained Eugene's indifference, of course. That explained his air of abstraction. He wasn't thinking of her, the miserable creature! He was thinking of someone else. Still she could not be sure, for she had no proof. Two adroit questions elicited the fact that no one in the shop had ever seen his wife. He had just gone out. A woman had called up.

Angela took her way home amid a whirling fire of conjecture. When she reached it Eugene was not there yet, for he sometimes delayed his coming, lingering, as he said, to look at the water. It was natural enough in an artist. She went upstairs and hung the broad-brimmed straw she had worn in the closet, and went into the kitchen to await his coming. Experience with him and the nature of her own temperament determined her to enact a rôle of subtlety. She would wait until he spoke, pretending that she had not been out. She would ask whether he had had a hard day, and see whether he disclosed the fact that he had been away from the factory. That would show her positively what he was doing and whether he was deliberately deceiving her.

Eugene came up the stairs, gay enough but anxious to deposit the scraps of paper where they would not be seen. No opportunity came for Angela was there to greet him.

"Did you have a hard job today?" she asked, noting that he made no preliminary announcement of any absence.

"Not very," he replied; "no. I don't look tired?"

"No," she said bitterly, but concealing her feelings; she wanted to see how thoroughly and deliberately he would lie. "But I thought maybe you might have. Did you stop to look at the water tonight?"

"Yes," he replied smoothly. "It's very lovely over there. I never get tired of it. The sun on the leaves these days now that they are turning yellow is so beautiful. They look a little like stained glass at certain angles."

Her first impulse after hearing this was to exclaim, "Why do you lie to me, Eugene?" for her temper was fiery, almost uncontrollable at times; but she restrained herself. She wanted to find out more—how she did not know, but time, if she could only wait a little, would help her. Eugene went to the bath, congratulating himself on the ease of his escape—the comfortable fact that he was not catechised very much; but in this temporary feeling of satisfaction he forgot the scraps of paper in his vest pocket—though not for long. He hung his coat and vest on a hook and started into the bedroom to get himself a fresh collar and tie. While he was in there Angela passed the bathroom door. She was always interested in Eugene's clothes, how they were wearing, but tonight there were other thoughts in her mind. Hastily and by intuition she went through his pockets, finding the torn scraps, then for excuse took his coat and vest down to clean certain spots. At the same moment Eugene thought of his letter. He came hurrying out to get it, or the pieces, rather, but Angela already had them and was looking at them curiously.

"What was that?" she asked, all her suspicious nature on the *qui vive* for additional proof. Why should he keep the torn fragments of a letter in his pocket? For days she had had a psychic sense of something impending. Everything about him seemed strangely to call for investigation. Now it was all coming out.

"Nothing," he said nervously. "A memorandum. Throw it in the paper box."

Angela noted the peculiarity of his voice and manner. She was taken by the guilty expression of his eyes. Something was wrong. It concerned these scraps of paper. Maybe it was in these she would be able to read the riddle of his conduct. The woman's name might be in here. Like a flash it came to her that she might piece these scraps together, but there was another thought equally swift which urged her to pretend indifference. That might help her. Pretend now and she would know more later. She threw them in the paper box, thinking to piece them together at her leisure. Eugene noted her hesitation, her suspicion. He was afraid she would do something, what he could not guess. He breathed more easily when the papers fluttered into the practically empty box, but he was nervous. If they were only burned! He did not think she would attempt to put them together, but he was afraid. He would have given anything if his sense of romance had not led him into this trap.

CHAPTER XXVII

Angela was quick to act upon her thought. No sooner had Eugene entered the bath than she gathered up the pieces, threw other bits of paper like them in their place and tried quickly to piece them together on the ironing board where she was. It was not difficult; the scraps were not small. On one triangular bit were the words, "Oh, Genie!" with a colon after it; on another the words, "The bridge," and on another "Roses." There was no doubt in her mind from this preliminary survey that this was a love note, and every nerve in her body tingled to the terrible import of it. Could it really be true? Could Eugene have found someone else? Was this the cause of his coolness and his hypocritical pretence of affection? and of his not wanting her to come to him? Oh, God! Would her sufferings never cease! She hurried into the front room, her face white, her hand clenching the tell-tale bits, and there set to work to complete her task. It did not take her long. In four minutes it was all together, and then she saw it all. A love note! From some demon of a woman. No doubt of it! Some mysterious woman in the background. "Ashes of Roses!" Now God curse her for a siren, a love thief, a hypnotizing snake, fascinating men with her evil eyes. And Eugene! The dog! The scoundrel! The vile coward! The traitor! Was there no decency, no morality, no kindness, no gratitude in his soul? After all her patience, all her suffering, all her loneliness, her poverty. To treat her like this! Writing that he was sick and lonely and unable to have her with him, and at the same time running around with a strange woman. "Ashes of Roses!" Oh, curses, curses, curses on her harlot's heart and brain! Might God strike her dead for her cynical, brutal seizing upon that sacred possession which belonged to another. She wrung her hands desperately.

Angela was fairly beside herself. Through her dainty little head ran a foaming torrent of rage, hate, envy, sorrow, self-commiseration, brutal desire for revenge. If she could only get at this woman! If she could only denounce Eugene now to his face! If she could only find them together and kill them! How she would like to strike her on the mouth! How tear her hair and her eyes out! Something of the forest cat's cruel rage shone in her gleaming eyes as she thought of her, for if she could have had Carlotta there alone she would have tortured her with hot irons, torn her tongue and teeth from their roots, beaten her into insensibility and an unrecognizable mass.

She was a real tigress now, her eyes gleaming, her red lips wet. She would kill her! kill her!! kill her!!! As God was judge, she would kill her if she could find her, and Eugene and herself. Yes, yes, she would. Better death than this agony of suffering. Better a thousand times to be dead with this beast of a woman dead beside her and Eugene than to suffer this way. She didn't deserve it. Why did God torture her so? Why was she made to bleed at every step by this her sacrificial love? Had she not been a good wife? Had she not laid every tribute of tenderness, patience, self-abnegation, self-sacrifice and virtue on the altar of love? What more could God ask? What more could man want? Had she not waited on Eugene in sickness and health? She had gone without clothes, gone without friends, hidden herself away in Blackwood the seven months while he was here frittering away his health and time in love and immorality, and what was her reward? In Chicago, in Tennessee, in Mississippi, had she not waited on him, sat up with him of nights, walked the floor with him when he was nervous, consoled him in his fear of poverty and failure, and here she was now, after seven long months of patient waiting and watching—eating her lonely heart out—forsaken. Oh, the inconceivable inhumanity of the human heart! To think anybody could be so vile, so low, so unkind, so cruel! To think that Eugene with his black eyes, his soft hair, his smiling face, could be so treacherous, so subtle, so dastardly! Could he really be as mean as this note proved him to be? Could he be as brutal, as selfish? Was she awake or asleep? Was this a dream? Ah, God! no, no it was not a dream. It was a cold, bitter, agonizing reality. And the cause of all her suffering was there in the bathroom now shaving himself.

For one moment she thought she would go in and strike him where he stood. She thought she could tear his heart out, cut him up, but then suddenly the picture of him bleeding and dead came to her and she recoiled. No, no, she could not do that! Oh, no, not Eugene—and yet and yet——

"Oh, God, let me get my hands on that woman!" she said to herself. "Let me get my hands on her. I'll kill her, I'll kill her! I'll kill her!"

This torrent of fury and self-pity was still raging in her heart when the bathroom knob clicked and Eugene came out. He was in his undershirt, trousers and shoes, looking for a clean white shirt. He was very nervous over the note which had been thrown in scraps into the box, but looking in the kitchen and seeing the pieces still there he was slightly reassured. Angela was not there; he could come back and get them when he found out where she was. He went on into the bedroom, looking into the front room as he did so. She appeared to be at the window waiting for him. After all, she was probably not as suspicious as he thought. It was his own imagination.

He was too nervous and sensitive. Well, he would get those pieces now if he could and throw them out of the window. Angela should not have a chance to examine them if she wanted to. He slipped out into the kitchen, made a quick grab for the little heap, and sent the pieces flying. Then he felt much better. He would never bring another letter home from anybody, that was a certainty. Fate was too much against him.

Angela came out after a bit, for the click of the bathroom knob had sobered her a little. Her rage was high, her pulse abnormal, her whole being shaken to its roots, but still she realized that she must have time to think. She must see who this woman was first. She must have time to find her. Eugene mustn't know. Where was she now? Where was this bridge? Where did they meet? Where did she live? She wondered for the moment why she couldn't think it all out, why it didn't come to her in a flash, a revelation. If she could only know!

In a few minutes Eugene came in, clean-shaven, smiling, his equanimity and peace of mind fairly well restored. The letter was gone. Angela could never know. She might suspect, but this possible burst of jealousy had been nipped in the bud. He came over toward her to put his arm round her, but she slipped away from him, pretending to need the sugar. He let this effort at love making go—the will for the deed, and sat down at the snow-white little table, set with tempting dishes and waited to be served. The day had been very pleasant, being early in October, and he was pleased to see a last lingering ray of light falling on some red and yellow leaves. This yard was very beautiful. This little flat, for all their poverty, very charming. Angela was neat and trim in a dainty house dress of mingled brown and green. A dark blue studio apron shielded her bosom and skirt. She was very pale and distraught-looking, but Eugene for the time was almost unconscious of it—he was so relieved.

"Are you very tired, Angela?" he finally asked sympathetically.

"Yes, I'm not feeling so well today," she replied.

"What have you been doing, ironing?"

"Oh, yes, and cleaning. I worked on the cupboard."

"You oughtn't to try to do so much," he said cheerfully. "You're not strong enough. You think you're a little horse, but you are only a colt. Better go slow, hadn't you?"

"I will after I get everything straightened out to suit me," she replied.

She was having the struggle of her life to conceal her real feelings. Never at any time had she undergone such an ordeal as this. Once in the studio, when she discovered those two letters, she thought she was suffering—but that, what was that to this? What were her suspicions concerning Frieda? What were the lonely longings at home, her grieving and worrying over his illness? Nothing, nothing! Now he was actually faithless to her. Now she had the evidence. This woman was here. She was somewhere in the immediate background. After these years of marriage and close companionship he was deceiving her. It was possible that he had been with this woman today, yesterday, the day before. The letter was not dated. Could it be that she was related to Mrs. Hibberdell? Eugene had said that there was a married daughter, but never that she was there. If she was there, why should he have moved? He wouldn't have. Was it the wife of the man he was last living with? No; she was too homely. Angela had seen her. Eugene would never associate with her. If she could only know! "Ashes of Roses!" The world went red before her eyes. There was no use bursting into a storm now, though. If she could only be calm it would be better. If she only had someone to talk to—if there were a minister or a bosom friend! She might go to a detective agency. They might help her. A detective could trace this woman and Eugene. Did she want to do this? It cost money. They were very poor now. Paugh! Why should she worry about their poverty, mending her dresses, going without hats, going without decent shoes, and he wasting his time and being upon some shameless strumpet! If he had money, he would spend it on her. Still, he had handed her almost all the money he had brought East with him intact. How was that?

All the time Eugene was sitting opposite her eating with fair heartiness. If the trouble about the letter had not come out so favorably he would have been without appetite, but now he felt at ease. Angela said she was not hungry and could not eat. She passed him the bread, the butter, the hashed brown potatoes, the tea, and he ate cheerfully.

"I think I am going to try and get out of that shop over there," he volunteered affably.

"Why?" asked Angela mechanically.

"I'm tired of it. The men are not so interesting to me now. I'm tired of them. I think Mr. Haverford will transfer me if I write to him. He said he would. I'd rather be outside with some section gang if I could. It's going to be very dreary in the shop when they close it up."

"Well, if you're tired you'd better," replied Angela. "Your mind needs diversion, I know that. Why don't you write to Mr. Haverford?"

"I will," he said, but he did not immediately. He went into the front room and lit the gas eventually, reading a paper, then a book, then yawning wearily. Angela came in after a time and sat down pale and tired. She went and secured a little workbasket in which were socks undarned and other odds and ends and began on those, but she revolted at the thought of doing anything for him and put them up. She got out a skirt of hers which she was making. Eugene watched her a little while lazily, his artistic eye measuring the various dimensions of her features. She had a well-balanced face, he finally concluded. He noted the effect of the light on her hair—the peculiar hue it gave it—and wondered if he could get that in oil. Night scenes were harder than those of full daylight. Shadows were so very treacherous. He got up finally.

"Well, I'm going to turn in," he said. "I'm tired. I have to get up at six. Oh, dear, this darn day labor business gives me a pain. I wish it were over."

Angela did not trust herself to speak. She was so full of pain and despair that she thought if she spoke she would cry. He went out, saying: "Coming soon?" She nodded her head. When he was gone the storm burst and she broke into a blinding flood of tears. They were not only tears of sorrow, but of rage and helplessness. She went out on a little balcony which was there and cried alone, the night lights shining wistfully about. After the first storm she began to harden and dry up again, for helpless tears were foreign to her in a rage. She dried her eyes and became white-faced and desperate as before.

The dog, the scoundrel, the brute, the hound! she thought. How could she ever have loved him? How could she love him now? Oh, the horror of life, its injustice, its cruelty, its shame! That she should be dragged through the mire with a man like this. The pity of it! The shame! If this was art, death take it! And yet hate him as she might—hate this hellish man-trap who signed herself "Ashes of Roses"—she loved him, too. She could not help it. She knew she loved him. Oh, to be crossed by two fevers like this! Why might she not die? Why not die, right now?

CHAPTER XXVIII

The hells of love are bitter and complete. There were days after that when she watched him, followed him down the pleasant lane from the house to the water's edge, slipping out unceremoniously after he had gone not more than eight hundred feet. She watched the bridge at Riverwood at one and six, expecting that Eugene and his paramour might meet there. It just happened that Carlotta was compelled to leave town for ten days with her husband, and so Eugene was safe. On two occasions he went downtown—into the heart of the great city, anxious to get a breath of the old life that so fascinated him, and Angela followed him only to lose track of him quickly. He did nothing evil, however, merely walked, wondering what Miriam Finch and Christina Channing and Norma Whitmore were doing these days and what they were thinking of him in his long absence. Of all the people he had known, he had only seen Norma Whitmore once and that was not long after he returned to New York. He had given her a garbled explanation of his illness, stated that he was going to work now and proposed to come and see her. He did his best to avoid observation, however, for he dreaded explaining the reason of his non-productive condition. Miriam Finch was almost glad that he had failed, since he had treated her so badly. Christina Channing was in opera, as he quickly discovered, for he saw her name blazoned one day the following November in the newspapers. She was a star of whose talent great hopes were entertained, and was interested almost exclusively in her career. She was to sing in "Bohème" and "Rigoletto."

Another thing, fortunate for Eugene at this time, was that he changed his work. There came to the shop one day an Irish foreman, Timothy Deegan, master of a score of "guineas," as he called the Italian day laborers who worked for him, who took Eugene's fancy greatly. He was of medium height, thick of body and neck, with a cheerful, healthy red face, a keen, twinkling gray eye, and stiff, closely cropped gray hair and mustache. He had come to lay the foundation for a small dynamo in the engine room at Speonk, which was to supply the plant with light in case of night work, and a car of his had been backed in, a tool car, full of boards, barrows, mortar boards, picks and shovels. Eugene was amused and astonished at his insistent, defiant attitude and the brisk manner in which he was handing out orders to his men.

"Come, Matt! Come, Jimmie! Get the shovels now! Get the picks!" he heard him shout. "Bring some sand here! Bring some stone! Where's the cement now? Where's the cement? Jasus Christ! I must have some cement. What arre ye all doing? Hurry now, hurry! Bring the cement."

"Well, he knows how to give orders," commented Eugene to Big John, who was standing near. "He certainly does," replied the latter.

To himself Eugene observed, hearing only the calls at first, "the Irish brute." Later he discovered a subtle twinkle in Deegan's eyes as he stood brazenly in the door, looking defiantly about. There was no brutality in it, only self-confidence and a hearty Irish insistence on the necessity of the hour.

"Well, you're a dandy!" commented Eugene boldly after a time, and laughed.

"Ha! ha! ha!" mocked Deegan in return. "If you had to work as harred as these men you wouldn't laugh."

"I'm not laughing at them. I'm laughing at you," explained Eugene.

"Laugh," said Deegan. "Shure you're as funny to me as I am to you."

Eugene laughed again. The Irishman agreed with himself that there was humor in it. He laughed too. Eugene patted his big rough shoulder with his hands and they were friends immediately. It did not take Deegan long to find out from Big John why he was there and what he was doing.

"An arrtist!" he commented. "Shewer he'd better be outside than in. The loikes of him packin' shavin's and him laughin' at me."

Big John smiled.

"I believe he wants to get outside," he said.

"Why don't he come with me, then? He'd have a foine time workin' with the guineas. Shewer 'twould make a man av him—a few months of that"—and he pointed to Angelo Esposito shoveling clay.

Big John thought this worth reporting to Eugene. He did not think that he wanted to work with the guineas, but he might like to be with Deegan. Eugene saw his opportunity. He liked Deegan.

"Would you like to have an artist who's looking for health come and work for you, Deegan?" Eugene asked genially. He thought Deegan might refuse, but it didn't matter. It was worth the trial.

"Shewer!" replied the latter.

"Will I have to work with the Italians?"

"There'll be plenty av work for ye to do without ever layin' yer hand to pick or shovel unless ye want to. Shewer that's no work fer a white man to do."

"And what do you call them, Deegan? Aren't they white?"

"Shewer they're naat."

"What are they, then? They're not black."

"Nagurs, of coorse."

"But they're not negroes."

"Will, begad, they're naat white. Any man kin tell that be lookin' at thim."

Eugene smiled. He understood at once the solid Irish temperament which could draw this hearty conclusion. There was no malice in it. Deegan did not underestimate these Italians. He liked his men, but they weren't white. He didn't know what they were exactly, but they weren't white. He was standing over them a moment later shouting, "Up with it! Up with it! Down with it! Down with it!" as though his whole soul were intent on driving the last scrap of strength out of these poor underlings, when as a matter of fact they were not working very hard at all. His glance was roving about in a general way as he yelled and they paid little attention to him. Once in a while he would interpolate a "Come, Matt!" in a softer key—a key so soft that it was entirely out of keeping with his other voice. Eugene saw it all clearly. He understood Deegan.

"I think I'll get Mr. Haverford to transfer me to you, if you'll let me come," he said at the close of the day when Deegan was taking off his overalls and the "Eyetalians," as he called them, were putting the things back in the car.

"Shewer!" said Deegan, impressed by the great name of Haverford. If Eugene could accomplish that through such a far-off, wondrous personality, he must be a remarkable man himself. "Come along. I'll be glad to have ye. Ye can just make out the O. K. blanks and the repoarts and watch over the min sich times as I'll naat be there and—well—all told, ye'll have enough to keep ye busy."

Eugene smiled. This was a pleasant prospect. Big John had told him during the morning that Deegan went up and down the road from Peekskill on the main line, Chatham on the Midland Division, and Mt. Kisco on a third branch to New York City. He built wells, culverts, coal bins, building piers—small brick buildings—anything and everything, in short, which a capable foreman-mason ought to be able to build, and in addition he was fairly content and happy in his task. Eugene could see it. The atmosphere of the man was wholesome. He was like a tonic—a revivifying dynamo to this sickly overwrought sentimentalist.

That night he went home to Angela full of the humor and romance of his new situation. He liked the idea of it. He wanted to tell her about Deegan—to make her laugh. He was destined unfortunately to another kind of reception.

For Angela, by this time, had endured the agony of her discovery to the breaking point. She had listened to his pretences, knowing them to be lies, until she could endure it no longer. In following him she had discovered nothing, and the change in his work would make the chase more difficult. It was scarcely possible for anyone to follow him, for he himself did not know where he would be from day to day. He would be here, there, and everywhere. His sense of security as well as of his unfairness made him sensitive about being nice in the unimportant things. When he thought at all he was ashamed of what he was doing—thoroughly ashamed. Like the drunkard he appeared to be mastered by his weakness, and the psychology of his attitude is so best interpreted. He caressed her sympathetically, for he thought from her drawn, weary look that she was verging on some illness. She appeared to him to be suffering from worry for him, overwork, or approaching malady.

But Eugene in spite of his unfaithfulness did sympathize with Angela greatly. He appreciated her good qualities—her truthfulness, economy, devotion and self-sacrifice in all things which related to him. He was sorry that his own yearning for freedom crossed with her desire for simple-minded devotion on his part. He could not love her as she wanted him to, that he knew, and yet he was at times sorry for it, very. He would look at her when she was not looking at him, admiring her industry, her patience, her pretty figure, her geniality in the face of many difficulties, and wish that she could have had a better fate than to have met and married him.

Because of these feelings on his part for her he could not bear to see her suffer. When she appeared to be ill he could not help drawing near to her, wanting to know how she was, endeavoring to make her feel better by those sympathetic, emotional demonstrations which he knew meant so much to her. On this particular evening, noting the still drawn agony of her face, he was moved to insist. "What's the matter with you, Angelface, these days? You look so tired. You're not right. What's troubling you?"

"Oh, nothing," replied Angela wearily.

"But I know there is," he replied. "You can't be feeling well. What's ailing you? You're not like yourself at all. Won't you tell me, sweet? What's the trouble?"

He was thinking because Angela said nothing that it must be a real physical illness. Any emotional complaint vented itself quickly.

"Why should you care?" she asked cautiously, breaking her self-imposed vow of silence. She was thinking that Eugene and this woman, whoever she was, were conspiring to defeat her and that they were succeeding. Her voice had changed from one of weary resignation to subtle semi-concealed complaint and offense, and Eugene noted it. Before she could add any more, he had observed, "Why shouldn't I? Why, how you talk! What's the matter now?"

Angela really did not intend to go on. Her query was dragged out of her by his obvious sympathy. He was sorry for her in some general way. It made her pain and wrath all the greater. And his additional inquiry irritated her the more.

"Why should you?" she asked weepingly. "You don't want me. You don't like me. You pretend sympathy when I look a little bad, but that's all. But you don't care for me. If you could get rid of me, you would. That is so plain."

"Why, what are you talking about?" he asked, astonished. Had she found out anything? Was the incident of the scraps of paper really closed? Had anybody been telling her anything about Carlotta? Instantly he was all at sea. Still he had to pretend.

"You know I care," he said. "How can you say that?"

"You don't. You know you don't!" she flared up suddenly. "Why do you lie? You don't care. Don't touch me. Don't come near me. I'm sick of your hypocritical pretences! Oh!" And she straightened up with her finger nails cutting into her palms.

Eugene at the first expression of disbelief on her part had laid his hand soothingly on her arm. That was why she had jumped away from him. Now he drew back, nonplussed, nervous, a little defiant. It was easier to combat rage than sorrow; but he did not want to do either.

"What's the matter with you?" he asked, assuming a look of bewildered innocence. "What have I done now?"

"What haven't you done, you'd better ask. You dog! You coward!" flared Angela. "Leaving me to stay out in Wisconsin while you go running around with a shameless woman. Don't deny it! Don't dare to deny it!"—

this apropos of a protesting movement on the part of Eugene's head—"I know all! I know more than I want to know. I know how you've been acting. I know what you've been doing. I know how you've been lying to me. You've been running around with a low, vile wretch of a woman while I have been staying out in Blackwood eating my heart out, that's what you've been doing. Dear Angela! Dear Angelface! Dear Madonna Doloroso! Ha! What have you been calling her, you lying, hypocritical coward! What names have you for her, Hypocrite! Brute! Liar! I know what you've been doing. Oh, how well I know! Why was I ever born?—oh, why, why?"

Her voice trailed off in a wail of agony. Eugene stood there astonished to the point of inefficiency. He could not think of a single thing to do or say. He had no idea upon what evidence she based her complaint. He fancied that it must be much more than had been contained in that little note which he had torn up. She had not seen that—of that he was reasonably sure—or was he? Could she have taken it out of the box while he was in the bath and then put it back again? This sounded like it. She had looked very bad that night. How much did she know? Where had she secured this information? Mrs. Hibberdell? Carlotta? No! Had she seen her? Where? When?

"You're talking through your hat," he said aimlessly and largely in order to get time. "You're crazy! What's got into you, anyhow? I haven't been doing anything of the sort."

"Oh, haven't you!" she sneered. "You haven't been meeting her at bridges and road houses and street cars, have you? You liar! You haven't been calling her 'Ashes of Roses' and 'River Nymph' and 'Angel Girl.'" Angela was making up names and places out of her own mind. "I suppose you used some of the pet names on her that you gave to Christina Channing, didn't you? She'd like those, the vile strumpet! And you, you dog, pretending to me—pretending sympathy, pretending loneliness, pretending sorrow that I couldn't be here! A lot you cared what I was doing or thinking or suffering. Oh, I hate you, you horrible coward! I hate her! I hope something terrible happens to you. If I could get at her now I would kill her and you both—and myself. I would! I wish I could die! I wish I could die!"

Eugene was beginning to get the measure of his iniquity as Angela interpreted it. He could see now how cruelly he had hurt her. He could see now how vile what he was doing looked in her eyes. It was bad business—running with other women—no doubt of it. It always ended in something like this—a terrible storm in which he had to sit by and hear himself called brutal names to which there was no legitimate answer. He had heard of this in connection with other people, but he had never thought it would come to him. And the worst of it was that he was guilty and deserving of it. No doubt of that. It lowered him in his own estimation. It lowered her in his and her own because she had to fight this way. Why did he do it? Why did he drag her into such a situation? It was breaking down that sense of pride in himself which was the only sustaining power a man had before the gaze of the world. Why did he let himself into these situations? Did he really love Carlotta? Did he want pleasure enough to endure such abuse as this? This was a terrible scene. And where would it end? His nerves were tingling, his brain fairly aching. If he could only conquer this desire for another type and be faithful, and yet how dreadful that seemed! To confine himself in all his thoughts to just Angela! It was not possible. He thought of these things, standing there enduring the brunt of this storm. It was a terrible ordeal, but it was not wholly reformatory even at that.

"What's the use of your carrying on like that, Angela?" he said grimly, after he had listened to all this. "It isn't as bad as you think. I'm not a liar, and I'm not a dog! You must have pieced that note I threw in the paper box together and read it. When did you do it?"

He was curious about that and about how much she knew. What were her intentions in regard to him? What in regard to Carlotta? What would she do next?

"When did I do it?" she replied. "When did I do it? What has that to do with it? What right have you to ask? Where is this woman, that's what I want to know? I want to find her. I want to face her. I want to tell her what a wretched beast she is. I'll show her how to come and steal another woman's husband. I'll kill her. I'll kill her and I'll kill you, too. Do you hear? I'll kill you!" And she advanced on him defiantly, blazingly.

Eugene was astounded. He had never seen such rage in any woman. It was wonderful, fascinating, something like a great lightning-riven storm. Angela was capable of hurling thunderbolts of wrath. He had not known that. It raised her in his estimation—made her really more attractive than she would otherwise have been, for power, however displayed, is fascinating. She was so little, so grim, so determined! It was in its way a test of great capability. And he liked her for it even though he resented her abuse.

"No, no, Angela," he said sympathetically and with a keen wish to alleviate her sorrow. "You would not do anything like that. You couldn't!"

"I will! I will!" she declared. "I'll kill her and you, too!"

And then having reached this tremendous height she suddenly broke. Eugene's big, sympathetic understanding was after all too much for her. His brooding patience in the midst of her wrath, his innate sorrow for what he could not or would not help (it was written all over his face), his very obvious presentation of the fact by his attitude that he knew that she loved him in spite of this, was too much for her. It was like beating her hands against a stone. She might kill him and this woman, whoever she was, but she would not have changed his attitude toward her, and that was what she wanted. A great torrent of heart-breaking sobs broke from her, shaking her frame like a reed. She threw her arms and head upon the kitchen table, falling to her knees, and cried and cried. Eugene stood there contemplating the wreck he had made of her dreams. Certainly it was hell, he said to himself; certainly it was. He was a liar, as she said, a dog, a scoundrel. Poor little Angela! Well, the damage had been done. What could he do now? Anything? Certainly not. Not a thing. She was broken—heart-broken. There was no earthly remedy for that. Priests might shrive for broken laws, but for a broken heart what remedy was there?

"Angela!" he called gently. "Angela! I'm sorry! Don't cry! Angela!! Don't cry!"

But she did not hear him. She did not hear anything. Lost in the agony of her situation, she could only sob convulsively until it seemed that her pretty little frame would break to pieces.

CHAPTER XXIX

Eugene's feelings on this occasion were of reasonable duration. It is always possible under such circumstances to take the victim of our brutalities in our arms and utter a few sympathetic or repentant words. The real kindness and repentance which consists in reformation is quite another matter. One must see with eyes too pure to behold evil to do that. Eugene was not to be reformed by an hour or many hours of agony on anyone's part. Angela was well within the range of his sympathetic interests. He suffered with her keenly, but not enough to outrun or offset his own keen desire for what he considered his spiritual right to enjoy beauty. What harm did it do, he would have asked himself, if he secretly exchanged affectionate looks and feelings with Carlotta or any other woman who fascinated him and in turn was fascinated by him? Could an affinity of this character really be called evil? He was not giving her any money which Angela ought to have, or very little. He did not want to marry her—and she really did not want to marry him, he thought—there was no chance of that, anyhow. He wanted to associate with her. And what harm did that do Angela? None, if she did not know. Of course, if she knew, it was very sad for her and for him. But, if the shoe were on the other foot, and Angela was the one who was acting as he was acting now he would not care, he thought. He forgot to add that if he did not care it would be because he was not in love, and Angela was in love. Such reasoning runs in circles. Only it is not reasoning. It is sentimental and emotional anarchy. There is no will toward progress in it.

When Angela recovered from her first burst of rage and grief it was only to continue it further, though not in quite the same vein. There can only be one superlative in any field of endeavor. Beyond that may be mutterings and thunderings or a shining after-glow, but no second superlative. Angela charged him with every weakness and evil tendency, only to have him look at her in a solemn way, occasionally saying: "Oh, no! You know I'm not as bad as that," or "Why do you abuse me in that way? That isn't true," or "Why do you say that?"

"Because it is so, and you know it's so," Angela would declare.

"Listen, Angela," he replied once, with a certain amount of logic, "there is no use in brow-beating me in this way. It doesn't do any good to call me names. You want me to love you, don't you? That's all that you want. You don't want anything else. Will calling me names make me do it? If I can't I can't, and if I can I can. How will fighting help that?"

She listened to him pitifully, for she knew that her rage was useless, or practically so. He was in the position of power. She loved him. That was the sad part of it. To think that tears and pleadings and wrath might not really avail, after all! He could only love her out of a desire that was not self-generated. That was something she was beginning to see in a dim way as a grim truth.

Once she folded her hands and sat white and drawn, staring at the floor. "Well, I don't know what to do," she declared. "I suppose I ought to leave you. If it just weren't for my family! They all think so highly of the marriage state. They are so naturally faithful and decent. I suppose these qualities have to be born in people. They can't be acquired. You would have to be made over."

Eugene knew she would not leave him. He smiled at the superior condescension of the last remark, though it was not intended as such by her. To think of his being made over after the model Angela and her relatives would lay down!

"I don't know where I'd go or what I'd do," she observed. "I can't go back to my family. I don't want to go there. I haven't been trained in anything except school teaching, and I hate to think of that again. If I could only study stenography or book-keeping!" She was talking as much to clear her own mind as his. She really did not know what to do.

Eugene listened to this self-demonstrated situation with a shamed face. It was hard for him to think of Angela being thrown out on the world as a book-keeper or a stenographer. He did not want to see her doing anything like that. In a way, he wanted to live with her, if it could be done in his way—much as the Mormons might, perhaps. What a lonely life hers would be if she were away from him! And she was not suited to it. She was not suited to the commercial world—she was too homey, too housewifely. He wished he could assure her now that she would not have further cause for grief and mean it, but he was like a sick man wishing he could do the things a hale man might. There was no self-conviction in his thoughts, only the idea that if he tried to do right in this matter he might succeed, but he would be unhappy. So he drifted.

In the meanwhile Eugene had taken up his work with Deegan and was going through a very curious experience. At the time Deegan had stated that he would take him he had written to Haverford, making a polite request for transfer, and was immediately informed that his wishes would be granted.

Haverford remembered Eugene kindly. He hoped he was improving. He understood from inquiry of the Superintendent of Buildings that Deegan was in need of a capable assistant, anyhow, and that Eugene could well serve in that capacity. The foreman was always in trouble about his reports. An order was issued to Deegan commanding him to receive Eugene, and another to Eugene from the office of the Superintendent of Buildings ordering him to report to Deegan. Eugene went, finding him working on the problem of constructing a coal bin under the depot at Fords Centre, and raising as much storm as ever. He was received with a grin of satisfaction.

"So here ye arre. Will, ye're just in time. I want ye to go down to the ahffice."

Eugene laughed. "Sure," he said. Deegan was down in a freshly excavated hole and his clothes were redolent of the freshly turned earth which surrounded him. He had a plumb bob in his hand and a spirit level, but he laid them down. Under the neat train shed to which he crawled when Eugene appeared and where they stood, he fished from a pocket of his old gray coat a soiled and crumpled letter which he carefully unfolded with his thick and clumsy fingers. Then he held it up and looked at it defiantly.

"I want ye to go to Woodlawn," he continued, "and look after some bolts that arre theyer—there's a keg av thim—an' sign the bill fer thim, an' ship thim down to me. They're not miny. An' thin I waant ye to go down to the ahffice an' take thim this O. K." And here he fished around and produced another crumpled slip. "It's nonsinse!" he exclaimed, when he saw it. "It's onraisonable! They're aalways yillen fer thim O. K. blanks. Ye'd think, begad, I was goin' to steal thim from thim. Ye'd think I lived on thim things. O. K. blanks, O. K. blanks. From mornin' 'til night O. K. blanks. It's nonsinse! It's onraisonable!" And his face flushed a defiant red.

Eugene could see that some infraction of the railroad's rules had occurred and that Deegan had been "called down," or "jacked up" about it, as the railroad men expressed it. He was in a high state of dudgeon—as defiant and pugnacious as his royal Irish temper would allow.

"I'll fix it," said Eugene. "That's all right. Leave it to me."

Deegan showed some signs of approaching relief. At last he had a man of "intilligence," as he would have expressed it. He flung a parting shot though at his superior as Eugene departed.

"Tell thim I'll sign fer thim when I git thim and naat before!" he rumbled.

Eugene laughed. He knew no such message would be accepted, but he was glad to give Deegan an opportunity to blow off steam. He entered upon his new tasks with vim, pleased with the out-of-doors, the sunshine, the opportunity for brief trips up and down the road like this. It was delightful. He would soon be all right now, that he knew.

He went to Woodlawn and signed for the bolts; went to the office and met the chief clerk (delivering the desired O. K. blanks in person) who informed him of the chief difficulty in Deegan's life. It appeared that there were some twenty-five of these reports to be made out monthly, to say nothing of endless O. K. blanks to be filled in with acknowledgments of material received. Everything had to be signed for in this way, it mattered not whether it was a section of a bridge or a single bolt or a pound of putty. If a man could sit down and reel off a graphic report of what he was doing, he was the pride of the chief clerk's heart. His doing the work properly was taken as a matter of course. Deegan was not efficient at this, though he was assisted at times by his wife and all three of his children, a boy and two girls. He was constantly in hot water.

"My God!" exclaimed the chief clerk, when Eugene explained that Deegan had thought that he might leave the bolts at the station where they would be safe until he needed them and then sign for them when he took them out. He ran his hands distractedly through his hair. "What do you think of that?" he exclaimed. "He'll leave them there until he needs them, will he? What becomes of my reports? I've got to have those O. K.'s. You tell Deegan he ought to know better than that; he's been long enough on the road. You tell him that I said that I want a signed form for everything consigned to him the moment he learns that it's waiting for him. And I want it without fail. Let him go and get it. The gall! He's got to come to time about this, or something's going to drop. I'm not going to stand it any longer. You'd better help him in this. I've got to make out my reports on time."

Eugene agreed that he would. This was his field. He could help Deegan. He could be really useful.

Time passed. The weather grew colder, and while the work was interesting at first, like all other things it began after a time to grow monotonous. It was nice enough when the weather was fine to stand out under the trees, where some culvert was being built to bridge a small rivulet or some well to supply the freight engines with water, and survey the surrounding landscape; but when the weather grew colder it was not so nice. Deegan was always interesting. He was forever raising a ruction. He lived a life of hard, narrow activity laid among boards, wheelbarrows, cement, stone, a life which concerned construction and had no particular joy in fruition. The moment a thing was nicely finished they had to leave it and go where everything would be torn up again. Eugene used to look at the wounded ground, the piles of yellow mud, the dirty Italians, clean enough in their spirit, but soiled and gnarled by their labor, and wonder how much longer he could stand it. To think that he, of all men, should be here working with Deegan and the *guineas*! He became lonesome at times—terribly, and sad. He longed for Carlotta, longed for a beautiful studio, longed for a luxurious, artistic life. It seemed that life had wronged him terribly, and yet he could do nothing about it. He had no money-making capacity.

About this time the construction of a rather pretentious machine shop, two hundred by two hundred feet and four storeys high was assigned to Deegan, largely because of the efficiency which Eugene contributed to Deegan's work. Eugene handled his reports and accounts with rapidity and precision, and this so soothed the division management that they had an opportunity to see Deegan's real worth. The latter was beside himself with excitement, anticipating great credit and distinction for the work he was now to be permitted to do.

"'Tis the foine time we'll have, Eugene, me bye," he exclaimed, "puttin' up that buildin'. 'Tis no culvert we'll be after buildin' now. Nor no coal bin. Wait till the masons come. Then ye'll see somethin'.'"

Eugene was pleased that their work was progressing so successfully, but of course there was no future in it for him. He was lonely and disheartened.

Besides, Angela was complaining, and rightfully enough, that they were leading a difficult life—and to what end, so far as she was concerned? He might recover his health and his art (by reason of his dramatic shake-up and changes he appeared to be doing so), but what would that avail her? He did not love her. If he became prosperous again it might be to forsake her, and at best he could only give her money and position if he ever attained these, and how would that help? It was love that she wanted—his love. And she did not have that, or only a mere shadow of it. He had made up his mind after this last fatal argument that he would not pretend to anything he did not feel in regard to her, and this made it even harder. She did believe that he sympathized with her in his way, but it was an intellectual sympathy and had very little to do with the heart. He was sorry for her. Sorry! Sorry! How she hated the thought of that! If he could not do any better than that, what was there in all the years to come but misery?

A curious fact to be noted about this period was that suspicion had so keyed up Angela's perceptions that she could almost tell, and that without knowing, when Eugene was with Carlotta or had been. There was something about his manner when he came in of an evening, to say nothing of those subtler thought waves which passed from him to her when he was with Carlotta, which told her instantly where he had been and what he had been doing. She would ask him where he had been and he would say: "Oh, up to White Plains" or "out to Scarborough," but nearly always when he had been with Carlotta she would flare up with, "Yes, I know where you've been. You've been out again with that miserable beast of a woman. Oh, God will punish her yet! You will be punished! Wait and see."

Tears would flood her eyes and she would berate him roundly.

Eugene stood in profound awe before these subtle outbreaks. He could not understand how it was that Angela came to know or suspect so accurately. To a certain extent he was a believer in spiritualism and the mysteries of a subconscious mind or self. He fancied that there must be some way of this subconscious self seeing or apprehending what was going on and of communicating its knowledge in the form of fear and suspicion to Angela's mind. If the very subtleties of nature were in league against him, how was he to continue or profit in this career? Obviously it could not be done. He would probably be severely punished for it. He was half terrified by the vague suspicion that there might be some laws which tended to correct in this way all the abuses in nature. There might be much vice and crime going seemingly unpunished, but there might also be much correction going on, as the suicides and deaths and cases of insanity seemed to attest. Was this true? Was there no escape from the results of evil except by abandoning it entirely? He pondered over this gravely.

Getting on his feet again financially was not such an easy thing. He had been out of touch now so long with things artistic—the magazine world and the art agencies—that he felt as if he might not readily be able to get in touch again. Besides he was not at all sure of himself. He had made sketches of men and things at Speonk, and of Deegan and his gang on the road, and of Carlotta and Angela, but he felt that they were weak in their import—lacking in the force and feeling which had once characterized his work. He thought of trying his hand at newspaper work if he could make any sort of a connection—working in some obscure newspaper art department until he should feel himself able to do better; but he did not feel at all confident that he could get that. His severe breakdown had made him afraid of life—made him yearn for the sympathy of a woman like Carlotta, or of a larger more hopeful, more tender attitude, and he dreaded looking for anything anywhere. Besides he hated to spare the time unless he were going to get somewhere. His work was so pressing. But he knew he must quit it. He thought about it wearily, wishing he were better placed in this world; and finally screwed up his courage to leave this work, though it was not until something else was quite safely in his hands.

CHAPTER XXX

It was only after a considerable lapse of time, when trying to live on nine dollars a week and seeing Angela struggle almost hopelessly in her determination to live on what he earned and put a little aside, that he came to his senses and made a sincere effort to find something better. During all this time he had been watching her narrowly, seeing how systematically she did all her own house work, even under these adverse and trying circumstances, cooking, cleaning, marketing. She made over her old clothes, reshaping them so that they would last longer and still look stylish. She made her own hats, doing everything in short that she could to make the money in the bank hold out until Eugene should be on his feet. She was willing that he should take money and buy himself clothes when she was not willing to spend it on herself. She was living in the hope that somehow he would reform. Consciousness of what she was worth to him might some day strike him. Still she did not feel that things could ever be quite the same again. She could never forget, and neither could he.

The affair between Eugene and Carlotta, because of the various forces that were militating against it, was now slowly drawing to a close. It had not been able to endure all the storm and stress which followed its discovery. For one thing, Carlotta's mother, without telling her husband, made him feel that he had good cause to stay about, which made it difficult for Carlotta to act. Besides she charged her daughter constantly, much as Angela was charging Eugene, with the utmost dissoluteness of character and was as constantly putting her on the defensive. She was too hedged about to risk a separate apartment, and Eugene would not accept money from her to pay for expensive indoor entertainment. She wanted to see him but she kept hoping he would get to the point where he would have a studio again and she could see him as a star in his own field. That would be so much nicer.

By degrees their once exciting engagements began to lapse, and despite his grief Eugene was not altogether sorry. To tell the truth, great physical discomfort recently had painted his romantic tendencies in a very sorry light for him. He thought he saw in a way where they were leading him. That there was no money in them was obvious. That the affairs of the world were put in the hands of those who were content to get their life's happiness out of their management, seemed quite plain. Idlers had nothing as a rule, not even the respect of their fellow men. The licentious were worn threadbare and disgraced by their ridiculous and psychologically diseased propensities. Women and men who indulged in these unbridled relations were sickly sentimentalists, as a rule, and were thrown out or ignored by all forceful society. One had to be strong, eager, determined and abstemious if wealth was to come, and then it had to be held by the same qualities. One could not relax. Otherwise one became much what he was now, a brooding sentimentalist—diseased in mind and body.

So out of love-excitement and poverty and ill health and abuse he was coming to see or thought he was this one fact clearly,—namely that he must behave himself if he truly wished to succeed. Did he want to? He could not say that. But he had to—that was the sad part of it—and since apparently he had to, he would do the best he could. It was grim but it was essential.

At this time Eugene still retained that rather ultra artistic appearance which had characterized his earlier years, but he began to suspect that on this score he was a little bizarre and out of keeping with the spirit of the times. Certain artists whom he met in times past and recently, were quite commercial in their appearance—the very successful ones—and he decided that it was because they put the emphasis upon the hard facts of life and not upon the romance connected with their work. It impressed him and he decided to do likewise, abandoning the flowing tie and the rather indiscriminate manner he had of combing his hair, and thereafter affected severe simplicity. He still wore a soft hat because he thought it became him best, but otherwise he toned himself down greatly. His work with Deegan had given him a sharp impression of what hard, earnest labor meant. Deegan was nothing but a worker. There was no romance in him. He knew nothing about romance. Picks and shovels and mortar boards and concrete forms—such was his life, and he never complained. Eugene remembered commiserating him once on having to get up at four A. M. in order to take a train which would get to work by seven. Darkness and cold made no difference to him, however.

"Shewer, I have to be theyre," he had replied with his quizzical Irish grin. "They're not payin' me me wages fer lyin' in bed. If ye were to get up that way every day fer a year it would make a man of ye!"

"Oh, no," said Eugene teasingly.

"Oh, yes," said Deegan, "it would. An' yere the wan that's needin' it. I can tell that by the cut av ye."

Eugene resented this but it stayed by him. Deegan had the habit of driving home salutary lessons in regard to work and abstemiousness without really meaning to. The two were wholly representative of him—just those two things and nothing more.

One day he went down into Printing House Square to see if he could not make up his mind to apply at one of the newspaper art departments, when he ran into Hudson Dula whom he had not seen for a long while. The latter was delighted to see him.

"Why, hello, Witla!" he exclaimed, shocked to see that he was exceptionally thin and pale. "Where have you been all these years? I'm delighted to see you. What have you been doing? Let's go over here to Hahn's and you tell me all about yourself."

"I've been sick, Dula," said Eugene frankly. "I had a severe case of nervous breakdown and I've been working on the railroad for a change. I tried all sorts of specialists, but they couldn't help me. So I decided to go to work by the day and see what that would do. I got all out of sorts with myself and I've been pretty near four years getting back. I think I am getting better, though. I'm going to knock off on the road one of these days and try my hand at painting again. I think I can do it."

"Isn't that curious," replied Dula reminiscently, "I was just thinking of you the other day and wondering where you were. You know I've quit the art director game. *Truth* failed and I went into the lithographic business. I have a small interest in a plant that I'm managing down in Bond Street. I wish you'd come in and see me some day."

"I certainly will," said Eugene.

"Now this nervousness of yours," said Dula, as they strolled into the restaurant where they were dining. "I have a brother-in-law that was hit that way. He's still doctoring around. I'm going to tell him about your case. You don't look so bad."

"I'm feeling much better," said Eugene. "I really am but I've had a bad spell of it. I'm going to come back in the game, though, I feel sure of it. When I do I'll know better how to take care of myself. I over-worked on that first burst of pictures."

"I must say that was the best stuff of that kind I ever saw done in this country," said Dula. "I saw both your shows, as you remember. They were splendid. What became of all those pictures?"

"Oh, some were sold and the rest are in storage," replied Eugene.

"Curious, isn't it," said Dula. "I should have thought all those things would have been purchased. They were so new and forceful in treatment. You want to pull yourself together and stay pulled. You're going to have a great future in that field."

"Oh, I don't know," replied Eugene pessimistically. "It's all right to obtain a big reputation, but you can't live on that, you know. Pictures don't sell very well over here. I have most of mine left. A grocer with one delivery wagon has the best artist that ever lived backed right off the board for financial results."

"Not quite as bad as that," said Dula smilingly. "An artist has something which a tradesman can never have—you want to remember that. His point of view is worth something. He lives in a different world spiritually. And then financially you can do well enough—you can live, and what more do you want? You're received everywhere. You have what the tradesman cannot possibly attain—distinction; and you give the world a standard of merit—you will, at least. If I had your ability I would never sit about envying any butcher or baker. Why, all the artists know you now—the good ones, anyhow. It only remains for you to do more, to obtain more. There are lots of things you can do."

"What, for instance?" asked Eugene.

"Why, ceilings, mural decorations. I was saying to someone the other day what a mistake it was the Boston Library did not assign some of their panels to you. You would make splendid things of them."

"You certainly have a world of faith in me," replied Eugene, tingling warmly. It was like a glowing fire to hear this after all the dreary days. Then the world still remembered him. He was worth while.

"Do you remember Oren Benedict—you used to know him out in Chicago, didn't you?"

"I certainly did," replied Eugene. "I worked with him."

"He's down on the *World* now, in charge of the art department there. He's just gone there." Then as Eugene exclaimed over the curious shifts of time, he suddenly added, "Why wouldn't that be a good idea for you? You say you're just about to knock off. Why don't you go down and do some pen work to get your hand in? It would be a good experience for you. Benedict would be glad to put you on, I'm sure."

Dula suspected that Eugene might be out of funds, and this would be an easy way for him to slip into something which would lead back to studio work. He liked Eugene. He was anxious to see him get along. It flattered him to think he had been the first to publish his work in color.

"That isn't a bad idea," said Eugene. "I was really thinking of doing something like that if I could. I'll go up and see him maybe today. It would be just the thing I need now,—a little preliminary practise. I feel rather rusty and uncertain."

"I'll call him up, if you want," said Dula generously. "I know him well. He was asking me the other day if I knew one or two exceptional men. You wait here a minute."

Eugene leaned back in his chair as Dula left. Could it be that he was going to be restored thus easily to something better? He had thought it would be so hard. Now this chance was coming to lift him out of his sufferings at the right time.

Dula came back. "He says 'Sure,'" he exclaimed. "'Come right down!' You'd better go down there this afternoon. That'll be just the thing for you. And when you are placed again, come around and see me. Where are you living?"

Eugene gave him his address.

"That's right, you're married," he added, when Eugene spoke of himself and Angela having a small place. "How is Mrs. Witla? I remember her as a very charming woman. Mrs. Dula and I have an apartment in Gramercy Place. You didn't know I had tied up, did you? Well, I have. Bring your wife and come to see us. We'll be delighted. I'll make a dinner date for you two."

Eugene was greatly pleased and elated. He knew Angela would be. They had seen nothing of artistic life lately. He hurried down to see Benedict and was greeted as an old acquaintance. They had never been very chummy but always friendly. Benedict had heard of Eugene's nervous breakdown.

"Well, I'll tell you," he said, after greeting and reminiscences were over, "I can't pay very much—fifty dollars is high here just at present, and I have just one vacancy now at twenty-five which you can have if you want to try your hand. There's a good deal of hurry up about at times, but you don't mind that. When I get things straightened out here I may have something better."

"Oh, that's all right," replied Eugene cheerfully. "I'm glad to get that." (He was very glad indeed.) "And I don't mind the hurry. It will be good for a change."

Benedict gave him a friendly handshake in farewell. He was glad to have him, for he knew what he could do.

"I don't think I can come before Monday. I have to give a few days' notice. Is that all right?"

"I could use you earlier, but Monday will do," said Benedict, and they parted genially.

Eugene hurried back home. He was delighted to tell Angela, for this would rob their condition of part of its gloom. It was no great comfort to him to be starting in as a newspaper artist again at twenty-five dollars a week, but it couldn't be helped, and it was better than nothing. At least it was putting him back on the track again. He was sure to do still better after this. He could hold this newspaper job, he felt, and outside that he didn't care very much for the time being; his pride had received some severe jolts. It was vastly better than day labor, anyway. He hurried up the four flights of stairs to the cheap little quarters they occupied, saying when he saw Angela at the gas range: "Well, I guess our railroad days are over."

"What's the trouble?" asked Angela apprehensively.

"No trouble," he replied. "I have a better job."

"What is it?"

"I'm going to be a newspaper artist for a while on the *World*."

"When did you find that out?" she asked, brightening, for she had been terribly depressed over their state.

"This afternoon. I'm going to work Monday. Twenty-five dollars will be some better than nine, won't it?"

Angela smiled. "It certainly will," she said, and tears of thanksgiving filled her eyes.

Eugene knew what those tears stood for. He was anxious to avoid painful reminiscences.

"Don't cry," he said. "Things are going to be much better from now on."

"Oh, I hope so, I hope so," she murmured, and he patted her head affectionately as it rested on his shoulder.

"There now. Cheer up, girlie, will you! We're going to be all right from now on."

Angela smiled through her tears. She set the table, exceedingly cheerful.

"That certainly is good news," she laughed afterward. "But we're not going to spend any more money for a long while, anyhow. We're going to save something. We don't want to get in this hole again."

"No more for mine," replied Eugene gaily, "not if I know my business," and he went into the one little combination parlor, sitting room, reception room and general room of all work, to open his evening newspaper and whistle. In his excitement he almost forgot his woes over Carlotta and the love question in general. He was going to climb again in the world and be happy with Angela. He was going to be an artist or a business man or something. Look at Hudson Dula. Owning a lithographic business and living in Gramercy Place. Could any artist he knew do that? Scarcely. He would see about this. He would think this art business over. Maybe he could be an art director or a lithographer or something. He had often thought while he was with the road that he could be a good superintendent of buildings if he could only give it time enough.

Angela, for her part, was wondering what this change really spelled for her. Would he behave now? Would he set himself to the task of climbing slowly and surely? He was getting along in life. He ought to begin to place himself securely in the world if he ever was going to. Her love was not the same as it had formerly been. It was crossed with dislike and opposition at times, but still she felt that he needed her to help him. Poor Eugene—if he only were not cursed with this weakness. Perhaps he would overcome it? So she mused.

CHAPTER XXXI

The work which Eugene undertook in connection with the art department of the *World* was not different from that which he had done ten years before in Chicago. It seemed no less difficult for all his experience—more so if anything, for he felt above it these days and consequently out of place. He wished at once that he could get something which would pay him commensurately with his ability. To sit down among mere boys—there were men there as old as himself and older, though, of course, he did not pay so much attention to them—was galling. He thought Benedict should have had more respect for his talent than to have offered him so little, though at the same time he was grateful for what he had received. He undertook energetically to carry out all the suggestions given him, and surprised his superior with the speed and imagination with which he developed everything. He surprised Benedict the second day with a splendid imaginative interpretation of "the Black Death," which was to accompany a Sunday newspaper article upon the modern possibilities of plagues. The latter saw at once that Eugene could probably only be retained a very little while at the figure he had given him. He had made the mistake of starting him low, thinking that Eugene's talent after so severe an illness might be at a very low ebb. He did not know, being new to the art directorship of a newspaper, how very difficult it was to get increases for those under him. An advance of ten dollars to anyone meant earnest representation and an argument with the business manager, and to double and treble the salary, which should have been done in this case, was out of the question. Six months was a reasonable length of time for anyone to wait for an increase—such was the dictate of the business management—and in Eugene's case it was ridiculous and unfair. However, being still sick and apprehensive, he was content to abide by the situation, hoping with returning strength and the saving of a little money to put himself right eventually.

Angela, of course, was pleased with the turn of affairs. Having suffered so long with only prospects of something worse in store, it was a great relief to go to the bank every Tuesday—Eugene was paid on Monday—and deposit ten dollars against a rainy day. It was agreed between them that they might use six for clothing, which Angela and Eugene very much needed, and some slight entertainment. It was not long before Eugene began to bring an occasional newspaper artist friend up to dinner, and they were invited out. They had gone without much clothing, with scarcely a single visit to the theatre, without friends—everything. Now the tide began slowly to change; in a little while, because they were more free to go to places, they began to encounter people whom they knew.

There was six months of the drifting journalistic work, in which as in his railroad work he grew more and more restless, and then there came a time when he felt as if he could not stand that for another minute. He had been raised to thirty-five dollars and then fifty, but it was a terrific grind of exaggerated and to him thoroughly meretricious art. The only valuable results in connection with it were that for the first time in his life he was drawing a moderately secure living salary, and that his mind was fully occupied with details which gave him no time to think about himself. He was in a large room surrounded by other men who were as sharp as knives in their thrusts of wit, and restless and greedy in their attitude toward the world. They wanted to live brilliantly, just as he did, only they had more self-confidence and in many cases that extreme poise which comes of rare good health. They were inclined to think he was somewhat of a poseur at first, but later they came to like him—all of them. He had a winning smile and his love of a joke, so keen, so body-shaking, drew to him all those who had a good story to tell.

"Tell that to Witla," was a common phrase about the office and Eugene was always listening to someone. He came to lunching with first one and then another, then three or four at a time; and by degrees Angela was compelled to entertain Eugene and two or three of his friends twice and sometimes three times a week. She objected greatly, and there was some feeling over that, for she had no maid and she did not think that Eugene ought to begin so soon to put the burden of entertainment upon their slender income. She wanted him to make these things very formal and by appointment, but Eugene would stroll in genially, explaining that he had Irving Nelson with him, or Henry Hare, or George Beers, and asking nervously at the last minute whether it was all right. Angela would say, "Certainly, to be sure," in front of the guests, but when they were alone there would be tears and reproaches and firm declarations that she would not stand it.

"Well, I won't do it any more," Eugene would apologize. "I forgot, you know."

Still he wanted Angela to get a maid and let him bring all who would come. It was a great relief to get back into the swing of things and see life broadening out once more.

It was not so long after he had grown exceedingly weary of his underpaid relationship to the *World* that he heard of something which promised a much better avenue of advancement. Eugene had been hearing for some time from one source and another of the development of art in advertising. He had read one or two articles on the subject in the smaller magazines, had seen from time to time curious and sometimes beautiful series of ads run by first one corporation and then another, advertising some product. He had always fancied in looking at these things that he could get up a notable series on almost any subject, and he wondered who handled these things. He asked Benedict one night, going up on the car with him, what he knew about it.

"Why so far as I know," said Benedict, "that is coming to be quite a business. There is a man out in Chicago, Saljerian, an American Syrian—his father was a Syrian, but he was born over here—who has built up a tremendous business out of designing series of ads like that for big corporations. He got up that Molly Maguire series for the new cleaning fluid. I don't think he does any of the work himself. He hires artists to do it. Some of the best men, I understand, have done work for him. He gets splendid prices. Then some of the big advertising agencies are taking up that work. One of them I know. The Summerville Company has a big art department in connection with it. They employ fifteen to eighteen men all the time, sometimes more. They turn out some fine ads, too, to my way of thinking. Do you remember that Korno series?"—Benedict was referring to a breakfast food which had been advertised by a succession of ten very beautiful and very clever pictures.

"Yes," replied Eugene.

"Well, they did that."

Eugene thought of this as a most interesting development. Since the days in which he worked on the Alexandria *Appeal* he had been interested in ads. The thought of ad creation took his fancy. It was newer than anything else he had encountered recently. He wondered if there would not be some chance in that field for him. His paintings were not selling. He had not the courage to start a new series. If he could make some money first, say ten thousand dollars, so that he could get an interest income of say six or seven hundred dollars a year, he might be willing to risk art for art's sake. He had suffered too much—poverty had scared him so that he was very anxious to lean on a salary or a business income for the time being.

It was while he was speculating over this almost daily that there came to him one day a young artist who had formerly worked on the *World*—a youth by the name of Morgenbau—Adolph Morgenbau—who admired

Eugene and his work greatly and who had since gone to another paper. He was very anxious to tell Eugene something, for he had heard of a change coming in the art directorship of the Summerville Company and he fancied for one reason and another that Eugene might be glad to know of it. Eugene had never looked to Morgenbau like a man who ought to be working in a newspaper art department. He was too self-poised, too superior, too wise. Morgenbau had conceived the idea that Eugene was destined to make a great hit of some kind and with that kindling intuition that sometimes saves us whole he was anxious to help Eugene in some way and so gain his favor.

"I have something I'd like to tell you, Mr. Witla," he observed.

"Well, what is it?" smiled Eugene.

"Are you going out to lunch?"

"Certainly, come along."

They went out together and Morgenbau communicated to Eugene what he had heard—that the Summerfield Company had just dismissed, or parted company with, or lost, a very capable director by the name of Freeman, and that they were looking for a new man.

"Why don't you apply for that?" asked Morgenbau. "You could hold it. You're doing just the sort of work that would make great ads. You know how to handle men, too. They like you. All the young fellows around here do. Why don't you go and see Mr. Summerfield? He's up in Thirty-fourth Street. You might be just the man he's looking for, and then you'd have a department of your own."

Eugene looked at this boy, wondering what had put this idea in his head. He decided to call up Dula and did so at once, asking him what he thought would be the best move to make. The latter did not know Summerville [*sic*], but he knew someone who did.

"I'll tell you what you do, Eugene," he said. "You go and see Baker Bates of the Satina Company. That's at the corner of Broadway and Fourth Street. We do a big business with the Satina Company, and they do a big business with Summerfield. I'll send a letter over to you by a boy and you take that. Then I'll call Bates up on the phone, and if he's favorable he can speak to Summerfield. He'll want to see you, though."

Eugene was very grateful and eagerly awaited the arrival of the letter. He asked Benedict for a little time off and went to Mr. Baker Bates. The latter had heard enough from Dula to be friendly. He had been told by the latter that Eugene was potentially a great artist, slightly down on his luck, but that he was doing exceedingly well where he was and would do better in the new place. He was impressed by Eugene's appearance, for the latter had changed his style from the semi-artistic to the practical. He thought Eugene looked capable. He was certainly pleasant.

"I'll talk to Mr. Summerfield for you," he said, "though I wouldn't put much hope in what will come of it if I were you. He's a difficult man and it's best not to appear too eager in this matter. If he can be induced to send for you it will be much better. You let this rest until tomorrow. I'll call him up on another matter and take him out to lunch, and then I'll see how he stands and who he has in mind, if he has anyone. He may have, you know. If there is a real opening I'll speak of you. We'll see."

Eugene went away once more, very grateful. He was thinking that Dula had always meant good luck to him. He had taken his first important drawing. The pictures he had published for him had brought him the favor of M. Charles. Dula had secured him the position that he now had. Would he be the cause of his getting this one?

On the way down town on the car he encountered a cross-eyed boy. He had understood from someone recently that cross-eyed boys were good luck—cross-eyed women bad luck. A thrill of hopeful prognostication passed over him. In all likelihood he was going to get this place. If this sign came true this time, he would believe in signs. They had come true before, but this would be a real test. He stared cheerfully at the boy and the latter looked him full in the eyes and grinned.

"That settles it!" said Eugene. "I'm going to get it."

Still he was far from being absolutely sure.

CHAPTER XXXII

The Summerfield Advertising Agency, of which Mr. Daniel C. Summerfield was president, was one of those curious exfoliations or efflorescences of the personality of a single individual which is so often met with in the business world, and which always means a remarkable individual behind them. The ideas, the enthusiasm, the strength of Mr. Daniel C. Summerfield was all there was to the Summerfield Advertising Agency. It was true there was a large force of men working for him, advertising canvassers, advertising writers, financial accountants, artists, stenographers, book-keepers and the like, but they were all as it were an emanation or irradiation of the personality of Mr. Daniel C. Summerfield. He was small, wiry, black-haired, black-eyed, black-mustached, with an olive complexion and even, pleasing, albeit at times wolfish, white teeth which indicated a disposition as avid and hungry as a disposition well might be.

Mr. Summerfield had come up into his present state of affluence or comparative affluence from the direst poverty and by the directest route — his personal efforts. In the State in which he had originated, Alabama, his family had been known, in the small circle to which they were known at all, as poor white trash. His father had been a rather lackadaisical, half-starved cotton planter who had been satisfied with a single bale or less of cotton to the acre on the ground which he leased, and who drove a lean mule very much the worse for age and wear, up and down the furrows of his leaner fields the while he complained of "the misery" in his breast. He was afflicted with slow consumption or thought he was, which was just as effective, and in addition had hook-worm, though that parasitic producer of hopeless tiredness was not yet discovered and named.

Daniel Christopher, his eldest son, had been raised with scarcely any education, having been put in a cotton mill at the age of seven, but nevertheless he soon manifested himself as the brain of the family. For four years he worked in the cotton mill, and then, because of his unusual brightness, he had been given a place in the printing shop of the Wickham Union, where he was so attractive to the slow-going proprietor that he soon became foreman of the printing department and then manager. He knew nothing of printing or newspapers at the time, but the little contact he obtained here soon cleared his vision. He saw instantly what the newspaper business was, and decided to enter it. Later, as he grew older, he suspected that no one knew very much about advertising as yet, or very little, and that he was called by God to revise it. With this vision of a still wider field of usefulness in his mind, he began at once to prepare himself for it, reading all manner of advertising literature and practicing the art of display and effective statement. He had been through such bitter things as personal fights with those who worked under him, knocking one man down with a heavy iron form key; personal altercation with his own father and mother in which he frankly told them that they were failures, and that they had better let him show them something about regulating their hopeless lives. He had quarreled with his younger brothers, trying to dominate them, and had succeeded in controlling the youngest, principally for the very good reason that he had become foolishly fond of him; this younger brother he later introduced into his advertising business. He had religiously saved the little he had earned thus far, invested a part of it in the further development of the Wickham *Union*, bought his father an eight acre farm, which he showed him how to work, and finally decided to come to New York to see if he could not connect himself with some important advertising concern where he could learn something more about the one thing that interested him. He was already married, and he brought his young wife with him from the South.

He soon connected himself as a canvasser with one of the great agencies and advanced rapidly. He was so smiling, so bland, so insistent, so magnetic, that business came to him rapidly. He became the star man in this New York concern and Alfred Cookman, who was its owner and manager, was soon pondering what he could do to retain him. No individual or concern could long retain Daniel C. Summerfield, however, once he understood his personal capabilities. In two years he had learned all that Alfred Cookman had to teach him and more than he could teach him. He knew his customers and what their needs were, and where the lack was in the service which Mr. Cookman rendered them. He foresaw the drift toward artistic representation of saleable products, and decided to go into that side of it. He would start an agency which would render a service so complete and dramatic that anyone who could afford to use his service would make money.

When Eugene first heard of this agency, the Summerfield concern was six years old and rapidly growing. It was already very large and profitable and as hard and forceful as its owner. Daniel C. Summerfield, sitting in his private office, was absolutely ruthless in his calculations as to men. He had studied the life of Napoleon and had come to the conclusion that no individual life was important. Mercy was a joke to be eliminated from business. Sentiment was silly twaddle. The thing to do was to hire men as cheaply as possible, to drive them as vigorously as possible, and to dispose of them quickly when they showed signs of weakening under the strain. He had already had five art directors in as many years, had "hired and fired," as he termed it, innumerable canvassers, ad writers, book-keepers, stenographers, artists—getting rid of anyone and everyone who showed the least sign of incapacity or inefficiency. The great office floor which he maintained was a model of cleanliness, order—one might almost say beauty of a commercial sort, but it was the cleanliness, order and beauty of a hard, polished and well-oiled machine. Daniel C. Summerfield was not much more than that, but he had long ago decided that was what he must be in order not to be a failure, a fool, and as he called it, "a mark," and he admired himself for being so.

When Mr. Baker Bates at Hudson Dula's request went to Mr. Summerfield in regard to the rumored vacancy which really existed, the latter was in a most receptive frame of mind. He had just come into two very important advertising contracts which required a lot of imagination and artistic skill to execute, and he had lost his art director because of a row over a former contract. It was true that in very many cases—in most cases, in fact—his customers had very definite ideas as to what they wanted to say and how they wanted to say it, but not always. They were almost always open to suggestions as to modifications and improvements, and in a number of very important cases they were willing to leave the entire theory of procedure to the Summerfield Advertising Company. This called for rare good judgment not only in the preparation, but in the placing of these ads, and it was in the matter of their preparation—the many striking ideas which they should embody—that the judgment and assistance of a capable art director of real imagination was most valuable.

As has already been said, Mr. Summerfield had had five art directors in almost as many years. In each case he had used the Napoleonic method of throwing a fresh, unwearied mind into the breach of difficulty, and when it wearied or broke under the strain, tossing it briskly out. There was no compunction or pity connected with any detail of this method. "I hire good men and I pay them good wages," was his favorite comment. "Why shouldn't I expect good results?" If he was wearied or angered by failure he was prone to exclaim—"These Goddamned cattle of artists! What can you expect of them? They don't know anything outside their little theory of how things ought to look. They don't know anything about life. Why, God damn it, they're like a lot of children. Why should anybody pay any attention to what they think? Who cares what they think? They give me a pain in the neck." Mr. Daniel C. Summerfield was very much given to swearing, more as a matter of habit than of foul intention, and no picture of him would be complete without the interpolation of his favorite expressions.

When Eugene appeared on the horizon as a possible applicant for this delightful position, Mr. Daniel C. Summerfield was debating with himself just what he should do in connection with the two new contracts in question. The advertisers were awaiting his suggestions eagerly. One was for the nation-wide advertising of a new brand of sugar, the second for the international display of ideas in connection with a series of French perfumes, the sale of which depended largely upon the beauty with which they could be interpreted to the lay mind. The latter were not only to be advertised in the United States and Canada, but in Mexico also, and the fulfilment of the contracts in either case was dependent upon the approval given by the advertisers to the designs for newspaper, car and billboard advertising which he should submit. It was a ticklish business, worth two hundred thousand dollars in ultimate profits, and naturally he was anxious that the man who should sit in the seat of authority in his art department should be one of real force and talent—a genius if possible, who should, through his ideas, help him win his golden harvest.

The right man naturally was hard to find. The last man had been only fairly capable. He was dignified, meditative, thoughtful, with considerable taste and apprehension as to what the material situation required in driving home simple ideas, but he had no great imaginative grasp of life. In fact no man who had ever sat in the director's chair had ever really suited Mr. Summerfield. According to him they had all been weaklings. "Dubs; fakes; hot air artists," were some of his descriptions of them. Their problem, however, was a hard one, for they had to think very vigorously in connection with any product which he might be trying to market, and to offer him endless suggestions as to what would be the next best thing for a manufacturer to say or do to attract attention to what he had to sell. It might be a catch phrase such as "Have You Seen This New Soap?" or "Do You Know Soresda?—It's Red." It might be that a novelty in the way of hand or finger, eye or mouth was all that was required, carrying some appropriate explanation in type. Sometimes, as in the case of very practical products, their very practical display in some clear, interesting, attractive way was all that was needed. In most cases, though, something radically new was required, for it was the theory of Mr. Summerfield that his ads must not only arrest the eye, but fix themselves in the memory, and convey a fact which was or at least could be made to seem important to the reader. It was a struggling with one of the deepest and most interesting phases of human psychology.

The last man, Older Freeman, had been of considerable use to him in his way. He had collected about him a number of fairly capable artists—men temporarily down on their luck—who like Eugene were willing to take a working position of this character, and from them he had extracted by dint of pleading, cajoling, demonstrating and the like a number of interesting ideas. Their working hours were from nine to five-thirty, their pay meagre— eighteen to thirty-five, with experts drawing in several instances fifty and sixty dollars, and their tasks innumerable and really never-ending. Their output was regulated by a tabulated record system which kept account of just how much they succeeded in accomplishing in a week, and how much it was worth to the concern. The ideas on which they worked were more or less products of the brains of the art director and his superior, though they occasionally themselves made important suggestions, but for their proper execution, the amount of time spent on them, the failures sustained, the art director was more or less responsible. He could not carry to his employer a poor drawing of a good idea, or a poor idea for something which required a superior thought, and long hope to retain his position. Mr. Daniel C. Summerfield was too shrewd and too exacting. He was really tireless in his energy. It was his art director's business, he thought, to get him good ideas for good drawings and then to see that they were properly and speedily executed.

Anything less than this was sickening failure in the eyes of Mr. Summerfield, and he was not at all bashful in expressing himself. As a matter of fact, he was at times terribly brutal. "Why the hell do you show me a thing like that?" he once exclaimed to Freeman. "Jesus Christ; I could hire an ashman and get better results. Why, God damn it, look at the drawing of the arm of that woman. Look at her ear. Whose going to take a thing like that? It's tame! It's punk! It's a joke! What sort of cattle have you got out there working for you, anyhow? Why, if the Summerfield Advertising Company can't do better than that I might as well shut up the place and go fishing. We'll be a joke in six weeks. Don't try to hand me any such God damned tripe as that, Freeman. You know better. You ought to know our advertisers wouldn't stand for anything like that. Wake up! I'm paying you five thousand a year. How do you expect I'm going to get my money back out of any such arrangement as that? You're simply wasting my money and your time letting a man draw a thing like that. Hell!!"

The art director, whoever he was, having been by degrees initiated into the brutalities of the situation, and having—by reason of the time he had been employed and the privileges he had permitted himself on account of his comfortable and probably never before experienced salary—sold himself into bondage to his now fancied necessities, was usually humble and tractable under the most galling fire. Where could he go and get five thousand dollars a year for his services? How could he live at the rate he was living if he lost this place? Art directorships were not numerous. Men who could fill them fairly acceptably were not impossible to find. If he thought at all and was not a heaven-born genius serene in the knowledge of his God-given powers, he was very apt to hesitate, to worry, to be humble and to endure a good deal. Most men under similar circumstances do the same thing. They think before they fling back into the teeth of their oppressors some of the slurs and brutal characterizations which so frequently issue therefrom. Most men do. Besides there is almost always a high percentage of truth in the charges made. Usually the storm is for the betterment of mankind. Mr. Summerfield knew this. He knew also the yoke of poverty and the bondage of fear which most if not all his men were under. He had no compunctions about using these weapons, much as a strong man might use a club. He had had a hard life himself. No one had sympathized with him very much. Besides you couldn't sympathize and succeed. Better look the facts in the face, deal only with infinite capacity, roughly weed out the incompetents and proceed along the line of least resistance, in so far as your powerful enemies were concerned. Men might theorize and theorize until the crack of doom, but this was the way the thing had to be done and this was the way he preferred to do it.

Eugene had never heard of any of these facts in connection with the Summerfield Company. The idea had been flung at him so quickly he had no time to think, and besides if he had had time it would have made no difference. A little experience of life had taught him as it teaches everyone else to mistrust rumor. He had applied for the place on hearing and he was hoping to get it. At noon the day following his visit to Mr. Baker Bates, the latter was speaking for him to Mr. Summerfield, but only very casually.

"Say," he asked, quite apropos of nothing apparently, for they were discussing the chances of his introducing his product into South America, "do you ever have need of an art director over in your place?"

"Occasionally," replied Summerfield guardedly, for his impression was that Mr. Baker Bates knew very little of art directors or anything else in connection with the art side of advertising life. He might have heard of his present need and be trying to palm off some friend of his, an incompetent, of course, on him. "What makes you ask?"

"Why, Hudson Dula, the manager of the Triple Lithographic Company, was telling me of a man who is connected with the *World* who might make a good one for you. I know something of him. He painted some rather remarkable views of New York and Paris here a few years ago. Dula tells me they were very good."

"Is he young?" interrupted Summerfield, calculating.

"Yes, comparatively. Thirty-one or two, I should say."

"And he wants to be an art director, does he. Where is he?"

"He's down on the *World*, and I understand he wants to get out of there. I heard you say last year that you were looking for a man, and I thought this might interest you."

"What's he doing down on the *World*?"

"He's been sick, I understand, and is just getting on his feet again."

The explanation sounded sincere enough to Summerfield.

"What's his name?" he asked.

"Witla, Eugene Witla. He had an exhibition at one of the galleries here a few years ago."

"I'm afraid of these regular high-brow artists," observed Summerfield suspiciously. "They're usually so set up about their art that there's no living with them. I have to have someone with hard, practical sense in my work. Someone that isn't a plain damn fool. He has to be a good manager—a good administrator, mere talent for drawing won't do—though he has to have that, or know it when he sees it. You might send this fellow around sometime if you know him. I wouldn't mind looking at him. I may need a man pretty soon. I'm thinking of making certain changes."

"If I see him I will," said Baker indifferently and dropped the matter. Summerfield, however, for some psychological reason was impressed with the name. Where had he heard it? Somewhere apparently. Perhaps he had better find out something about him.

"If you send him you'd better give him a letter of introduction," he added thoughtfully, before Bates should have forgotten the matter. "So many people try to get in to see me, and I may forget."

Baker knew at once that Summerfield wished to look at Witla. He dictated a letter of introduction that afternoon to his stenographer and mailed it to Eugene.

"I find Mr. Summerfield apparently disposed to see you," he wrote. "You had better go and see him if you are interested. Present this letter. Very truly yours."

Eugene looked at it with astonishment and a sense of foregoneness so far as what was to follow. Fate was fixing this for him. He was going to get it. How strange life was! Here he was down on the *World* working for fifty dollars a week, and suddenly an art directorship, a thing he had thought of for years, was coming to him out of nowhere! Then he decided to telephone Mr. Daniel Summerfield, saying that he had a letter from Mr. Baker Bates and asking when he could see him. Later he decided to waste no time, but to present the letter direct without phoning. At three in the afternoon he received permission from Benedict to be away from the office between three and five, and at three-thirty he was in the anteroom of the general offices of the Summerfield Advertising Company, waiting for a much desired permission to enter.

CHAPTER XXXIII

When Eugene called, Mr. Daniel C. Summerfield was in no great rush about any particular matter, but he had decided in this case as he had in many others that it was very important that anyone who wanted anything from him should be made to wait. Eugene was made to wait a solid hour before he was informed by an underling that he was very sorry but that other matters had so detained Mr. Summerfield that it was now impossible for him to see him at all this day, but that tomorrow at twelve he would be glad to see him. Eugene was finally admitted on the morrow, however, and then, at the first glance, Mr. Summerfield liked him. "A man of intelligence," he thought, as he leaned back in his chair and stared at him. "A man of force. Young still, wide-eyed, quick, clean looking. Perhaps I have found someone in this man who will make a good art director." He smiled, for Summerfield was always good-natured in his opening relationships—usually so in all of them, and took most people (his employees and prospective employees particularly) with an air of superior but genial condescension.

"Sit down! Sit down!" he exclaimed cheerfully and Eugene did so, looking about at the handsomely decorated walls, the floor which was laid with a wide, soft, light brown rug, and the mahogany desk, flat-topped, glass covered, on which lay handsome ornaments of silver, ivory and bronze. This man looked so keen, so dynamic, like a polished Japanese carving, hard and smooth.

"Now tell me all about yourself," began Summerfield. "Where do you come from? Who are you? What have you done?"

"Hold! Hold!" said Eugene easily and tolerantly. "Not so fast. My history isn't so much. The short and simple annals of the poor. I'll tell you in two or three sentences."

Summerfield was a little taken back at this abruptness which was generated by his own attitude; still he liked it. This was something new to him. His applicant wasn't frightened or apparently even nervous so far as he could judge. "He is droll," he thought, "sufficiently so—a man who has seen a number of things evidently. He is easy in manner, too, and kindly."

"Well," he said smilingly, for Eugene's slowness appealed to him. His humor was something new in art directors. So far as he could recall, his predecessors had never had any to speak of.

"Well, I'm an artist," said Eugene, "working on the *World*. Let's hope that don't militate against me very much."

"It don't," said Summerfield.

"And I want to become an art director because I think I'd make a good one."

"Why?" asked Summerfield, his even teeth showing amiably.

"Well, because I like to manage men, or I think I do. And they take to me."

"You know that?"

"I do. In the next place I know too much about art to want to do the little things that I'm doing. I can do bigger things."

"I like that also," applauded Summerfield. He was thinking that Eugene was nice and good looking, a little pale and thin to be wholly forceful, perhaps, he wasn't sure. His hair a little too long. His manner, perhaps, a bit too deliberate. Still he was nice. Why did he wear a soft hat? Why did artists always insist on wearing soft hats, most of them? It was so ridiculous, so unbusinesslike.

"How much do you get?" he added, "if it's a fair question."

"Less than I'm worth," said Eugene. "Only fifty dollars. But I took it as a sort of health cure. I had a nervous breakdown several years ago—better now, as Mulvaney used to say—and I don't want to stay at that. I'm an art director by temperament, or I think I am. Anyhow, here I am."

"You mean," said Summerfield, "you never ran an art department before?"

"Never."

"Know anything about advertising?"

"I used to think so."

"How long ago was that?"

"When I worked on the Alexandria, Illinois, *Daily Appeal*."

Summerfield smiled. He couldn't help it.

"That's almost as important as the Wickham *Union*, I fancy. It sounds as if it might have the same wide influence."

"Oh, much more, much more," returned Eugene quietly. "The Alexandria *Appeal* had the largest exclusively country circulation of any county south of the Sangamon."

"I see! I see!" replied Summerfield good-humoredly. "It's all day with the Wickham *Union*. Well, how was it you came to change your mind?"

"Well, I got a few years older for one thing," said Eugene. "And then I decided that I was cut out to be the greatest living artist, and then I came to New York, and in the excitement I almost lost the idea."

"I see."

"But I have it again, thank heaven, tied up back of the house, and here I am."

"Well, Witla, to tell you the truth you don't look like a real live, every day, sure-enough art director, but you might make good. You're not quite art-y enough according to the standards that prevail around this office. Still I might be willing to take one gosh-awful chance. I suppose if I do I'll get stung as usual, but I've been stung so often that I ought to be used to it by now. I feel sort of spotted at times from the hornets I've hired in the past. But, be that as it may, what do you think you could do with a real live art directorship if you had it?"

Eugene mused. This persiflage entertained him. He thought Summerfield would hire him now that they were together.

"Oh, I'd draw my salary first and then I'd see that I had the proper system of approach so that any one who came to see me would think I was the King of England, and then I'd — —"

"I was really busy yesterday," interpolated Summerfield apologetically.

"I'm satisfied of that," replied Eugene gaily. "And finally I might condescend, if I were coaxed enough, to do a little work."

This speech at once irritated and amused Mr. Summerfield. He liked a man of spirit. You could do something with someone who wasn't afraid, even if he didn't know so much to begin with. And Eugene knew a good deal, he fancied. Besides, his talk was precisely in his own sarcastic, semi-humorous vein. Coming from Eugene it did not sound so hard as it would have coming from himself, but it had his own gay, bantering attitude of mind in it. He believed Eugene could make good. He wanted to try him, instanter, anyhow.

"Well, I'll tell you what, Witla," he finally observed. "I don't know whether you can run this thing or not—the probabilities are all against you as I have said, but you seem to have some ideas or what might be made some under my direction, and I think I'll give you a chance. Mind you, I haven't much confidence. My personal likes usually prove very fatal to me. Still, you're here, and I like your looks and I haven't seen anyone else, and so——"

"Thanks," said Eugene.

"Don't thank me. You have a hard job ahead of you if I take you. It's no child's play. You'd better come with me first and look over the place," and he led the way out into the great central room where, because it was still noon time, there were few people working, but where one could see just how imposing this business really was.

"Seventy-two stenographers, book-keepers, canvassers and writers and trade-aid people at their desks," he observed with an easy wave of his hand, and moved on into the art department, which was in another wing of the building where a north and east light could be secured. "Here's where you come in," he observed, throwing open the door where thirty-two artists' desks and easels were ranged. Eugene was astonished.

"You don't employ that many, do you?" he asked interestedly. Most of the men were out to lunch.

"From twenty to twenty-five all the time, sometimes more," he said. "Some on the outside. It depends on the condition of business."

"And how much do you pay them, as a rule?"

"Well, that depends. I think I'll give you seventy-five dollars a week to begin with, if we come to an understanding. If you make good I'll make it a hundred dollars a week inside of three months. It all depends. The others we don't pay so much. The business manager can tell you."

Eugene noticed the evasion. His eyes narrowed. Still there was a good chance here. Seventy-five dollars was considerably better than fifty and it might lead to more. He would be his own boss—a man of some consequence. He could not help stiffening with pride a little as he looked at the room which Summerfield pointed out to him as his own if he came—a room where a large, highly polished oak desk was placed and where some of the Summerfield Advertising Company's art products were hung on the walls. There was a nice rug on the floor and some leather-backed chairs.

"Here's where you will be if you come here," said Summerfield.

Eugene gazed round. Certainly life was looking up. How was he to get this place? On what did it depend? His mind was running forward to various improvements in his affairs, a better apartment for Angela, better clothes for her, more entertainment for both of them, freedom from worry over the future; for a little bank account would soon result from a place like this.

"Do you do much business a year?" Eugene asked curiously.

"Oh, about two million dollars' worth."

"And you have to make drawings for every ad?"

"Exactly, not one but six or eight sometimes. It depends upon the ability of the art director. If he does his work right I save money."

Eugene saw the point.

"What became of the other man?" he asked, noting the name of Older Freeman on the door.

"Oh, he quit," said Summerville, "or rather he saw what was coming and got out of the way. He was no good. He was too weak. He was turning out work here which was a joke—some things had to be done over eight and nine times."

Eugene discovered the wrath and difficulties and opposition which went with this. Summerfield was a hard man, plainly. He might smile and joke now, but anyone who took that chair would hear from him constantly. For a moment Eugene felt as though he could not do it, as though he had better not try it, and then he thought, "Why shouldn't I? It can't hurt me. If worst comes to worst, I have my art to fall back on."

"Well, so it goes," he said. "If I don't make good, the door for mine, I suppose?"

"No, no, nothing so easy," chuckled Summerfield; "the coal chute."

Eugene noticed that he champed his teeth like a nervous horse, and that he seemed fairly to radiate waves of energy. For himself he winced the least bit. This was a grim, fighting atmosphere he was coming into. He would have to fight for his life here—no doubt of that.

"Now," said Summerfield, when they were strolling back to his own office. "I'll tell you what you might do. I have two propositions, one from the Sand Perfume Company and another from the American Crystal Sugar Refining Company which may mean big contracts for me if I can present them the right line of ideas for advertising. They want to advertise. The Sand Company wants suggestions for bottles, labels, car ads, newspaper ads, posters, and so on. The American Crystal Company wants to sell its sugar in small packages, powdered, grained, cubed, hexagoned. We want package forms, labels, posters ads, and so on for that. It's a question of how much novelty, simplicity and force we can put in the smallest possible space. Now I depend upon my art director to tell me something about these things. I don't expect him to do everything. I'm here and I'll help him. I have men in the trade aid department out there who are wonders at making suggestions along this line, but the art director is supposed to help. He's the man who is supposed to have the taste and can execute the proposition in its last form. Now suppose you take these two ideas and see what you can do with them. Bring me some suggestions. If they suit me and I think you have the right note, I'll hire you. If not, well then I won't, and no harm done. Is that all right?"

"That's all right," said Eugene.

Mr. Summerfield handed him a bundle of papers, catalogues, prospectuses, communications. "You can look these over if you want to. Take them along and then bring them back."

Eugene rose.

"I'd like to have two or three days for this," he said. "It's a new proposition to me. I think I can give you some ideas—I'm not sure. Anyhow, I'd like to try."

"Go ahead! Go ahead!" said Summerfield, "the more the merrier. And I'll see you any time you're ready. I have a man out there—Freeman's assistant—who's running things for me temporarily. Here's luck," and he waved his hand indifferently.

Eugene went out. Was there ever such a man, so hard, so cold, so practical! It was a new note to him. He was simply astonished, largely because he was inexperienced. He had not yet gone up against the business world as those who try to do anything in a big way commercially must. This man was getting on his nerves already, making him feel that he had a tremendous problem before him, making him think that the quiet realms of art were merely the backwaters of oblivion. Those who did anything, who were out in the front row of effort, were fighters such as this man was, raw products of the soil, ruthless, superior, indifferent. If only he could be that way, he thought. If he could be strong, defiant, commanding, what a thing it would be. Not to wince, not to quail, but to stand up firm, square to the world and make people obey. Oh, what a splendid vision of empire was here before him.

CHAPTER XXXIV

The designs or suggestions which Eugene offered his prospective employer for the advertising of the products of M. Sand et Cie and the American Crystal Sugar Refining Company, were peculiar. As has been indicated, Eugene had one of those large, effervescent intelligences which when he was in good physical condition fairly bubbled ideas. His imaginings, without any effort on his part, naturally took all forms and shapes. The call of Mr. Summerfield was for street car cards, posters and newspaper ads of various sizes, and what he wanted Eugene specifically to supply was not so much the lettering or rather wording of the ads as it was their artistic form and illustrative point: what one particular suggestion in the form of a drawing or design could be made in each case which would arrest public attention. Eugene went home and took the sugar proposition under consideration first. He did not say anything of what he was really doing to Angela, because he did not want to disappoint her. He pretended that he was making sketches which he might offer to some company for a little money and because it amused him. By the light of his green shaded working lamp at home he sketched designs of hands holding squares of sugar, either in the fingers or by silver and gold sugar tongs, urns piled high with crystalline concoctions, a blue and gold after-dinner cup with one lump of the new form on the side against a section of snow white table cloth, and things of that character. He worked rapidly and with ease until he had some thirty-five suggestions on this one proposition alone, and then he turned his attention to the matter of the perfumery.

His first thought was that he did not know all the designs of the company's bottles, but he originated peculiar and delightful shapes of his own, some of which were afterwards adopted by the company. He designed boxes and labels to amuse himself and then made various still-life compositions such as a box, a bottle, a dainty handkerchief and a small white hand all showing in a row. His mind slipped to the manufacture of perfume, the growing of flowers, the gathering of blossoms, the type of girls and men that might possibly be employed, and then he hurried to the great public library the next day to see if he could find a book or magazine article which would tell him something about it. He found this and several articles on sugar growing and refining which gave him new ideas in that direction.

He decided that in each case he would put a beautifully designed bottle of perfume or a handsome package of sugar, say, in the upper right or lower left-hand corner of the design, and then for the rest show some scene in the process of its manufacture. He began to think of men who could carry out his ideas brilliantly if they were not already on his staff, letterers, character artists, men with a keen sense of color combination whom he might possibly hire cheaply. He thought of Jerry Mathews of the old Chicago *Globe* days—where was he now?—and Philip Shotmeyer, who would be almost ideal to work under his direction, for he was a splendid letterer, and Henry Hare, still of the *World*, with whom he had frequently talked on the subject of ads and posters. Then there was young Morgenbau, who was a most excellent character man, looking to him for some opportunity, and eight or ten men whose work he had admired in the magazines—the best known ones. He decided first to see what could be done with the staff that he had, and then to eliminate and fill in as rapidly as possible until he had a capable working group. He had already caught by contact with Summerfield some of that eager personage's ruthlessness and began to manifest it in his own attitude. He was most impressionable to things advantageous to himself, and this chance to rise to a higher level out of the slough of poverty in which he had so greatly suffered nerved him to the utmost effort. In two days he had a most impressive mass of material to show his prospective employer, and he returned to his presence with considerable confidence. The latter looked over his ideas carefully and then began to warm to his attitude of mind.

"I should say!" he said generously, "there's some life to this stuff. I can see you getting the five thousand a year all right if you keep on. You're a little new, but you've caught the drift." And he sat down to show him where some improvements from a practical point of view could be made.

"Now, professor," he said finally when he was satisfied that Eugene was the man he wanted, "you and I might as well call this a deal. It's pretty plain to me that you've got something that I want. Some of these things are fine. I don't know how you're going to make out as a master of men, but you might as well take that desk out there and we'll begin right now. I wish you luck. I really do. You're a live wire, I think."

Eugene thrilled with satisfaction. This was the result he wanted. No half-hearted commendation, but enthusiastic praise. He must have it. He always felt that he could command it. People naturally ran after him. He was getting used to it by now—taking it as a matter of course. If he hadn't broken down, curse the luck, think where he could have been today. He had lost five years and he was not quite well yet, but thank God he was getting steadily better, and he would try and hold himself in check from now on. The world demanded it.

He went out with Summerfield into the art room and was there introduced by him to the various men employed. "Mr. Davis, Mr. Witla; Mr. Hart, Mr. Witla; Mr. Clemens, Mr. Witla," so it went, and the staff was soon aware of who he was. Summerfield then took him into the next room and introduced him to the various heads of departments, the business manager who fixed his and his artists' salaries, the cashier who paid him, the manager of the ad writing department, the manager of the trade aid department, and the head of the stenographic department, a woman. Eugene was a little disgusted with what he considered the crassness of these people. After the quality of the art atmosphere in which he had moved these people seemed to him somewhat raw and voracious, like fish. They had no refinement. Their looks and manners were unduly aggressive. He resented particularly the fact that one canvasser with whom he shook hands wore a bright red tie and had on yellow shoes. The insistence on department store models for suits and floor-walker manners pained him.

"To hell with such cattle," he thought, but on the surface he smiled and shook hands and said how glad he would be to work with them. Finally when all the introductions were over he went back to his own department, to take up the work which rushed through here like a living stream, pellmell. His own staff was, of course, much more agreeable to him. These artists who worked for him interested him, for they were as he suspected men very much like himself, in poor health probably, or down on their luck and compelled to do this. He called for his assistant, Mr. Davis, whom Summerfield had introduced to him as such, and asked him to let him see how the work stood.

"Have you a schedule of the work in hand?" he asked easily.

"Yes, sir," said his new attendant.

"Let me see it."

The latter brought what he called his order book and showed him just how things worked. Each particular piece of work, or order as it was called, was given a number when it came in, the time of its entry marked on the slip, the name of the artist to whom it was assigned, the time taken to execute it, and so forth. If one artist only put two hours on it and another took it and put four, this was noted. If the first drawing was a failure and a second begun, the records would show all, the slips and errors of the office as well as its speed and capacity. Eugene perceived that he must see to it that his men did not make many mistakes.

After this order book had been carefully inspected by him, he rose and strolled about among the men to see how they were getting on. He wanted to familiarize himself at once with the styles and methods of his men. Some were working on clothing ads, some on designs illustrative of the beef industry, some on a railroad travel series for the street cars, and so forth. Eugene bent over each one graciously, for he wanted to make friends with these people and win their confidence. He knew from experience how sensitive artists were—how they could be bound by feelings of good fellowship. He had a soft, easy, smiling manner which he hoped would smooth his way for him. He leaned over this man's shoulder and that asking what the point was, how long a piece of work of that character ought to take, suggesting where a man appeared to be in doubt what he thought would be advisable. He was not at all certain of himself—this line of work being so new—but he was hopeful and eager. It was a fine sensation, this being a boss, if one could only triumph at it. He hoped to help these men to help themselves; to make them make good in ways which would bring them and him more money. He wanted more money—that five thousand, no less.

"I think you have the right idea there," he said to one pale, anæmic worker who looked as though he might have a lot of talent.

The man, whose name was Dillon, responded to the soothing, caressing tone of his voice. He liked Eugene's appearance, though he was not at all disposed to pass favorable judgment as yet. It was already rumored that he had had an exceptional career as an artist. Summerfield had attended to that. He looked up and smiled and said, "Do you think so?"

"I certainly do," said Eugene cheerfully. "Try a touch of yellow next to that blue. See if you don't like that."

The artist did as requested and squinted at it narrowly. "It helps it a lot, don't it," he observed, as though it were his own.

"It certainly does," said Eugene, "that's a good idea," and somehow Dillon felt as though he had thought of it. Inside of twenty minutes the whole staff was agreeing with itself that he was a nice man to all outward appearances and that he might make good. He appeared to be so sure. They little knew how perturbed he was inwardly, how anxious he was to get all the threads of this in his hand and to see that everything came to an ideal fruition. He dreaded the hour when he might have something to contend with which was not quite right.

Days passed at this new work and then weeks, and by degrees he grew moderately sure of himself and comparatively easy in his seat, though he realized that he had not stepped into a bed of roses. He found this a most tempestuous office to work in, for Summerfield was, as he expressed it, "on the job" early and late, and tireless in his insistence and enthusiasm. He came down from his residence in the upper portion of the city at eight-fifty in the morning and remained almost invariably until six-thirty and seven and not infrequently until eight and nine in the evening. He had the inconsiderate habit of keeping such of his staff as happened to be working upon the thing in which he was interested until all hours of the night; sometimes transferring his deliberations to his own home and that without dinner or the proffer of it to those whom he made to work. He would talk advertising with one big merchant or another until it was time to go home, and would then call in the weary members of his staff before they had time to escape and begin a long and important discussion of something he wanted done. At times, when anything went wrong, he would fly into an insane fury, rave and curse and finally, perhaps, discharge the one who was really not to blame. There were no end of labored and irritating conferences in which hard words and sarcastic references would fly about, for he had no respect for the ability or personality of anyone who worked for him. They were all more or less machines in his estimation and rather poorly constructed ones at that. Their ideas were not good enough unless for the time being they happened to be new, or as in Eugene's case displaying pronounced talent.

He could not fathom Eugene so readily, for he had never met anyone of his kind. He was looking closely in his case, as he was in that of all the others, to see if he could not find some weakness in his ideas. He had a gleaming, insistent, almost demoniac eye, a habit of chewing incessantly and even violently the stub end of a cigar, the habit of twitching, getting up and walking about, stirring things on his desk, doing anything and everything to give his restless, generative energy a chance to escape.

"Now, professor," he would say when Eugene came in and seated himself quietly and unobtrusively in some corner, "we have a very difficult thing here to solve today. I want to know what you think could be done in such and such a case," describing a particular condition.

Eugene would brace himself up and begin to consider, but rumination was not what Summerfield wanted from anyone.

"Well, professor! well! well!" he would exclaim.

Eugene would stir irritably. This was so embarrassing—in a way so degrading to him.

"Come to life, professor," Summerfield would go on. He seemed to have concluded long before that the gad was the most effective commercial weapon.

Eugene would then make some polite suggestion, wishing instead that he could tell him to go to the devil, but that was not the end of it. Before all the old writers, canvassers, trade aid men—sometimes one or two of his own artists who might be working upon the particular task in question, he would exclaim: "Lord! what a poor suggestion!" or "can't you do any better than that, professor?" or "good heavens, I have three or four ideas better than that myself." The best he would ever say in conference was, "Well, there may be something in that," though privately, afterwards, he might possibly express great pleasure. Past achievements counted for nothing; that was so plain. One might bring in gold and silver all day long; the next day there must be more gold and silver and in larger quantities. There was no end to the man's appetite. There was no limit to the speed at which he wished to drive his men. There was no limit to the venomous commercial idea as an idea. Summerfield set an example of nagging and irritating insistence, and he urged all his employees to the same policy. The result was a bear-garden, a den of prize-fighters, liars, cutthroats and thieves in which every man was for himself openly and avowedly and the devil take the hindmost.

CHAPTER XXXV

Still time went by, and although things did not improve very much in his office over the standards which he saw prevailing when he came there, he was obviously getting things much better arranged in his private life. In the first place Angela's attitude was getting much better. The old agony which had possessed her in the days when he was acting so badly had modified as day by day she saw him working and conducting himself with reasonable circumspection. She did not trust him as yet. She was not sure that he had utterly broken with Carlotta Wilson (she had never found out who his paramour was), but all the evidence seemed to attest it. There was a telephone down stairs in a drug store by which, during his days on the *World*, Angela would call him up at any time, and whenever she had called him up he was always in the office. He seemed to have plenty of time to take her to the theatre if she wished to go, and to have no especial desire to avoid her company. He had once told her frankly that he did not propose to pretend to love her any more, though he did care for her, and this frightened her. In spite of her wrath and suffering she cared for him, and she believed that he still sympathized with her and might come to care for her again—that he ought to.

She decided to play the rôle of the affectionate wife whether it was true or not, and to hug and kiss him and fuss over him if he would let her, just as though nothing had happened. Eugene did not understand this. He did not see how Angela could still love him. He thought she must hate him, having such just grounds, for having by dint of hard work and absence come out of his vast excitement about Carlotta he was beginning to feel that he had done her a terrific injustice and to wish to make amends. He did not want to love her, he did not feel that he could, but he was perfectly willing to behave himself, to try to earn a good living, to take her to theatre and opera as opportunity permitted, and to build up and renew a social relationship with others which should act as a substitute for love. He was beginning to think that there was no honest or happy solution to any affair of the heart in the world. Most people so far as he could see were unhappily married. It seemed to be the lot of mankind to make mistakes in its matrimonial selections. He was probably no more unhappy than many others. Let the world wag as it would for a time. He would try to make some money now, and restore himself in the eyes of the world. Later, life might bring him something—who could tell?

In the next place their financial condition, even before he left the *World*, was so much better than it had been. By dint of saving and scraping, refusing to increase their expenses more than was absolutely necessary, Angela had succeeded by the time he left the *World* in laying by over one thousand dollars, and since then it had gone up to three thousand. They had relaxed sufficiently so that now they were wearing reasonably good clothes, were going out and receiving company regularly. It was not possible in their little apartment which they still occupied to entertain more than three or four at the outside, and two was all that Angela ever cared to consider as either pleasurable or comfortable; but they entertained this number frequently. There were some slight recoveries of friendship and of the old life—Hudson Dula, Jerry Mathews, who had moved to Newark; William McConnell, Philip Shotmeyer. MacHugh and Smite were away, one painting in Nova Scotia, the other working in Chicago. As for the old art crowd, socialists and radicals included, Eugene attempted to avoid them as much as possible. He knew nothing of the present whereabouts of Miriam Finch and Norma Whitmore. Of Christina Channing he heard much, for she was singing in Grand Opera, her pictures displayed in the paper and upon the billboards. There were many new friends, principally young newspaper artists like Adolph Morgenbau, who took to Eugene and were in a sense his disciples.

Angela's relations showed up from time to time, among them David Blue, now a sub-lieutenant in the army, with all the army officer's pride of place and station. There were women friends of Angela's for whom Eugene cared little—Mrs. Desmas, the wife of the furniture manufacturer at Riverwood, from whom they had rented their four rooms there; Mrs. Wertheim, the wife of the multimillionaire, to whom M. Charles had introduced them; Mrs. Link, the wife of the West Point army captain who had come to the old Washington Square studio with Marietta and who was now stationed at Fort Hamilton in Brooklyn; and a Mrs. Juergens, living in a neighboring apartment. As long as they were very poor, Angela was very careful how she revived acquaintances; but when they began to have a little money she decided that she might indulge her predilection and so make life less lonesome for herself. She had always been anxious to build up solid social connections for Eugene, but as yet she did not see how it was to be done.

When Eugene's new connection with the Summerfield company was consummated, Angela was greatly astonished and rather delighted to think that if he had to work in this practical field for long it was to be under such comforting auspices—that is, as a superior and not as an underling.

Long ago she had come to feel that Eugene would never make any money in a commercial way. To see him mounting in this manner was curious, but not wholly reassuring. They must save money; that was her one cry. They had to move soon, that was very plain, but they mustn't spend any more than they had to. She delayed until the attitude of Summerfield, upon an accidental visit to their flat, made it commercially advisable.

Summerfield was a great admirer of Eugene's artistic ability. He had never seen any of his pictures, but he was rather keen to, and once when Eugene told him that they were still on display, one or two of them at Pottle Frères, Jacob Bergman's and Henry LaRue's, he decided to visit these places, but put it off. One night when he was riding uptown on the L road with Eugene he decided because he was in a vagrom mood to accompany him home and see his pictures there. Eugene did not want this. He was chagrined to be compelled to take him into their very little apartment, but there was apparently no way of escaping it. He tried to persuade him to visit Pottle Frères instead, where one picture was still on view, but Summerfield would none of that.

"I don't like you to see this place," finally he said apologetically, as they were going up the steps of the five-story apartment house. "We are going to get out of here pretty soon. I came here when I worked on the road."

Summerfield looked about at the poor neighborhood, the inlet of a canal some two blocks east where a series of black coal pockets were and to the north where there was flat open country and a railroad yard.

"Why, that's all right," he said, in his direct, practical way. "It doesn't make any difference to me. It does to you, though, Witla. You know, I believe in spending money, everybody spending money. Nobody gets anywhere by saving anything. Pay out! Pay out—that's the idea. I found that out for myself long ago. You'd better move when you get a chance soon and surround yourself with clever people."

Eugene considered this the easy talk of a man who was successful and lucky, but he still thought there was much in it. Summerfield came in and viewed the pictures. He liked them, and he liked Angela, though he wondered how Eugene ever came to marry her. She was such a quiet little home body. Eugene looked more like a Bohemian or a club man now that he had been worked upon by Summerfield. The soft hat had long since been discarded for a stiff derby, and Eugene's clothes were of the most practical business type he could find. He looked more like a young merchant than an artist. Summerfield invited them over to dinner at his house, refusing to stay to dinner here, and went his way.

Before long, because of his advice they moved. They had practically four thousand by now, and because of his salary Angela figured that they could increase their living expenses to say two thousand five hundred or even three thousand dollars. She wanted Eugene to save two thousand each year against the day when he should decide to return to art. They sought about together Saturday afternoons and Sundays and finally found a charming apartment in Central Park West overlooking the park, where they thought they could live and entertain beautifully. It had a large dining-room and living-room which when the table was cleared away formed one great room. There was a handsomely equipped bathroom, a nice kitchen with ample pantry, three bedrooms, one of which Angela turned into a sewing room, and a square hall or entry which answered as a temporary reception room. There were plenty of closets, gas and electricity, elevator service with nicely uniformed elevator men, and a house telephone. It was very different from their last place, where they only had a long dark hall, stairways to climb, gas only, and no phone. The neighborhood, too, was so much better. Here were automobiles and people walking in the park or promenading on a Sunday afternoon, and obsequious consideration or polite indifference to your affairs from everyone who had anything to do with you.

"Well, the tide is certainly turning," said Eugene, as they entered it the first day.

He had the apartment redecorated in white and delft-blue and dark blue, getting a set of library and dining-room furniture in imitation rosewood. He bought a few choice pictures which he had seen at various exhibitions to mix with his own, and set a cut-glass bowl in the ceiling where formerly the commonplace chandelier had been. There were books enough, accumulated during a period of years, to fill the attractive white bookcase with its lead-paned doors. Attractive sets of bedroom furniture in bird's-eye maple and white enamel were secured, and the whole apartment given a very cosy and tasteful appearance. A piano was purchased outright and dinner and breakfast sets of Haviland china. There were many other dainty accessories, such as rugs, curtains, portières, and so forth, the hanging of which Angela supervised. Here they settled down to a comparatively new and attractive life.

Angela had never really forgiven him his indiscretions of the past, his radical brutality in the last instance, but she was not holding them up insistently against him. There were occasional scenes even yet, the echoes of a far-off storm; but as long as they were making money and friends were beginning to come back she did not propose to quarrel. Eugene was very considerate. He was very, very hard-working. Why should she nag him? He would sit by a window overlooking the park at night and toil over his sketches and ideas until midnight. He was up and dressed by seven, down to his office by eight-thirty, out to lunch at one or later, and only back home at eight or nine o'clock at night. Sometimes Angela would be cross with him for this, sometimes rail at Mr. Summerfield for an inhuman brute, but seeing that the apartment was so lovely and that Eugene was getting along so well, how could she quarrel? It was for her benefit as much as for his that he appeared to be working. He did not think about spending money. He did not seem to care. He would work, work, work, until she actually felt sorry for him.

"Certainly Mr. Summerfield ought to like you," she said to him one day, half in compliment, half in a rage at a man who would exact so much from him. "You're valuable enough to him. I never saw a man who could work like you can. Don't you ever want to stop?"

"Don't bother about me, Angelface," he said. "I have to do it. I don't mind. It's better than walking the streets and wondering how I'm going to get along"—and he fell to his ideas again.

Angela shook her head. Poor Eugene! If ever a man deserved success for working, he certainly did. And he was really getting nice again—getting conventional. Perhaps it was because he was getting a little older. It might turn out that he would become a splendid man, after all.

CHAPTER XXXVI

There came a time, however, when all this excitement and wrath and quarreling began to unnerve Eugene and to make him feel that he could not indefinitely stand the strain. After all, his was the artistic temperament, not that of a commercial or financial genius. He was too nervous and restless. For one thing he was first astonished, then amused, then embittered by the continual travesty on justice, truth, beauty, sympathy, which he saw enacted before his eyes. Life stripped of its illusion and its seeming becomes a rather deadly thing to contemplate. Because of the ruthless, insistent, inconsiderate attitude of this employer, all the employees of this place followed his example, and there was neither kindness nor courtesy—nor even raw justice anywhere. Eugene was compelled to see himself looked upon from the beginning, not so much by his own staff as by the other employees of the company, as a man who could not last long. He was disliked forsooth because Summerfield displayed some liking for him, and because his manners did not coincide exactly with the prevailing standard of the office. Summerfield did not intend to allow his interest in Eugene to infringe in any way upon his commercial exactions, but this was not enough to save or aid Eugene in any way. The others disliked him, some because he was a true artist to begin with, because of his rather distant air, and because in spite of himself he could not take them all as seriously as he should.

Most of them seemed little mannikins to him—little second, third, and fourth editions or copies of Summerfield. They all copied that worthy's insistent air. They all attempted to imitate his briskness. Like children, they were inclined to try to imitate his bitter persiflage and be smart; and they demanded, as he said they should, the last ounce of consideration and duty from their neighbors. Eugene was too much of a philosopher not to take much of this with a grain of salt, but after all his position depended on his activity and his ability to get results, and it was a pity, he thought, that he could expect neither courtesy nor favor from anyone. Departmental chiefs stormed his room daily, demanding this, that, and the other work immediately. Artists complained that they were not getting enough pay, the business manager railed because expenses were not kept low, saying that Eugene might be an improvement in the matter of the quality of the results obtained and the speed of execution, but that he was lavish in his expenditure. Others cursed openly in his presence at times, and about him to his employer, alleging that the execution of certain ideas was rotten, or that certain work was delayed, or that he was slow or discourteous. There was little in these things, as Summerfield well knew from watching Eugene, but he was too much a lover of quarrels and excitement as being productive of the best results in the long run to wish to interfere. Eugene was soon accused of delaying work generally, of having incompetent men (which was true), of being slow, of being an artistic snob. He stood it all calmly because of his recent experience with poverty, but he was determined to fight ultimately. He was no longer, or at least not going to be, he thought, the ambling, cowardly, dreaming Witla he had been. He was going to stand up, and he did begin to.

"Remember, you are the last word here, Witla," Summerfield had told him on one occasion. "If anything goes wrong here, you're to blame. Don't make any mistakes. Don't let anyone accuse you falsely. Don't run to me. I won't help you."

It was such a ruthless attitude that it shocked Eugene into an attitude of defiance. In time he thought he had become a hardened and a changed man—aggressive, contentious, bitter.

"They can all go to hell!" he said one day to Summerfield, after a terrific row about some delayed pictures, in which one man who was animated by personal animosity more than anything else had said hard things about him. "The thing that's been stated here isn't so. My work is up to and beyond the mark. This individual here"—pointing to the man in question—"simply doesn't like me. The next time he comes into my room nosing about I'll throw him out. He's a damned fakir, and you know it. He lied here today, and you know that."

"Good for you, Witla!" exclaimed Summerfield joyously. The idea of a fighting attitude on Eugene's part pleased him. "You're coming to life. You'll get somewhere now. You've got the ideas, but if you let these wolves run over you they'll do it, and they'll eat you. I can't help it. They're all no good. I wouldn't trust a single God-damned man in the place!"

So it went. Eugene smiled. Could he ever get used to such a life? Could he ever learn to live with such cheap, inconsiderate, indecent little pups? Summerfield might like them, but he didn't. This might be a marvellous business policy, but he couldn't see it. Somehow it seemed to reflect the mental attitude and temperament of Mr. Daniel C. Summerfield and nothing more. Human nature ought to be better than that.

It is curious how fortune sometimes binds up the wounds of the past, covers over the broken places as with clinging vines, gives to the miseries and mental wearinesses of life a look of sweetness and comfort. An illusion of perfect joy is sometimes created where still, underneath, are cracks and scars. Here were Angela and Eugene living together now, beginning to be visited by first one and then the other of those they had known in the past, seemingly as happy as though no storm had ever beset the calm of their present sailing. Eugene, despite all his woes, was interested in this work. He liked to think of himself as the captain of a score of men, having a handsome office desk, being hailed as chief by obsequious subordinates and invited here and there by Summerfield, who still liked him. The work was hard, but it was so much more profitable than anything he had ever had before. Angela was happier, too, he thought, than she had been in a long time, for she did not need to worry about money and his prospects were broadening. Friends were coming back to them in a steady stream, and they were creating new ones. It was possible to go to a seaside resort occasionally, winter or summer, or to entertain three or four friends at dinner. Angela had a maid. The meals were served with considerable distinction under her supervision. She was flattered to hear nice things said about her husband in her presence, for it was whispered abroad in art circles with which they were now slightly in touch again that half the effectiveness of the Summerfield ads was due to Eugene's talent. It was no shame for him to come out now and say where he was, for he was getting a good salary and was a department chief. He, or rather the house through him, had made several great hits, issuing series of ads which attracted the attention of the public generally to the products which they advertised. Experts in the advertising world first, and then later the public generally, were beginning to wonder who it was that was primarily responsible for the hits.

The Summerfield company had not had them during the previous six years of its history. There were too many of them coming close together not to make a new era in the history of the house. Summerfield, it was understood about the office, was becoming a little jealous of Eugene, for he could not brook the presence of a man with a reputation; and Eugene, with his five thousand dollars in cash in two savings banks, with practically two thousand five hundred dollars' worth of tasteful furniture in his apartment and with a ten-thousand life-insurance policy in favor of Angela, was carrying himself with quite an air. He was not feeling so anxious about his future.

Angela noted it. Summerfield also. The latter felt that Eugene was beginning to show his artistic superiority in a way which was not entirely pleasant. He was coming to have a direct, insistent, sometimes dictatorial manner. All the driving Summerfield had done had not succeeded in breaking his spirit. Instead, it had developed him. From a lean, pale, artistic soul, wearing a soft hat, he had straightened up and filled out until now he looked more like a business man than an artist, with a derby hat, clothes of the latest cut, a ring of oriental design on his middle finger, and pins and ties which reflected the prevailing modes.

Eugene's attitude had not as yet changed completely, but it was changing. He was not nearly so fearsome as he had been. He was beginning to see that he had talents in more directions than one, and to have the confidence of this fact. Five thousand dollars in cash, with two or three hundred dollars being added monthly, and interest at four per cent, being paid upon it, gave him a reserve of self-confidence. He began to joke Summerfield himself, for he began to realize that other advertising concerns might be glad to have him. Word had been brought to him once that the Alfred Cookman Company, of which Summerfield was a graduate, was considering making him an offer, and the Twine-Campbell Company, the largest in the field, was also interested in what he was doing. His own artists, mostly faithful because he had sought to pay them well and to help them succeed, had spread his fame greatly. According to them, he was the sole cause of all the recent successes which had come to the house, which was not true at all.

A number, perhaps the majority, of things recently had started with him; but they had been amplified by Summerfield, worked over by the ad-writing department, revised by the advertisers themselves, and so on and so forth, until notable changes had been effected and success achieved. There was no doubt that Eugene was directly responsible for a share of this. His presence was inspiring, constructive. He keyed up the whole tone of the Summerfield Company merely by being there; but he was not all there was to it by many a long step. He realized this himself.

He was not at all offensively egotistic—simply surer, calmer, more genial, less easily ruffled; but even this was too much. Summerfield wanted a frightened man, and seeing that Eugene might be getting strong enough to slip away from him, he began to think how he should either circumvent his possible sudden flight, or discredit his fame, so that if he did leave he would gain nothing by it. Neither of them was directly manifesting any ill-will or indicating his true feelings, but such was the situation just the same. The things which Summerfield thought he might do were not easy to do under any circumstances. It was particularly hard in Eugene's case. The man was beginning to have an air. People liked him. Advertisers who met him, the big manufacturers, took note of him. They did not understand him as a trade figure, but thought he must have real force. One man—a great real estate plunger in New York, who saw him once in Summerfield's office— spoke to the latter about him.

"That's a most interesting man you have there, that man Witla," he said, when they were out to lunch together. "Where does he come from?"

"Oh, the West somewhere!" replied Summerfield evasively. "I don't know. I've had so many art directors I don't pay much attention to them."

Winfield (ex-Senator Kenyon C. Winfield, of Brooklyn) perceived a slight undercurrent of opposition and belittling. "He looks like a bright fellow," he said, intending to drop the subject.

"He is, he is," returned Summerfield; "but like all artists, he's flighty. They're the most unstable people in the world. You can't depend upon them. Good for one idea today—worth nothing tomorrow—I have to handle them like a lot of children. The weather sometimes makes all the difference in the world."

Winfield fancied this was true. Artists generally were worth nothing in business. Still, he remembered Eugene pleasantly.

As Summerfield talked here, so was it in the office and elsewhere. He began to say in the office and out that Eugene was really not doing as well as he might, and that in all likelihood he would have to drop him. It was sad; but all directors, even the best of them, had their little day of ability and usefulness, and then ran to seed. He did not see why it was that all these directors failed so, but they did. They never really made good in the company. By this method, his own undiminished ability was made to stand out free and clear, and Eugene was not able to appear as important. No one who knew anything about Eugene, however, at this time believed this; but they did believe—in the office—that he might lose his position. He was too bright—too much of a leader. They felt that this condition could not continue in a one-man concern; and this made the work harder, for it bred disloyalty in certain quarters. Some of his men were disposed to counsel with the enemy.

But as time passed and in spite of the change of attitude which was coming over Summerfield, Eugene became even stronger in his own self-esteem. He was not getting vainglorious as yet—merely sure. Because of his art work his art connections had revived considerably, and he had heard again from such men as Louis Deesa, M. Charles, Luke Severas, and others who now knew where he was and wondered why he did not come back to painting proper. M. Charles was disgusted. "A great error," he said. He always spoke of him to others as a great loss to art. Strange to relate, one of his pictures was sold the spring following his entry into the Summerfield Company, and another the following winter. Each netted him two hundred and fifty dollars, Pottle Frères being the agents in one case, Jacob Bergman in the other. These sales with their consequent calls for additional canvases to show, cheered him greatly. He felt satisfied now that if anything happened to him he could go back to his art and that he could make a living, anyhow.

There came a time when he was sent for by Mr. Alfred Cookman, the advertising agent for whom Summerfield had worked; but nothing came of that, for the latter did not care to pay more than six thousand a year and Summerfield had once told Eugene that he would eventually pay him ten thousand if he stayed with him. He did not think it was fair to leave him just then, and, besides, Cookman's firm had not the force and go and prestige which Summerfield had at this time. His real chance came some six months later, when one of the publishing houses of Philadelphia having an important weekly to market, began looking for an advertising manager.

It was the policy of this house to select young men and to select from among all the available candidates just the one particular one to suit the fancy of the owner and who had a record of successful effort behind him. Now Eugene was not any more an advertising manager by experience than he was an art director, but having worked for Summerfield for nearly two years he had come to know a great deal about advertising, and the public thought he knew a great deal more. He knew by now just how Summerfield had his business organized. He knew how he specialized his forces, giving this line to one and that line to another. He had been able to learn by sitting in conferences and consultations what it was that advertisers wanted, how they wanted their goods displayed, what they wanted said. He had learned that novelty, force and beauty were the keynotes and he had to work these elements out under the most galling fire so often that he knew how it ought to be done. He knew also about commissions, rebates, long-time contracts, and so forth. He had fancied more than once that he might run a little advertising business of his own to great profit if he only could find an honest and capable business manager or partner. Since this person was not forthcoming, he was content to bide his time.

But the Kalvin Publishing Company of Philadelphia had heard of him. In his search for a man, Obadiah Kalvin, the founder of the company, had examined many individuals through agents in Chicago, in St. Louis, in Baltimore, Boston, and New York, but he had not yet made up his mind. He was slow in his decisions, and always flattered himself that once he made a selection he was sure of a good result. He had not heard of Eugene until toward the end of his search, but one day in the Union Club in Philadelphia, when he was talking to a big advertising agent with whom he did considerable business, the latter said:

"I hear you are looking for an advertising manager for your weekly."

"I am," he said.

"I heard of a man the other day who might suit you. He's with the Summerfield Company in New York. They've been getting up some very striking ads of late, as you may have noticed."

"I think I have seen some of them," replied Kalvin.

"I'm not sure of the man's name—Witla, or Gitla, or some such thing as that; but, anyhow, he's over there, and they say he's pretty good. Just what he is in the house I don't know. You might look him up."

"Thanks; I will," replied Kalvin. He was really quite grateful, for he was not quite satisfied with any of those he had seen or heard of. He was an old man, extremely sensitive to ability, wanting to combine force with refinement if he could; he was a good Christian, and was running Christian, or rather their happy correlatives, decidedly conservative publications. When he went back to his office he consulted with his business partner, a man named Fredericks, who held but a minor share in the company, and asked him if he couldn't find out something about this promising individual. Fredericks did so. He called up Cookman, in New York, who was delighted to injure his old employee, Summerfield, to the extent of taking away his best man if he could. He told Fredericks that he thought Eugene was very capable, probably the most capable young man in the field, and in all likelihood the man he was looking for—a hustler.

"I thought once of hiring him myself here not long ago," he told Fredericks. "He has ideas, you can see that."

The next thing was a private letter from Mr. Fredericks to Mr. Witla asking if by any chance he could come over to Philadelphia the following Saturday afternoon, indicating that there was a business proposition of considerable importance which he wished to lay before him.

From the paper on which it was written Eugene could see that there was something important in the wind, and laid the matter before Angela. The latter's eyes glistened.

"I'd certainly go if I were you," she advised. "He might want to make you business manager or art director or something. You can be sure they don't intend to offer you less than you're getting now, and Mr. Summerfield certainly has not treated you very well, anyhow. You've worked like a slave for him, and he's never kept his agreement to raise your salary as much as he said he would. It may mean our having to leave New York; but that doesn't make any difference for a while. You don't intend to stay in this field, anyhow. You only want to stay long enough to get a good sound income of your own."

Angela's longing for Eugene's art career was nevertheless being slightly stilled these days by the presence and dangled lure of money. It was a great thing to be able to go downtown and buy dresses and hats to suit the seasons. It was a fine thing to be taken by Eugene Saturday afternoons and Sundays in season to Atlantic City, to Spring Lake, and Shelter Island.

"I think I will go over," he said; and he wrote Mr. Fredericks a favorable reply.

The latter met him at the central station in Philadelphia with his auto and took him out to his country place in the Haverford district. On the way he talked of everything but business—the state of the weather, the condition of the territory through which they were traveling, the day's news, the nature and interest of Eugene's present work. When they were in the Fredericks house, where they arrived in time for dinner, and while they were getting ready for it, Mr. Obadiah Kalvin dropped in—ostensibly to see his partner, but really to look at Eugene without committing himself. He was introduced to Eugene, and shook hands with him cordially. During the meal he talked with Eugene a little, though not on business, and Eugene wondered why he had been called. He suspected, knowing as he did that Kalvin was the president of the company, that the latter was there to look at him. After dinner Mr. Kalvin left, and Eugene noted that Mr. Fredericks was then quite ready to talk with him.

"The thing that I wanted you to come over and see me about is in regard to our weekly and the advertising department. We have a great paper over here, as you know," he said. "We are intending to do much more with it in the future than we have in the past even. Mr. Kalvin is anxious to get just the man to take charge of the advertising department. We have been looking for someone for quite a little while. Several people have suggested your name, and I'm rather inclined to think that Mr. Kalvin would be pleased to see you take it. His visit here today was purely accidental, but it was fortunate. He had a chance to look at you, so that if I should propose your name he will know just who you are. I think you would find this company a fine background for your efforts. We have no penny-wise-and-pound-foolish policy over here. We know that any successful thing is made by the men behind it, and we are willing to pay good money for good men. I don't know what you are getting where you are, and I don't care very much. If you are interested I should like to talk to Mr. Kalvin about you, and if he is interested I should like to bring you two together for a final conference. The salary will be made right, you needn't worry about that. Mr. Kalvin isn't a small man. If he likes a man—and I think he might like you—he'll offer you what he thinks you're worth and you can take it or leave it. I never heard anyone complain about the salary he offered."

Eugene listened with extreme self-gratulation. He was thrilling from head to toe. This was the message he had been expecting to hear for so long. He was getting five thousand now, he had been offered six thousand. Mr. Kalvin could do no less than offer him seven or eight—possibly ten. He could easily ask seven thousand five hundred.

"I must say," he said innocently, "the proposition sounds attractive to me. It's a different kind of thing—somewhat—from what I have been doing, but I think I could handle it successfully. Of course, the salary will determine the whole thing. I'm not at all badly placed where I am. I've just got comfortably settled in New York, and I'm not anxious to move. But I would not be opposed to coming. I have no contract with Mr. Summerfield. He has never been willing to give me one."

"Well, we are not keen upon contracts ourselves," said Mr. Fredericks. "It's not a very strong reed to lean upon, anyhow, as you know. Still a contract might be arranged if you wish it. Supposing we talk a little further to Mr. Kalvin today. He doesn't live so far from here," and with Eugene's consent he went to the phone.

The latter had supposed that the conversation with Mr. Kalvin was something which would necessarily have to take place at some future date; but from the conversation then and there held over the phone it appeared not. Mr. Fredericks explained elaborately over the phone—as though it was necessary—that he had been about the work of finding an advertising manager for some time, as Mr. Kalvin knew, and that he had some difficulty in finding the right man.

"I have been talking to Mr. Witla, whom you met here today, and he is interested in what I have been telling him about the *Weekly*. He strikes me from my talk with him here as being possibly the man you are looking for. I thought that you might like to talk with him further."

Mr. Kalvin evidently signified his assent, for the machine was called out and they traveled to his house, perhaps a mile away. On the way Eugene's mind was busy with the possibilities of the future. It was all so nebulous, this talk of a connection with the famous Kalvin Publishing Company; but at the same time it was so significant, so potential. Could it be possible that he was going to leave Summerfield, after all, and under such advantageous circumstances? It seemed like a dream.

Mr. Kalvin met them in the library of his house, which stood in a spacious lawn and which save for the lights in the library was quite dark and apparently lonely. And here their conversation was continued. He was a quiet man—small, gray-haired, searching in his gaze. He had, as Eugene noted, little hands and feet, and appeared as still and composed as a pool in dull weather. He said slowly and quietly that he was glad that Eugene and Mr. Fredericks had had a talk. He had heard a little something of Eugene in the past; not much. He wanted to know what Eugene thought of current advertising policies, what he thought of certain new developments in advertising method, and so on, at some length.

"So you think you might like to come with us," he observed drily toward the end, as though Eugene had proposed coming.

"I don't think I would object to coming under certain conditions," he replied.

"And what are those conditions?"

"Well, I would rather hear what you have to suggest, Mr. Kalvin. I really am not sure that I want to leave where I am. I'm doing pretty well as it is."

"Well, you seem a rather likely young man to me," said Mr. Kalvin. "You have certain qualities which I think I need. I'll say eight thousand for this year, and if everything is satisfactory one year from this time I'll make it ten. After that we'll let the future take care of itself."

"Eight thousand! Ten next year!" thought Eugene. The title of advertising manager of a great publication! This was certainly a step forward!

"Well, that isn't so bad," he said, after a moment's apparent reflection. "I'd be willing to take that, I think."

"I thought you would," said Mr. Kalvin, with a dry smile. "Well, you and Mr. Fredericks can arrange the rest of the details. Let me wish you good luck," and he extended his hand cordially.

Eugene took it.

It did not seem as he rode back in the machine with Mr. Fredericks to the latter's house—for he was invited to stay for the night—that it could really be true. Eight thousand a year! Was he eventually going to become a great business man instead of an artist? He could scarcely flatter himself that this was true, but the drift was strange. Eight thousand this year! Ten the next if he made good; twelve, fifteen, eighteen—— He had heard of such salaries in the advertising field alone, and how much more would his investments bring him. He foresaw an apartment on Riverside Drive in New York, a house in the country perhaps, for he fancied he would not always want to live in the city. An automobile of his own, perhaps; a grand piano for Angela; Sheraton or Chippendale furniture; friends, fame—what artist's career could compare to this? Did any artist he knew enjoy what he was enjoying now, even? Why should he worry about being an artist? Did they ever get anywhere? Would the approval of posterity let him ride in an automobile now? He smiled as he recalled Dula's talk about class superiority—the distinction of being an artist, even though poor. Poverty be hanged! Posterity could go to the devil! He wanted to live now—not in the approval of posterity.

CHAPTER XXXVII

The best positions are not always free from the most disturbing difficulties, for great responsibility goes with great opportunity; but Eugene went gaily to this new task, for he knew that it could not possibly be much more difficult than the one he was leaving. Truly, Summerfield had been a terrible man to work for. He had done his best by petty nagging, insisting on endless variations, the most frank and brutal criticism, to break down Eugene's imperturbable good nature and make him feel that he could not reasonably hope to handle the situation without Summerfield's co-operation and assistance. But he had only been able, by so doing, to bring out Eugene's better resources. His self-reliance, coolness under fire, ability to work long and ardently even when his heart was scarcely in it, were all strengthened and developed.

"Well, luck to you, Witla," he said, when Eugene informed him one morning that he was going to leave and wished to give him notice.

"You needn't take me into consideration. I don't want you to stay if you're going to go. The quicker the better. These long drawn-out agonies over leaving don't interest me. There's nothing in that. Clinch the job today if you want it. I'll find someone."

Eugene resented his indifference, but he only smiled a cordial smile in reply. "I'll stay a little while if you want me to—one or two weeks—I don't want to tie up your work in any way."

"Oh, no, no! You won't tie up my work. On your way, and good luck!"

"The little devil!" thought Eugene; but he shook hands and said he was sorry. Summerfield grinned imperturbably. He wound up his affairs quickly and got out. "Thank God," he said the day he left, "I'm out of that hell hole!" But he came to realize afterward that Summerfield had rendered him a great service. He had forced him to do his best and utmost, which no one had ever done before. It had told in his character, his spiritual make-up, his very appearance. He was no longer timid and nervous, but rather bold and determined-looking. He had lost that fear of very little things, for he had been sailing through stormy seas. Little storms did not—could never again—really frighten him. He had learned to fight. That was the one great thing Summerfield had done for him.

In the offices of the Kalvin Company it was radically different. Here was comparative peace and quiet. Kalvin had not fought his way up by clubbing little people through little difficulties, but had devoted himself to thinking out a few big things, and letting them because of their very bigness and newness make their own way and his. He believed in big men, honest men—the biggest and most honest he could find. He saw something in Eugene, a tendency toward perfection perhaps which attracted him.

The formalities of this new arrangement were soon concluded, and Eugene came into his new and beautiful offices, heralded by the word recently passed about that he was a most charming man. He was greeted by the editor, Townsend Miller, in the most cordial manner. He was met by his assembled staff in the most friendly spirit. It quite took Eugene's breath away to realize that he was the responsible head of some fifteen capable advertising men here in Philadelphia alone, to say nothing of eight more in a branch office in Chicago and traveling canvassers in the different parts of the country—the far West, the South, the Southwest, the Canadian Northwest. His material surroundings were much more imposing than they had been with the Summerfield Company. The idea of all these men was to follow up business, to lay interesting propositions before successful merchants and manufacturers who had not yet tried the columns of the *North American Weekly*, to make contracts which should be mutually advantageous to the advertiser and the *Weekly*, and to gain and retain good-will according to the results rendered. It was no very difficult task in connection with the *North American Weekly* to do this, because owing to a novel and appealing editorial policy it was already in possession of a circulation of five hundred thousand a week, and was rapidly gaining more. It was not difficult, as Eugene soon found, to show advertisers in most cases that this was a proposition in which worth-while results could be obtained. What with Eugene's fertility in suggesting new methods of advertising, his suaveness of approach and geniality in laying before the most recalcitrant his very desirable schemes, his ability to get ideas and suggestions out of his men in conference, he was really in no danger of not being able to hold his own, and indeed was destined to make a rather remarkable showing.

Eugene and Angela settled into what might have been deemed a fixed attitude of comfort and refinement. Without much inconvenience to himself and with little friction among those about, he had succeeded in reorganizing his staff along lines which were eminently satisfactory to himself. Some men who were formerly with the Summerfield Company were now with him. He had brought them because he found he could inculcate in them the spirit of sympathetic relationship and good understanding such as Kalvin desired. He was not making the progress which Summerfield was making with really less means at his command, but then, on the other hand, this was a rich company which did not ask or expect any such struggle as that which Summerfield had been and was still compelled to make for himself. The business ethics of this company were high. It believed in clean methods, good salaries, honest service. Kalvin liked him, and he had one memorable conversation with Eugene some time after he came there—almost a year— which stuck in his memory and did him much good. Kalvin saw clearly wherein both his strength and his weakness lay, and once said to Fredericks, his business manager: "The one thing I like about that man is his readiness with ideas. He always has one, and he's the most willing man to try I ever knew. He has imagination. He needs to be steadied in the direction of sober thought, so that he doesn't promise more than he can fulfil. Outside this I see nothing the matter with him."

Fredericks agreed. He liked Eugene also. He did as much as he could to make things smooth, but of course Eugene's task was personal and to be worked out by him solely. Kalvin said to him when it became necessary to raise his salary:

"I've watched your work for a year now and I'm going to keep my word and raise your salary. You're a good man. You have many excellent qualities which I want and need in the man who sits at that desk; but you have also some failings. I don't want you to get offended. A man in my position is always like a father who sits at the head of a family, and my lieutenants are like my sons. I have to take an interest in them because they take an interest in me. Now you've done your work well—very well, but you are subject to one fault which may sometime lead into trouble. You're a little too enthusiastic. I don't think you stop to think enough. You have a lot of ideas. They swarm in your head like bees, and sometimes you let them all out at once and they buzz around you and confuse you and everyone else connected with you. You would really be a better man if you had, not less ideas—I wouldn't say that—but better control of them. You want to do too many things at once. Go slow. Take your time. You have lots of time. You're young yet. Think! If you're in doubt, come down and consult with me. I'm older in this business than you are, and I'll help you all I can."

Eugene smiled and said: "I think that's true."

"It is true," said Kalvin; "and now I want to speak of another thing which is a little more of a personal matter, and I don't want you to take offence, for I'm saying it for your benefit. If I'm any judge of men, and I flatter myself sometimes that I am, you're a man whose greatest weakness lies—and, mind you, I have no actual evidence to go upon, not one scrap—your greatest weakness lies perhaps not so much in the direction of women as in a love of luxury generally, of which women might become, and usually are, a very conspicuous part."

Eugene flushed the least bit nervously and resentfully, for he thought he had conducted himself in the most circumspect manner here—in fact, everywhere since the days he had begun to put the Riverwood incident behind him.

"Now I suppose you wonder why I say that. Well, I raised two boys, both dead now, and one was just a little like you. You have so much imagination that it runs not only to ideas in business, but ideas in dress and comfort and friends and entertainment. Be careful of the kind of people you get in with. Stick to the conservative element. It may be hard for you, but it's best for you, materially speaking. You're the kind of man, if my observations and intuitions are correct, who is apt to be carried away by his ideals of anything—beauty, women, show. Now I have no ascetic objections to women, but to you they are dangerous, as yet. At bottom, I don't think you have the making of a real cold business man in you, but you're a splendid lieutenant. I'll tell you frankly I don't think a better man than you has ever sat, or could sit, in that chair. You are very exceptional, but your very ability makes you an uncertain quantity. You're just on the threshold of your career. This additional two thousand dollars is going to open up new opportunities to you. Keep cool. Keep out of the hands of clever people. Don't let subtle women come near. You're married, and for your sake I hope you love your wife. If you don't, pretend to, and stay within the bounds of convention. Don't let any scandal ever attach to you. If you do it will be absolutely fatal so far as I am concerned. I have had to part with a number of excellent men in my time because a little money turned their heads and they went wild over some one woman, or many women. Don't you be that way. I like you. I'd like to see you get along. Be cold if you can. Be careful. Think. That's the best advice I can give you, and I wish you luck."

He waved him a dismissal, and Eugene rose. He wondered how this man had seen so clearly into his character. It was the truth, and he knew it was. His inmost thoughts and feelings were evidently written where this man could see them. Fittingly was he president of a great company. He could read men.

He went back into his office and decided to take this lesson to heart. He must keep cool and sane always. "I guess I've had enough experience to know that, though, by now," he said and dismissed the idea from his mind.

For this year and the year following, when his salary was raised to twelve thousand, Eugene flourished prodigiously. He and Miller became better friends than ever. Miller had advertising ideas which were of value to Eugene. Eugene had art and editorial ideas which were of value to Miller. They were together a great deal at social functions, and were sometimes hailed by their companions as the "Kalvin Kids," and the "Limelight Twins." Eugene learned to play golf with Miller, though he was a slow student and never good, and also tennis. He and Mrs. Miller, Angela and Townsend, frequently made a set on their own court or over at Miller's. They automobiled and rode a great deal. Eugene met some charming women, particularly young ones, at dances, of which he had become very fond, and at dinners and receptions. They and the Millers were invited to a great many affairs, but by degrees it became apparent to him, as it did to Miller and Mrs. Miller, that his presence was much more desired by a certain type of smart woman than was that of his wife.

"Oh, he is so clever!" was an observation which might have been heard in various quarters. Frequently the compliment stopped there and nothing was said of Angela, or later on it would come up that she was not quite so nice. Not that she was not charming and worthy and all that, "But you know, my dear, she isn't quite so available. You can't use her as you can some women."

It was at this time that Angela first conceived the notion seriously that a child might have a sobering effect on Eugene. She had, in spite of the fact that for some time now they had been well able to support one or more, and in spite also of the fact that Eugene's various emotional lapses indicated that he needed a sobering weight of some kind, steadily objected in her mind to the idea of subjecting herself to this ordeal. To tell the truth, aside from the care and worry which always, owing to her early experience with her sister's children, had been associated in her mind with the presence of them, she was decidedly afraid of the result. She had heard her mother say that most girls in their infancy showed very clearly whether they were to be good healthy mothers or not—whether they were to have children—and her recollection was that her mother had once said that she would not have any children. She half believed it to be impossible in her case, though she had never told this to Eugene, and she had guarded herself jealously against the chance of having any.

Now, however, after watching Eugene all these years, seeing the drift of his present mood, feeling the influence of prosperity on him, she wished sincerely that she might have one, without great danger or discomfort to herself, in order that she might influence and control him. He might learn to love it. The sense of responsibility involved would have its effect. People would look to him to conduct himself soberly under these circumstances, and he probably would—he was so subject to public opinion now. She thought of this a long time, wondering, for fear and annoyance were quite strong influences with her, and she did nothing immediately. She listened to various women who talked with her from time to time about the child question, and decided that perhaps it was very wrong not to have children— at least one or two; that it was very likely possible that she could have one, if she wanted to. A Mrs. Sanifore who called on her quite frequently in Philadelphia—she met her at the Millers'—told her that she was sure she could have one even if she was past the usual age for first babies; for she had known so many women who had.

"If I were you, Mrs. Witla, I would see a doctor," she suggested one day. "He can tell you. I'm sure you can if you want to. They have so many ways of dieting and exercising you which make all the difference in the world. I'd like to have you come some day and see my doctor, if you will."

Angela decided that she would, for curiosity's sake, and in case she wished to act in the matter some time; and was informed by the wiseacre who examined her that in his opinion there was no doubt that she could. She would have to subject herself to a strict regimen. Her muscles would have to be softened by some form of manipulation. Otherwise, she was apparently in a healthy, normal condition and would suffer no intolerable hardship. This pleased and soothed Angela greatly. It gave her a club wherewith to strike her lord—a chain wherewith to bind him. She did not want to act at once. It was too serious a matter. She wanted time to think. But it was pleasant to know that she could do this. Unless Eugene sobered down now——

During the time in which he had been working for the Summerfield Company and since then for the Kalvin Company here in Philadelphia, Eugene, in spite of the large salary he was receiving—more each year—really had not saved so much money. Angela had seen to it that some of his earnings were invested in Pennsylvania Railroad stock, which seemed to her safe enough, and in a plot of ground two hundred by two hundred feet at Upper Montclair, New Jersey, near New York, where she and Eugene might some day want to live. His business engagements had necessitated considerable personal expenditures, his opportunity to enter the Baltusrol Golf Club, the Yere Tennis Club, the Philadelphia Country Club, and similar organizations had taken annual sums not previously contemplated, and the need of having a modest automobile, not a touring car, was obvious. His short experience with that served as a lesson, however, for it was found to be a terrific expense, entirely disproportionate to his income. After paying for endless repairs, salarying a chauffeur wearisomely, and meeting with an accident which permanently damaged the looks of his machine, he decided to give it up. They could rent autos for all the uses they would have. And so that luxury ended there.

It was curious, too, how during this time their Western home relations fell rather shadowily into the background. Eugene had not been home now for nearly two years, and Angela had seen only David of all her family since she had been in Philadelphia. In the fall of their third year there Angela's mother died and she returned to Blackwood for a short time. The following spring Eugene's father died. Myrtle moved to New York; her husband, Frank Bangs, was connected with a western furniture company which was maintaining important show rooms in New York. Myrtle had broken down nervously and taken up Christian Science, Eugene heard. Henry Burgess, Sylvia's husband, had become president of the bank with which he had been so long connected, and had sold his father's paper, the Alexandria *Appeal*, when the latter suddenly died. Marietta was promising to come to Philadelphia next year, in order, as she said, that Eugene might get her a rich husband; but Angela informed him privately that Marietta was now irrevocably engaged and would, the next year, marry a wealthy Wisconsin lumber man. Everyone was delighted to hear that Eugene was doing so well, though all regretted the lapse of his career as an artist. His fame as an advertising man was growing, and he was thought to have considerable weight in the editorial direction of the *North American Weekly*. So he flourished.

CHAPTER XXXVIII

It was in the fall of the third year that the most flattering offer of any was made him, and that without any seeking on his part, for he was convinced that he had found a fairly permanent berth and was happy among his associates. Publishing and other trade conditions were at this time in a peculiar condition, in which lieutenants of any importance in any field might well be called to positions of apparently extraordinary prominence and trust. Most of the great organizations of Eugene's day were already reaching a point where they were no longer controlled by the individuals who had founded and constructed them, but had passed into the hands of sons or holding companies, or groups of stockholders, few of whom knew much, if anything, of the businesses which they were called to engineer and protect.

Hiram C. Colfax was not a publisher at all at heart. He had come into control of the Swinton-Scudder-Davis Company by one of those curious manipulations of finance which sometimes give the care of sheep into the hands of anything but competent or interested shepherds. Colfax was sufficiently alert to handle anything in such a way that it would eventually make money for him, even if that result were finally attained by parting with it. In other words, he was a financier. His father had been a New England soap manufacturer, and having accumulated more or less radical ideas along with his wealth, had decided to propagandize in favor of various causes, the Single Tax theory of Henry George for one, Socialism for another, the promotion of reform ideas in politics generally. He had tried in various ways to get his ideas before the public, but had not succeeded very well. He was not a good speaker, not a good writer, simply a good money maker and fairly capable thinker, and this irritated him. He thought once of buying or starting a newspaper in Boston, but investigation soon showed him that this was a rather hazardous undertaking. He next began subsidizing small weeklies which should advocate his reforms, but this resulted in little. His interest in pamphleteering did bring his name to the attention of Martin W. Davis of the Swinton-Scudder-Davis Company, whose imprint on books, magazines and weeklies was as common throughout the length and breadth of the land as that of Oxford is upon the English bible.

The Swinton-Scudder-Davis Company was in sad financial straits. Intellectually, for various reasons, it had run to seed. John Jacob Swinton and Owen V. Scudder, the men with book, magazine and true literary instincts, were long since dead. Mr. Davis had tried for the various heirs and assigns involved to run it intelligently and honestly, but intelligence and honesty were of little value in this instance without great critical judgment. This he had not. The house had become filled with editors, readers, critics, foremen of manufacturing and printing departments, business managers, art directors, traveling salesmen and so on without end, each of whom might be reasonably efficient if left alone, but none of whom worked well together and all of whom used up a great deal of money.

The principal literary publication, a magazine of great prestige, was in the hands of an old man who had been editor for nearly forty years. A weekly was being run by a boy, comparatively, a youth of twenty-nine. A second magazine, devoted to adventure fiction, was in the hands of another young man of twenty-six, a national critical monthly was in the hands of salaried critics of great repute and uncompromising attitude. The book department was divided into the hands of a juvenile editor, a fiction editor, a scientific and educational editor and so on. It was Mr. Davis' task to see that competent overseers were in charge of all departments so that they might flourish and work harmoniously under him, but he was neither sufficiently wise or forceful to fill the rôle. He was old and was veered about first by one theory and then by another, and within the house were rings and cliques. One of the most influential of these—the most influential, in fact—was one which was captained and led by Florence J. White, an Irish-American, who as business manager (and really more than that, general manager under Davis) was in charge of the manufacturing and printing departments, and who because of his immense budgets for paper, ink, printing, mailing and distribution generally, was in practical control of the business.

He it was who with Davis' approval said how much was to be paid for paper, ink, composition, press work, and salaries generally. He it was who through his henchman, the head of the printing department, arranged the working schedules by which the magazines and books were to reach the presses, with the practical power to say whether they were to be on time or not. He it was who through another superintendent supervised the mailing and the stock room, and by reason of his great executive ability was coming to have a threatening control over the advertising and circulation departments.

The one trouble with White, and this was something which would affect any man who should come in through Davis' auspices, was that he knew nothing of art, literature, or science, and cared less, his only interest being in manufacture. He had risen so rapidly on the executive side that his power had outrun his financial means. Davis, the present head above him, had no means beyond his own depreciated share. Because of poor editorial judgment, the books and magazines were tottering through a serious loss of prestige to eventual failure. Something had to be done, for at that time the expenditure for three years past had been much greater than the receipts.

So Marshall P. Colfax, the father of Hiram Colfax, had been appealed to, because of his interest in reform ideas which might be to a certain extent looked upon as related to literature, and because he was reported to be a man of great wealth. Rumor reported his fortune as being anywhere between six and eight millions. The proposition which Davis had to put before him was this: that he buy from the various heirs and assigns the whole of the stock outside his (Davis') own, which amounted to somewhere about sixty-five per cent, and then come in as managing director and reorganize the company to suit himself. Davis was old. He did not want to trouble himself about the future of this company or risk his own independent property. He realized as well as anyone that what the company needed was new blood. A receivership at this juncture would injure the value of the house imprint very much indeed. White had no money, and besides he was so new and different that Davis scarcely understood what his ambitions or his true importance might be. There was no real intellectual sympathy between them. In the main, he did not like White's temperament, and so in considering what might be done for the company he passed him by.

Various consultations were held. Colfax was greatly flattered to think that this proposition should be brought to his attention at all. He had three sons, only one of whom was interested in the soap business. Edward and Hiram, the two youngest, wanted nothing to do with it. He thought this might be an outlet for the energies of one or both of them, preferably Hiram, who was more of an intellectual and scientific turn than the others, though his chief interests were financial; and besides these books and publications would give him the opportunity which he had long been seeking. His personal prestige might be immensely heightened thereby. He examined carefully into the financial phases of the situation, using his son Hiram, whose financial judgment he had faith in, as an accountant and mouthpiece, and finally, after seeing that he could secure the stock on a long-time consideration for a very moderate valuation—$1,500,000, while it was worth $3,000,000—he had his son Hiram elected director and president and proceeded to see what could be done with the company.

In this approaching transaction Florence J. White had seen his opportunity and seized it. He had realized on sight that Hiram would need and possibly appreciate all the information and assistance he could get, and being in a position to know he had laid all the facts in connection with the house plainly before him. He saw clearly where the trouble lay, the warring factions, the lack of editorial judgment, the poor financial manipulations. He knew exactly where the stock was and by what representations it could be best frightened and made to release itself cheaply. He worked vigorously for Hiram because he liked him and the latter reciprocated his regard.

"You've been a prince in this transaction, White," he said to that individual one day. "You've put things practically in my hands. I'm not going to forget it."

"Don't mention it," said White. "It's to my interest to see a real live man come in here."

"When I become president, you become vice-president, and that means twenty-five thousand a year." White was then getting twelve.

"When I become vice-president nothing will ever happen to your interests," returned the other man grimly. White was six feet tall, lean, savage, only semi-articulate. Colfax was small, wiry, excitable, with enough energy to explode a cartridge by yelling at it. He was eager, vainglorious, in many respects brilliant. He wanted to shine in the world, and he did not know how to do it as yet exactly.

The two shook hands firmly.

Some three months later Colfax was duly elected director and president, and the same meeting that elected him president elected Florence J. White vice-president. The latter was for clearing out all the old elements and letting in new blood. Colfax was for going slow, until he could see for himself what he wanted to do. One or two men were eliminated at once, an old circulation man and an old advertising man. In six months, while they were still contemplating additional changes and looking for new men, Colfax senior died, and the Swinton-Scudder-Davis Company, or at least Mr. Colfax's control of it, was willed to Hiram. So he sat there, accidentally president, and in full charge, wondering how he should make it a great success, and Florence J. White was his henchman and sworn ally.

At the time that Colfax first heard of Eugene he had been in charge of the Swinton-Scudder-Davis Company (which he was planning to reincorporate as "The United Magazines Corporation") for three years. He had made a number of changes, some radical, some conservative. He had put in an advertising man whom he was now finding unsatisfactory, and had made changes in the art and editorial departments which were more the result of the suggestions of others, principally of White, than the thoughts of his own brain. Martin W. Davis had retired. He was old and sick, and unwilling to ruminate in a back-room position. Such men as the editor of the *National Review, Swinton's Magazine,* and *Scudder's Weekly* were the only figures of importance about the place, and they were now of course immensely subsidiary to Hiram Colfax and Florence White.

The latter had introduced a rather hard, bitter atmosphere into the place. He had been raised under difficult conditions himself in a back street in Brooklyn, and had no sympathy with the airs and intellectual insipidities which characterized the editorial and literary element which filled the place. He had an Irishman's love of organization and politics, but far and away above that he had an Irishman's love of power. Because of the trick he had scored in winning the favor of Hiram Colfax at the time when the tremendous affairs of the concern were in a state of transition, he had become immensely ambitious. He wanted to be not nominally but actually director of the affairs of this house under Colfax, and he saw his way clear to do it by getting editors, art directors, department heads and assistants generally who were agreeable to him. But unfortunately he could not do this directly, for while Colfax cared little about the details of the business his hobby was just this one thing—men. Like Obadiah Kalvin, of the Kalvin Publishing Company, who, by the way, was now his one great rival, Colfax prided himself on his ability to select men. His general idea was that if he could find one more man as good as Florence White to take charge of the art, editorial and book end of the business, not from the manufacturing and commercial, but from the intellectual and spiritual ends—a man with ideas who would draw to him authors, editors, scientific writers and capable assistants generally—the fortune of the house would be made. He thought, sanely enough from some points of view, that this publishing world could be divided in this way. White bringing the inside manufacturing, purchasing and selling interests to a state of perfection; the new man, whoever he might be, bringing the ideas of the house and their literary and artistic representation up to such a state of efficiency that the whole country would know that it was once more powerful and successful. He wanted to be called the foremost publisher of his day, and then he could retire gracefully or devote himself to other financial matters as he pleased.

He really did not understand Florence J. White as well as he did himself. White was a past master at dissembling. He had no desire to see any such thing as Colfax was now planning come to pass. He could not do the things intellectually and spiritually which Colfax wanted done, nevertheless he wanted to be king under this emperor, the real power behind the throne, and he did not propose to brook any interference if he could help it. It was in his power, having the printing and composing room in his hands, to cause any man whom he greatly disliked to suffer severely. Forms could be delayed, material lost, complaints lodged as to dilatoriness in the matter of meeting schedules, and so on, ad infinitum. He had the Irishman's love of chicanery in the matter of morals. If he could get at an enemy's record and there was a flaw in it, the facts were apt to become mysteriously known at the most inconvenient times. He demanded the utmost loyalty of those who worked under him. If a man did not know enough instinctively to work intelligently for his interests, while at the same time appearing to serve the interests of the house at large only, he was soon dismissed on one pretext or another. Intelligent department heads, not sure of their own strength and seeing which way the wind was blowing, soon lined up in his course. Those whom he liked and who did his will prospered. Those whom he disliked suffered greatly in their duties, and were forever explaining or complaining to Colfax, who was not aware of White's subtlety and who therefore thought them incompetent.

Colfax, when he first heard of Eugene, was still cherishing his dream of a literary and artistic primate who should rank in power with White. He had not found him as yet, for all the men he sincerely admired and thought fitted for the position were in business for themselves. He had sounded one man after another, but to no satisfactory end. Then it became necessary to fill the position of advertising manager with someone who would make a conspicuous success of it, and he began to sound various authorities. Naturally he looked at the different advertising men working for various publications, and quickly came to the name of Eugene Witla. The latter was rumored to be making a shining success of his work. He was well liked where he was. Two different business men told Colfax that they had met him and that he was exceptionally clever. A third told him of his record with Summerfield, and through a fourth man who knew Eugene, and who was having him to lunch at the Hardware Club a few weeks later, Colfax had a chance to meet him without appearing to be interested in him in any way.

Not knowing who Colfax was, or rather very little, other than that he was president of this great rival publishing concern, Eugene was perfectly free and easy in his manner. He was never affected at any time, decidedly eager to learn things from anybody and supremely good natured.

"So you're Swinton, Scudder and Davis, are you?" he said to Colfax on introduction. "That trinity must have shrunk some to get condensed into you, but I suppose the power is all there."

"I don't know about that! I don't know about that!" exclaimed Colfax electrically. He was always ready like a greyhound to run another a race. "They tell me Swinton and Scudder were exceptionally big men. If you have as much force as you have length there's nothing the matter with you, though."

"Oh, I'm all right," said Eugene, "when I'm by myself. These little men worry me, though. They are so darned smart."

Colfax cackled ecstatically. He liked Eugene's looks. The latter's manner, easy and not in any way nervous or irritable but coupled with a heavenly alertness of eye, took his fancy. It was a fit companion for his own terrific energy, and it was not unduly soft or yielding.

"So you're the advertising manager of the *North American*. How'd they ever come to tie you down to that?"

"They didn't tie me," said Eugene. "I just lay down. But they put a nice fat salary on top of me to keep me there. I wouldn't lie down for anything except a salary."

He grinned smartly.

Colfax cackled.

"Well, my boy, it doesn't seem to be hurting your ribs, does it? They've not caved in yet. Ha! Ha!—Ha! Ha! They've not, have they? Ha! Ha!"

Eugene studied this little man with great interest. He was taken by his sharp, fierce, examining eye. He was so different from Kalvin, who was about his size, but so much more quiet, peaceful, dignified. Colfax was electric, noisy, insistent, like a pert jack-in-the-box; he seemed to be nothing but energy. Eugene thought of him as having an electric body coated over with some thin veneer of skin. He seemed as direct as a flash of lightning.

"Doing pretty good over there, are you?" he asked. "I've heard a little something about you from time to time. Not much. Not much. Just a little. Not unfavorable, though. Not unfavorable."

"I hope not," said Eugene easily. He wondered why Colfax was so interested in him. The latter kept looking him over much as one might examine a prize animal. Their eyes would meet and Colfax's would gleam with a savage but friendly fire.

"Well?" said Eugene to him finally.

"I'm just thinking, my boy! I'm just thinking!" he returned, and that was all Eugene could get out of him.

It was not long after this very peculiar meeting which stuck in Eugene's memory that Colfax invited him over to his house in New York to dinner. "I wish," he wrote one day not long after this meeting, "that the next time you are in New York you would let me know. I would like to have you come to my house to dine. You and I ought to be pretty good friends. There are a number of things I would like to talk to you about."

This was written on the paper of the United Magazines Corporation, which had just been organized to take over the old company of Swinton, Scudder and Davis, and was labeled "The Office of the President."

Eugene thought this was significant. Could Colfax be going to make him an offer of some kind? Well, the more the merrier! He was doing very well indeed, and liked Mr. Kalvin very much, in fact, all his surroundings, but, as an offer was a testimonial to merit and could be shown as such, he would not be opposed to receiving it. It might strengthen him with Kalvin if it did nothing else. He made an occasion to go over, first talking the letter over with Angela, who was simply curious about the whole thing. He told her how much interested Colfax appeared to be the first time they met and that he fancied it might mean an offer from the United Magazines Corporation at some time or other.

"I'm not particularly anxious about it," said Eugene, "but I'd like to see what is there."

Angela was not sure that it was wise to bother with it. "It's a big firm," she said, "but it isn't bigger than Mr. Kalvin's, and he's been mighty nice to you. You'd better not do anything to injure yourself with him."

Eugene thought of this. It was sound advice. Still he wanted to hear.

"I won't do anything," he said. "I would like to hear what he has to say, though."

A little later he wrote that he was coming on the twentieth and that he would be glad to take dinner with Colfax.

The first meeting between Eugene and Colfax had been conclusive so far as future friendship was concerned. These two, like Eugene and Summerfield, were temperamentally in accord, though Colfax was very much superior to Summerfield in his ability to command men.

This night when they met at dinner at Colfax's house the latter was most cordial. Colfax had invited him to come to his office, and together they went uptown in his automobile. His residence was in upper Fifth Avenue, a new, white marble fronted building with great iron gates at the door and a splendid entry set with small palms and dwarf cedars. Eugene saw at once that this man was living in that intense atmosphere of commercial and financial rivalry which makes living in New York so keen. You could feel the air of hard, cold order about the place, the insistence on perfection of appointment, the compulsion toward material display which was held in check only by that sense of fitness, which knowledge of current taste and the mode in everything demanded. His automobile was very large and very new, the latest model, a great dark blue affair which ran as silently as a sewing machine. The footman who opened the door was six feet tall, dressed in knee breeches and a swallow-tailed coat. The valet was a Japanese, silent, polite, attentive. Eugene was introduced to Mrs. Colfax, a most graceful but somewhat self-conscious woman. A French maid later presented two children, a boy and a girl.

Eugene by now had become used to luxury in various forms, and this house was not superior to many he had seen; but it ranked with the best. Colfax was most free in it. He threw his overcoat to the valet carelessly and tossed his babies in the air by turn, when they were presented to him by the French maid. His wife, slightly taller than himself, received a resounding smack.

"There, Ceta," he exclaimed (a diminutive for Cecile, as Eugene subsequently learned), "how do you like that, eh? Meet Mr. Witla. He's an artist and an art director and an advertising manager and——"

"A most humble person," put in Eugene smilingly. "Not half as bad as you may think. His report is greatly exaggerated."

Mrs. Colfax smiled sweetly. "I discount much that he says at once," she returned. "More later. Won't you come up into the library?"

They ascended together, jesting. Eugene was pleased with what he saw. Mrs. Colfax liked him. She excused herself after a little while and Colfax talked life in general. "I'm going to show you my house now, and after dinner I'm going to talk a little business to you. You interest me. I may as well tell you that."

"Well, you interest me, Colfax," said Eugene genially, "I like you."

"You don't like me any more than I like you, that's a sure thing," replied the other.

CHAPTER XXXIX

The results of this evening were most pleasant, but in some ways disconcerting. It became perfectly plain that Colfax was anxious to have Eugene desert the Kalvin Company and come over to him.

"You people over there," he said to him at one stage of the conversation, "have an excellent company, but it doesn't compare with this organization which we are revising. Why, what are your two publications to our seven? You have one eminently successful one—the one you're on—and no book business whatsoever! We have seven publications all doing excellently well, and a book business that is second to none in the country. You know that. If it hadn't been that the business had been horribly mismanaged it would never have come into my hands at all. Why, Witla, I want to tell you one little fact in connection with that organization which will illustrate everything else which might be said in connection with it before I came here! They were wasting twenty thousand dollars a year on ink alone. We were publishing a hundred absolutely useless books that did not sell enough to pay for the cost of printing, let alone the paper, plates, typework and cost of distribution. I think it's safe to say we lost over a hundred thousand dollars a year that way. The magazines were running down. They haven't waked up sufficiently yet to suit me. But I'm looking for men. I'm really looking for one man eventually who will take charge of all that editorial and art work and make it into something exceptional. He wants to be a man who can handle men. If I can get the right man I will even include the advertising department, for that really belongs with the literary and art sections. It depends on the man."

He looked significantly at Eugene, who sat there stroking his upper lip with his hand.

"Well," he said thoughtfully, "that ought to make a very nice place for someone. Who have you in mind?"

"No one as yet that I'm absolutely sure of. I have one man in mind who I think might come to fill the position after he had had a look about the organization and a chance to study its needs a little. It's a hard position to hold. It requires a man with imagination, tact, judgment. He would have to be a sort of vice-Colfax, for I can't give my attention permanently to that business. I don't want to. I have bigger fish to fry. But I want someone who will eventually be my other self in these departments, who can get along with Florence White and the men under him and hold his own in his own world. I want a sort of bi-partisan commission down there—each man supreme in his own realm."

"It sounds interesting," said Eugene thoughtfully. "Who's your man?"

"As I say, he isn't quite ready yet, in my judgment, but he is near it, and he's the right man! He's in this room now. You're the man I'm thinking about, Witla."

"No," said Eugene quietly.

"Yes; you," replied Colfax.

"You flatter me," he said, with a deprecatory wave of his hand. "I'm not so sure that he is."

"Oh, yes, he is, if he thinks he is!" replied Colfax emphatically. "Opportunity doesn't knock in vain at a real man's door. At least, I don't believe it will knock here and not be admitted. Why the advertising department of this business alone is worth eighteen thousand dollars a year to begin with."

Eugene sat up. He was getting twelve. Could he afford to ignore that offer? Could the Kalvin Company afford to pay him that much? They were paying him pretty well as it was. Could the Kalvin Company offer him the prospects which this company was offering him?

"What is more, I might say," went on Colfax, "the general publishing control of this organization—the position of managing publisher, which I am going to create and which when you are fitted for it you can have, will be worth twenty-five thousand dollars a year, and that oughtn't to be so very far away, either."

Eugene turned that over in his mind without saying anything. This offer coming so emphatically and definitely at this time actually made him nervous and fearsome. It was such a tremendous thing to talk about—the literary, art and advertising control of the United Magazines Corporation. Who was this man White? What was he like? Would he be able to agree with him? This man beside him was so hard, so brilliant, so dynamic! He would expect so much.

And then his work with Townsend Miller and under Mr. Kalvin. How much he had learned of the editorial game by merely talking and planning with those two men! He had got the whole idea of timely topics, of big progressive, national forecasts and features, of odd departments and interesting pieces of fiction and personality studies, from talking with Miller alone. Kalvin had made clear to him what constituted great craftsmen. Of course, long before, he had suspected just how it was, but in Philadelphia he had sat in conference with Miller and Kalvin, and knew. He had practically managed the former's little art department for him without paying much attention to it either. Couldn't he really handle this greater thing if he tried? If he didn't, someone else would. Would the man who would, be so much greater than himself?

"I'm not anxious that you should act hastily," said Colfax soothingly, after a little bit, for he saw that Eugene was debating the question solemnly and that it was a severe problem for him. "I know how you feel. You have gone into the Kalvin Company and you've made good. They've been nice to you. It's only natural that they should be. You hate to leave. Well, think it over. I won't tempt you beyond your best judgment. Think it over. There's a splendid chance here. Just the same, I like you, and I think you are the man to get away with it. Come down to my place tomorrow and let me show you what we have. I want to show our resources. I don't think you know how big this thing really is."

"Yes, I do," replied Eugene, smiling. "It certainly is a fascinating proposition. But I can't make up my mind about it now. It's something I want to think about. I'd like to take my time, and I'll let you know."

"Take all the time you want, my boy! Take all the time you want!" exclaimed Colfax. "I'll wait for you a little while. I'm in no life-or-death hurry. This position can't be filled satisfactorily in a minute. When you're ready, let me know what you decide. And now let's go to the theatre—what do you say?"

The automobile was called, Mrs. Colfax and her guest, Miss Genier, appeared. There was an interesting evening in a box, with Eugene talking gaily and entertainingly to all, and then an after-theatre bite at Sherry's. The next morning, for he stayed all night at Colfax's, they visited the United Magazines Corporation building together, and at noon Eugene returned to Philadelphia.

His head was fairly seething and ringing with all he had seen and heard. Colfax was a great man, he thought, greater in some respects than Kalvin. He was more forceful, more enthusiastic, younger—more like himself, than Kalvin. He could never fail, he was too rich. He would make a success of this great corporation—a tremendous success—and if he went he might help make it with him. What a thing that would be! Very different from working for a corporation with whose success he had never had anything to do. Should he ignore this offer? New York, a true art and literary standing;

a great executive and social standing; fame; money—all these were calling. Why, on eighteen or twenty-five thousand he could have a splendid studio apartment of his own, say on Riverside Drive; he could entertain magnificently; he could keep an automobile without worrying about it. Angela would cease feeling that they had to be careful. It would be the apex of lieutenantship for him. Beyond that he would take stock in the company, or a business of his own. What a long distance he had come from the days when, here as a boy, he had walked the streets, wondering where he would find a $3 room, and when as an art failure he carried his paintings about and sold them for ten and fifteen dollars. Dear Heaven, what peculiar tricks fortune could play!

The discussion with Angela of this proposition led to some additional uncertainty, for although she was greatly impressed with what Colfax offered, she was afraid Eugene might be making a mistake in leaving Kalvin. The latter had been so nice to Eugene. He had never associated with him in any intimate way, but he and Angela had been invited to his home on several formal occasions, and Eugene had reported that Kalvin was constantly giving him good advice. His attitude in the office was not critical but analytic and considerate.

"He's been mighty nice to me," Eugene said to her one morning at breakfast; "they all have. It's a shame to leave him. And yet, now that I look at it, I can see very plainly that there is never going to be the field here that there will be with the United Company. They have the publications and the book business, and the Kalvin Company hasn't and won't have. Kalvin is too old. They're in New York, too; that's one thing I like about it. I'd like to live in New York again. Wouldn't you?"

"It would be fine," said Angela, who had never really cared for Philadelphia and who saw visions of tremendous superiority in this situation. Philadelphia had always seemed a little out of the way of things after New York and Paris. Only Eugene's good salary and the comforts they had experienced here had made it tolerable. "Why don't you speak to Mr. Kalvin and tell him just what Mr. Colfax says," she asked. "It may be that he'll offer to raise your salary so much that you'll want to stay when he hears of this."

"No danger," replied Eugene. "He may raise it a bit, but he never can pay me twenty-five thousand dollars a year. There isn't any reason for paying it. It takes a corporation like the United to do it. There isn't a man in our place gets that, unless it is Fredericks. Besides, I could never be anything more here, or much more, than advertising manager. Miller has that editorial job sewed up. He ought to have it, too, he's a good man. This thing that Colfax offers lets me out into a new field. I don't want to be an advertising manager all my days if I can help it!"

"I don't want you to be, either, Eugene," sighed Angela. "It's a shame you can't quit entirely and take up your art work. I've always thought that if you were to stop now and go to painting you would make a success of it. There's nothing the matter with your nerves now. It's just a question of whether we want to live more simply for a while and let you work at that. I'm sure you'd make a big success of it."

"Art doesn't appeal to me so much as it did once," replied Eugene. "I've lived too well and I know a lot more about living than I once did. Where could I make twelve thousand a year painting? If I had a hundred thousand or a couple of hundred thousand laid aside, it would be a different thing, but I haven't. All we have is that Pennsylvania Railroad stock and those lots in Montclair eating their merry little heads off in taxes, and that Steel common stock. If we go back to New York we ought to build on that Montclair property, and rent it if we don't want to live in it. If I quit now we wouldn't have more than two thousand dollars a year outside of what I could earn, and what sort of a life can you live on that?"

Angela saw, disappearing under those circumstances, the rather pleasant world of entertainment in which they were disporting themselves. Art distinction might be delightful, but would it furnish such a table as they were sitting at this morning? Would they have as nice a home and as many friends? Art was glorious, but would they have as many rides and auto trips as they had now? Would she be able to dress as nicely? It took money to produce a variety of clothing—house, street, evening, morning and other wear. Hats at thirty-five and forty dollars were not in the range of artists' wives, as a rule. Did she want to go back to a simpler life for his art's sake? Wouldn't it be better to have him go with Mr. Colfax and make $25,000 a year for a while and then have him retire?

"You'd better talk to Mr. Kalvin," she counseled. "You'll have to do that, anyhow. See what he says. After that you can decide what you must do."

Eugene hesitated, but after thinking it all over he decided that he would.

One morning not long after, when he met Mr. Kalvin in the main hall on the editorial floor, he said, "I'd like to talk to you for a few moments some time today alone, Mr. Kalvin, if you can spare me the time."

"Certainly. I'm not busy now," returned the president. "Come right down. What is it you want to see me about?"

"Well, I'll tell you," said Eugene, when they had reached the former's office and he had closed the door. "I've had an offer that I feel that I ought to talk to you about. It's a pretty fascinating proposition and it's troubling me. I owe it to you as well as to myself to speak about it."

"Yes; what is it?" said Kalvin considerately.

"Mr. Colfax of the United Magazines Corporation came to me not long ago and wanted to know if I would not come with him. He offers me eighteen thousand dollars a year as advertising manager to begin with, and a chance to take charge of all the art and editorial ends as well a little later at twenty-five thousand dollars. He calls it the managing-publishing end of the business. I've been thinking of it seriously, for I've handled the art and advertising ends here and at the Summerfield Company, and I have always imagined that I knew something of the book and magazine business. I know it's a rather large proposition, but I'm not at all sure that I couldn't handle it.".

Mr. Kalvin listened quietly. He saw what Colfax's scheme was and liked it as a proposition. It was a good idea, but needed an exceptional man for the position. Was Eugene the man? He wasn't sure of that, and yet perchance he might be. Colfax, he thought, was a man of excellent financial if not publishing judgment. He might, if he could get the proper person, make an excellent success of his business. Eugene interested him, perhaps more at first flash than he would later. This man before him had a most promising appearance. He was clean, quick, with an alert mind and eye. He could see how, because of Eugene's success here, Colfax was thinking of him being even more exceptional than he was. He was a good man, a fine man, under direction. Would Colfax have the patience, the interest, the sympathy, to work with and understand him?

"Now, let's think about that a little, Witla," he said quietly. "It's a flattering offer. You'd be foolish if you didn't give it careful consideration. Do you know anything about the organization of that place over there?"

"No," replied Eugene, "nothing except what I learned by casually going over it with Mr. Colfax."

"Do you know much about Colfax as a man?"

"Very little. I've only met him twice. He's forceful, dramatic, a man with lots of ideas. I understand he's very rich, three or four millions, someone told me."

Kalvin's hand moved indifferently. "Do you like him?"

"Well, I can't say yet absolutely whether I do or don't. He interests me a lot. He's wonderfully dynamic. I'm sure I'm favorably impressed with him."

"And he wants to give you charge eventually of all the magazines and books, the publishing end?"

"So he says," said Eugene.

"I'd go a little slow if I were saddling myself with that responsibility. I'd want to be sure that I knew all about it. You want to remember, Witla, that running one department under the direction and with the sympathetic assistance and consideration of someone over you is very different from running four or five departments on your own responsibility and with no one over you except someone who wants intelligent guidance from you. Colfax, as I understand him, isn't a publisher, either by tendency or training or education. He's a financier. He'll want you, if you take that position, to tell him how it shall be done. Now, unless you know a great deal about the publishing business, you have a difficult task in that. I don't want to appear to be throwing cold water on your natural ambition to get up in the world. You're entitled to go higher if you can. No one in your circle of acquaintances would wish you more luck than I will if you decide to go. I want you to think carefully of what you are doing. Where you are here you are perfectly safe, or as nearly safe as any man is who behaves himself and maintains his natural force and energy can be. It's only natural that you should expect more money in the face of this offer, and I shall be perfectly willing to give it to you. I intended, as you possibly expected, to do somewhat better for you by January. I'll say now that if you want to stay here you can have fourteen thousand now and possibly sixteen thousand in a year or a year and a half from now. I don't want to overload this department with what I consider an undue salary. I think sixteen thousand dollars, when it is paid, will be high for the work that is done here, but you're a good man and I'm perfectly willing to pay it to you.

The thing for you to do is to make up your mind whether this proposition which I now make you is safer and more in accord with your desires than the one Mr. Colfax makes you. With him your eighteen thousand begins at once. With me sixteen thousand is a year away, anyhow. With him you have promise of an outlook which is much more glittering than any you can reasonably hope for here, but you want to remember that the difficulties will be, of course, proportionately greater. You know something about me by now. You still—and don't think I want to do him any injustice; I don't—have to learn about Mr. Colfax. Now, I'd advise you to think carefully before you act. Study the situation over there before you accept it. The United

Magazines Corporation is a great concern. I have no doubt that under Mr. Colfax's management it has a brilliant future in store for it. He is an able man. If you finally decide to go, come and tell me and there will be no hard feelings one way or the other. If you decide to stay, the new salary arrangement goes into effect at once. As a matter of fact, I might as well have Mr. Fredericks credit that up to you so that you can say that you have drawn that sum here. It won't do you any harm. Then we can run along as before. I know it isn't good business as a rule to try and keep a man who has been poisoned by a bigger offer, and because I know that is the reason why I am only offering you fourteen thousand dollars this year. I want to be sure that you are sure that you want to stay. See?"

He smiled.

Eugene arose. "I see," he said. "You are one of the best men I have ever known, Mr. Kalvin. You have constantly treated me with more consideration than I ever expected to receive anywhere. It has been a pleasure and a privilege to work for you. If I stay, it will be because I want to because I value your friendship."

"Well," said Kalvin quietly, "that's very nice, I'm sure, and I appreciate it. But don't let your friendship for me or your sense of gratitude stop you from doing something you think you ought to do. Go ahead if you feel like it. I won't feel the least bit angry with you. I'll feel sorry, but that's neither here nor there. Life is a constant condition of readjustment, and every good business man knows it."

He took Eugene's extended hand.

"Good luck," he said, "whatever you do"—his favorite expression.

CHAPTER XL

The upshot of Eugene's final speculation was that he accepted the offer of the United Magazines Corporation and left Mr. Kalvin. Colfax had written one day to his house asking him what he thought he would do about it. The more he had turned it over in his mind, the more it had grown in attraction. The Colfax company was erecting a tremendous building, eighteen stories high, in the heart of the middle business district in New York near Union Square, to house all their departments. Colfax had said at the time Eugene took dinner with him that the sixteenth, seventeenth and eighteenth floors would be devoted to the editorial, publication, circulation, art, and advertising departments. He had asked Eugene what he had thought would be a good floor arrangement, and the latter, with his usual facility for scheming such things, had scratched on a piece of paper a tentative layout for the various departments. He had put the editorial and art departments on the topmost floor, giving the publisher, whoever he might eventually prove to be, a commanding position in a central room on the western side of the building which overlooked all the city between the Square and Hudson River, and showed that magnificent body of water as a panorama for the eye to feast upon. He had put the advertising and some overflow editorial rooms on the seventeenth floor, and the circulation with its attendant mailing and cabinet record rooms on the sixteenth. The publisher's and editor's rooms he laid out after an old Flemish scheme he had long had in mind, in which green, dark blue, blood-red and black walnut shades contrasted richly with the flood of light which would be available.

"You might as well do this thing right if you do it at all," he had said to Colfax. "Nearly all the editorial offices I have ever seen have been the flimsiest makeshifts. A rich-looking editorial, art and advertising department would help your company a great deal. It has advertising value."

He recalled as he spoke Summerfield's theory that a look of prosperity was about the most valuable asset a house could have.

Colfax agreed with him, and said when the time came that he wished Eugene would do him the favor to come and look the thing over. "I have two good architects on the job," he explained, "but I would rather trust your ideas as to how those rooms should be laid out."

When he was considering this final call for a decision he was thinking how this floor would look—how rich it would be. Eventually, if he succeeded, his office would be the most sumptuous thing in it. He would be the most conspicuous figure in the great, new building, apart from Colfax himself.

Thoughts of this kind, which ought to have had but very little share in any commercial speculation, were nevertheless uppermost in Eugene's mind; for he was not a business man—he was primarily an artist, and for all his floundering round in the commercial world he remained an artist still. His sense of his coming dignity and standing before the world was almost greater than his sense of the terrifying responsibility which it involved. Colfax was a hard man, he knew, harder even than Summerfield, for he talked less and acted more; but this did not sink into Eugene's consciousness sufficiently to worry him. He fancied he was a strong man, able to hold his own anywhere.

Angela was really not very much opposed to the change, though her natural conservatism made her worry and hesitate to approve. It was a great step forward if Eugene succeeded, but if he failed it would be such a loss.

"Colfax has so much faith in me," he told her. "He's convinced that I can do it, and faith like that is a great help. I'd like to try it, anyhow. It can't do me any harm. If I think I can't handle the publishing proposition I'll stick to the advertising end."

"All right," said Angela, "but I scarcely know what to advise. They've been so nice to you over here."

"I'll try it," said Eugene determinedly. "Nothing venture, nothing have," and he informed Kalvin the same day.

The latter looked at him solemnly, his keen gray eyes contemplating the situation from all points of view. "Well, Eugene," he said, "you're shouldering a great responsibility. It's difficult. Think carefully of everything that you do. I'm sorry to see you go. Good-bye."

He had the feeling that Eugene was making a mistake—that he would do better to rest a while where he was; but persuasion was useless. It would only give Eugene the notion that he was more important than he was— make matters more difficult in the future.

Kalvin had heard a number of things concerning Colfax recently, and he fancied that Eugene might find it hard to deal with him later. The general impression was that he was subject to sudden likes and dislikes which did not bear the test of time. He was said to be scarcely human enough to be the effective head of a great working corporation.

The truth was that this general opinion was quite correct. Colfax was as hard as steel but of a smiling and delightful presence to those he fancied. Vanity was really his other name, and ambition with him knew no bounds. He hoped to make a tremendous success of his life, to be looked up to as an imposing financier, and he wanted *men*—only strong men about him. Eugene seemed to Colfax to be a strong man, and the day he finally communicated with him saying that he thought that he would accept his offer but that he wished to talk to him further, Colfax threw his hat up in the air, slapped his side partner White on the back, and exclaimed: "Whee! Florrie! There's a trick I've scored for this corporation. There's a man, unless I am greatly mistaken, will do something here. He's young but he's all right. He's got the looks on you and me, Florrie, but we can stand that, can't we?"

White eyed him, with a show of joy and satisfaction which was purely simulated. He had seen many editors and many advertising men in his time. To his judgment they were nearly all lightweights, men who were easily satisfied with the little toy wherewith he or anyone might decide to gratify their vanity. This was probably another case in point, but if a real publisher were coming in here it would not be so well with him. He might attempt to crowd in on his authority or at least divide it with him. That did not appeal to his personal vanity. It really put a stumbling block in his path, for he hoped to rule here some day alone. Why was it that Colfax was so eager to have the authority in this house divided? Was it because he was somewhat afraid of him? He thought so, and he was exceedingly close to the truth when he thought so.

"Florrie's a good lieutenant," Colfax said to himself, "but he needs to be counterbalanced here by someone who will represent the refinements and that intellectual superiority which the world respects."

He wanted this refinement and intellectual superiority to be popular with the public, and to produce results in the shape of increased circulation for his magazines and books. These two would then act as checks each to the other, thus preventing the house from becoming overweighted in either direction. Then he could drive this team as a grand master—the man who had selected both, whose ideas they represented, and whose judgment they respected. The world of finance and trade would know they were nothing without him.

What Eugene thought and what White thought of this prospective situation was that the other would naturally be the minor figure, and that he under Colfax would be the shining light. Eugene was convinced that the house without proper artistic and intellectual dominance was nothing. White was convinced that without sane commercial management it was a failure and that this was the thing to look to. Money could buy brains.

Colfax introduced Eugene to White on the morning he arrived to take charge, for on the previous occasions when he had been there White was absent. The two looked at each other and immediately suspended judgment, for both were able men. Eugene saw White as an interesting type—tall, leathery, swaggering, a back-street bully evolved into the semblance of a gentleman. White saw in Eugene a nervous, refined, semi-emotional literary and artistic type who had, however, a curious versatility and virility not common among those whom he had previously encountered. He was exceedingly forceful but not poised. That he could eventually undermine him if he could not dominate him he did not doubt. Still he was coming in with the backing of Colfax and a great reputation, and it might not be easy. Eugene made him feel nervous. He wondered as he looked at him whether Colfax would really make him general literary, artistic and advertising administrator, or whether he would remain simply advertising manager as he now entered. Colfax had not accepted Eugene for more than that.

"Here he is, Florrie," Colfax had said of Eugene, in introducing him to White. "This is the man I've been talking about. Witla—Mr. White. White—Mr. Witla. You two want to get together for the good of this house in the future. What do you think of each other?"

Eugene had previously noted the peculiarity of this rowdy, rah! rah! attitude on the part of Colfax. He seemed to have no sense of the conventions of social address and conference at any time.

"Now, by God," Colfax exclaimed, striking his right fist against his left palm, "unless I am greatly mistaken, this house is going to begin to move! I'm not positive that I have the man I want, but I think I have. White, let's stroll around and introduce him."

White swaggered to the office door.

"Sure," he said quietly. "An exceptional man," he said to himself.

Colfax was almost beside himself with satisfaction, for he was subject to emotional flushes which, however, related to self-aggrandizement only. He walked with a great stride (little as he was), which was his wont when he was feeling particularly satisfied. He talked in a loud voice, for he wanted everyone to know that he, Hiram Colfax, was about and as forceful as the lord of so great an institution should be. He could yell and scream something like a woman in a paroxysm of rage when he was thwarted or irritated. Eugene did not know that as yet.

"Here's one of the printing floors," he said to Eugene, throwing open a door which revealed a room full of thundering presses of giant size. "Where's Dodson, boy? Where's Dodson? Tell him to come here. He's foreman of our printing department," he added, turning to Eugene, as the printer's devil, who had been working at a press, scurried away to find his master. "I told you, I guess, that we have thirty of these presses. There are four more floors just like this."

"So you did," replied Eugene. "It certainly is a great concern. I can see that the possibilities of a thing like this are almost limitless."

"Limitless—I should say! It depends on what you can do with this," and he tapped Eugene's forehead. "If you do your part right, and he does his"—turning to White—"there won't be any limit to what this house can do. That remains to be seen."

Just then Dodson came bustling up, a shrewd, keen henchman of White's, and looked at Eugene curiously.

"Dodson, Mr. Witla, the new advertising manager. He's going to try to help pay for all this wasteful presswork you're doing. Witla, Mr. Dodson, manager of the printing department."

The two men shook hands. Eugene felt in a way as though he were talking to an underling, and did not pay very definite attention to him. Dodson resented his attitude somewhat, but gave no sign. His loyalty was to White, and he felt himself perfectly safe under that man's supervision.

The next visit was to the composing room where a vast army of men were working away at type racks and linotype machines. A short, fat, ink-streaked foreman in a green striped apron that looked as though it might have been made of bed ticking came forward to greet them ingratiatingly. He was plainly nervous at their presence, and withdrew his hand when Eugene offered to take it.

"It's too dirty," he said. "I'll take the will for the deed, Mr. Witla."

More explanations and laudations of the extent of the business followed.

Then came the circulation department with its head, a tall dark man who looked solemnly at Eugene, uncertain as to what place he was to have in the organization and uncertain as to what attitude he should ultimately have to take. White was "butting into his affairs," as he told his wife, and he did not know where it would end. He had heard rumors to the effect that there was to be a new man soon who was to have great authority over various departments. Was this he?

There came next the editors of the various magazines, who viewed this triumphal procession with more or less contempt, for to them both Colfax and White were raw, uncouth upstarts blazoning their material superiority in loud-mouthed phrases. Colfax talked too loud and was too vainglorious. White was too hard, bitter and unreasoning. They hated them both with a secret hate but there was no escaping their domination. The need of living salaries held all in obsequious subjection.

"Here's Mr. Marchwood," Colfax said inconsiderately of the editor of the *International Review*. "He thinks he's making a wonderful publication of that, but we don't know whether he is yet or not."

Eugene winced for Marchwood. He was so calm, so refined, so professional.

"I suppose we can only go by the circulation department," he replied simply, attracted by Eugene's sympathetic smile.

"That's all! That's all!" exclaimed Colfax.

"That is probably true," said Eugene, "but a good thing ought to be as easily circulated as a poor one. At least it's worth trying."

Mr. Marchwood smiled. It was a bit of intellectual kindness in a world of cruel comment.

"It's a great institution," said Eugene finally, on reaching the president's office again. "I'll begin now and see what I can do."

"Good luck, my boy. Good luck!" said Colfax loudly. "I'm laying great stress on what you're going to do, you know."

"Don't lean too hard," returned Eugene. "Remember, I'm just one in a great organization."

"I know, I know, but *the one* is all I need up there—*the one*, see?"

"Yes, yes," laughed Eugene, "cheer up. We'll be able to do a little something, I'm sure."

"A great man, that," Colfax declared to White as he went away. "The real stuff in that fellow, no flinching there you notice. He knows how to think. Now, Florrie, unless I miss my guess you and I are going to get somewhere with this thing."

White smiled gloomily, almost cynically. He was not so sure. Eugene was pretty good, but he was obviously too independent, too artistic, to be really stable and dependable. He would never run to him for advice, but he would probably make mistakes. He might lose his head. What must he do to offset this new invasion of authority? Discredit him? Certainly. But he needn't worry about that. Eugene would do something. He would make mistakes of some kind. He felt sure of it. He was almost positive of it.

CHAPTER XLI

The opening days of this their second return to New York were a period of great joy to Angela. Unlike that first time when she was returning after seven months of loneliness and unhappiness to a sick husband and a gloomy outlook, she was now looking forward to what, in spite of her previous doubts, was a glorious career of dignity, prosperity and abundance. Eugene was such an important man now. His career was so well marked and in a way almost certified. They had a good bit of money in the bank. Their investments in stocks, on which they obtained a uniform rate of interest of about seven per cent., aggregated $30,000. They had two lots, two hundred by two hundred, in Montclair, which were said to be slowly increasing in value and which Eugene now estimated to be worth about six thousand. He was talking about investing what additional money he might save in stocks bearing better interest or some sound commercial venture. When the proper time came, a little later, he might even abandon the publishing field entirely and renew his interest in art. He was certainly getting near the possibility of this.

The place which they selected for their residence in New York was in a new and very sumptuous studio apartment building on Riverside Drive near Seventy-ninth Street, where Eugene had long fancied he would like to live. This famous thoroughfare and show place with its restricted park atmosphere, its magnificent and commanding view of the lordly Hudson, its wondrous woods of color and magnificent sunsets had long taken his eye. When he had first come to New York it had been his delight to stroll here watching the stream of fashionable equipages pour out towards Grant's Tomb and return. He had sat on a park bench many an afternoon at this very spot or farther up, and watched the gay company of horsemen and horsewomen riding cheerfully by, nodding to their social acquaintances, speaking to the park keepers and road scavengers in a condescending and superior way, taking their leisure in a comfortable fashion and looking idly at the river. It seemed a wonderful world to him at that time. Only millionaires could afford to live there, he thought—so ignorant was he of the financial tricks of the world. These handsomely garbed men in riding coats and breeches; the chic looking girls in stiff black hats, trailing black riding skirts, yellow gloved, and sporting short whips which looked more like dainty canes than anything else, took his fancy greatly. It was his idea at that time that this was almost the apex of social glory—to be permitted to ride here of an afternoon.

Since then he had come a long way and learned a great deal, but he still fancied this street as one of the few perfect expressions of the elegance and luxury of metropolitan life, and he wanted to live on it. Angela was given authority, after discussion, to see what she could find in the way of an apartment of say nine or eleven rooms with two baths or more, which should not cost more than three thousand or three thousand five hundred. As a matter of fact, a very handsome apartment of nine rooms and two baths including a studio room eighteen feet high, forty feet long and twenty-two feet wide was found at the now, to them, comparatively moderate sum of three thousand two hundred. The chambers were beautifully finished in old English oak carved and stained after a very pleasing fifteenth century model, and the walls were left to the discretion of the incoming tenant. Whatever was desired in the way of tapestries, silks or other wall furnishing would be supplied.

Eugene chose green-brown tapestries representing old Rhine Castles for his studio, and blue and brown silks for his wall furnishings elsewhere. He now realized a long cherished dream of having the great wooden cross of brown stained oak, ornamented with a figure of the bleeding Christ, which he set in a dark shaded corner behind two immense wax candles set in tall heavy bronze candlesticks, the size of small bed posts. These when lighted in an otherwise darkened room and flickering ruefully, cast a peculiar spell of beauty over the gay throngs which sometimes assembled here. A grand piano in old English oak occupied one corner, a magnificent music cabinet in French burnt woodwork, stood near by. There were a number of carved and fluted high back chairs, a carved easel with one of his best pictures displayed, a black marble pedestal bearing a yellow stained marble bust of Nero, with his lascivious, degenerate face, scowling grimly at the world, and two gold plated candelabra of eleven branches each hung upon the north wall.

Two wide, tall windows with storm sashes, which reached from the floor to the ceiling, commanded the West view of the Hudson. Outside one was a small stone balcony wide enough to accommodate four chairs, which gave a beautiful, cool view of the drive. It was shielded by an awning in summer and was nine storeys above the ground. Over the water of the more or less peaceful stream were the stacks and outlines of a great factory, and in the roadstead lay boats always, war vessels, tramp freighters, sail boats, and up and down passed the endless traffic of small craft always so pleasant to look upon in fair or foul weather. It was a beautiful apartment, beautifully finished in which most of their furniture, brought from Philadelphia, fitted admirably. It was here that at last they settled down to enjoy the fruit of that long struggle and comparative victory which brought them so near their much desired goal—an indestructible and unchangeable competence which no winds of ill fortune could readily destroy.

Eugene was quite beside himself with joy and satisfaction at thus finding himself and Angela eventually surrounded by those tokens of luxury, comfort and distinction which had so long haunted his brain. Most of us go through life with the furniture of our prospective castle well outlined in mind, but with never the privilege of seeing it realized. We have our pictures, our hangings, our servitors well and ably selected. Eugene's were real at last.

CHAPTER XLII

The affairs of the United Magazines Corporation, so far as the advertising, commercial and manufacturing ends at least were concerned, were not in such an unfortunate condition by any means as to preclude their being quickly restored by tact, good business judgment and hard work. Since the accession to power of Florence White in the commercial and financial ends, things in that quarter at least had slowly begun to take a turn for the better. Although he had no judgment whatsoever as to what constituted a timely article, an important book or a saleable art feature, he had that peculiar intuition for right methods of manufacture, right buying and right selling of stock, right handling of labor from the cost and efficiency point of view, which made him a power to be reckoned with. He knew a good manufacturing man to employ at sight. He knew where books could be sold and how. He knew how to buy paper in large quantities and at the cheapest rates, and how to print and manufacture at a cost which was as low as could possibly be figured. All waste was eliminated. He used his machines to their utmost capacity, via a series of schedules which saved an immense amount of waste and demanded the least possible help. He was constantly having trouble with the labor unions on this score, for they objected to a policy which cut out duplication of effort and so eliminated their men. He was an iron master, however, coarse, brutal, foul when dealing with them, and they feared and respected him.

In the advertising end of the business things had been going rather badly, for the reason that the magazines for which this department was supposed to get business had not been doing so well editorially. They were out of touch with the times to a certain extent—not in advance of the feelings and emotions of the period, and so the public was beginning to be inclined to look elsewhere for its mental pabulum. They had had great circulation and great prestige. That was when they were younger, and the original publishers and editors in their prime. Since then days of weariness, indifference and confusion had ensued. Only with the accession of Colfax to power had hope begun to return. As has been said, he was looking for strong men in every quarter of this field, but in particular he was looking for one man who would tell him how to govern them after he had them. Who was to dream out the things which would interest the public in each particular magazine proposition? Who was to draw great and successful authors to the book end of the house? Who was to inspire the men who were directing the various departments with the spirit which would bring public interest and success? Eugene might be the man eventually he hoped, but how soon? He was anxious to hurry his progress now that he had him.

It was not long after Eugene was seated in his advertising managerial chair that he saw how things lay. His men, when he gathered them in conference, complained that they were fighting against falling circulations.

"You can talk all you want, Mr. Witla," said one of his men gloomily, "but circulation and circulation only is the answer. They have to keep up the magazines here. All these manufacturers know when they get results. We go out and get new business all the time, but we don't keep it. We can't keep it. The magazines don't bring results. What are you going to do about that?"

"I'll tell you what we are going to do," replied Eugene calmly, "we're going to key up the magazines. I understand that a number of changes are coming in that direction. They are doing better already. The manufacturing department, for one thing, is in splendid shape. I know that. In a short time the editorial departments will be. I want you people to put up, at this time, the best fight you know how under the conditions as they are. I'm not going to make any changes here if I can help it. I'm going to show you how it can be done—each one separately. I want you to believe that we have the greatest organization in the world, and it can be made to sweep everything before it. Take a look at Mr. Colfax. Do you think he is ever going to fail? We may, but he won't."

The men liked Eugene's manner and confidence. They liked his faith in them, and it was not more than ten days before he had won their confidence completely. He took home to the hotel where he and Angela were stopping temporarily all the magazines, and examined them carefully. He took home a number of the latest books issued, and asked Angela to read them. He tried to think just what it was each magazine should represent, and who and where was the man who would give to each its proper life and vigor. At once, for the adventure magazine, he thought of a man whom he had met years before who had since been making a good deal of a success editing a Sunday newspaper magazine supplement, Jack Bezenah. He had started out to be a radical writer, but had tamed down and become a most efficient newspaper man. Eugene had met him several times in the last few years and each time had been impressed by the force and subtlety of his judgment of life. Once he had said to him, "Jack, you ought to be editing a magazine of your own."

"I will be, I will be," returned that worthy. Now as he looked at this particular proposition Bezenah stuck in his mind as the man who should be employed. He had seen the present editor, but he seemed to have no force at all.

The weekly needed a man like Townsend Miller—where would he find him? The present man's ideas were interesting but not sufficiently general in their appeal. Eugene went about among the various editors looking at them, ostensibly making their acquaintance, but he was not satisfied with any one of them.

He waited to see that his own department was not needing any vast effort on his part before he said to Colfax one day:

"Things are not right with your editorial department. I've looked into my particular job to see that there is nothing so radically behindhand there but what it can be remedied, but your magazines are not right. I wish, aside from salary proposition entirely, that you would let me begin to make a few changes. You haven't the right sort of people upstairs. I'll try not to move too fast, but you couldn't be worse off than you are now in some instances."

"I know it!" said Colfax. "I know it! What do you suggest?"

"Simply better men, that's all," replied Eugene. "Better men with newer ideas. It may cost you a little more money at present, but it will bring you more back in the long run."

"You're right! You're right!" insisted Colfax enthusiastically. "I've been waiting for someone whose judgment I thought was worth two whoops to come and tell me that for a long time. So far as I'm concerned you can take charge right now! The salary that I promised you goes with it. I want to tell you something, though! I want to tell you something! You're going in there now with full authority, but don't you fall or stub your toe or get sick or make any mistakes. If you do, God help you! if you do, I'll eat you alive! I'm a good employer, Witla. I'll pay any price for good men, within reason, but if I think I'm being done, or made a fool of, or a man is making a mistake, then there's no mercy in me—not a single bit. I'm a plain, everyday blank, blank, blank" (and he used a term so foul that it would not bear repetition in print), "and that's all there is to me. Now we understand each other."

Eugene looked at the man in astonishment. There was a hard, cold gleam in his blue eyes which he had seen there before. His presence was electric—his look demoniac.

"I've had a remark somewhat of that nature made to me before," commented Eugene. He was thinking of Summerfield's "the coal shute for yours." He had hardly expected to hear so cold and definite a proposition laid down so soon after his entry upon his new duties, but here it was, and he had to face it. He was sorry for the moment that he had ever left Kalvin.

"I'm not at all afraid of responsibility," replied Eugene grimly. "I'm not going to fall down or stub my toe or make any mistakes if I can help it. And if I do I won't complain to you."

"Well, I'm only telling you," said Colfax, smiling and good-natured again. The cold light was gone. "And I mean it in the best way in the world. I'll back you up with all power and authority, but if you fail, God help you; I can't."

He went back to his desk and Eugene went upstairs. He felt as though the red cap of a cardinal had been put upon his head, and at the same time an axe suspended over him. He would have to think carefully of what he was doing from now on. He would have to go slow, but he would have to go. All power had been given him—all authority. He could go upstairs now and discharge everybody in the place. Colfax would back him up, but he would have to replace them. And that quickly and effectively. It was a trying hour, notable but grim.

His first move was to send for Bezenah. He had not seen him for some time, but his stationery which he now had headed "The United Magazines Corporation," and in one corner "Office of the Managing Publisher," brought him fast enough. It was a daring thing to do in a way thus to style himself managing publisher, when so many able men were concerned in the work, but this fact did not disturb him. He was bound and determined to begin, and this stationery—the mere engraving of it—was as good a way as any of serving notice that he was in the saddle. The news flew like wild fire about the building, for there were many in his office, even his private stenographer, to carry the news. All the editors and assistants wondered what it could mean, but they asked no questions, except among themselves. No general announcement had been made. On the same stationery he sent for Adolph Morgenbau, who had exhibited marked skill at Summerfield's as his assistant, and who had since become art editor of *The Sphere*, a magazine of rising importance. He thought that Morgenbau might now be fitted to handle the art work under him, and he was not mistaken. Morgenbau had developed into a man of considerable force and intelligence, and was only too glad to be connected with Eugene again. He also talked with various advertising men, artists and writers as to just who were the most live editorial men in the field at that time, and these he wrote to, asking if they would come to see him. One by one they came, for the fact that he had come to New York to take charge not only of the advertising but the editorial ends of the United Magazines Corporation spread rapidly over the city. All those interested in art, writing, editing and advertising heard of it. Those who had known something of him in the past could scarcely believe their ears. Where did he get the skill?

Eugene stated to Colfax that he deemed it advisable that a general announcement be made to the staff that he was in charge. "I have been looking about," he said, "and I think I know what I want to do."

The various editors, art directors, advertising men and book workers were called to the main office and Colfax announced that he wished to make a statement which affected all those present. "Mr. Witla here will be in charge of all the publishing ends of this business from now on. I am withdrawing from any say in the matter, for I am satisfied that I do not know as much about it as he does. I want you all to look to him for advice and counsel just as you have to me in the past. Mr. White will continue in charge of the manufacturing and distributing end of the business. Mr. White and Mr. Witla will work together. That's all I have to say."

The company departed, and once more Eugene returned to his office. He decided at once to find an advertising man who could work under him and run that branch of the business as well as he would. He spent some time looking for this man, and finally found him working for the Hays-Rickert Company, a man whom he had known something of in the past as an exceptional worker. He was a strong, forceful individual of thirty-two, Carter Hayes by name, who was very anxious to succeed in his chosen work, and who saw a great opportunity here. He did not like Eugene so very well—he thought that he was over-estimated—but he decided to work for him. The latter put him in at ten thousand a year and then turned his attention to his new duties completely.

The editorial and publishing world was entirely new to Eugene from the executive side. He did not understand it as well as he did the art and advertising worlds, and because it was in a way comparatively new and strange to him he made a number of initial mistakes. His first was in concluding that all the men about him were more or less weak and inefficient, principally because the magazines were weak, when, as a matter of fact, there were a number of excellent men whom conditions had repressed, and who were only waiting for some slight recognition to be of great value. In the next place, he was not clear as to the exact policies to be followed in the case of each publication, and he was not inclined to listen humbly to those who could tell him. His best plan would have been to have gone exceedingly slow, watching the men who were in charge, getting their theories and supplementing their efforts with genial suggestions. Instead he decided on sweeping changes and not long after he had been in charge he began to make them. Marchwood, the editor of the *Review*, was removed, as was Gailer of the *Weekly*. The editorship of the *Adventure Story Magazine* was given to Bezenah.

In any organization of this kind, however, great improvements cannot be effected in a moment, and weeks and months must elapse before any noticeable change can be shown. Instead of throwing the burden of responsibility on each of his assistants and leaving it there, making occasional criticisms, Eugene undertook to work with each and all of them, endeavoring to direct the policy intimately in each particular case. It was not easy, and to him at times it was confusing. He had a great deal to learn. Still he did have helpful ideas in a score of directions daily and these told. The magazines were improved. The first issues which were affected by his judgment and those of his men were inspected closely by Colfax and White. The latter was particularly anxious to see what improvement had been made, and while he could not judge well himself, he had the means of getting opinions. Nearly all these were favorable, much to his disappointment, for he hoped to find things to criticize.

Colfax, who had been watching Eugene's determined air, the energy with which he went about his work and the manner in which he freely accepted responsibility, came to admire him even more than he had before. He liked him socially—his companionship after business hours—and began to invite him up to the house to dinner. Unlike Kalvin, on most of these occasions he did not take Angela into consideration, for having met her he was not so very much impressed with her. She was nice, but not of the same coruscating quality as her husband. Mrs. Colfax expressed a derogatory opinion, and this also made it difficult. He sincerely wished that Eugene were single.

Time passed. As Eugene worked more and more with the various propositions which this situation involved, he became more and more at his ease. Those who have ever held an executive position of any importance know how easy it is, given a certain degree of talent, to attract men and women of ability and force according to that talent. Like seeks like and those who are looking for advancement in their world according to their talents naturally drift to those who are more highly placed and who are much like themselves. Advertising men, artists, circulation men, editors, book critics, authors and all those who were sufficiently in his vein to understand or appreciate him sought him out, and by degrees he was compelled to learn to refer all applicants to the heads of departments. He was compelled to learn to rely to a certain degree on his men, and having learned this he was inclined to go to the other extreme and rely too much. In the case of Carter Hayes, in the advertising department, he was particularly impressed with the man's efficiency, and rested on him heavily for all the details of that work, merely inspecting his programs of procedure and advising him in difficult situations. The latter appreciated this, for he was egotistic to the roots, but it did not develop a sense of loyalty in him. He saw in Eugene a man who had risen by some fluke of fortune, and who was really not an advertising man at heart. He hoped some day that circumstances would bring it about that he could be advertising manager in fact, dealing directly with Colfax and White, whom, because of their greater financial interest in the business, he considered Eugene's superiors, and whom he proposed to court. There were others in the other departments who felt the same way.

The one great difficulty with Eugene was that he had no great power of commanding the loyalty of his assistants. He had the power of inspiring them—of giving them ideas which would be helpful to themselves—but these they used, as a rule, merely to further their own interests, to cause them to advance to a point where they deemed themselves beyond him. Because in his manner he was not hard, distant, bitter, he was considered, as a rule, rather easy. The men whom he employed, and he had talent for picking men of very exceptional ability, sometimes much greater than his own in their particular specialties, looked upon him not so much as a superior after a time, as someone who was in their path and to whose shoes they might properly aspire. He seemed so good natured about the whole work—so easy going. Now and then he took the trouble to tell a man that he was getting too officious, but in the main he did not care much. Things were going smoothly, the magazines were improving, the advertising and circulation departments were showing marked gains, and altogether his life seemed to have blossomed out into comparative perfection. There were storms and daily difficulties, but they were not serious. Colfax advised with him genially when he was in doubt, and White pretended a friendship which he did not feel.

CHAPTER XLIII

The trouble with this situation was that it involved more power, comfort, ease and luxury than Eugene had ever experienced before, and made him a sort of oriental potentate not only among his large company of assistants but in his own home. Angela, who had been watching his career all these years with curiosity, began to conceive of him at last as a genius in every respect—destined to some great pre-eminence, in art or finance or the publishing world or all three. She did not relax her attitude in regard to his conduct, being more convinced than ever that to achieve the dizzy eminence to which he was now so rapidly ascending, he must be more circumspect than ever. People were watching him so closely now. They were so obsequious to him, but still so dangerous. A man in his position must be so careful how he dressed, talked, walked.

"Don't make so much fuss," he used to say to her. "For heaven's sake, let me alone!" This merely produced more quarrels, for Angela was determined to regulate him in spite of his wishes and in his best interests.

Grave men and women in various walks of life—art, literature, philanthropy, trade, began to seek him out, because in the first place he had an understanding mind and because in the next place, which was much more important, he had something to give. There are always those in all walks of life who are seeking something through those avenues which a successful person represents, whatever they may be, and these together with those others who are always intensely eager to bask in the reflected glory of a rising luminary, make a retinue for every successful man. Eugene had his retinue, men and women of his own station or beneath it, who would eagerly shake his hand with an "Oh, yes, indeed. Managing Publisher of the United Magazines Corporation! Oh, yes, yes!" Women particularly were prone to smile, showing him even white teeth and regretting that all good looking and successful men were married.

In July following his coming from Philadelphia the United Magazines Corporation moved into its new building, and then he was installed into the most imposing office of his career. A subtle assistant, wishing to ingratiate the staff in Eugene's good graces, suggested that a collection be taken up for flowers. His room, which was done in white, blue and gold with rose wood furniture, to set it apart from the prevailing decorative scheme and so make it more impressive, was scattered with great bouquets of roses, sweet peas and pinks, in beautiful and ornate vases of different colors, countries and schools. His great rosewood flat-topped desk, covered with a thick, plate glass through which the polished wood shone brightly, was decorated with flowers. On the morning of his entry he held an impromptu reception, on which occasion he was visited by Colfax and White, who after going to look at their new rooms, came to his. A general reception which followed some three weeks later, and in which the successful representatives of various walks of life in the metropolis took part, drew to the building a great crowd, artists, writers, editors, publishers, authors and advertising men who saw him in all his glory. On this occasion, Eugene, with White and Colfax did the receiving. He was admired at a distance by striplings who wondered how he had ever accomplished such great results. His rise had been so meteoric. It seemed so impossible that a man who had started as an artist should change and become a dominant factor in literature and art from a publishing point of view.

In his own home his surroundings were equally showy; he was as much a figure as he was in his office. When he was alone with Angela, which was not so often, for naturally they did a great deal of entertaining, he was a figure even to her. Long ago she had come to think of him as someone who would some day dominate in the art world; but to see him an imposing factor in the city's commercial life, its principal publishers' representative, having a valet and an automobile, riding freely in cabs, lunching at the most exclusive restaurants and clubs, and associating constantly with someone who was of importance, was a different matter.

She was no longer so sure of herself with him, not so certain of her power to control him. They quarreled over little things, but she was not so ready to begin these quarrels. He seemed changed now and deeper still. She was afraid, even yet, that he might make a mistake and lose it all, that the forces of ill will, envy and jealousy which were everywhere apparent in life, and which blow about so easily like gusts of wind, would work him harm. Eugene was apparently at ease, though he was troubled at times for his own safety, when he thought of it, for he had no stock in the company, and was as beholden to Colfax as any hall boy, but he did not see how he could easily be dispensed with. He was *making good*.

Colfax was friendly to him. He was surprised at times to see how badly the manufacturing arrangements could go awry, affecting his dates of issue, but White invariably had a good excuse. Colfax took him to his house in the country, his lodge in the mountains, on short yachting and fishing trips, for he liked to talk to him, but he rarely if ever invited Angela. He did not seem to think it was necessary to do this, and Eugene was afraid to impress the slight upon his attention, much as he dreaded the thoughts which Angela must be thinking. It was Eugene here and Eugene there, with constant calls of "where are you, old man?" from Colfax, who appeared not to want to be away from him.

"Well, old man," he would say, looking him over much as one might a blood horse or a pedigree dog, "you're getting on. This new job agrees with you. You didn't look like that when you came to me," and he would feel the latest suit Eugene might be wearing, or comment on some pin or tie he had on, or tell him that his shoes were not as good as he could really get, if he wanted to be perfect in dress. Colfax was for grooming his new prize much as one might groom a blood horse, and he was always telling Eugene little details of social life, the right things to do, the right places to be seen, the right places to go, as though Eugene knew little or nothing.

"Now when we go down to Mrs. Savage's Friday afternoon, you get a Truxton Portmanteau. Have you seen them? Well, there's the thing. Got a London coat? Well, you ought to have one. Those servants down there go through your things and they size you up accordingly. Nothing less than two dollars each goes, and five dollars to the butler, remember that."

He assumed and insisted after a fashion which Eugene resented quite as much as he did his persistent ignoring of Angela, but he did not dare comment on it. He could see that Colfax was variable, that he could hate as well as love, and that he rarely took any intermediate ground. Eugene was his favorite now.

"I'll send my car around for you at two Friday," he would say, as though Eugene did not keep a car, when he was planning one of his week-end excursions. "You be ready."

At two, on that day, Colfax's big blue touring car would come speeding up to the entrance of the apartment house and Eugene's valet would carry down his bags, golf sticks, tennis racket and the various paraphernalia that go with a week-end's entertainment, and off the car would roll. At times Angela would be left behind, at times taken, when Eugene could arrange it; but he found that he had to be tactful and accede to Colfax's indifference mostly. Eugene would always explain to her how it was. He was sorry for her in a way, and yet he felt there was some justice in the distinction. She was not exactly suited to that topmost world in which he was now beginning to move. These people were colder, sharper, shrewder, than Angela. They had more of that intense sophistication of manner and experience than she could achieve. As a matter of fact, Angela had as much grace and more than many of the four hundred, but she did lack that quickness of wit or that shallow self-sufficiency and assurance which are the almost invariable traits of those who shine as members of the smart set. Eugene was able to assume this manner whether he felt it or not.

"Oh, that's all right," she would say, "as long as you're doing it for business reasons."

She resented it nevertheless, bitterly, for it seemed such an uncalled for slur. Colfax had no compunctions in adjusting his companionship to suit his moods. He thought Eugene was well suited to this high life. He thought Angela was not. He made the distinction roughly and went his way.

It was in this manner that Eugene learned a curious fact about the social world, and that was that frequently in these highest circles a man would be received where his wife would not and vice versa, and that nothing very much was thought of it, if it could be managed.

"Oh, is that Birkwood," he heard a young swell once remark, concerning an individual in Philadelphia. "Why do they let him in? His wife is charming, but he won't do," and once in New York he heard a daughter ask her mother, of a certain wife who was announced—her husband being at the same table—"who invited her?"

"I'm sure I don't know," replied her mother; "I didn't. She must have come of her own accord."

"She certainly has her nerve with her," replied the daughter—and when the wife entered Eugene could see why. She was not good looking and not harmoniously and tastefully dressed. It gave Eugene a shock, but in a way he could understand. There were no such grounds of complaint against Angela. She was attractive and shapely. Her one weakness was that she lacked the blasé social air. It was too bad, he thought.

In his own home and circle, however, he thought to make up for this by a series of entertainments which grew more and more elaborate as time went on. At first when he came back from Philadelphia it consisted of a few people in to dinner, old friends, for he was not quite sure of himself and did not know how many would come to share his new honors with him. Eugene had never got over his love for those he had known in his youth. He was not snobbish. It was true that now he was taking naturally to prosperous people, but the little ones, the old-time ones, he liked for old lang syne's sake as well as for themselves. Many came to borrow money, for he had associated with many ne'er do wells in his time, but many more were attracted by his fame.

Eugene knew intimately and pleasantly most of the artistic and intellectual figures of his day. In his home and at his table there appeared artists, publishers, grand opera stars, actors and playwrights. His large salary, for one thing, his beautiful apartment and its location, his magnificent office and his friendly manner all conspired to assist him. It was his self-conscious boast that he had not changed. He liked nice people, simple people, natural people he said, for these were the really great ones, but he could not see how far he had come in class selection. Now he naturally gravitated to the wealthy, the reputed, the beautiful, the strong and able, for no others interested him. He hardly saw them. If he did it was to pity or give alms.

It is difficult to indicate to those who have never come out of poverty into luxury, or out of comparative uncouthness into refinement, the veil or spell which the latter comes eventually to cast over the inexperienced mind, coloring the world anew. Life is apparently striving, constantly, to perfect its illusions and to create spells. There are, as a matter of fact, nothing but these outside that ultimate substance or principle which underlies it all. To those who have come out of inharmony, harmony is a spell, and to those who have come out of poverty, luxury is a dream of delight. Eugene, being primarily a lover of beauty, keenly responsive to all those subtleties of perfection and arrangement which ingenuity can devise, was taken vastly by the nature of this greater world into which, step by step apparently, he was almost insensibly passing. Each new fact which met his eye or soothed his sensibilities was quickly adjusted to all that had gone before. It seemed to him as though all his life he had naturally belonged to this perfect world of which country houses, city mansions, city and country clubs, expensive hotels and inns, cars, resorts, beautiful women, affected manners, subtlety of appreciation and perfection of appointment generally were the inherent concomitants. This was the true heaven—that material and spiritual perfection on earth, of which the world was dreaming and to which, out of toil, disorder, shabby ideas, mixed opinions, non-understanding and all the ill to which the flesh is heir, it was constantly aspiring.

Here was no sickness, no weariness apparently, no ill health or untoward circumstances. All the troubles, disorders and imperfections of existence were here carefully swept aside and one saw only the niceness, the health and strength of being. He was more and more impressed as he came farther and farther along in the scale of comfort, with the force and eagerness with which life seems to minister to the luxury-love of the human mind. He learned of so many, to him, lovely things, large, wellkept, magnificent country places, scenes of exquisite beauty where country clubs, hotels, seaside resorts of all descriptions had been placed. He found sport, amusement, exercise, to be tremendously well organized and that there were thousands of people who were practically devoting their lives to this. Such a state of social ease was not for him yet, but he could sit at the pleasures, so amply spread, between his hours of work and dream of the time to come when possibly he might do nothing at all. Yachting, motoring, golfing, fishing, hunting, riding, playing tennis and polo, there were experts in all these fields he found. Card playing, dancing, dining, lounging, these seemed to occupy many people's days constantly. He could only look in upon it all as upon a passing show, but that was better than nothing. It was more than he had ever done before. He was beginning to see clearly how the world was organized, how far were its reaches of wealth, its depths of poverty. From the lowest beggar to the topmost scene—what a distance!

Angela scarcely kept pace with him in all these mental peregrinations. It was true that now she went to the best dressmakers only, bought charming hats, the most expensive shoes, rode in cabs and her husband's auto, but she did not feel about it as he did. It seemed very much like a dream to her—like something that had come so suddenly and so exuberantly that it could not be permanent. There was running in her mind all the time that Eugene was neither a publisher, nor an editor, nor a financier at heart, but an artist and that an artist he would remain. He might attain great fame and make much money out of his adopted profession, but some day in all likelihood he would leave it and return to art. He seemed to be making sound investments—at least, they seemed sound to her, and their stocks and bank accounts, principally convertible stocks, seemed a safe enough margin for the future to guarantee peace of mind, but they were not saving so much, after all. It was costing them something over eight thousand dollars a year to live, and their expenses were constantly growing larger rather than smaller. Eugene appeared to become more and more extravagant.

"I think we are doing too much entertaining," Angela had once protested, but he waived the complaint aside. "I can't do what I'm doing and not entertain. It's building me up. People in our position have to." He threw open the doors finally to really remarkable crowds and most of the cleverest people in all walks of life—the really exceptionally clever—came to eat his meals, to drink his wines, to envy his comfort and wish they were in his shoes.

During all this time Eugene and Angela instead of growing closer together, were really growing farther and farther apart. She had never either forgotten or utterly forgiven that one terrific lapse, and she had never believed that Eugene was utterly cured of his hedonistic tendencies. Crowds of beautiful women came to Angela's teas, lunches and their joint evening parties and receptions. Under Eugene's direction they got together interesting programmes, for it was no trouble now for him to command musical, theatrical, literary and artistic talent. He knew men and women who could make rapid charcoal or crayon sketches of people, could do feats in legerdemain, and character representation, could sing, dance, play, recite and tell humorous stories in a droll and off-hand way. He insisted that only exceptionally beautiful women be invited, for he did not care to look at the homely ones, and curiously he found dozens, who were not only extremely beautiful, but singers, dancers, composers, authors, actors and playwrights in the bargain. Nearly all of them were brilliant conversationalists and they helped to entertain themselves—made their own entertainment, in fact. His table very frequently was a glittering spectacle. One of his "Stunts" as he called it was to bundle fifteen or twenty people into three or four automobiles after they had lingered in his rooms until three o'clock in the morning and motor out to some out-of-town inn for breakfast and "to see the sun rise." A small matter like a bill for $75.00 for auto hire or thirty-five dollars for a crowd for breakfast did not trouble him. It was a glorious sensation to draw forth his purse and remove four or five or six yellow backed ten dollar bills, knowing that it made little real difference. More money was coming to him from the same source. He could send down to the cashier at any time and draw from five hundred to a thousand dollars. He always had from one hundred and fifty to three hundred dollars in his purse in denominations of five, ten and twenty dollar bills. He carried a small check book and most frequently paid by check. He liked to assume that he was known and frequently imposed this assumption on others.

"Eugene Witla! Eugene Witla! George! he's a nice fellow,"—or "it's remarkable how he has come up, isn't it?" "I was at the Witlas' the other night. Did you ever see such a beautiful apartment? It's perfect! That view!"

People commented on the interesting people he entertained, the clever people you met there, the beautiful women, the beautiful view. "And Mrs. Witla is so charming."

But down at the bottom of all this talk there was also much envy and disparagement and never much enthusiasm for the personality of Mrs. Witla. She was not as brilliant as Eugene—or rather the comment was divided. Those who liked clever people, show, wit, brilliance, ease, liked Eugene and not Angela quite so much. Those who liked sedateness, solidity, sincerity, the commoner virtues of faithfulness and effort, admired Angela. All saw that she was a faithful handmaiden to her husband, that she adored the ground he walked on.

"Such a nice little woman—so homelike. It's curious that he should have married her, though, isn't it? They are so different. And yet they appear to have lots of things in common, too. It's strange—isn't it?"

CHAPTER XLIV

It was in the course of his final upward progress that Eugene came once more into contact with Kenyon C. Winfield, Ex-State Senator of New York, President of the Long Island Realty Company, land developer, real estate plunger, financier, artist, what not—a man very much of Eugene's own type and temperament, who at this time was doing rather remarkable things in a land speculative way. Winfield was tall and thin, black haired, black eyed, slightly but not offensively hook nosed, dignified, gracious, intellectual, magnetic, optimistic. He was forty-eight years of age. Winfield was a very fair sample of your man of the world who has ideas, dreams, fancies, executive ability, a certain amount of reserve and judgment, sufficient to hold his own in this very complicated mortal struggle. He was not really a great man, but he was so near it that he gave the impression to many of being so. His deep sunken black eyes burned with a peculiar lustre, one might almost have fancied a tint of red in them. His pale, slightly sunken face had some of the characteristics of your polished Mephisto, though not too many. He was not at all devilish looking in the true sense of the word, but keen, subtle, artistic. His method was to ingratiate himself with men who had money in order to get from them the vast sums which he found it necessary to borrow to carry out the schemes or rather dreams he was constantly generating. His fancies were always too big for his purse, but he had such lovely fancies that it was a joy to work with them and him.

Primarily Winfield was a real estate speculator, secondarily he was a dreamer of dreams and seer of visions. His visions consisted of lovely country areas near some city stocked with charming country houses, cut up with well paved, tree shaded roads, provided with sewers, gas, electricity, suitable railway service, street cars and all the comforts of a well organized living district which should be at once retired, exclusive, pleasing, conservative and yet bound up tightly with the great Metropolitan heart of New York which he so greatly admired. Winfield had been born and raised in Brooklyn. He had been a politician, orator, insurance dealer, contractor, and so on. He had succeeded in organizing various suburban estates—Winfield, Sunnyside, Ruritania, The Beeches—little forty, fifty, one hundred and two hundred acre flats which with the help of "O. P. M." as he always called other people's money he had divided off into blocks, laying out charmingly with trees and sometimes a strip of green grass running down the centre, concrete sidewalks, a set of noble restrictions, and so forth. Anyone who ever came to look at a lot in one of Winfield's perfect suburbs always found the choicest piece of property in the centre of this latest burst of improvement set aside for the magnificent house which Mr. Kenyon C. Winfield, the president of the company, was to build and live in. Needless to say they were never built. He had been round the world and seen a great many things and places, but Winfield or Sunnyside or Ruritania or The Beeches, so the lot buyers in these places were told, had been finally selected by him deliberately as the one spot in all the world in which he hoped to spend the remainder of his days.

At the time Eugene met him, he was planning Minetta Water on the shores of Gravesend Bay, which was the most ambitious of all his projects so far. He was being followed financially, by a certain number of Brooklyn politicians and financiers who had seen him succeed in small things, taking a profit of from three to four hundred per cent, out of ten, twenty and thirty acre flats, but for all his brilliance it had been slow work. He was now worth between three and four hundred thousand dollars and, for the first time in his life, was beginning to feel that freedom in financial matters which made him think that he could do almost anything. He had met all sorts of people, lawyers, bankers, doctors, merchants, the "easy classes" he called them, all with a little money to invest, and he had succeeded in luring hundreds of worth-while people into his projects. His great dreams had never really been realized, however, for he saw visions of a great warehouse and shipping system to be established on Jamaica Bay, out of which he was to make millions, if it ever came to pass, and also a magnificent summer resort of some kind, somewhere, which was not yet clearly evolved in his mind. His ads were scattered freely through the newspapers: his signs, or rather the signs of his towns, scattered broadcast over Long Island.

Eugene had met him first when he was working with the Summerfield Company, but he met him this time quite anew at the home of the W. W. Willebrand on the North Shore of Long Island near Hempstead. He had gone down there one Saturday afternoon at the invitation of Mrs. Willebrand, whom he had met at another house party and with whom he had danced. She had been pleased with his gay, vivacious manner and had asked him if he wouldn't come. Winfield was here as a guest with his automobile.

"Oh, yes," said Winfield pleasantly. "I recall you very well. You are now with the United Magazines Corporation,—I understand—someone was telling me—a most prosperous company, I believe. I know Mr. Colfax very well. I once spoke to Summerfield about you. A most astonishing fellow, that, tremendously able. You were doing that series of sugar plantation ads for them or having them done. I think I copied the spirit of those things in advertising Ruritania, as you may have noticed. Well, you certainly have improved your condition since then. I once tried to tell Summerfield that he had an exceptional man in you, but he would have nothing of it. He's too much of an egoist. He doesn't know how to work with a man on equal terms."

Eugene smiled at the thought of Summerfield.

"An able man," he said simply. "He did a great deal for me."

Winfield liked that. He thought Eugene would criticize him. He liked Eugene's genial manner and intelligent, expressive face. It occurred to him that when next he wanted to advertise one of his big development projects, he would go to Eugene or the man who had done the sugar plantation series of pictures and get him to give him the right idea for advertising.

Affinity is such a peculiar thing. It draws people so easily, apart from volition or consciousness. In a few moments Eugene and Winfield, sitting side by side on the veranda, looking at the greenwood before them, the long stretch of open sound, dotted with white sails and the dim, distant shore of Connecticut, were talking of real estate ventures in general, what land was worth, how speculations of this kind turned out, as a rule. Winfield was anxious to take Eugene seriously, for he felt drawn to him and Eugene studied Winfield's pale face, his thin, immaculate hands, his suit of soft, gray cloth. He looked as able as his public reputation made him out to be— in fact, he looked better than anything he had ever done. Eugene had seen Ruritania and The Beeches. They did not impress him vastly as territorial improvements, but they were pretty, nevertheless. For middle-class people, they were quite the thing he thought.

"I should think it would be a pleasure to you to scheme out a new section," he said to him once. "The idea of a virgin piece of land to be converted into streets and houses or a village appeals to me immensely. The idea of laying it out and sketching houses to fit certain positions, suits my temperament exactly. I wish sometimes I had been born an architect."

"It is pleasant and if that were all it would be ideal," returned Winfield. "The thing is more a matter of financing than anything else. You have to raise money for land and improvements. If you make exceptional improvements they are expensive. You really can't expect to get much, if any, of your money back, until all your work is done. Then you have to wait. If you put up houses you can't rent them, for the moment you rent them, you can't sell them as new. When you make your improvements your taxes go up immediately. If you sell a piece of property to a man or woman who isn't exactly in accord with your scheme, he or she may put up a house which destroys the value of a whole neighborhood for you. You can't fix the details of a design in a contract too closely. You can only specify the minimum price the house is to cost and the nature of the materials to be used. Some people's idea of beauty will vary vastly from others. Taste in sections may change. A whole city like New York may suddenly decide that it wants to build west when you are figuring on its building east. So—well, all these things have to be taken into consideration."

"That sounds logical enough," said Eugene, "but wouldn't the right sort of a scheme just naturally draw to itself the right sort of people, if it were presented in the right way? Don't you fix the conditions by your own attitude?"

"You do, you do," replied Winfield, easily. "If you give the matter sufficient care and attention it can be done. The pity is you can be too fine at times. I have seen attempts at perfection come to nothing. People with taste and tradition and money behind them are not moving into new additions and suburbs, as a rule. You are dealing with the new rich and financial beginners. Most people strain their resources to the breaking point to better their living conditions and they don't always know. If they have the money, it doesn't always follow that they have the taste to grasp what you are striving for, and if they have the taste they haven't the money. They would do better if they could, but they can't. A man in my position is like an artist and a teacher and a father confessor and financier and everything all rolled into one. When you start to be a real estate developer on a big scale you must be these things. I have had some successes and some notable failures. Winfield is one of the worst. It's disgusting to me now."

"I have always wished I could lay out a seaside resort or a suburb," said Eugene dreamily. "I've never been to but one or two of the resorts abroad, but it strikes me that none of the resorts here—certainly none near New York—are right. The opportunities are so wonderful. The things that have been done are horrible. There is no plan, no detail anywhere."

"My views exactly," said Winfield. "I've been thinking of it for years. Some such place could be built, and I suppose if it were done right it would be successful. It would be expensive, though, very, and those who come in would have a long wait for their money."

"It would be a great opportunity to do something really worth while, though," said Eugene. "No one seems to realize how beautiful a thing like that could be made."

Winfield said nothing, but the thought stuck in his mind. He was dreaming a seaside improvement which should be the most perfect place of its kind in the world—a monument to himself if he did it. If Eugene had this idea of beauty he might help. At least he might talk to him about it when the time came. Perhaps Eugene might have a little money to invest. It would take millions to put such a scheme through, but every little would help. Besides Eugene might have ideas which should make money both for himself and for Winfield. It was worth thinking about. So they parted, not to meet again for weeks and months, but they did not forget each other.